C0-ARB-726

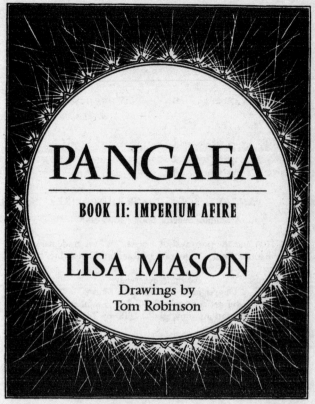

PANGAEA

BOOK II: IMPERIUM AFIRE

LISA MASON

Drawings by
Tom Robinson

INCLUDES THE COMPLETE ORB OF ETERNITY

BANTAM BOOKS
New York Toronto London Sydney Auckland

PANGAEA: BOOK II IMPERIUM AFIRE

A Bantam Spectra Book / May 2000

SPECTRA and the portrayal of a boxed "s" are trademarks of
Bantam Books, a division of Random House, Inc.

ISBN 0-553-58166-X

Published simultaneously in the United States and Canada

Bantam Books are published by Bantam Books, a division of Random
House, Inc. Its trademark, consisting of the words "Bantam Books"
and the portrayal of a rooster, is Registered in U.S. Patent and Trademark Office and in other countries. Marca Registrada. Bantam
Books, 1540 Broadway, New York, New York 10036.

PRINTED IN THE UNITED STATES OF AMERICA

OPM   10   9   8   7   6   5   4   3   2   1

CONTENTS

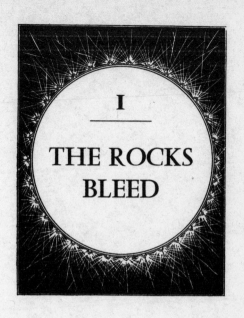

I

THE ROCKS
BLEED

FACET 16

Volcano: Release or cataclysm.
The sharer punishes the corrupted child,
    who thrashes a younger sibling.
The action is forcefulness.
The forbearance is paroxysm.

The Orb of Eternity

Commentaries:
Councillor Sausal: Stillness is the natural state of
the world, as tranquility is the fundamental state
of the Imperium. As volcanic eruption is disruptive and destructive, so rebellion is deviant and
offensive.

So, too, the Imperium observes the law of
proximity since the divinity of things embodies
the natural order of the world. Observing the
laws of the Imperium, however, requires vigilance
since such laws embody humanity's artifice.

Therefore the prudent person should dishonor
rebellion among higher pures and punish rebellion among lower pures. Above all, restrain rebellion in your heart . . . [*Deleted from The
Contemporary Commentaries of Sausal (15th
Ed.)* unless rebellion is vital.]
Guttersage (usu. considered vulgar): Terror is as
terror does.

*Our City of Atlan, a league below Northwest Market-
place. Blackblood Cavern, main tentsite of the impure,
West Ingress:*

Only after she'd returned from the village of Al-Muud did Salit Zehar discover the answer. And the question? It was the question that had vexed all Pangaea since the world began to change last summer.

Salit gripped a devil star. Her last. The six-pointed semisentient knife vibrated in her fist—or maybe it was her own trembling. She ran her tongue tip over her lip and tasted salt and grit and fear.

Rumor said the rocks had bled since the eruption in the Hercynian Sea. Magma surged from the ocean floor over wreckage of the famous Floating Towers. From the sea rose a cineritious caldera. Isle of Pyrber, the High Council called the forsaken place: Emerged from Fire.

In Atlan to the south and Blackblood Cavern below the streets, the smell of sulfur and a haze of ashes choked the air. Winter was approaching, the breadfruit leaves turning gold, and Our Sacred Imperium of Pangaea pondered ever-present death, emerging life, and ineluctable change.

Salit crouched behind a tumble of boulders. The earthshock that had devastated the world last summer—some said the Big Shock prophesied by the Apocalyptists—had dislodged chunks of the granite walls. Rockfalls littered West Ingress, forming crawl spaces like the one where she hid. Scattered torches cast pools of fitful amber light.

A squad of walkabout vigiles marched past her no more than a handbreadth away. Tall, golden-haired magister pures, the vigiles swung golden-skinned faces back and forth, surveilling the ingress with penetrating blue eyes. Imperial weapons dangled from their belts—crossbows, daggers, firebolts. Fine uniforms of indigo-blue flattered bulging muscles in their formidable arms and thighs.

Sweat poured down Salit's neck, sliding in ticklish trails beneath her chameleon cloak. The cloak obeyed her for a change, wrapping its draperies around her. She glanced down at herself and saw a ripple of rock and shadows. A decent camouflaging for once.

Cursed vigiles, what are you doing in impure terri-

tory? Raiding my people for Atlan Prefecture? Round-ing up hostages for Vigilance torturers?

A vigile swung his head around and cocked it, and Salit realized she'd been whispering aloud. *So alone.* Alone too long since Horan Zehar had died beneath the knife of Lieutenant Captain Regim Deuceman. Too long the journey from Al-Muud to Atlan. Too many days of evading Vigilance, hiding on the cliffs, sleeping on Sausal Beach, before she dared return to Blackblood Cavern, searching for Asif.

A pretty vigile not much older than Salit's seventeen years unfurled a scroll and proceeded to post it. *Bang bang bang bang,* four efficient hammer strikes on four iron spikes. A dozen scrolls were tucked beneath her brawny arm. The smallest of the squad, the pretty vigile stood twice as tall as Salit and easily tipped the scales at three stone more.

Salit had always had trouble keeping enough meat on her frail bones. *Way* too many days since she'd en-joyed a square meal. Yesterday she had dined on three tiny speckled eggs she'd found in a seabird's nest. She had crunched eggshells in her teeth, swallowed raw yolks, and wished there had been more.

The most regal vigile of the squad wrinkled her slope of a nose and yawned, bored and disdainful. "Hai, my officers," announced this fine specimen of the magister purity, "I cannot bear this vile place another moment. Let's begone. Our young Assayev will post the rest, won't you, officer?"

The vigiles glanced among themselves in the peculiar way people of the purities often did: dreamy-eyed and withdrawn.

When the pures look as if they're gone into a trance, they have entered sharemind, Horan had taught her. *We of the impure possess no sharemind. We invoke no Imperial sharemind. We do not dream in the Mind of the World. We possess no sharemind among the purities or among the impure, not even between our bonded ones. We possess no security numbers, no protocol chips, no sharelock chips. But don't despair, my daugh-*

*ter. We may be all alone, each within our own minds,
but we are free.*

And the question vexing all Pangaea loomed before
Salit: *If I am impure, and I cannot dream in the Mind
of the World, then how could I have appeared in the
dream of a famous angel? The eminent Milord Lucyd,
whom I've never even met before?*

The regal vigile said, "Look lively, Officer Assayev,
and watch your back. The impure are nasty little beasts,
even those not of the terrorist clans." She made the sign
of the Imperial star. "They're the Fallen of Inim, servants of the Supreme Adversary. We should pray for
them but we should also be wary."

"Yes, my sergeant," barked the pretty vigile, nearly
toppling when she clicked her bootheels.

The vigiles chuckled at their puppy of a colleague.
Awareness left their eyes as they entered sharemind
again.

Salit frowned, and sorrow coiled around her heart.
She had no notion what the pures communicated in
their shared consciousness. Or how, exactly. Or what it
felt like.

She only knew she was excluded.

"Report to me at Vigilance when you're done, Assayev," the sergeant vigile said. "I've got a batch of new
protocol regulations I need you to post in Allpure
Square."

"Yes, my sergeant."

The squad turned and marched up West Ingress
toward Marketplace, leaving the pretty vigile to her
task.

The vigile glanced imperiously at the rough-hewn
walls, searching for a place to post another scroll. She
withdrew one from beneath her arm and a handful of
spikes from a pouch at her belt. She lazily nailed the
scroll to the wall, obeying her orders as if nothing could
possibly harm her.

Here, in impure territory.

My territory.

Since when has Vigilance become so arrogant?

The vigile withdrew another scroll and sauntered deeper down the ingress, whistling a popular tune. What were the scrolls, anyway? From her hiding place, Salit glimpsed an impure face, bold kaligraphs splashed across the parchment.

Smug vigile, pretty and fair, you dare post the face of one of my people at the very entrance to our tentsite?

Salit's fingers found her slingshot and slung a stone in the leather pouch. She spun the leather cord, and flung it.

The stone struck the wall twenty paces ahead and clattered to the ground in a burst of dust. The vigile whipped around, startled, and dashed to the spot where the stone had struck.

Salit darted in a parallel path.

She cocked her head. *What was that?*

From deep within the cavern came the *pitter-patter* of footsteps. Two impure children scampered up, bound for fresh air or a treasure hunt amid the wastebins of Marketplace. Tiny and misshapen as only the impure could be—a clubfoot here, a milky eye there—the children stopped in their tracks at the sight of the vigile. And, yelping in terror, scampered back down West Ingress as fast as their stubby legs could gallop.

"Halt, I command you," the vigile shouted. "I'll teach you to throw stones at me. I'll show you how Vigilance deals with impure brats."

The vigile dashed after them, overcoming them in three swift strides. She seized one by the hood of his cloak and smashed him against the wall as if he were a stray animal that needed putting down.

Bone struck rock with a dull *crack*. The child fell, eyes wide, limbs limp. Blood pooled on the ground behind his skull.

The second child ran shrieking into the cavern.

Salit wanted to shriek. But she didn't.

The vigile stood over the corpse, frowning. She gingerly lifted it by the hood and flung it behind the rocks where Salit hid. She kicked gravel over the child's blood.

The vigile looked around, realization dawning.

She had suddenly found herself thirty paces deeper into West Ingress. The torches shone dimmer there. The shadows fell darker. The ashy air clung. An earthshock rumbled somewhere along Sausal Coast, tremors vivid in this place between sunlit surfaces and sunless depths.

A brace of bloodbats scuttled overhead, leathery wings shuddering against the ceiling.

The vigile glanced up in alarm.

Getting frightened, pretty vigile? Have a little more respect for where you are? All alone, a murderer like you?

With me?

Salit leapt from behind the outcrop and flung the devil star the way her father had taught her. The sliver whizzed through the air, struck the vigile's shoulder, and flipped open. Six startips commenced their devouring dance, puncturing linen, penetrating flesh, piercing bone. Depositing poison deep within each wound.

To Salit's surprise the vigile didn't scream but only gasped, then bit back even that sound. She dropped the scrolls, the hammer, the spikes, and yanked out her firebolt. She warily pirouetted as she searched for her target.

The chameleon cloak shivered. Horan Zehar had bequeathed it to Salit in his dying moment, but she had yet to master her cantankerous bequest. She glanced around. After her leap, the rock and shadows surrounding her had changed. She willed the cloak to adjust, fiercely summoning a new camouflage.

The vigile's eyes darted toward her, darted away.

Darted back.

An imperfect camouflaging, but better than before.

"Tell me, vigile," Salit said in the mocking singsong Horan had used to taunt his enemies. "How *does* Vigilance deal with impure brats?"

She was quick. "With fifty lashes of an ox whip till your back is a sack of blood."

The vigile staggered and struck the wall. The impact caught the devil star at its center point, cracking the weapon in half. The disabled star ceased its pillage but the halves remained impaled just below the vigile's rib cage, decorating each side of her spine.

The vigile clenched her firebolt.

Only a dagger and a couple of caltrops hung from Salit's belt. She yanked off a caltrop and flung it.

It was a sweet little metal ball bristling with spikes, but the caltrop had no sentience. It caught the vigile below her kneecap and plunged through skin and muscle well enough. But only hung there, its work done.

The vigile reached down, plucked it out.

And flung the caltrop at Salit, shooting the firebolt at the same time. *Good move. Study a skillful enemy and you may outlive her,* Horan had said. Dodging the caltrop, Salit dived straight into the line of fire. She jerked back, the cloak swirling out before her, creating the illusion she'd gone farther than she had.

Which gave her just enough time to slam herself across a boulder and drop down before the vigile fired again.

Bullets of flame burst all around Salit, raining red-hot drops of liquid fire. The vigile vaulted over the boulder and fired again, saturating the crawl space with a sheet of flames.

Salit wriggled around the boulder on her hands and knees, regaining the ingress and heaving for breath. She fumbled at her belt, glanced back. There lay her caltrops, her dagger, where she'd dislodged them in her haste.

The vigile staggered around the boulder, coming after her.

Salit lurched to her feet, dashed across the ingress to the vigile's pile of abandoned scrolls. She picked one up, feverishly unrolled it, and studied the kaligraphs.

Had she really seen what she thought she'd seen?

FOR THE MURDER OF DAME CLERE TWINE NAITRE
SECUNDUS ADJUNCT PREFECT OF OUR SACRED CITY OF

ATLAN, CONSECRATED SHARER OF LIEUTENANT CAPTAIN
REGIM DEUCEMAN, DAUGHTER OF COUNCILLOR CLAREN
TWINE, CHIEF ADVISOR ON IMPURE ACTIVITIES TO THE
HIGH COUNCIL OF OUR SACRED IMPERIUM OF PANGAEA
WANTED DEAD OR ALIVE
SALIT ZEHAR OF THE HEAVEN'S DEVILS CLAN

Salit dropped to her knees and bowed her head,
brandishing the warrant like a flag of surrender. "Please
don't fire, kind vigile."

The pretty vigile reeled across the corridor, face
flushed and slick. The poison in the startips didn't take
long.

"Is it true, then?" She stared at the warrant, stared at
Salit. She edged closer, thrust the muzzle of her firebolt
under Salit's chin, and shoved her face up. "Are you
really—?"

"I am Salit Zehar." She raised her hands in supplica-
tion. "Spare me, I beg you."

"Dear Pan, you really *are* that ugly. It's hard to believe." The vigile blinked. "Why should I spare you?"

"Think of the rewards you'll reap if you capture
me," Salit whimpered. "No one need know about the
child. He was only impure. Think of your glory when
you march me into Marketplace."

The vigile barked with laughter. She raised the
firebolt in an unsteady fist. "It says 'Dead or Alive,'
stupid girl. You know what I think? I think my glory
will be greater if I march into Marketplace with your
corpse slung over my shoulder."

Salit flung the warrant in the vigile's face. "Death to
the Imperium! The Apocalypse is here!" She seized the
hammer, leapt to her feet, and slammed the hammer-
head on the vigile's left breast. *A vigorous blow directly
to the heart will stun the strongest,* Horan Zehar had
taught her, *and then you may kill at your leisure.*

The vigile bawled, dropped the firebolt, and fell.

Salit seized a spike and slammed the hammer again,

plunging the metal shaft deep in the vigile's heart and lung. She shut her eyes as blood geysered.

Blood blinds, her father had warned her.

The vigile's screams echoed down West Ingress.

Salit winced. Once she would have relished a blooding like this, but since Al-Muud she'd had enough of death. It was terrible, the things a Heaven's Devil had to do to wage the holy war against the Imperium.

Her revulsion transformed into a sneer. "You know what *I* think, vigile?" She ripped apart the warrant and stuffed the shreds into the vigile's mouth. "I think I don't want to die."

"Salit! Salit Zehar," came the reedy cry, and the rap of an impatient fist on the tent flap. "Haul your lazy bum out here and come quickly. A stranger's come to see you."

"A stranger?" Salit sat up on Asif's bedroll and stubbed out her cheroot. *Way* too many days since she'd had a good smoke. She had begged Asif to buy her a tin of bacco, which she'd incinerated down to the last knobby roll. She was scheming how she could persuade him to buy her another.

"Go fish, Tiki," Asif called through the flap. "Salit rests."

Asif's tent, perched on a low ridge above his family's tentsite, was a huddle of black sacking amid countless thousands in Blackblood Cavern. Asif had stood at the tent flap, tense and watchful, for a dawn and a day while Salit had collapsed in boneless exhaustion.

"Gah, rest," the boy said. "I thought you Heaven's Devils will never rest till the Imperium falls."

"Watch your tongue, Tiki. Who's to say Salit's a Devil?"

"*I* say. You are, too, Asif."

"You'll lose that tongue if it gets too loose, boy."

"Hush," Salit whispered. "Don't be harsh. Tiki used to run errands for my father. He knows we're Devils."

"Feed your tongue to the fish, Asif," Tiki said and

kicked the tent flap. "I know Salit's there. I can smell her cheroot, and you never touch the wasting weed. Let me speak to her."

Salit held up her hands, and Asif pulled her to her feet. She flung back the tent flap. "All right, Tiki. Who is this stranger?"

The boy grinned, all lopsided lips and protruding ears. "Some serv, butting his head into Granmam's tent. Says he's a midwife from the Imperial Natalries. Won't get till he sees you." The boy added, "He's got a sack with 'im."

Salit snapped her fingers. "Of course I'll see him. Give him a jar of beer, and Asif will fetch him in a moment."

"Hurry up, will you? Granmam's fit to be trussed. My sisters are cackling like hens around a rooster."

Salit grinned. She knew exactly who the stranger was. "Black hair tied back with a thong? Black eyes to match? Spends time on the gamefields from the look of his brawn?"

Asif raised an eyebrow.

"That's the one," Tiki said. "Gah, a midwife-natalist. Lackey of the Imperium!"

The neighbor boy dashed away, leaving Salit alone with Asif in sultry semidarkness. As an unbonded impure man twenty years of age and a full-fledged assassin of the Heaven's Devils clan, Asif Zehest was entitled to his own private tent. Salit looked him over as he retied the tent flap. His wrists were gnarled, his feet enormous, his eyes mismatched as all impure eyes were. His golden brown complexion stretched tight over uneven cheekbones. His left ear was a prominent funnel, his right ear a funny stub.

He was the most beautiful thing Salit had ever seen.

How long I've longed for my comrade!

"Thank you for sheltering me, Asif."

"Well, I'd better, my little comrade. Vigilance has tripled the bounty on your lovely head."

"I would rather die than place you in jeopardy. If there's another Vigilance raid—"

"If there's another Vigilance raid, I'll hide you like before."

When vigiles had swept into Blackblood Cavern seeking the slayer of the officer found in West Ingress, Salit had crawled inside the false bottom Asif had excavated beneath his foodpit. He had doused the pit with mint oil, stuffed bags of buckwheat meal on top. And she had lain, breathless, while vigiles tramped over her. It was a miracle they hadn't found her, with their keen powers of surveillance and Imperial training.

But they hadn't. Half a dozen surprise raids in a dawn and a day, and they hadn't found her.

Salit had said nothing of the vigile's blooding, not even to Asif. *What would the Dark Ones say, what would they do, if they knew I have executed a vigile of my own will—again—and not by their command?*

Best not to dwell on *that* question. She resolved to leave an offering of food and money for the grieving family of the murdered child.

"If there's another raid, I'll go."

"Don't be foolish. You belong here with me." Asif sat next to her. "Little comrade, don't you know I'd do anything for you?" He took her in his arms and rocked her, stroking her head. She hadn't scraped her scalp bald in days. White-gold and vermilion bristles sprouted on the domes and ridges of her skull.

"Oh, Asif," she whispered, "it was horrible at Al-Muud."

The dust, the wailing of the druds, and the buzz of flies on newly butchered flesh. The hands of the jarmaker, the hands of his whole family. Salit's half-pure cousin, Whieta, the jarmaker's sharer, fleeing for her life. And Whieta's two little girls, what Regim had done to them. . . .

Over the scene of the atrocity an Imperial banner waved—

ALL YE WHO PASS
THIS PLACE OF DESECRATION
WITNESS WHAT HAPPENS
TO THOSE WHO COLLABORATE WITH HEAVEN'S DEVILS

"It's all my f-fault," Salit said.

"Hush. Regim Deuceman wielded his blade, not you."

"If only I hadn't gone to see Whieta—"

"If you hadn't gone to see Whieta, the druds of Al-Muud would still believe Vigilance atrocities in Atlan are idle complaints of cityfolk, too terrible to be true. They know better now. You've struck another blow against the Imperium. I'm sorry your half kin suffered, but you made no mistake."

She nodded, only half-convinced. "I should have taken Regim's life when I had the chance."

"Salit, you know damn well the Dark Ones have forbidden you to take the vigile's life. Put aside your vow of vengeance."

"Regim has vowed against *me* for the death of Clere. What do the Dark Ones have to say about that?"

"No one can know what the Dark Ones will say. Not me. Not you."

She couldn't resist a barb. "My devoted comrade will do anything save defy the Dark Ones?"

Asif kissed her forehead. "Little Salit, you're braver than you're wise. I swear I will never let Regim carry out his vow."

He looked so serious Salit had to smile. Fierce yearning pierced her, flew to him, and circled back to her again. She could *feel* it, the lance of their affinity, invisible yet as tangible as the air she breathed. Was this what the purities meant when they spoke of Pannish love? Love that endured for Eternity? The Ideal Ecstasy that inspired the generation of a family grown in an Imperial Natalry?

No. Salit knew nothing of Pannish love. None of the impure did. The unborn of the impure weren't grown in natalries.

She had been a child of five when Horan Zehar first took her to Marketplace. Drayer children had tussled over a tossball in the drud quadrant. As she'd stood, admiring their copper skin, well-knit limbs, and glossy muscles, a drayer girl had caught sight of her. Had pointed and jeered.

Lookit! Lookit the impure freak.

That was when Salit had taken up a looking glass for the first time. "Why didn't you drown me?" she'd shouted at her father. "Druds fit only for pulling wagons are prettier than me. Why didn't you grow me in a natalry? Why didn't you let me die?"

Horan Zehar had dried her tears. *My daughter, the impure have never permitted the perpetuation of our people by the Imperium's technology, however good that technology may seem. You're beautiful just the way you are.*

"I love to see you smile, Salit." Asif stood as if he'd discerned her confusion and meant to untangle it. He removed his weapons, belt, tunic, and slippers. A ring of gold gleamed over his heart: the clan band of the Heaven's Devils piercing his left nipple. He bent and through the fabric of her tunic kissed the clan band piercing her.

"Asif, I love you," she said. "You're all that matters to me in this fleeting life."

Except avenging my father's death.

But she didn't want to think about vengeance at the moment.

Asif reached for his discarded tunic and searched in the pocket. He withdrew two gold rings carved with kaligraphs. Each ring had been cut, and the cut ends sharpened into points. "I've been carrying these with me since we parted on the night your father died."

Salit caught her breath.

"Before no witnesses other than your Essence and mine," he said, whispering the ritual question, and handed her a ring. "Will you wear my bond band and live with me as my bonded one?"

"Before no witnesses other than my Essence and

yours, I say yes, I will live with you as your bonded one, as you shall live with me," she said, whispering the ritual answer. "I only have eyes for thee, Asif."

"And I only have eyes for thee. As Darkness is our witness at the beginning and at the end, I hereby bond with thee for all the world to see."

He seized his dirk, pierced her left eyebrow, and inserted a ring through her skin. He squeezed the pointed ends shut.

She wiped away the trickle of blood, took the dirk from his hand, and pierced his left eyebrow. She inserted the second ring through his skin and squeezed it shut. "As Darkness is our witness at the beginning and at the end, I hereby bond with thee for all the world to see."

He pulled off his leggings. Long through the thigh was his right leg and stumpy below the knee. His left leg was just the opposite. But both were strong. Strong and reliable. Salit knew she could always depend on those legs. Asif lay beside her, his lean body stretching half again as long as hers. He eased off her tunic and leggings, and she nestled against him, fitting into a place that had been waiting for her.

Where she'd always wanted to be.

"Beloved comrade and bonded one," she whispered, "may death alone part us."

"Beloved comrade and bonded one," he answered, "even death will never part us. I'll follow you into the Flames of Inim."

"Ho, Dubban Quartermain." Salit appraised the midwife-natalist. He was very handsome, yes, but no other man could move her with Asif's seed inside her and his bond band piercing her brow. "How dare you rouse me from my bonded one's bed?"

"I'm sorry." Dubban clutched an empty beer jar and slowly set it down. His deep voice throbbed with apprehension. "I didn't mean to disturb you."

They sat cross-legged on a saddle blanket in front of

the tent. Asif stood five steps away, observing their huddled conference with a watchful eye. Devil stars, dirk, and dagger decorated his belt once more.

Dubban stole an anxious glance at Asif's weapons, at the bloodbats stirring on the ceiling. Rumor said that the impure ate filth and slept in filth, but it wasn't true. The impure were scrupulously tidy with what little they possessed.

Still, the cavern was filled with many dark things.

"Have you got the threads of disease you promised me?" At his nod, Salit extended her hand. "Give them to me."

But Dubban didn't hand the threads over; he stood decisively, and Salit saw a changed man. No longer the serv who had cowered before her when she'd confronted him at Quartius Natalry. She saw someone bold. Assured. Maybe corrupt, by Imperial standards. He certainly had become a thief.

She liked that.

"These threads," he said, "were cut out of the birthpods of magister unborns. From magister pures, Salit Zehar. Magisters."

"I heard you the first time." She eyed him. "How did you get them? I thought you told me you couldn't set foot in Secundus Natalry 'cause you're just a midwife and a serv and not pure enough. Otherwise, you could have shown me how to poison every magister growing there, like I asked you."

His eyes hardened. "I stole them from an orderly. She was about to incinerate the filth. I took them instead."

No longer a tethered ox led by the nose, indeed. She waggled her fingers. "So let me see this filth."

He withdrew from the burlap sack a copper carrying rack. Stacked within were seven crystal dishes with lids. Within each dish lay slivers of crystal smeared with some nasty-looking fluid.

Salit reached for it, but he held the rack away.

"I want my debt to you, and to your late father, erased in full."

"Well, I don't know, midwife. That was a lot of qut Horan sold you. Two hundred and twenty ores' worth."

"Before Pan and the Imperium, I've done the worst I can do. Release me. I demand it!"

She gnawed her thumbnail. "Half your debt is released."

"I can do no more. I *will* do no more."

"Yet I may ask more."

Dubban glowered so fiercely that Asif stepped closer, a hand on his dagger. She smiled up at her bonded one, expecting his wink of approval.

To her surprise Asif said, "Release him, Salit. He's a decent sort. A serv pure, but not our enemy."

"But I may have further need of him. Half is released," she said stubbornly, toying with her own dagger. "And I'll not trouble you for the other half unless I have urgent need of your services. Agreed?"

Dubban heaved an exasperated sigh. "Do I have a choice?"

"No." She withdrew a pouch on a thong around her neck, smiled slyly, and proffered a greasy little bundle of the bitter herb. "Need a quid of qut, midwife?"

"No." His hands shook, and his eyes filmed over with a haunted look. But the haunting passed, and he stared back again, stern. "I am no longer in the grip of the demon herb. That's how I dug myself into this ditch in the first place."

"A pity." She hooked her thumb beneath another thong around her neck, extracting four enormous faceted orbs. The atlantium glittered a translucent purple. Kaligraphs carved on the facets glowed, and strange little glyphs shimmered all around them. "How about this, then? Do you gamble? Can I interest you in an Orb of Eternity?"

He flinched at the sight. "I don't traffic in witchery."

"What a wilting rose you are. And a good Imperial pure. Do you fear the High Council's ban? Another pity. Our smugglers can't sell enough illegal orbs to you pures."

"Laugh as you will. I've seen and heard all I need to about the Orb of Eternity."

So had Salit. *Sometimes the orb foretells. Sometimes it does more than foretell.* So Tahliq had said when Salit had first met her on the Imperial Planet of Sanguine. And Tahliq ought to know. The erotician was an accomplished orbcaster.

Salit tucked the orbs into the neckline of her tunic, relishing the way they stung her skin. "Tell me something, Dubban Quartermain. You didn't have to seek out magister threads. You could've given me serv threads. Why have you done the worst you can do for me?"

"Because," he said, "I finally have something to live for."

"What's that?"

"The love of a woman."

"Ho! A sacred sharer?" she said sardonically. "Is it Pannish love, supreme and pure, that's got your blood all fired up?"

"No. I love a woman forbidden to me by the Imperium."

Salit laughed and clapped her hands with delight. "Tell you what. I'll release two-thirds of your debt."

She stood, unhooked the chameleon cloak, and drew the draperies apart. She opened a pocket inside—the mnemon pocket. A little sheet of white light—the mnemon that recorded Dubban's debt—glimmered where she'd tied it through the pocket's buttonhole. "Two hundred and twenty ores," said her father's voice, emanating from the mnemon.

"Make that seventy-five ores you owe me." Salit tore off a corner of the mnemon and released it. The bit spiraled away like a firewing escaping a jar. She rethreaded the tattered remains through the buttonhole and retied it, a restless little bow of white light.

"You have something to live for?" she said. "You know what, Dubban? So do I."

•   •   •

"But what in hell *is* it?" Asif frowned at the burlap sack Salit had slung over her shoulder. "What's it *really* worth? What can we *do* with it?"

"We'll have to find out, won't we?"

She pulled the hood of the chameleon cloak over her head, concealing her face and scalp fuzz. She preferred not to announce to all the impure that Salit Zehar had returned to Atlan. Yet achieving invisibility the way her father had so masterfully done—anytime, anywhere— was still far beyond her command.

Old-fashioned concealment would have to do. She and Asif had escorted Dubban to South Ingress and bade him farewell.

Asif plunked his lanky frame on a pile of tumbled rocks in the ingress and pensively studied his newly bonded one. "I don't know, Salit. All this trouble for a bit of scum."

She squatted opposite him and set down the sack. "This is not scum, my bonded one, it is contraband." She lifted out the rack and examined the crystal dishes. "Some of the best contraband ever!"

Asif touched one of the dishes as if it might bite him. "But they look empty. Except for the slop in the bottom."

Salit smirked, pleased *some*thing was going right for a change. "Well, they're not empty. You simply need a viewglass to see the poxy stuff inside."

"A viewglass? What's that?"

"It's an Imperial device for seeing tiny, tiny things. It looks like a column or tube of really thick crystal that's stuck into a metal frame with a bunch of knobs that make the tiny things look bigger." All Salit knew of viewglasses she had gleaned from her father's mnemon showing Dubban peering through the device while he worked at the natalries. "That's what's in these dishes, Asif. Tiny, tiny things."

"You called them threads of disease."

"Yes. Very dangerous. And very valuable, if everything Dubban told me is true."

"But if we can't see them, how do we know Dubban didn't cheat you?"

"Now, *that* is a very good question." She cautiously untied the tattered mnemon that recorded the midwife's debt. "Show me Dubban Quartermain again."

The sheet of white light lofted itself out of her fingertips and hovered. Salit leaned forward, listening intently. There was something Horan Zehar had recorded, something he'd said, that tickled her recollection.

Viewglass might be worth appropriating, his voice murmured from the mnemon, *but who besides the Alchemist knows how to use one? And for what? What does our fine Dubban do with the viewglass? Whatever it is, may be worth much more. . . .*

She snapped her fingers. "The Alchemist! The Alchemist knows many dark things. We must take our dishes of scum to him. He'll know what to do."

Asif sprang to his feet. "You and the Alchemist may know about viewglasses but *I* know that the Alchemist moved his tentsite from Blackblood Cavern to Big Derelict Duct." Asif playfully ran his fingernails through her scalp fuzz, his equanimity restored. "It's half a day's journey. Come, let's return to my tent and rest awhile." His eyes filled with mischief. "We'll pack extra provisions and—"

A commotion burst forth at the mouth of South Ingress—a clamor of shouts, children's shrieks, the dreadful *clang* of weapons. A covey of bloodbats shot up out of the cavern, wings casting weird shadows as the beasts scrambled away in desperate flight.

Suddenly a huge bloodbat swooped before Salit and slammed to the ground. The beast butted its snout against her breast and bowled her over before she could think or shout.

Dumbfounded, she fell flat on her back, arms and legs sprawling. The bloodbat leapt on her, straddling her waist. It bared curved yellow fangs stuck in rheumy red gums that reeked powerfully of rotten meat. Peering down at her, the bat searched her face, muttering and hissing.

Asif drew his dagger, lunged.

"Wait!" Salit stared back into those predatory eyes. She and Asif had lived around bloodbats all their lives. Bloodbats fed upon people and sometimes killed—but only when their easier prey of packbeasts was scarce.

If the bloodbat meant to kill her, it would have done so at once. Instead the beast seemed to want something other than blood.

Salit waited. She smiled nervously, encouraging it.

"Sah lah. Zeeeeerrrrr?" the bloodbat said. "Sah lah. Zeeeeerrrrr?"

"Yes," she whispered, comprehending. "I am Salit Zehar."

The bloodbat lifted its paw from her arm and handed her a scroll. The bony wings beat, levitating the beast in a maelstrom of dirt and gravel. It hovered for a moment, then took off, soaring out of South Ingress with a sound like knives being sharpened on a grindstone.

Salit unrolled the scroll. Stylized kaligraphs with strange serifs blazed before her eyes:

VIGILANCE COMES FOR YOU

Harsh vigile voices echoed up the ingress. "Peace and calm. You are all under arrest."

"Someone warns us, Asif!" Salit said.

"Let's make haste." He pulled her to her feet and they ran for their lives. "I wonder, who could it be?"

Salit was ever hungry but the pot of gruel slung over cookstones turned her stomach with its sour odor. The hag stirred, then rapped her ladle on the rim.

"The Alchemist, did ye say? Gah, there's a strange one. Keeps moving his camp here and there. Ever since the Big Shock, he don't want to settle down."

The hag, grey-haired and worry-grooved, was no

more than a handful of years older than Salit. But the
burden of life weighed heavily on her. Surrounded by
four clutching children, she cupped her belly, weirdly
distended beneath her billowing qaftan.

Salit tried not to stare.

She's growing an unborn inside her body. A gravid
woman was a disturbing sight never seen among the
purities.

On their quest to find the Alchemist, she and Asif
had stumbled across a confinement camp. Storytellers
among the impure still told of the Morn of Savagery:
the dawn a hundred seasons ago when Vigilance had
raided Blackblood Cavern and murdered every gravid
woman and nursing babe.

Since then, the impure sequestered their gravid
women, fed and provisioned them, moving the camps
from secret cavern to secret cavern. Heavily armed clan
guards had intercepted Salit and Asif at this camp's perimeter.

*I must brew the cleansing tea as soon as we make
camp,* Salit thought with a twinge of guilt as she gazed
at the hag. Since her mother was dead, Horan had
taught her the herbal recipe that prevented an unborn
from growing inside *her*. She should have drunk some
tea right away, she knew, after she'd lain with Asif. But
between Dubban's visit and the Vigilance raid, there
hadn't been time.

The hag said, "Not likely the Alchemist'll let ye
close. Anyway, don't know what business you youngsters have got with him." She pulled down the bodice of
her qaftan and gave each sagging breast to the hungry
mouths of the two youngest children.

Salit averted her eyes. Another sight never seen
among the purities: a woman feeding her offspring with
her body. From angel to drud, babes of the purities
drank from jars the way everyone drank, the youngest
sucking from soft spouts.

"Riftside Ledge, that's where ye want to go," the hag
said, pointing north. "But you're wasting your time.
The Alchemist, he don't see no one."

• • •

They hiked north along the subterranean waterway, adjusting their eyes to the light leaking through the duct's cracked ceiling. After two leagues they confronted a mountain of fallen rock that impeded all further passage. Water gushed beneath the debris, bound for some unknown outlet.

"If water goes through," Asif said, securing his weapons more tightly to his belt, "so can we."

They stripped off their stockings and tied them into a makeshift rope. Asif tied one end to the back of his belt, the other end to the front buckle of Salit's belt. The burlap sack with dishes and threads he nestled against his chest, securely buttoning his tunic over the contraband.

They plunged in and swept beneath the debris, bobbing up into spaces between rock and water to fill their lungs. Then down again into watery darkness, arms and legs pumping, and up at the next airspace. "Bloody hell!" Salit shouted when she scraped her forehead and skinned the tip of her nose.

Abruptly the ruins ended. They bobbed up and swept out into a rush of open currents. The clamor of water was deafening. Salit spied a curious paleness in the darkness ahead and the line of a horizon, as if the waterway came to an end. Yet that could not be since the tumult had loudened into a rampaging roar. She swam abreast of Asif, seized his arm, and dragged him with her toward the bank.

He struggled against her. "What in hell are you doing? We're wet anyway. We'll get there quicker with the current."

"Get out," she shouted. "Now! To shore!"

He seized her and, with three powerful strokes, propelled them both to the slippery bank. He gripped her waist, boosted her up, then climbed out himself. Shivering and wringing water from their clothes, they crept toward the thunderous crash.

Over the brink of a newly made cliff plunged a vast

cataract, chutes and flumes spewing from lesser ledges and chimneys through the rock.

"By all Darkness, Salit," Asif shouted and pulled her into a stunned embrace. "You saved our lives!"

"Beloved comrade," she shouted back, "it's not our destiny to die so soon."

The stonework floor north of a monstrous fracture had sunk a quarter league or more. Finding fingerholds and toeholds, they scaled down the rock face. Soaked to the skin, they hiked another half a league. A deepening darkness and an invading chill told them night was descending in the world above.

They stood at last at the brink of Riftside Ledge.

There, too, the Big Shock had ripped open the duct floor, thrusting one colossal edge of rock above the opposite one and exposing a length of the rift. The Apocalyptists preached that when the Imperium came to an end, the world would crack apart and plunge into the Eternal Flames of Inim. Gazing down into the steaming chasm, Salit could believe it.

She cupped her hands around her mouth and shouted, "Ho, Alchemist! It's me, Salit Zehar, and my newly bonded one, Asif Zehest. We must speak with you."

Her voice echoed into the darkness. The ground trembled beneath her feet, and Salit smelled the reek of rotting eggs. She heard a roar and a crackling. Heat blasted out of the chasm, and red-hot magma gouted deep within the rift. *Then it's true. The rocks bleed beneath Atlan.*

Movement stirred in the murk above them. Lamplight flared in erratic shafts and reflected off the cavernous ceiling.

"So, Salit Zehar." The Alchemist's rasping whisper seemed to fill the whole duct, a sound that reminded her eerily of the time she had stood before the Dark Ones in the Chamber of Reckoning. "I've heard the news from Al-Muud. You have a knack for inviting trouble nearly equal to your late father's knack for avoiding it."

Asif said, "What happened at Al-Muud was not Salit's fault, Alchemist."

"That's not what rumor says, my gallant young comrade."

"Will you listen to the chatter of distant druds or the truth told by your own comrade standing before you?"

Salit squeezed Asif's hand. "No, you're right, Alchemist," she called across the chasm. "Regim Deuceman would never have journeyed all the way to Al-Muud just to torment jarmakers. He went looking for me. But you know all that, don't you? Do you, like the Dark Ones, forbid my vow of vengeance?"

The Alchemist's laughter rang out. "No one wants that damned vigile's head on a post in Marketplace more than me, little Salit. Next to the head of his father-in-lock, Councillor Claren Twine."

A narrow rope-and-plank bridge slowly swung over the chasm. Asif caught the end and secured the planks on the cliff's edge.

"Well, come on up, you young Devils. Newly bonded, are you? Maybe that will tame some of the wildness in your blood. What brings you all the way out to Riftside Ledge this fine evening besides the singular pleasure of my company?"

Salit said, "Something only you among all those of the shadow sector will understand, esteemed Alchemist."

"Splendid. I expected nothing less of you. I don't suppose you've got any cheroots."

"I may have one last one in my pocket, if the waterway didn't steal it. It'll be soaked."

"It'll dry. Slow and steady on my little bridge. I recommend that you don't look down."

She gripped the ropes and placed a trembling foot onto the plank. Naked fear swept over her. She always had detested heights. Just then the magma seethed, shooting a spray of molten rock up the chasm walls. Her slim foot slipped into a gap next to the plank.

Asif caught her. "Do be careful, my love."

•   •   •

The Alchemist slouched in an oxhide slingchair, sipping a shot of d'ka. He was intently studying an Orb of Eternity and didn't so much as glance up when they strode into his tentsite. The atlantium facets sparkled in the light of a lone magmalamp. He waved at a jug on a side table, inviting them to help themselves.

Salit caught her breath. This was the man who had sprinted into Blackblood Cavern three seasons ago, pursued by furious vigiles. Blood had streamed down his face when he burst into their tent, and Horan Zehar had hidden him in the crawl space beneath Salit's bedroll. After the vigiles had marched on empty-handed, Horan had hidden him in sanctuaries so secret Salit herself had never known exactly where the Alchemist slept.

This was the man who had concocted lethal cherry laurel gas and loaded the inferno bolts. This, the man who had accompanied Horan Zehar on the most infamous of Heaven's Devils' bloodings—the daring assassination of Milady Danti and the angels in the Hanging Gardens of Appalacia.

Cluttering a low table were bubbling retorts, colanders dripping with reddish green weeds, and crystal tubes rigged up in a heady amalgam of scientific industry and artistic abandon. More distilling equipment, an elegant caf brewer, and a full-sized mattress on a fancy sleep platform were visible through the open front flap of his tent.

How did he transport all this across the barrier? Down the cascade? Over the rift?

But his tentsite wasn't the only astonishing thing about the Alchemist.

The man wore nothing but a gaudy vest over his bare chest and the short leggings of a tourist at the beach. He was as huge and muscular as a high magister subpure, as silver-blond and gorgeous as an angel. His long finger- and toenails were painted with amethyst polish. He wore no diamond-shaped sharelock chips embedded in the backs of his hands. Not a sharer, then.

He wore his extreme age as lightly as silk and as profoundly as Imperial armor. Seventy years? A hundred? More? Who could tell with such a high pure?

His only visible flaw was a scar the shape and circumference of an ore-coin that bored deeply into his right biceps.

The Alchemist laid the orb on the table, raised vivid blue-green eyes, and studied them curiously. Salit shrank before his incisive gaze.

"Well, what have you got for me?" he said.

Asif removed the burlap sack from beneath his tunic and handed it to Salit. She withdrew the copper carrying rack and handed over the crystal dishes.

"There's this midwife who owed my father a qut debt. After Horan died, I went to collect. Dubban and me, we struck a deal. He says these are threads of disease cut out of magister birthpods growing in the tanks at Secundus Natalry. The midwife does this himself. He cuts threads like these—*prunes* them, he calls it—out of seeded pods. He uses a viewglass. Women of the purities just hand over their birthpods to the Imperium, and men hand over their seed. 'Imperial materia,' isn't that the polite name?"

"That's the polite name." The Alchemist seized a dish, strode to the table, and shoved aside a mortar and pestle. He pulled out his own viewglass—Salit *knew* he would have one—and turned up the wick on a magma-lamp. He carefully unscrewed the lid, placed the dish beneath the viewglass, and peered in, fiddling with the knobs.

Silence. Silence for a long time. Salit and Asif traded troubled glances. *Have we been swindled?*

The Alchemist exclaimed, "Of course I've always suspected. Everyone's always suspected. But to find proof. Proof!"

"Are the threads there?" Salit said.

"Threads? Oh, yes, these are generative chains of recombinant acidic—Never mind. Threads will do. Hard to tell just what sort of threads, though."

"Damn," Asif muttered. "The midwife *did* cheat us."

"Oh, I'll pay you, if that's what you're worried about," the Alchemist said. "I know very well you didn't come here for the singular pleasure of my company. Two hundred and fifty ores, will that do?"

Salit could barely contain her glee. The sum was enough to pay off the qut smugglers who'd supplied her father and leave an excellent profit jingling in her pocket.

"If I can make use of them to strike a blow against the Imperium," the Alchemist added, "I'll pay more."

"Done!" Salit clapped her hands. She glanced at Asif, expecting his grin.

But her bonded one gazed at the viewglass, furrowing his brow. "Alchemist, how do the threads get into the birthpods if midwife-natalists keep cutting them out? Wouldn't pure birthpods be free of disease threads by now?"

"An excellent question, Asif. I was never privy to all the secrets of the natalries, in spite of my purity. The Twines and other magisters secreted that knowledge away long ago while my ancestors feasted and drank and danced. Wastrels," he muttered. "Wastrels, with their prestigious name."

They waited while the Alchemist poured more d'ka.

"Near as I can tell, my young Devils," he said, "there are so many threads in every birthpod that even the Imperium can't keep track of them all. The threads recombine with each new linkage of male seed and female birthpod. And there are always impurities. *Good* impurities. Perhaps they're the reason the Imperium has survived, in spite of its technology."

He beckoned Salit to the viewglass.

"There are grains inside every birthpod," he said. "The grains affect the linked threads in myriad ways. The Imperium simply cannot eliminate them all. And *will* not. The grains are necessary for all the threads to grow. Yet they cause further linkages among the threads that no one can predict. You know what? These lively little grains are very much like people of the impure. They stir things up. Even the Imperium cannot control the mystery of life for all Eternity."

Salit peered into the viewglass, thrumming with anticipation. But all she saw was a disappointing jumble. "What else could they be if not disease threads?"

"Oh, just about anything," the Alchemist said. "It will take some study. I may ask that you go to the midwife for more."

She nodded, glad she'd been firm with Dubban. "Alchemist?" The renegade pure knew many dark things. Perhaps her father had shared secrets with the Alchemist. Secrets Horan hadn't shared with her. "You're of the purities. You dream the angels' dreams in the Mind of the World, don't you? Tell me how I appeared in Milord Lucyd's dream?"

To her dismay and astonishment, the Alchemist's eyes filmed with tears. "I don't know, Salit. Why don't you ask the mnemon pocket if your father recorded a mnemon on the subject?"

"You know about my father's mnemons?"

"Oh, certainly. Horan told me all about the cloak and the pocket, and showed me quite a few mnemons. But we never discussed dreams in the Mind of the World. Go ahead. Ask."

Salit hesitated, unwilling to be humiliated. "I've tried and tried but the pocket won't obey me. It spits out whatever mnemon it wants to, no matter what I ask. I had to tie the mnemon about Dubban's debt to the buttonhole so I wouldn't lose it in the pocket."

"Try again. And, Salit, try asking politely for once in your life."

She wanted to stamp her foot and tell the Alchemist to go stuff it, but he smiled at her in such a kindly way, she restrained herself. Very well, politely.

She opened the cloak. The mnemon pocket yawned opposite her heart like a tiny black abyss. She cleared her throat.

"Dear pocket," she said, feeling distinctly ridiculous. "Could you please show me a mnemon that explains how I appeared in Milord Lucyd's dream in the Mind of the World?"

Nothing happened. She bit back a surge of rage. "I *said* please, you moldy scum-spattered piece of worthless—"

"Politely," the Alchemist reminded her.

She sighed. "Please, dear pocket. Please, please?"

A glimmering sheet of white light slipped out, flickering with images, rustling with sounds.

The cluster of commercial cloudscrapers at Marketplace. Vigilance Authority, the Security Number Administration, an Imperial treasury. Among them, a monolith, its hematite facade reflecting the street like a silver mirror: the Temple of the Mind of the World.

Inside, daub-and-wattle cubicles line a maze of labyrinthine hallways. Custodians on their knees slowly push their hands along the baseboards, their fingers like the rags of a mop.

Horan Zehar's whisper: "They only audit dreams, the acolyte-auditors. Cannot cast them the way the angels do."

The tiny hutch of an acolyte-auditor's work cubicle. On a desk, stained caf cups, family pictures, an ashtray overflowing with cheroot butts. A half-chewed quid of qut, too. "This is where Sami Triademe labors," Horan says. "His qut debt to me? Five hundred ores. Pays in installments, not always on time. Vain about his position, but hates the labor. Excellent corruption potential. Who would believe what he let me do this morning before the Big Shock struck? Only took a touch of persuasion from a devil star. His aetheric shell is worth killing for, if only you could smuggle the thing out."

Salit studied the supine figure of Sami Triademe, his eyes closed, mouth pursed in concentration. His chest rose and fell with the rhythm of his breath. He lay inside a device that resembled nothing so much as a coffin made of cookpot metal.

"You know what, Alchemist?" Salit whispered. "I think I've discovered the answer to the question."

FACET 17

Lake: Ownership or greed.
The angel drives the pauper off her property,
    but gives him a loaf of bread.
The action is amassing wealth.
The forbearance is selfishness.

The Orb of Eternity

Commentaries:

Councillor Sausal: As Pan is the source of all things, so all things are distributed according to proximity to Pan. Once distribution according to proximity occurs, however, things disperse according to chance, opportunity, violence . . . [*Deleted from The Contemporary Commentaries of Sausal (15th Ed.*) or application of Imperial law.]

    As angels and magisters exchange wealth with the Imperium for labor, so the lower purities exchange labor for wealth.

    Therefore the prudent person should conserve resources for personal and family needs and contribute any excess to the needy.

Guttersage (usu. considered vulgar): When you've got it, don't let anybody take it.

    When you haven't got it, take what you can get.

Our City of Atlan, the crest of Prime Hill. Milord Lucyd's cloudscraper, the Villa de Reve:

Someone else was there. *Inside* Lucyd's dream. Fear jolted him so sharply, he nearly woke.

Not an acolyte-auditor from the Temple of the Mind of the World. A strange presence intruded *inside* his dream. The Honorable Milord Lucyd Sol naitre Primus, aetherist of the angels, felt it as surely as he felt the racing of his pulse.

But he did not wake. How could he?

It was his Imperial duty to dream:

The Mind of the World stretches before the dream-eye, a glimmering panorama. The glimmer coalesces, and images solidify.

Lucyd stands, a slender angel in a black-silk robe, before the Pyramid of Perpetuities. He admires the soaring granite slopes, the mountain of skulls, the frescoes depicting Eternal Bliss and Eternal Torment.

Milady Danti stands beside him. But she is only a preserved corpse displayed in a translucent sarcophagus. Wires move her lips, and her face forms a smile.

No more dreams of Danti alive the way he'd dreamed of her after she'd been murdered. All Pangaea knew her smile was a gesture she made from Eternity. A gesture of the dead.

Sizzle of magma surging from a crevice, moan of the winter wind, susurration of two hundred million shareminds partaking the dream—these are the only sounds.

Lucyd says, as he was told to say, "As she was born to this world, so she is born to Eternity."

"And so I shall see you again, my beloved sharer," Danti's corpse intones, *"when you join me in Eternity."*

Reclining in his aetheric shell, Lucyd stifled a skeptical snort. Who believed such lies anymore? Danti had vanished from the world. He would never see her again.

A furtive figure darts around the corner of the pyramid.

Lucyd jolted. Anxiety furrowed his high-domed forehead. His noble face grew as cool as carved ivory, a substance it resembled more closely than skin. He had always lain motionless when he dreamed but tonight he

tossed and turned. Even a whiff of hypnolia did not
soothe him. Thankfully the aetheric shell beamed his
dream into the Mind of the World as effortlessly as it
always had. An elegant silver ovoid the size and shape
of a capacious coffin set in the center of his dreamchamber, the shell had beamed dreams for his angelic
ancestors since times lost to antiquity.

The diamond-shaped scars in Lucyd's hands ached.
After Danti had succumbed to the murderous stars of
Heaven's Devils, he had ordered his house physician to
remove his sharelock chips. Now summer and autumn
had come and gone, and still Vigilance had not apprehended the terrorists. It was a disgrace and an outrage.
The Hanging Gardens of Appalacia had always been a
sanctum for angels, not a slaughterhouse for foes.

*He dashes after the elusive figure and shouts, "Say,
you! I didn't dream you. Where are you? Show yourself, you coward."*

*He trembles with fear and fury, but there is nothing.
No one confronts him. No one flees across the flagstones. The grounds are empty.*

The temple magisters would be furious. Fear and
fury had no place in Lucyd's dreams. His were the finest: lovely visions depicting the joys of Pannish love.
Edifying visions showing the Imperial duties of sacred
sharelock and destined labor according to one's purity.
Every pure and subpure in Pangaea partook of Lucyd's
dreams. All became better citizens when they did.

There. The patter of footsteps.

*He shouts again, "Damn you, this is my dream! I
won't let you ruin it. No one will ever infiltrate my
dreams again."*

For this was the dream of Milady Danti's consecration to Eternity, not the terrible dream of Darkness last
summer. A commissioned dream paid for by the Temple
of the Mind of the World. He had his instructions. He
was to dream of high pures honoring Danti, proving
their reverence for Pan and their belief in her everlasting
Essence.

At the actual consecration last summer, high pures

had honored Danti. Angels had come and magisters from every bureaucracy plaguing the Imperium. Councillors of the First Families. Rogues of newly wealthy vigile clans. They sullied Danti's consecration with their magister arrogance.

Danti would have been appalled. She had despised the magister purity. And the consecration? The ceremony had been ludicrous, a charade, humiliating and pathetic. Why pretend a living spirit spoke through the wired lips of a corpse?

Because who would believe in Eternity otherwise? Who would believe a lifetime of servitude to the Imperium was justified by the promise of Eternal Bliss? Who would serve and obey?

Few angels had distinguished themselves amid those hulking vigiles and councillors. No angel had made the brilliant impression those of the highest purity ought to make. Since when had angels become so puny, so blanched, so debilitated?

Come forth, angels! And vibrant angels stride into Lucyd's dream, robust angels with fiery eyes, blushing cheeks, and broad shoulders. They walk with a stride worthy of those who cast dreams in the Mind of the World.

Much better. *Now* he was dreaming properly.

But a sudden movement outside the shell distracted him. Another earthshock? So many shocks, great and small, troubled these times. They jostled the megalopolis nearly every day, rattling the fractured foundation of Villa de Reve. Lucyd had hoped the Big Shock that devastated Atlan last summer would be the last, but it hadn't been. Inside the aetheric shell, he clasped his hands more tightly over his chest, half-praying, half-concentrating on his dream—

She leaps out from behind the pyramid.

Lucyd shouts in terror, leaps back.

The girl! The same girl who invaded his dream of Darkness! She wears a sweeping cloak that swirls around her as if the garment has a spirit of its own. Her grotesque face twists in a mocking leer. Her misshapen eyes gleam with malice. She unhooks a sliver from her belt and flicks it. Six startips snap out.

Lucyd backs away, searching for a weapon.

"Wait," he cries. "You can't do this in my dream."

The girl flings the devil star with an expert flip of her wrist. The star whirls, hissing, and slices off Lucyd's forearm. Blood spurts from his severed elbow. The star whirls again, orbiting him. Startips plunge into his chest and cartwheel, carving bloody spirals from neck to navel.

"Welcome, Heaven's Devils," she sings in a ragged soprano, "who wreak wrack and ruin on the Imperium!"

He gasps, falls to his knees.

The girl brandishes an Orb of Eternity. She turns a facet toward the dream-eye, and Lucyd sees the image of an erupting volcano. Red-hot magma spews out of the facet, splattering his face.

The girl shouts, "The Apocalypse is here!"

Lucyd punched open the lid of the aetheric shell and leapt out as he'd never leapt in his sixty-seven years. The girl's song, her shout, echoed horribly in his ears. His right kneecap cracked, propelling hot pain up his leg. Both knees buckled, and he nearly fell the way he'd fallen in his dream.

Shaking, he glanced down, hardly daring to look.

His forearm was intact, his chest unharmed. Yet the dream had been so vivid, the wounds so horrifying, pain gnawed through his elbow and stitched spirals across his abdomen.

He leaned against the aetheric shell, shuddering. His trusted handmaid stood beside him, bearing his customary cup of caf and a vial of nopaine. He held out his hand. "My dear Dote, will you help me?"

"Yes, milord," Dote replied, observing proper protocol the way she always did. But her steadying hand was cool and perfunctory.

Sitla and Arvel, his beloved sphinxes, crouched at the handmaid's feet. The pets squabbled and spit over a honeycomb though they knew very well Lucyd forbade them to quarrel.

Every pure in Pangaea, even heavily shaped druds like the sphinxes, had been behaving peculiarly since the Big Shock. The Bureau of Ground Control had promised to stop the shocks with Imperial technology, but they hadn't. The world might not have come to an end the way the Apocalyptists said, but a recklessness infected everyone in Atlan.

"Dote, take the honeycomb away from my sphinxes and send them to bed without supper," Lucyd said. It saddened him that trusted servants and beloved pets—whom he'd always treated with kindness and generosity—should regard him with distance and defiance.

Lucyd heard the sound of a throat being politely cleared. An acolyte-auditor in the silver livery of the Temple of the Mind of the World stood at the doorway of his dreamchamber. An entourage of temple vigiles flanked her.

"Greetings, Milord Lucyd," the acolyte-auditor said with an ironic bow that managed to satisfy protocol while conveying depthless contempt. "Her Holiness, Dame Cardinal of the Mind of the World, requests that you appear before her and a Grand Jurare this evening."

At another time, in an earlier day, if such a low-middle pure had dared clear her throat before an angel deigned to notice her, Lucyd would have commanded his majordomo to thrash her.

But he didn't do that. Instead Lucyd smoothed his gold-sateen bodysuit over his long, slender limbs. Ran trembling fingers through his platinum curls. Since the dream of Darkness last summer, he had anticipated an interview with the Cardinal. He'd dreaded the summons, but fully expected it.

He had *not* expected the Cardinal to summon him before a Grand Jurare.

"On what charge?" he asked softly.

"*Charges,* milord. Contamination of the Mind of the World. Breach of an aetherist's Imperial duty. Collusion with Heaven's Devils. And, milord, the heresy of Apocalyptism."

"All Pangaea knows I lost my codreamer, Dame Cardinal," Lucyd said to the Grand Jurare as humbly as he could, though outrage nearly overwhelmed him. "No thanks to Vigilance Authority," he added acidly.

He hung within a suspension in the Chamber for Pure Thoughts, dangling in midair like any interrogee of the lowest purity. He crossed his arms over his chest and pressed his legs together, determined to sustain a dignified stance in this supremely undignified predicament. The suspension simultaneously pulled him up by the roots of his hair and dragged him down by his toes. If the Cardinal decided to, she could accelerate the opposing forces within the suspension. She could tear an interrogee in two.

Twelve ranks of interrogators stood upon the colossal marble dais surrounding the suspension. The suspension could elevate the interrogee above the interrogators or thrust him down into a well below them, depending upon his pure and subpure and its relation to magisters of the temple functionary subpure. The Grand Jurare had observed enough of protocol to raise Lucyd's suspension to a height befitting an angel. He gazed down at upturned faces, accusatory eyes, merciless mouths.

"Vigilance Authority," the Cardinal replied imperiously, "is doing its utmost to exterminate the Heaven's Devils." Short-legged for a magister pure, the supreme arbiter of the Mind of the World was built as massively as a drayer, but without a drayer's tautness from ceaseless physical labor. Flesh hung in drapes from her stocky bones. "Vigilance Authority is not at issue here," she said, matching his caustic tone. "*You* are, milord. On charges of the gravest nature. Do you understand?"

"Of course." Mildly, mildly. *Pan grant me patience.*

"I should hope so, milord. The Mind of the World is one of the Imperium's finest achievements. Next to the purities, it is a cornerstone of the Imperium's glory and perpetuity."

"As Pan is the source of all existence, so the Mind of the World is the source of all thought." Lucyd repeated the Imperial propaganda, supplying his own addendum. "And as the great dreamers who created the Mind of the World in antiquity were angels, so the angels cast dreams in the Mind of the World to this day."

"To *this* day," the Cardinal replied. "Who knows what tomorrow will bring?"

Her seditious words stunned Lucyd into silence.

Other than elevating the level at which he hung in the suspension, the Grand Jurare had observed little else of propriety toward an aetherist of the highest pure and subpure. The magisters had not permitted Lucyd's protocol advisor, commercial manager, or Imperial liaison to the proceeding. Had not permitted a fellow aetherist or another angel to appear as advocate or witness. And most distressing of all, had forced him to disembark from his cherished windship.

He shivered in the chill air shifting inside the suspension.

The distraught windship hovered within a cordon of armed temple vigiles. Its multicolored wings crowning the translucent blue teardrop fluttered with anguish. If Lucyd summoned the ship, it would fly to him, envelop him, pump heat and hypnolia into its inner atmosphere. Embrace him as tenderly as a caretaker embraces a child.

He dared not summon the ship. He had no notion what the temple vigiles would do to it. Or him.

What power do angels possess if the purities disrespect our blessed proximity to Pan? What defenses do we have left without our cloudscrapers and windships and dreams?

He wondered if he would swoon.

Would they release him then? Or thrust smelling salts in his face and continue this disgraceful interrogation?

He would not give them the satisfaction.

"Surely you do not mean to confess," the Cardinal

said, "that the eminent Milord Lucyd has relied upon a codreamer for the purity of his renowned dreams?"

"A codreamer content to be the puppet of her sharer's dreams?" added a temple magister, brightly blond despite a low, brutish forehead and jutting jaw. "With no dreams of her own?"

How could he possibly explain to these beasts what Milady Danti had meant to him?

That she was my Essence. My muse. That I could dream of no one else after the sacred surgeons inserted our sharelock chips.

He said nothing. Not because he would not, even to these bullying magisters, but because he didn't know what the truth was anymore. *Who was Danti, really?* Now that the sharelock chips were gone, Lucyd had begun to recall Danti in deeply disturbing ways. Layers of memory peeled away, revealing a Danti he'd scarcely known.

"Yes, I depended on Danti as my codreamer," he finally said. "She was the most beloved woman in the Mind of the World."

And he unleashed his angel's sharemind, most powerful of the purities. Dreams of Danti exploded in their puny magister shareminds: ten thousand exquisite smiles, a hundred thousand of her songs, a million passionate glances of her slanting sapphire eyes.

Lucyd loathed entering mutual consciousness with lesser shareminds. He'd feel as if he'd been strapped into a straitjacket and dipped in sewage. He had known only two people with whom entering sharemind was not a torment, and one had been Danti. But this small demonstration was worth it. The magisters clapped shut their flapping jaws. The blond brute-face collapsed in a swoon.

As swiftly as he'd unleashed it, Lucyd withdrew his sharemind. One flicker was enough.

"Of *course* we recognize D-Danti's exaltation in the Mind of the World, milord," the Cardinal stammered.

"Then shame on this Jurare for ridiculing her memory and castigating me." The Cardinal mumbled apologies, but Lucyd waved them away. "Aetherists often rely on the steadying influence of a codreamer. The late Milady Faro had quite an unusual one." Lucyd had despised the aetherist who had perished in the Hercynian eruption nearly as much as he despised her dreams of torture, but his tastes were hardly the Jurare's concern at the moment. "She relied on a pet sphinx."

Stunned gasps rang out. Faro's tiny, white-haired sphinx had been as famous as her mistress. And scandalous since owning lower pures was illegal these days. Who could have suspected that a drud could serve as an angel's codreamer?

"Dreaming is a difficult undertaking," Lucyd said. "It is nothing like the random musings you recall from your slumber. Dreaming in the Mind of the World is ever a trial and a burden. I don't mind telling you that practice of the blessed art exacts its toll. I myself must take nopaine after I dream. Sometimes I feel like I'm dying."

"We are terribly sorry," the Cardinal murmured. "Then, milord, you do not subscribe to the heresy of Apocalyptism?"

"Of course not. I do not dream that the world is coming to an end." Lucyd rubbed his forehead, which was beginning to throb. "It is only when that devilish girl invades my dreams that Darkness and horror appear."

"And you cannot account for that invasion? For the impure girl? The Orb of Eternity?"

Lucyd was, this time, prepared for the accusation. He recalled his dream of this evening and shuddered anew. "I have never met that girl. I have never even *seen* an actual orb. I certainly do not now possess a device banned by the High Council three seasons ago. I do not wish for the same sort of ruin that befell Councillor Sausal."

"Then, milord, how is it that you dream of these things?"

"Come, Dame Cardinal. It is *your* acolyte-auditors

who interrupt my dreams again and again. It is within *your* purview to discover how this terrorist wreaks havoc in the Mind of the World. I swear before this Grand Jurare that I am as much a victim of this terrorism as every Pangaean. I have sworn the same to Lieutenant Captain Regim Deuceman."

The magisters flinched at the mention of Regim's name. Lucyd smiled grimly. *Frightened of one of your own purity, are you?* He was not the only one who had cringed before the newly appointed Special Investigator of Impure Activities at Vigilance. Every Pangaean had entered the stylized gloss of a crier's sharemind and witnessed Regim's torture of the jarmakers at Al-Muud. Lucyd had never thought about jarmakers one way or the other till he'd witnessed the atrocity.

He could well imagine what Danti would have done. She would have thrown back her beautiful head and laughed. He could almost hear her derisive chuckle, how she would have clapped her hands and said, "Look at *that* one squirm." And Lucyd would have laughed with her. In the intimacy of sharers' sharemind, he would have shared her cruel amusement.

Alone, without sharelock chips, he had not laughed. He had sent a beck-and-call man to Al-Muud with a thousand ores for the jarmaker and his family. Had refused to cast dreams celebrating Regim's atrocity as a blow against the foes.

"You accuse me of shirking my Imperial duty," Lucyd said. "Of Apocalyptism. Know that I welcome an investigation of my dreams. Yet if neither I nor the integrity of my aetheric shell can be held accountable, then I demand that you, Dame Cardinal, commence your investigation *here*. In your temple."

If he had blatantly accused the temple magisters of treason, he could not have provoked a more furious outcry. Lucyd gazed down on averted faces, fearful eyes, trembling lips.

The Cardinal shouted, "Silence!" At her gesture, the temple vigiles stepped forward, brandishing crossbows. "We shall commence an internal investigation at once.

As for you, milord, I am satisfied you are the trusted aetherist Pangaea loves best and dreams with. The temple, therefore, respectfully submits a request."

Lucyd raised an eyebrow. "What request?"

"A new commission of dreams." The Cardinal retrieved contracts from the flat hands of a document bearer. "Our Imperial Bureau of Ground Control has not fulfilled the High Council's mandate to stop the earthshocks. The High Council is displeased. As is Ground Control, you may well imagine. Every day, a new heretic is discovered. The bureau, and its advisors at Sausal Academy, are scrambling to implement a new strategy."

"As well they should be," Lucyd said.

"Then you agree," the Cardinal said, "that these incessant earthshocks are dreadful?"

"Disastrous. Every time I try to repair my house, another shock ruins the effort."

"Disruptive of the Imperium?"

"Catastrophic to the Imperium. Ceaseless destruction compromises the purities' faith in Pan's benevolence."

"Then the temple requests that you dream of happy days ahead." The Cardinal brandished the contracts. "Dream of how Ground Control's new strategy will stop earthshocks, once and for all. Of how the Imperium will restore the peace and calm we and our ancestors have enjoyed all our lives. That our children and their children will enjoy all their lives. Find a new codreamer, milord, if that's what you require. But dream of happy days."

Dream of lies. "Release me from this suspension and restore my windship to me."

"I will. But, first, are we agreed?"

"Yes, yes. I agree." He was so tired of the Imperium's lies. Find a new codreamer? After Danti, he didn't know where to begin.

•   •   •

Lucyd heard a scream.

Night had fallen in earnest. A stunning crescent moon hung in the midheaven and Our Imperial Planet of Sanguine sparkled, a tantalizing plum-red orb to the north. Lucyd braked the windship at Villa de Reve's front door and stepped out, slipping down the ship's slick stairs in his haste.

Another scream rent the villa's hush, hurling out of the southwest salon.

Lucyd sprinted up the grand staircase spiraling from ground floor to second to third. He hadn't moved so quickly in decades. No, wrong. He'd been a dreamer his whole life. He'd *never* moved so quickly. His lungs burned as he heaved for breath.

He flung the gilt doors open.

And strode into his favorite salon. Settees uphol-stered in white glove-leather and hand-carved peyr-wood chairs had been arranged in graceful suites. Silk tapestries of seaside scenes softened the whitewashed walls. There Lucyd displayed his collection of antique ivory trifles from pre-mandate Tasman, the largest of its kind in Our City of Atlan.

The side tables had been set with porcelain dishes bearing honey puddings and rosenut cakies. Crystal goblets brimmed with golden kapfo wine and milky d'ka.

Blood spattered the bleached-fleece carpet.

Danatia crouched on the floor, pressing fingers to her lower lip, her exquisite face paler than the rich, pale furnishings. Her platinum hair straggled down the stem of her neck. The décolletage of her gown had been wrenched over her shoulder.

Tonel stood over her, his face—so like Lucyd's in repose—contorted with rage. His cheeks had flushed nearly as scarlet as the blood leaking from Danatia's lip. He swayed slightly, eyes blurred with intoxication, fists clenched.

The sphinxes huddled behind a footstool, tiny arms wrapped around each other.

The handmaids, majordomo, and beck-and-call men

stood miserably at the periphery of the salon, eyes impassive or averted. Only Dote wrung the slabs of her hands, and Gingi, the good-hearted caretaker, openly wept. Lucyd had retained Gingi when he and Danti had dispatched his cloven sons to his villa in Siluria fifty years ago. She loved them well. Handmaid and caretaker risked severe punishment for protocol violations with such displays of emotion.

The other ten clovens reclined in settees and chairs, regarding their brother with a gamut of emotions from pained amusement to outraged contempt. Lucyd's sons—all so like him with their high-domed foreheads and sculpted cheekbones—had kept to their seats. Just as Lucyd's staff stood at unhappy attention.

Because Tonel was the eldest and their superior. He had emerged from his gestation tank at Primus Natalry a full seven hours before the others, first cloven of the most famous angel in Pangaea. Under purity protocol, neither brothers nor staff could raise a hand or speak a word against him.

But famed aetherist, elder, and father, Lucyd could.

He strode across his favorite salon and slapped his eldest cloven across the face as hard as he could. He had never slapped another human being in his life. Let alone his son.

Tonel staggered back, shock and another sort of rage twisting his expression. Lucyd's handprint blazed on his cheek. Tonel's fist drew back in an incipient counterblow and hung there, suspended. Trapped in Imperial protocol, relentless in its demand to tame ancient shames.

"I will have you whipped if you do," Lucyd whispered.

Grief welled in his chest at the venom in his son's eyes. Lucyd hadn't seen Tonel more than a half dozen times in fifty years, had entered sharemind with his progeny even less. When Tonel and the clovens had appeared at Danti's consecration so unexpectedly, Lucyd had been overcome with guilt. Overcome with shame at

Danti's hatred of his clovens—a hatred he had tolerated or ignored while he wore sharelock chips.

Why had Danti despised his clovens?

She had been barren. She'd wept for days when the Superior Mother and Superior Father had told her at Primus Natalry that her Imperial materia would not mingle with Lucyd's in the miracle of Pan. That her birthpod would not become fruitful with his seed, but that his seed, with the natalry's spark, could generate unborns. Generate many clovens.

Any other barren woman would have welcomed her sharer's clovens. Would have thanked Pan and the Imperium for the miracle of natalry technology. Not banished her sharer's progeny from her heart and her presence.

But Danti's behavior, however wretched, was no excuse for Tonel's shameful behavior.

"How dare you violate the serenity of my household?" Lucyd said.

"Milord is a fine one to speak of violations," Tonel said. "Fresh from a Grand Jurare, isn't that so? The devilish girl, again? And that thing, the Orb of Eternity? In a dream this very evening! Dote told us all about it when we returned from Marketplace."

"The Cardinal held me blameless."

"I see. And who has inquired lately about your sphinxes? Owning druds has been illegal since the repeal of the mandate of indenture. Or does milord consider himself above Imperial law?"

Sitla scampered to Lucyd's feet and pressed her pretty little face against his calf muscles. Arvel raised his furry arms in a supplicating gesture and mewed in consternation.

My sphinxes, loyal still. Lucyd smiled fondly at his pets, but he trembled at Tonel's accusation. "I treat my sphinxes as if they were my children," he said and immediately regretted it.

His clovens regarded him somberly, ten identical faces filled with sorrow. *I never meant to neglect you, my sons.*

Tonel laughed derisively. "Surely you must mean *better* than your children, milord. Else I shall have to report you for drud abuse, wouldn't you say, Dote?"

Dote moaned and wrung her hands.

"What? Speak up. I cannot hear you," Tonel said. "Or perhaps I should report milord to Vigilance for owning sphinxes. What do you think about that, Dote?"

Rage boiled up in Lucyd at his son's badgering of the drud handmaid. "That's enough, Tonel." He pointed at Danatia, who had not moved. "What is the meaning of your protocol violation against this angel?"

"*My* violation? It is *she* who committed a violation."

"What violation?"

"She swallowed her wine before I swallowed mine."

"Did she sip first?"

"No. I sipped first."

One of the clovens raised his finger. At Lucyd's nod, he said, "Our eldest brother made a show of savoring his wine, knowing full well Milady Danatia finds kapfo distasteful and would rather have spit it out than swallow it."

"Thank you, my son." Was this cloven Votrel or Tassem? Lucyd wasn't certain. Since Danti's consecration, he'd seen more of the clovens than he had in his whole life. But they still looked so alike to his eyes. To Tonel, "Swallowing her wine first after sipping second is hardly a violation calling for a beating."

"Oh, this was hardly a beating, milord. When I beat her, she will know it. I merely punished her insubordination. As is my prerogative as her pledged sharer and the superior subpure."

Lucyd drew himself up. "As master of this estate and *your* superior, I withdraw all prerogatives you may claim to punish anyone in my house. Let alone an angel of a subpure proximate to yours and a delicate person who deserves the shield of your hand, not the blow of your fist."

"Oh, milord, don't be deceived by her gentle wiles. She's as tough as an old plower. And hardly proximate.

Danatia is of the same low subpure as your dearly departed sharer. Any fool can see the resemblance. Like Danti and me, she is a worthless angel who cannot dream."

"Milady Danti was far more blessed by Pan than I. She codreamed because she chose to. You, on the other hand, have chosen not to dream at all."

"*I* do not dream because I cannot," Tonel said. "You may have given me your face, milord, but you were much too greedy to part with any of your gift."

"Whatever gift you may possess you have squandered on d'ka and bitterness. You will address me as your father. Do you understand me, my son?"

"Yes, my father," Tonel spit back.

Lucyd sighed deeply. If only Tonel or the other clovens *had* shown any signs of the gift for dreaming. If only they had delved deeper into their fine minds. Trained more assiduously. Meditated. Gone into seclusion. Even partaken of the intoxicants that sometimes released a latent gift, even if those intoxicants might release madness, too. *Any* of the ancient techniques would have satisfied Lucyd. He would have gladly chosen a new codreamer from among his clovens. A trusted family member would have been an ideal candidate.

But none had made the effort. Or perhaps truly none possessed any gift. And that, too, was as much the bleak harvest of his neglect as his sons' estrangement.

"I would have welcomed your dreams, Tonel," Lucyd said sadly. "You may leave. All of you, begone. Except Danatia. You will please stay, milady. I want a word with you."

His sons rose stiffly, his staff turned obediently, and the congregation silently shuffled from the salon.

"Planning to bed her after we're gone, my father?" Tonel called sardonically over his shoulder. "I'll warn you now, she's a dud in the sack. You're better off with a cold fish."

"You will respect your father and refrain from scurrilous speech, my son."

"Really, a man of your age and experience? You

must have spoiled your loins with skillful eroticians for decades. She'll be no match for your exotic tastes. My father."

"Majordomo?" Lucyd said.

"Yes, milord?"

"I have instructed my son to refrain from scurrilous speech. He has disobeyed me. I empower you to take Tonel to the punishment chamber and administer ten lashes with the leather whip. He may wear a shirt, but you must put your muscle into it. Do not spare him. Then have my physician treat his wounds, but he is to be administered no anodyne. I want him to feel pain."

"Yes, milord."

Tonel guffawed. "Remember, my father, she's pledged to me in sharelock. You may touch her body, but you'll never, ever, touch her Essence."

"Neither will you."

When they were alone, Lucyd stooped beside Danatia and gently pried her hand from her lip. "Let me see, milady."

"You needn't address me so, milord."

"But of course I must. You *are* Danti's cloven, aren't you? It's a miracle. Our natalry in Atlan had assured us Danti could never generate clovens or children. I never knew she had one."

"I am not her cloven, milord."

Surprise rippled through him. He studied her face. The platinum hair, ivory complexion, slanting sapphire eyes—so like Danti, his throat clenched every time he looked at her. The corner of her mouth was already swelling though there was only a small cleave in her lip where Tonel's fist had punched her flesh against her teeth. Still, her blood flowed freely the way Danti's had from the slightest nick in her finger or a tiny crack in her skin when the weather grew cold.

He lifted the young woman to her feet. She didn't flinch or tremble, but permitted him to move her as if she were lifeless. She seemed to gaze at something deep within herself instead of the world.

"Danatia," he said, "I wish to attend midnight revelations at the Pyramid of Perpetuities. Would you—? That is, if you're not too tired." He was unaccustomed to asking. "Would you please accompany me?"

"I would gladly accompany you anywhere, milord."

And as Lucyd's evening of dreaming had begun, so it ended at midnight: standing before the Pyramid of Perpetuities. The pyramid of the world, though, not a vision in a dream.

The world of flesh and time disappointed Lucyd, as it usually did. Reality never quite glowed the way his dreams did. He spied chinks in the granite slopes, water stains on the stones. The mountain of skulls was crude and poorly carved. And the frescoes depicting Eternal Bliss and Eternal Torment?

"Danatia," he said to the young woman who stood, wide-eyed, beside him, "tell me, what do you think of the frescoes?"

To his astonishment, she giggled, then clapped her hand over her wounded mouth and winced with pain. "I apologize, milord."

"Do not apologize. Tell me why you're laughing!"

For the first time since he'd met her at Danti's consecration, Danatia snapped out of her passivity. "I laugh in amazement that our powerful Imperium chooses to persuade reverence among the purities with images of suffering."

"I happen to agree with your delightful blasphemy, but we must both bear in mind *that*"—he pointed at the fresco—"is Eternal Bliss."

"I beg your pardon, but *that* is torment everlasting. To live forever, chaste, hands clasped in prayer, eyes stuck on Pan? While one's beloved, however sinful, is cast away forever into Inim's flames? I cannot imagine a worse Eternal Bliss."

"And Eternal Torment?"

She examined the frescoes of everlasting torture and slowly inflicted death. "They're vulgar. They invite contempt for a Supreme Being who would abuse the power of divinity to torment powerless subjects."

"But those subjects have transgressed against Pan."

"And that is how the big bully proposes to teach them the blessed way? They will never learn piety on a rack. Torture victims learn only to inflict more torture on those weaker than themselves. As the tavern wit says about Facet 16 of the Orb of Eternity, 'Terror is as terror does.'"

"Watch your tongue, milady, lest vigiles cut it out," he said in mock admonishment.

"For citing the Orb of Eternity?"

"For referring to contaminated philosophies that degrade the contemplation of Pan and will land you in jail."

"Ah, milord. Since the High Council banned the orb, my fellow students at Siluria Academy have become more fascinated than ever with orbcasting and oracles."

"But why, when they place themselves at risk?"

"I suppose human nature flies to the forbidden like a feltwing to a flame. Don't you agree?"

"Hush!" But Lucyd smiled. "Shall we ask for revelations from Milady Danti?"

"By all means." She wrapped her hand around his elbow.

They entered the Venerated Vestibule via the angels' queue. No angels attended the revelations tonight, but all shapes and sizes of pures and subpures crowded the other queues. Firefighters and fishers, millet threshers and pondplum pickers jostled each other and gawked at Lucyd.

Danatia glanced at him, admiration shining in her eyes. For once, Lucyd felt proud of his fame. He gazed back at her with admiration of his own. And jolted. Had he ever gazed at Danti this way? And if he had, would she have laughed scornfully, accused him of the bestial urge, and advised him to seek the services of an erotician?

Lucyd released Danatia's hand from his elbow and threaded his fingers through hers. They promenaded down the angels' gold-silk carpet to the Perpetual Peak. The pyramid within the pyramid rose in five thousand tiers. Hand-chiseled Tythys marble glowed a pale luminous green. Each tier bore five hundred translucent sarcophagi bearing mummified corpses of the greatest angels and magisters who had been consecrated to Eternity in the last ten decades. Here and there the modest sarcophagus of a brilliant scholar or a ferocious athlete had been set among the higher pures. At the Apex stood sarcophagi containing the oldest mummies among the consecrated, visible from where Lucyd and Danatia stood only as dwarfish lozenges of light.

"What happens when the memorializers run out of room on the tiers?" Danatia asked.

"Another impudent question, milady?"

"A practical one, milord."

He laughed. "So it is." After the long, difficult evening—another terrifying dream, the Grand Jurare, the confrontation with Tonel—how lighthearted she made him feel. "The pyramid's staff removes the longest dead to the preservation vaults below us."

"And when the vaults run out of room?"

"They shall have to dig deeper, won't they?"

"Perhaps they should place them on funeral pyres and permit them to return to Pan, body *and* Essence."

"You know," Lucyd said, "that's a splendid idea. I shall have to write it into my will. Hush now, and kneel with me."

They knelt together before Danti's station set upon the lowest tier of the Perpetual Peak. Lucyd gazed at the corpse in its translucent coffin. *Danti, so cherished once. My sharer and codreamer for fifty years. You were younger than this young woman beside me when we entered into sharelock. So young. So exquisite. I would have died for you then.*

Memorializers scurried around the coffin, bearing sticks of smoldering incense. Others manipulated the corpse's face and limbs with concealed wires. A mimicker crouched behind the sarcophagus, speaking into a trumpet. The mimicker's voice, only vaguely resembling Danti's, emanated from the corpse's mouth.

Supplicants thronged before the station.

"So if I pledge to Pan a tenth of my wage and a quarter of my inheritance," said a sorrowful man, a dancer from the look of his graceful limbs, "will that lift my sharer out of Eternal Torment into Toleration?"

"It will do for a start," the mimicker said. "Though your sharer should have taken precautions to purify herself before she died."

"How could she have taken precautions? She died by accident."

"You must always and ever be purified."

At any other time Lucyd would have listened intently to such revelations, the better to comprehend Pan. Now he saw nothing but the exquisite angel kneeling beside him.

"Danatia," he whispered as the mimickers droned on, "if you're not Danti's cloven, may I ask what are you?"

"Danti's full sister, milord. Our father's great-granddaughter and our mother's youngest grandniece generated Danti forty-five years ago with the materia of our father and mother. They were killed in the Rising of '02. Danti was never the cloven of our beautiful mother, though she liked to say so. She was a full-born of our father's seed and our mother's birthpods. As am I."

"But her debilities. Her sensitivity. Her barrenness. Her inability to dream."

"The poor heritage of angels, I'm afraid. Our mother and father were oh so pure. Our family preserved their Imperial materia in the Natalry Bank at Siluria for fifteen decades."

"A full sister." Lucyd pondered that. Another question plagued him. "Danatia, why you have pledged yourself in sharelock to Tonel?"

"He sought me out when he discovered that Danti's ancestors lived in Siluria. He offered a very generous begetting fee, which my eldest living sister and eldest aunt accepted. I'm afraid our family has lived off our estate for years without replenishing our inherited resources. It's quite banal. My family needs the money."

"So Tonel wreaks his revenge on Danti's sister because Danti refused to love him like a mother. By striking you, he strikes at the memory of my sharer."

"You're too harsh with your eldest cloven, milord."

"And you," he touched her lip, "are too soft."

"Perhaps. He didn't hate me at first. Tonel has had many disappointments in his life. He's a bitter man."

"Because of me."

"Because of his nature."

"And what is your nature, Danatia? Why do you withdraw into yourself? This is the first time you've spoken with me freely. No," he said as that distant look crept into her eyes and her face froze into a mask. "Do not leave me."

She shook her head, wincing with the effort. "I've always turned within myself. Isn't that the prerogative of angels? To dwell in the higher realms?"

"What realms are these?"

"The realms within, milord. Just within."

"Dear Pan, you are a dreamer," he whispered. "A natural dreamer." He fairly shook with excitement. "Danatia, have you ever dreamed in an aetheric shell?"

Her eyes widened with dismay. "Oh, no, of course not! Tonel is right. My subpure isn't of aetherists. Neither was Milady Danti's. *That's* why she never dreamed her own dreams."

"Doesn't matter. I taught Danti. I'll teach you," he said, surprising himself. In sixty-seven years, he had never been so impetuous. "We'll start next evening."

Her face flushed with alarm. "Tonel will never allow it."

"Tonel will have to allow it. I'm in urgent need of a codreamer for a commission issued by the Temple of the Mind of the World. Sweet angel," he said, smoothing a curl from her cheek, "I need someone just like you."

He wanted to enter sharemind with her at that very

moment. Convince her in mutual consciousness. He
could have easily, overwhelmingly, exercised his prerogative. *If she were Danti, I would compel her to lie in
the aetheric shell with me right now.*

His own vehemence took him aback. Had he really
been such a tyrant with Danti?

And what if he entered into sharemind with Danatia
only to find her consciousness lacking? To discover that
sharemind with her was a torment? The thought nearly
brought him to tears. He couldn't bear the disappointment.

Sunlight glimmered on the eastern horizon, bright
scarlet and deep purple from vapors and ash infusing
the air. A new Pangaean dawn as wounded as this
young angel's lip.

He summoned the windship. The translucent blue
teardrop met them at the Venerated Vestibule. The ship
opened its portal and extruded steps, and Lucyd
handed her inside. Then he boarded himself and fiddled
with the controls, suddenly nervous as a schoolboy to
be standing so near her.

The ship sped them to Villa de Reve, buffeted by the
winter winds. Lucyd had not slept all night but he felt
no trace of fatigue. He felt giddy and a little confused.
They disembarked at the front door. Lucyd summoned
his majordomo.

"Escort Milady Danatia to her sleep chamber and
post an armed guard at the door. Do not permit Tonel
near her. I hereby empower you to command my son,
however strenuously he attempts to exercise his prerogative."

"Yes, milord," the majordomo said.

Danatia said, "Thank you for everything, milord."

"You may call me Lucyd. Sleep well, Danatia."

Tonel would harm this young woman no more. Lucyd would challenge the pledge of his own cloven son
before the Temple of Sacred Sharelock. Before the High
Council. Before all Pangaea, if he had to.

He had never thought such daring thoughts in his
life. He needed to talk to someone, to share mutual

consciousness. Advice, that's what he needed. He'd kept his own counsel too long, secluding himself in his cloudscraper. Now that Danti was gone, he knew of only one person with whom entering sharemind had never been a torment.

He boarded his windship and set a course for Rancid Flats.

FACET 18

> Island: Sanctuary or prison.
> The hermit ponders the nature of existence
>   and tells no one.
> The action is contemplation.
> The forbearance is delusion.

The Orb of Eternity

Commentaries:
Councillor Sausal: As Pan permeates all space, so Pan dwells in the smallest place. And as the Imperium shapes the Mind of the World, so, too, the Imperium shapes every citizen's thoughts.

Therefore the prudent person should cultivate one's Essence, but beware of self-absorption.
Guttersage (usu. considered vulgar): Angels who behave strangely are eccentric.

Druds who behave strangely are crazy.

Our City of Atlan, the periphery of Northwest Marketplace, Rancid Flats. Jugglers Lane, the Salon of Shame:

Bam! Someone pounded on Tahliq's back door. The sun had torn itself loose of the eastern hills as the erotician climbed her spiral staircase. Bone-weary after the lively night, Tahliq headed toward her sleep chamber for a well-deserved rest.

Bam, bam, BAM.

"Mout? Dori?" she called to her handmaids. "Go see who's demolishing my back door. And tell the scoundrel to beat it. We're closed till midday." She sum-

moned purity sharemind and cast her questing
consciousness throughout the salon.

Where the devil were those lumbering druds? The
handmaids—she-bears both with their furry cheeks and
knob-knuckled hands—must have collapsed on their
straw pallets behind the laundry chamber. Tahliq had
often gone to rouse them and found the sisters spooned
together, snoring so soundly even the whip of her
sharemind couldn't disturb them.

She turned and strode downstairs, cursing softly.

Never in her thirty-five years as an Imperially li-
censed erotician had Tahliq Jahn Pentaput naitre Quintus endured such a strenuous evening. Not to mention
the demanding dawn. Across Jugglers Lane the Bawdy
Harridan had been rebuilt after the Big Shock, and pe-
destrian traffic between saloon and salon had just about
worn the cobblestones down to dirt.

Patrons of every purity and subpure staggered
through her rose-pink door. Brawny roadbuilders. Bel-
ligerent firefighters. Shy atlantium miners and brash academes. A dozen prefects, twice as many vigiles. Even
an angel or two.

So much lust unleashed. Such eagerness to abandon
protocol on Tahliq's pleasure couch. Calamity, apparently, inflamed the ancient shame.

And Tahliq entertained them all, fulfilling her Imperial duty as an erotician. Every now and then she en-
joyed her duty with a golden walkabout or a dashing
priest. As she had once delighted in every moment with
Regim.

*Dear Afrodite, no longer with Regim. Never, ever
again.*

Bam, bam, BAM!

Blast those handmaids! Who could it be? The vendors who delivered early left their wares in the dairy
chute and drove on.

"Either go away," she shouted, "or wait till I'm decent."

She hurried into the washroom off the foyer and un-
plaited her braids, permitting bronze tresses to cascade

down her severely shaped body. She found a handcloth and rubbed off the kohl rimming her ebony eyes, the scarlet beeswax staining her plush lips. She unstrapped her gigantic breasts from the leather corset and slipped on a camisole. Her waist ached, not tiny anymore. Her belly, never less than full, now dwarfed her ample hips and buttocks.

At first Tahliq had fretted that her burgeoning belly would offend her patrons, but her fears had proved groundless. Men and women alike had marveled over her new corpulence. Had paid for her company on the pleasure couch with praise and lavish tips.

Ardent patrons weren't all that stormed Tahliq's door.

Floods had drenched the flats after the Hercynian eruption. When the waters had receded at last, magma had boiled up out of a crevice newly cleaving South Fog Alley. A river of molten sludge had buried everything in its path. At Trap Corner and Low Way, Imperial Fire & Shock crews had excavated an impressive fire ditch, but magma had filled it and cooled. Fresh magma spurted from the crevice and surged over the new-made rock.

Heading straight for Jugglers Lane. For the Bawdy Harridan Saloon, the costermongers' market, and the Salon of Shame.

Tahliq had received the warnings from Ground Control, the pleas to evacuate. But she'd lived there her whole life. So had her mothers and their mothers and their mothers. Where would she go? Anyway, Fire & Shock promised to dig a new ditch.

Bam, bam, bam, bam, BAM.

"Knock it off before the neighbors summon Vigilance," she called as the frantic pounding continued. She drew on a dressing gown of dove-grey silk, clutched her abdomen, and groaned. The secret tucked inside her belly gave her nausea in the morning.

She strode to the door and unfastened the locks: two bolts, two chains, a latch at the top, and another at the bottom. In the flats, an erotician had to watch her back.

She flung the door open—

—and shrieked.

A hand like a claw clamped itself over her mouth, stifling her scream. An arm like an iron band wrapped itself around her waist, stilling her struggles.

A female held her in that iron grip—a very young, very scrawny girl. Mismatched eyes in a lopsided face glared ferociously. White-gold fuzz streaked with vermilion sprouted from her bony scalp.

As if *that* wasn't bad enough, she had a companion—a tall, young man as grotesque as the girl. Gold rings pierced their ragged eyebrows. Devil stars and daggers dangled from their belts. Both were little more than scrofulous skin and stringy muscles stretched over meager bones.

"Damn, erotician, let us in," the girl said. "We spotted vigiles just around the corner."

"*That's* a reason I should let you in?" she mumbled through the girl's fingers.

The Devil girl loosened her grip. "I'm asking politely, Dame Tahliq. Can't promise how I'll ask in another minute."

"You're still a very rude young lady, Salit Zehar."

"I try," she replied with a grin.

Tahliq recognized that face, all right. That face had snarled in Milord Lucyd's dreams. And on detainment posters nailed to every lamppost in Atlan. The young terrorist was wanted by the Imperium for murder and banditry of every description.

Thank goodness the creature considered Tahliq a friend!

The first time they'd met on Sanguine, the girl had shaved her head and decorated her face with hideous black paint. Since then, she'd scrubbed off the paint and grown a bit of hair. It was an improvement. The hair was kind of pretty.

Tahliq stepped aside and admitted the two Devils. The young man gripped two lengths of stout rope, which led from his fists to an object outside the door. With a grunt and a heave, he hauled in a streetsweepers' sledge. The Devil girl scurried around to the rear of the sledge, grasped the hindmost posts, and shoved as the young man pulled.

The tarpaulin they'd flung over sledge and cargo fell away as they feverishly heaved-and-shoved one last time. They yanked their burden into the foyer and fell back on their heels, mopping their brows.

Tahliq shut the door and shot home the locks. "Dear Afrodite. Could that possibly be what I think it is?"

The sledge bore a device the size and shape of a coffin made of cookpot metal. The thing bristled with antennae, glowing knobs, a vipers' nest of cables. Across the domed lid, security kaligraphs blinked. Gaping blue lips of security monitors mimed *wahoo wahoo,* but the Devils had managed to mute them.

Salit winked, fatigue etching her haggard young face. "And just what do you think it is, erotician?"

Tahliq whispered, "*That* is an aetheric shell."

"So we broke into the damn Temple of the Mind of the World and stole the poxy thing." Salit held out her cup for another splash of Tahliq's best skee. "An acolyte-auditor at the temple owed my father money. Terrible qut habit, has Sami Triademe. My father's qut buyers have turned out to be quite useful."

"Like me?" Tahliq said, corking the flagon lest the girl's companion thirst for a refill, too.

"You, too," the girl said, missing her sarcasm. "Anyway, I found Horan's mnemon in the pocket of my cloak." The cloak rustled on the hook where she'd hung it. "That's right, *my* cloak," she said warningly to the garment, which—Tahliq could swear—indignantly swished its draperies. "My father had collected a bit of Sami's debt. I decided to collect the rest."

Tahliq herself had always avoided the temple, a forbidding monolith with a facade like a mirror dipped in fog. The place unnerved her. "I'm amazed. The temple is heavily guarded."

"Ho, no temple of the Imperium is safe from

Heaven's Devils. The security was about as tight as an old fishing net. Wasn't hard at all, was it, Asif?"

The Devil girl punched her companion affectionately on his sinewy arm. He nodded, licking crumbs off his fingers, and reached for another crab roll.

"Horan's mnemon showed us the way to a duct that took us into the utility chamber," Asif said, between chews. "And the way to Sami's cubicle. Plus, what Horan had done there. No, breaking in wasn't hard. Slitting the throats of the door guards on the way out— *that* was hard."

"Ah, my bonded one, they were just druds."

"I don't like killing folk who aren't warriors."

Tahliq swallowed hard. *I'm a drud. And Salit knows it.* "Have a baked egg," she urged, "and take it easy with that skee." When Salit frowned, Tahliq admonished gently, "You're too young and much too thin for such strong drink. Eat, before you make yourself ill."

She proffered the tray of day-old crab rolls, quail eggs baked in millet cups, a wheel of cheese, chocolate cakies, and three flagons of that expensive skee.

After admitting the Devils, she'd found her handmaids snoring in the straw, as she'd suspected. She'd decided against waking the skittish creatures. Instead she'd plundered her pantry and flung together the makeshift breakfast, then joined the exhausted young Devils and their aetheric shell in the crawl space below the flagstones of her wine cellar.

A trapdoor hidden beneath the wattle floor mat took her into the crawl space—the most secret sanctuary in the salon. Tahliq had discovered the space fifteen years ago, dug deep in the building's foundation. She had considered constructing such a sanctuary herself just in case the High Council ever decided to make trouble for eroticians. She'd been gratified to discover her mothers had already taken the precaution.

If patrolling vigiles knocked on Tahliq's door and discovered her with Heaven's Devils and Imperial booty, she had no doubt what would happen to her.

The aetheric shell buzzed, a sound like a riled nest of

hornets. Of course Tahliq had heard the rumors whispered in cafés, in saloons. In her dallying chamber.

No one dared speak them aloud.

The Imperium teaches us that the Mind of the World issues from Pan, through the angels. That the Mind of the World is a phenomenon like space and time.

But what we see and believe about the Mind of the World is not reality. It is what the Imperium instructs us to see and believe. It is fabricated.

We can choose another way to see. Another way to believe.

That's what the Orb of Eternity counseled. Tahliq had known that since the day she'd seized the shiny purple bauble at her mother's feet and felt the power throb within it. In facet after facet, that is what the orb advised and what the Imperium could not tolerate: *Search for the truth with your own understanding. See reality with your own eyes.*

Proof of the rumors stood before Tahliq's eyes. "What do you intend to do with this thing?"

"Edict Two," the Devils answered together.

"I beg your pardon?"

Salit gulped skee and wiped her mouth on the back of her hand. "The Manifesto of the Apocalypse, Edict Two, says we must infiltrate the Mind of the World. Yet who among the foes ever possessed the means? Or knew what that *meant,* let alone how to *do* it?"

Asif nodded. "It was our philosophy. A battle cry. Something to stir us up."

"But now *I* do. *Me,* Salit Zehar, Heaven's Devil extraordinaire." She leapt to her feet and whipped a devil star off her belt, brandishing the weapon. "I have infiltrated the Mind of the World like the great Horan Zehar before me. The Apocalypse is here!"

Tahliq and Asif ducked at the same time.

Asif said, "Settle down, my bonded one. The Apocalypse can wait till I finish my crab roll."

Tahliq said, "What on earth are you raving about, girl?"

The Devil girl strode to the shell. She tugged at the

lid but the clasp wouldn't budge. She slammed the side of it with the flat of her hand. Asif sprang to his feet and joined her, punching the lid with both fists. The security kaligraphs flashed faster and faster, becoming an incomprehensible blur. Still the clasp stubbornly resisted. The shell rocked back and forth beneath their assault.

And then the clasp gave way and the lid sprang open with a furious *squeak*.

Tahliq tiptoed to it and peered inside.

Like a coffin built for two, two pallets lay within, two disheveled mattress pads, and two pillows yellow with sweat. Cheap cologne, cheroot smoke, and the greasy odor of doughrings topped off the overpowering smell of an ill-washed human body.

An astonishing display took up one interior panel, where the hinges of the lid met the hasps of the shell: luminous datascreens, skittering kaligraphs, bright pushpads, blinking clickers. Scarlet light washed across two other panels studded with kaligraphs:

WARNING UNAUTHORIZED ACCESS WARNING

The fourth panel, where the lid had been hinged to the body of the shell, remained an ominous pearly grey.

"*This* smelly box gives us dreams in the Mind of the World?" Tahliq said.

"Gives *you* dreams, drud," Salit said. "Everybody knows the impure don't dream the angels' dreams. We don't have sharemind."

"Yes. I wonder why." Tahliq touched the lid cautiously. "How does it work?"

"That's the question vexing all Pangaea, isn't it?" Salit grinned. "There are *two* pallets, see? The acolyte-auditor only used one. He'd tossed his lunch sack on the other. I'm afraid I sat on his potted cheese."

Tahliq stared. "You got *inside* with an acolyte-auditor?"

"Sure! I lay down, too. Just like my father had lain next to Sami on the morning of the Big Shock. I wish

Horan had told me. Maybe he hadn't been sure himself what had happened and wanted to try it again. He'd dreamed of me, you see."

"But you make no sense," Tahliq said. "How could Horan's dream have wound up in Milord Lucyd's dream?"

"Let's find out." The Devil girl hoisted herself onto the edge of the shell, swung her legs over, and rolled inside. She stretched out on a pallet, clasping her gnarled hands over her chest. "Join me, Dame Tahliq. Maybe between the two of us, we'll get this thing to work."

"Oh, no. I couldn't possibly."

Asif pushed her shoulder. "It's got to be you. I don't want Salit in there by herself. And I've got to stand guard."

"Well, if you're going to twist my arm," Tahliq murmured and made the hexagram of Afrodite over her breast. Excitement percolated through her as she lifted her dressing gown, gingerly climbed in, and lay next to Salit.

The Devil girl punched random buttons with her fist.

"Good heavens, Salit, you cannot expect to operate this device just by slapping at its controls."

"It's built to be slapped. Don't worry."

"I'm *very* worried—"

—and then pressure like a gigantic hand squeezed her, bearing down on toes, knees, legs, belly, breast, neck, face—

—and squeezed her clear out of her body!

Her consciousness careened to the ceiling. She gasped for breath, choking, trying to scream, but she had no lungs, no throat, no mouth.

She shot right through the ceiling, every beam and stone looming before her with preternatural clarity.

Suddenly she was gazing down at the rooftop of the Salon of Shame. She could see each chipped tile, the decayed leaves clogging the gutters, the chimneys stained by smoke. She soared higher and higher. Then she gazed down at the twisting lanes of Rancid Flats, telescoping tinier and tinier till they were no thicker than the lines on the palms of her hands. She saw the river of glowing magma, the swath of destruction in its wake.

Suddenly she hung, suspended, in a burning blue infinity. No horizon, no beginning, no end.

The line of her vision turned—

—and she saw Salit Zehar suspended beside her, mismatched eyes blazing with lunatic glee.

"This is it," she shouted, laughing wildly. "We've done it! We're inside the Mind of the World. Let's break into an angel's dream! Come on, before an auditor catches us. I've seen the paths, the dreampaths. Each path leads to a dream and—"

Suddenly Tahliq found her throat, and she screamed, a terrified cry echoing over and over—

—and then she lay, convulsing, in the aetheric shell again.

A hand gripped her shoulder, shaking her till her teeth rattled in her jaw. "Tahliq," Asif was saying in an urgent whisper. "Dame erotician, wake up. Sit up!"

Salit was guffawing as if she'd completely lost her wits. "H-h-how's that for a d-dream?"

"Get up, get *up,* my bonded one." Asif seized Salit and tossed her out of the shell. "You, too." He scooped an arm around Tahliq's waist, another beneath her knees, and lifted her out. "Someone's looking for you, erotician. Up *there.*" He jerked his thumb at the ceiling of the crawl space.

Footsteps clumped across the wine cellar floor. Mout's and Dori's panicked voices called, "Dame Tahliq, where are you? Come quickly! The Imperial inspectors are here."

"Then how do you account for this swelling of your bosom and belly, dame erotician?" demanded the inspector-physician.

Tahliq lay as she'd always lain at each new moon, unclothed and compliant on the table the inspectors had rigged up in her dallying chamber. "All this quaking in Our Sacred City stimulates the appetite, don't you agree?"

"You've got no other earnings to declare, erotician?" said the inspector-accountant, bending over Tahliq's books of account.

Tahliq had produced her records as she'd always produced them, the ones that didn't reflect her shadow-sector transactions. "Alas, this quaking depresses the urge to spend."

"And you've got nothing better than this in your larder this morning?" the first inspector-taster said, sniffing doubtfully at the last limp crab roll, which he proceeded to devour anyway.

"Or this?" The second inspector-taster uncorked her last bottle of wine languishing in a waterlogged ice bucket, poured a glass, and drained it. "An inferior vintage. Unworthy of you."

"A pity," she said agreeably. "But you'll stamp my license just the same."

The accountant obligingly took out the Imperial stamp and blotted the nub, but hesitated. Did he expect a bribe?

"I could have sworn we had more rolls 'n' such left over, my dame," Mout said, wrinkling her low forehead. "And them cakies, the good chocolate ones—"

"And skee," Dori said. "That tasty skee you like, my dame. Two or three whole flagons."

"This is all we've got left, tiny Mout and tinier Dori," Tahliq told the hulking handmaids in her don't-sass-me tone. She dared not command them in purity sharemind. Middle-pure inspectors would apprehend drud sharemind as effortlessly as they heard vendors extolling wares in the street. And the chief inspector? A formidable vigile subpure, she would apprehend and flagellate them all with her powerful magister's sharemind.

Tahliq climbed off the table, feigning a cheer she did not feel, and clutched her dressing gown. She had hastily climbed out of the crawl space, closed and latched the trapdoor behind her, and rearranged the wattle floor mat. She'd left Devils and shell behind and prayed the inspectors wouldn't demand to inspect the cellar.

"Did you fine inspectors wish to stay for breakfast and a morning's dalliance? As soon as my baker and dairymaid make their morning deliveries, I shall be happy to serve you."

"I think not, dame erotician," came a voice like a hammer striking metal. The chief inspector strode into the dallying chamber. "Get her back up on that table, physician."

"I believe the inspection is finished, Dame Chief."

"No, it isn't," the chief inspector said, seized her waist, and shoved her onto the table. The table was equipped with leather straps, though the inspector-physician had never bound Tahliq before. The chief inspector bound her now, thrusting her wrists and ankles into the straps and viciously buckling them shut. With the stout security club she carried the inspector struck Tahliq's burgeoning belly and each breast—*slap slap slap*.

"I've seen this deformity among the impure," the chief inspector told her cowering staff. "She's growing an unborn. Inside her body."

The inspectors gasped. The handmaids whimpered.

"How is that possible?" the inspector-physician whispered.

"Obviously she hasn't been purified," the chief inspector said. To Tahliq, "Isn't that true? You still possess your birth chamber. Your own birthpods. Quintus Natalry didn't remove them all."

"Of course it's true, Dame Chief. There are those who know I'm one of the few female pures in all Pangaea who bleeds at each full moon. The way She of the Ancient Ones once bled."

She of the Ancient Ones. An inspector-taster's hand strayed briefly, covertly, over her breast in the hexagram of Afrodite.

"Yet you haven't had your courses for nearly half a season, isn't that also true?" the chief inspector said.

"Of course I have. I always do." Tahliq still presided at the Motherwine Ceremony on Sanguine, where she would display a sacred sponge with her blood. Blood from a prick in her finger.

No one knew she hadn't had her courses in half a season.

Or did they?

Tahliq raised her head from the table and stared at her handmaids. Mout averted her opaque yellow eyes. Dori stared off at a ceiling cornice.

The handmaids attended Tahliq, night and day. They assisted her with her bath, perfumed her, dressed her, arranged her hair. They changed her bedsheets and laundered her clothes. Had simple handmaids possessed the wit to notice all traces of her courses were gone?

How Tahliq had coddled the she-bear sisters! Had overlooked their frustrating drud sharemind and huge appetites. She had treated them with kindness, and they'd rewarded her with betrayal. For what? An extra box of chocolate cakies?

Hot anger and bitterness overwhelmed her. "My handmaids spread lies. I denounce them. In any case, it's not possible. All my patrons are good pures. The regulations of my license require it. That means, Dame Chief, the men are purified. No one could have possibly given me his seed."

"*Some* subpures don't purify themselves till after they enter sharelock. Really, the High Council ought to ban the filthy practice. But I think you know that, erotician." The chief inspector loomed over her. "Who is he?"

"There is no one." Tahliq clamped her lips shut. She knew who the father of her child was. The mnemons Salit had described to her on Sanguine had proven that beyond a doubt.

"I want a list of your male patrons for the last three full moons."

"My list of patrons is confidential under Imperial regulations, as you well know. In any case, Dame Chief, I'm afraid you're mistaken."

"Am I?" She said to the physician, "Get your bag of instruments. We shall find out the truth."

The physician withdrew from her leather satchel an evil-looking device: four tapered metal tongs that spread open like an iron flower when a winch was turned. She took out a covered crystal dish, the same sort in which the natalries stored materia, and a long curette.

Tahliq's fingers numbed with apprehension. "What the devil do you think you're doing?" She pressed her knees together as tightly as she could.

The chief inspector smiled grimly. "We're going to remove the contents of your birth chamber, dame erotician. It's easy enough. I've seen the impure scrape out their women's bellies and discard their unborn like so much garbage."

"The impure *are* garbage," the physician murmured.

"We'll take the harvest to Quintus Natalry," the chief inspector said. "The natalist-physicians will want to examine it. If you're carrying an unborn, they may grow it in a ges tank. Or preserve it as they see fit. You may file a claim of kinship, of course, though you'll have to identify who contributed the male seed. Isn't that true, physician?"

"I'm afraid so," the physician said. "The source of the materia generating every unborn must be verified before the Imperium will issue a security number to a new citizen." She brandished the curette. Its razor edge gleamed.

Tahliq screamed. Every terror and loathing she'd ever felt in her life surged out of her throat. The accountant, the tasters, the handmaids started screaming, too.

The chief inspector bellowed, "Shut up, all of you!"

Tahliq flailed, kicking at the ankle straps, twisting at the wrist straps, bucking away from the physician's hands, pleading for mercy—

"What are you doing to my favorite erotician?" said a melodic masculine voice, cutting through the cacophony.

The most famous angel in all Pangaea stood in the doorway of the dallying chamber, his luminous violet eyes incisive. Tall and impossibly slender, he moved like a ray of light manifested in human form.

"Milord Lucyd," Tahliq cried. Fresh fear shimmered through her. Angels weren't known for their kindness. Yet hope seized her heart. Before Danti's death, milord and milady had patronized the Salon of Shame more times than Tahliq could count.

How long had the angel had been standing there? It was as if he had materialized out of the air.

He was alone. He bore no weapons. He wore only a bodysuit of platinum-colored mesh and a necklace of diamonds set in atlantium. Diamond-shaped scars branded the backs of his hands where his sharelock chips had been.

If the inspectors chose to seize him, they could easily overpower this frail angel. But Lucyd's intensity, his charisma, invaded the chamber like a force. Tahliq had never sensed such power in her patron before.

He's become more of an angel . . . and more of a man.

The handmaids prostrated themselves and pressed their furry faces to the floor. The inspectors—accountant, tasters, even the physician—sank to their knees. Only the chief inspector stood her ground, the slash of her mouth drawn down in a frown.

"I asked you a question, Dame Chief." Lucyd strode to the inspection table, unbuckled the straps, and handed Tahliq her dressing gown. "I do not hear you."

"I am harvesting her," said the chief inspector. "She's growing an illegal child."

"Nonsense."

"Look at her belly. Her bosom."

"Dame Tahliq looks lovelier than ever, as befits an Imperial erotician of her success and reputation. You have no right to harvest her under any protocol I know. Take your staff and the wretched handmaids and begone."

"I don't take commands from you, angel," the chief

inspector said. "This is an Imperial inspection. Under jurisdiction of the Prefecture of Our City of Atlan. *I* issue the commands here."

"I relieve you of your command," Lucyd said.

"I shall summon Vigilance. I shall have this erotician taken away in shackles. I shall have her flogged—"

"Dame Chief," Lucyd said, "did I grant you permission to speak further?"

And he unleashed his angel's sharemind.

Tahliq touched his hand, the tip of her thumb against his little finger, and her secret sharemind—all encompassing, all apprehending—joined his in a sublime merger. She trembled, a nub of consciousness swept into Lucyd's oceanic awareness. He overwhelmed her, but being overwhelmed was nothing like her ordeal in the aetheric shell. She delighted in his glorious vastness.

He withdrew his sharemind as swiftly as he'd cast it.

Gradually, though Tahliq was not certain how much time had actually fled, she became aware of sounds around her. The handmaids' terrified shrieks. The inspectors' amazed sobs. The chief inspector's anguished moans. Tahliq had no notion what torment the angel's sharemind had inflicted upon these lower pures.

Lucyd said mildly, "Good-bye, and Pan preserve you."

"Many thanks, milord." Tahliq knelt at the angel's feet. "I cannot tell you how grateful I am."

"Tahliq, what are angels for but to rescue beautiful eroticians in distress?"

She laughed, amazed. Lucyd had always been the most dour of proximicists. She couldn't remember if she'd ever seen him smile before. "I haven't seen you since Milady Danti's tragedy."

"Yes, it has been a while," he said nonchalantly. Another surprise. All Pangaea knew how the angel had grieved for his sharer of fifty years. "Please rise, Tahliq." He took her hand and helped her to her feet. "A pity your pantry is picked clean. A busy night last night, eh? My night was quite busy, too. Fortunately, I've brought my own pot of hazelnut caf and a tray of pastries from Marketplace. Everything is in your kitchen. I'll go fetch them." The angel laughed. "Then come and lie with me on your pleasure couch. I've been thinking about you all night."

Surprise upon surprise. Tahliq raised her eyebrow. "You've removed your sharelock chips, milord."

Lucyd returned, bearing the breakfast tray. "Indeed, I have. I feel like a new man."

She took the tray from him. "Permit me to serve you. Milord, are you sure you want to do this?"

"Share breakfast with an erotician, you mean?"

"Well, yes. I'm the most despised subpure in all Pangaea, you the most exalted. Unless you wish to pay my Imperial fee."

"And render this an Imperial transaction instead of a breakfast between old friends? No, though I'll gladly give you as much money as you'd like."

She feigned horror. "The proximity violation alone might land you in Primus Jail, milord."

"Ah, but I won't tell anyone if you won't."

Tahliq laughed again. Lucyd moved and spoke like an irreverent and virile young vigile, not an elderly Pannish propagandist. The transformation astounded her.

Before, the angel and his lady would arrive at the salon in the dawn after late-night revelers had succumbed to skee or sleep. They would come by windship, alight on the rooftop, and descend the steps to the dallying chamber.

"Come, Tahliq," Lucyd said, climbing onto the pleasure couch fully clothed the way he'd always been. He lay back gracefully.

She lay next to him, fully clothed as she'd always been.

Before, he would watch while Danti took her pleasure with Tahliq. Sometimes he would hold Tahliq's hand and she and Lucyd would enter her secret sharemind. She'd been as circumspect with the angel as she'd always been with Regim. She'd been certain the angel was unaware of her secret. As for Milady Danti, she had been interested in only one thing: the satiation of her shame. Yet she'd taken little interest in her sharer.

"I've always wanted to ask you." Lucyd took her hand now. "How is it you enter allpure sharemind with me?"

"But I do not! I cannot. I'm only a drud with a drud's tiny sharemind."

"Come now, Tahliq. I *know* you do. Please enter with me now."

"Very well." Tahliq closed her eyes.

They lie together on a sward of seabent grass atop the famous cliff of Lucyd's dreams. The waves of a great bay sparkle below them. Before the famous coppice of willows stands a young woman, an exquisite angel with streaming white-gold hair.

Milady Danti?

But she is not Danti. The woman does not boldly stride onto the cliff the way Danti once did. Shyly she steps back into the coppice and vanishes beneath the sweeping leaves.

Lucyd smiles, but his eyes are sorrowful. "You know many Secrets because of this sharemind, don't you, Tahliq? You know about the Doors to the moon and Sanguine. You know the truth about the atlantium miners and the streetsweepers who toil on the other worlds. You know the truth about Danti."

"Only you know the truth about Danti, milord."

He chuckles sadly. "She was not what she appeared to be, was she?"

"She was your sharer. Your cherished one—"

"—joined in sacred sharelock. Yes. In Pannish love. Cornerstone of the Imperium that inspires generation of the family in the natalries. I have dreamed of sharelock and Pannish love for fifty years, but I never touched Danti the way you did. And she never touched me. She said I was too pure."

He released her hand, and Tahliq plummeted out of sharemind.

"If you can enter fully into mutual consciousness

with me," Lucyd said, "you must be able to do so with anyone."

"Yes. Any pure, any subpure. But only when I touch."

"But how did you come to possess this sharemind?"

"Milord, I don't know. Or why the gift only comes through touch. I've taken pains over the years to keep my sharemind a secret. I never even told my mothers." She lowered her voice. "I've always thought my gift was a trick of the natalries. An experiment of some sort. Perhaps a mistake."

"The natalries!" He frowned. "But that cannot be, Tahliq. Sharemind is given by Pan. Sharemind is the natural destiny of each purity."

"Rumor says sharemind is given by the Imperium, milord."

"Rumor babbles many strange things."

"How do you explain my sharemind, then?"

His eyes flickered with apprehension. "I cannot. Even with my angelic sharemind, I cannot."

"Rumor says what the Imperium gives, the Imperium may take away."

"Then perhaps it's time we stopped taking what the Imperium gives."

She smiled at his blasphemy. "I've never seen you so vibrant, milord."

"It's all because of her. Did you see her standing by the willows?"

"I did. She looks the very image of Milady Danti."

"She is nothing like Danti, despite the resemblance. She is Danatia. She's pledged in sharelock to my cloven son Tonel."

"I never knew you had sons, milord, cloven or otherwise."

"Apparently, I've barely known myself." He brandished his long, slender hands and studied the diamond-shaped scars. "Two seasons have passed since I invited my sons to stay awhile and visit with me at Villa de Reve. I had hoped to heal old wounds. I think my sons *are* beginning to forgive me. All except Tonel.

He won't relent. And now Danatia has come between us."

"For shame! She tries to turn your son against you?"

"Oh, no, nothing like that. Danatia is gentle, kind, intelligent, humorous. Lovely in every way. And Tonel abuses her. It's terrible. I will tolerate his abuse no more. If I must choose between Danatia's friendship or Tonel's filiation, I must choose her. I've invited her to dream with me. Tonel will find it out soon enough."

"Is she Danti's cloven?"

"No, Danti's sister. Generated from Imperial materia harvested from the same ancestors, though the man and woman were long dead when Danti was generated. I nearly swooned when I saw her the first time. She stirs the strangest sensations in me."

"Let me see," Tahliq said with a teasing smile. "She's gentle, kind, intelligent, humorous. Lovely in every way, I believe is how you put it. Milord, you're in love. And I don't mean Pannish love."

The angel stared at her, astonished. "I assure you, Tahliq, defiling her is the furthest thing from my mind."

"Precisely. *This* is defilement." She seized his hand and pressed his palm over her breast. "You do not wish to purchase her the way you and Danti purchased me, do you, milord?"

"Certainly not!"

"Then you cherish her as you would cherish a sacred sharer?"

"Well, not exactly that, either." Milord actually blushed. "I may not wish to defile her but neither do I wish to repeat the distant relations I endured with Danti. She's a beautiful woman. Angel or not, I'm a man."

Tahliq clapped her hands with delight. "Then take her away from your horrid son, milord! Propose sharelock yourself. I've known many sharers who share far more than Pannist philosophy and their Imperial materia."

"But I'm her elder by forty-seven years."

"Never mind her years. You say she was generated

from the same ancestors as Danti? Then she's of Danti's generation. Danti's contemporary in Imperial materia. Under the law of proximity, Tonel is to her as a son would be to his mother. He's hardly the more suitable sharer. *You* are."

Lucyd's eyes misted with tears. "I would never have thought of that. I would never have *dared* think of that. You're magnificent, Tahliq."

"I aim to please. Have you entered sharemind with her?"

"No." He heaved a sigh. "I fear I'll be disappointed. The way I've been disappointed with everyone save Danti and you, Tahliq."

"Give her a chance! You must court her properly, milord. As the more powerful sharemind, defer to her gentleness. As her senior in years, treat her with respect for her youth. As the more experienced dreamer, praise the freshness of her vision. Believe me, milord," she said, "she will be unimpressed by the mean hierarchies of Pannish domination."

"Thank you for your insight, Tahliq. I don't know how I can repay you."

A chorus of shouts rose in Jugglers Lane.

Tahliq gathered her dressing gown around her and hurried to the window. She peered out and gasped.

Rivulets of magma surged down the lane. Sulfur fumes and dirty steam whirled up, forming foul clouds that hung above the cobblestones. Suddenly the lane grew strangely dark. Tahliq heard the malevolent hum of an Imperial force. She glanced up.

A gigantic Vigilance windship hovered overhead, blocking the morning sunlight and casting deep shadows over the lane.

Despite the ship's altitude, she saw him standing behind the pilot on the bridge. Once he'd been the most handsome man she had ever seen, a tall, golden vigile with eyes bluer than sapphires. Once he'd been her beloved, the only patron of her pleasure couch who had ever captured her heart.

Sharp dread needled down her spine. Lieutenant Captain Regim Deuceman.

Lucyd stood behind her, gazing up. The angel pointed at the bridge as the windship descended. "The chief inspector stands behind the lieutenant captain. I see the physician, as well, and your handmaids." He closed his eyes, his features relaxing briefly in angelic sharemind. "They've come for you, Dame Tahliq. And your unborn. Is it true, then? You carry a child?"

She clutched her belly. "I fear so." She shivered, recalling the curette poised over her. "You must go at once, Milord Lucyd. And I must hide."

"Hide? Where can you hide?"

"I've got a sanctuary."

"No, Vigilance will post a watch. They'll wait for you. They'll tear this place apart. You must flee, Tahliq."

The shouts outside became a tumult. Tahliq glanced out again. The windship touched down in the lane, just beyond the magmaflow. A loading ramp lowered. The chiseled faces of a Vigilance squad scowled behind the jut of gleaming metal.

"It's too late, milord," she said, groaning.

Lucyd gripped her hands. "I said I didn't know how I could repay you. I do now. Come quickly. My windship is on your roof. I can opaque the walls. The craft accommodates two. I've got enough power to take you to the Great Wall before Vigilance even discovers you've fled."

"You would do that for me, milord?"

"The Imperium is changing and, thanks in part to you, I am, too. Do hurry."

She dashed to her wardrobe, stripped off her dressing gown, and pulled on a linen tunic, trousers, and high-topped boots. She seized her cloak and her travel pouch, stuffed in necessities, her beloved beeswax and her little crescent knife. "Wait. There's something more, milord."

She sprinted to her sleep chamber, crawled beneath

the bed, and tore open the secret panel. She reached inside and retrieved her Orb of Eternity.

Lucyd was kneeling beside the bed when she scooted out. She didn't think the angel could look more amazed in one morning, but he did, his eyes as round as coins. "Is *that* an Orb of Eternity?"

"You mean to tell me you've never seen one?"

"Only in my dreams."

"Dear me, I've been an orbcaster since I was a child."

He touched the purple jewel with his fingertip. "Tahliq, would you cast an oracle for me?"

BAM. BAM. BAM.

The Salon of Shame shook, the windowpanes rattling. Not an earthshock, this time. The Vigilance squad was battering down her front door.

"I would be honored to cast an oracle for you. And milord? I believe I know who invaded your dreams, and how. If you'll take me beyond the city limits, I'll tell you everything I know."

The clatter of weapons sounded in the foyer below them.

"I'd be pleased to take you anywhere you want to go," Lucyd said.

She heard Regim's voice shouting, "Seize the erotician."

FACET 19

Tree: Providing nourishment or supplying poison.
The red fruit sustains one, sickens another.
The action is survival.
The forbearance is corruption.

The Orb of Eternity

Commentaries:
Councillor Sausal: As Pan is the forest, so Pan is
the trees with their myriad fruits. In times lost to
antiquity, the Ancient Ones learned which fruits
nourished and which poisoned.

So, too, the Imperium encompasses all Pangaea yet lives within every purity.

Therefore the prudent person should look
to Pan for divinity, the Imperium for the law,
the temple for moral instruction, the academy
for knowledge, vendors for goods, the family for
companionship, and the sacred sharer for Pannish
love.

Beware of false gods, cults, fortune tellers, the
shadow sector, revolutionaries, and casual companions.

Guttersage (usu. considered vulgar): If it ain't poison, eat it.

*Our City of Atlan, the periphery of Northwest Market-
place, Rancid Flats. Jugglers Lane, the Salon of Shame:*

"Find the drud witch," Regim Landom Deuceman naitre Secundus shouted. "Gag her and drag her to me by
her hair."

Hair the color of bronze, lustrous as the metal but soft as down when it tumbled down her back.

"Yes, lieutenant captain!" his vigiles barked.

Stop thinking about her! Regim ground his teeth. *Tahliq means nothing to me. Less than nothing.*

Did the erotician suspect the truth? She must have lain with two hundred patrons half a season ago. He hadn't been her only man.

"Never mind gagging her." He revised his command, furious at the trembling in his voice. "She's already confounded these fine inspectors with her lies. Cut out her tongue."

"Yes, lieutenant captain!" His vigiles unsheathed their daggers.

Her stirring contralto. Her flame kisses.

He'd been three-and-twenty years when he first walked into her accursed salon. Now, at nearly six-and-twenty, he'd escaped her clutches at last.

Tahliq, there was a time I risked everything to be with you. To see you one more time.

His vigiles marched into the salon, bootheels thundering on the hardwood floor. The handmaids cowered behind the chief inspector and her physician, who stood, pasty-faced, in the foyer.

"Why must we return with you to the salon, lieutenant captain?" the chief inspector had asked in a quavering voice.

Regim could see why she had never qualified for Vigilance. "To finish what you've started," he'd replied. In truth he didn't want her and her staff telling tales at Our City Hall till he confirmed or refuted their outrageous claim.

He still shook with astonishment. *Tahliq, carrying an unborn of perhaps half a season. Tahliq, refusing to name names of who might have given her the male seed.*

The child had to be his. He knew it the moment the words spilled from the physician's mouth. What man of any purity in Pangaea kept his seed anywhere other than in the freezing vaults of Natalry Bank? Only the impure relied on their mortal bodies, on the bestial act, to perpetuate their people.

And certain subpures. Magister subpures, vigiles like him, for instance. Magisters didn't trust the natalries. Why should they? The natalries were run by a pack of bungling physicians and priestesses.

But who knew? Despite the glare of publicity surrounding Clere's assassination, the Twine family would never have revealed that Regim had gone to his new sharer unpurified.

The erotician had refused to tell these feeble inspectors; well, she possessed the cunning to do that. But what would she reveal to Vigilance interrogators? How strong would her resolve be in the Chamber of Justice when she faced the rack and the vivisectionist's knife?

Regim balanced on his prosthetic left leg and kicked the rose-pink door with his right foot as hard as he could. The salaciously painted wood splintered. Pain struck the nerves in his booted toes, shimmering all the way up his leg. He savored the sensation. *Good pain. Honest pain. Pain that I command.*

Not like the throbbing of the unhealed wounds in his chest and belly left by Salit Zehar's devil star. Not like the burning, itching, crawling of ten thousand tiny claws that plagued his left hip socket, starting at the concavity where the physicians had hacked off his poisoned leg and extending—or so it felt—down to the floor.

Clere Twine's whisper from the dead curled into his consciousness. *I want to feel the wood shatter, my beloved Regim. I want to feel the glory of your violence.*

The advice of the priestess-facilitator from the Temple of Sacred Sharelock had been sound: *If you want to generate a family with Clere one day, leave the sharelock chips in your hands.*

So he had. And when the Superior Mother and Superior Father had mingled his materia and Clere's at their Rite of Begetting, he had felt her presence, and he had believed. Clere lived forever. When the veil between the world and Eternity swept aside now and then, she could speak to him in sharers' sharemind through the share-lock chips he wore.

Sometimes, though, the diamond shapes embedded between his carpal bones throbbed so acutely he felt dizzy and despondent. He would reach for Clere in the intimacy of sharers' sharemind and find her gone, her last screams of rage and agony shrill in his memory.

Suddenly he realized the trembling wasn't just his own.

"Earthshock!" someone shouted.

A huge shock slammed through Rancid Flats. He heard the shatter of glass as windows popped out of their frames, the clatter of beams, terrified shrieks in Jugglers Lane. Heat stung his skin and a blast of sulfur fumes and smoke whipped through the foyer.

Regim swayed on his prosthesis. His bodyguards steadied him, two fierce-eyed, well-armed servs. The Twine family had procured them. They fit precisely beneath his armpits, turquoise protocol chips winking between their brows.

How I loathe it when they treat me like I'm weak.

Sometimes he wanted to whip the bodyguards, the wholeness of their bodies making a mockery of his maimed one.

"There's been an eruption at the vent!" someone shouted.

A crier staggered by the ruins of the rose-pink door. Regim seized her by her scrawny neck and invoked crier sharemind. He *saw* the flume of magma spraying from the crevice ten blocks away, fresh molten rock feeding the stream winding down the lane. "Oh, splendid," he muttered and released the crier, shoving her back into the street and the chaotic crowd.

"Lieutenant captain," his sergeant said, saluting smartly, "this area is directly in the path of the magma. I recommend that we evacuate immediately."

"Then I recommend you find the erotician sooner than that."

The sergeant's face blanched. "Yes, lieutenant captain."

Overturned furniture crashed and doors banged open, but two by two his vigiles marched back, empty-handed, woefully shaking their heads.

"Idiots," he raged. "Incompetents. I'll have you all demoted. I'll have you flogged. I'll do it myself."

How they despised him, these arrogant Atlanean vigiles. He discerned their hatred as surely as he felt the heat. Lowly walkabouts for decades, they thought he didn't deserve his mercuric promotion to lieutenant captain.

I'll show you who deserves this command.

"Take me to the erotician's library," and his body-guards swiftly bore him there. He searched the softly lit sanctum, examining the book-lined walls filled with forbidden texts, the rich settees, the circular carpet where he had coupled with Tahliq. The place filled him with shame and longing. How could he have known *she* had never been purified? That she could receive his magister seed?

The erotician carries a monster, my Regim. Clere's whisper crackled with outrage. The whisper had grown more strident since their Rite of Begetting. *A sacrilege, cursed by Pan and the Imperium.*

Clere was right, but something in him protested. *What she carries is half-mine. Once I shared bliss with Tahliq. I tried to shun her, but I couldn't. She tried to heal me. She tried to love me.*

He thrust the blasphemous thoughts away, praying Clere had not discerned them.

But of course she had. She might dwell in Eternity, but Clere Twine inhabited him more completely than she ever had in life. *Do you mean to tell me you bedded this drud beast more than once? More than once, you gave her your pure magister seed?*

He gripped his forehead with both hands, ignoring the curiosity flickering in his bodyguards' eyes. *Cherished Clere, I'm sorry, I'm sorry.*

On and on her whisper berated him, insulting him, accusing him, till it occurred to him: *Wearing the sharelock chips of a jealous sharer who is dead is driving me mad.*

"Lieutenant captain, we *must* go," his sergeant said.

"Not till I find the erotician. Bring me her handmaids."

The sergeant herded the great downy she-beasts into the library. They clutched each other, weeping dirty yellow tears.

"Separate them. You," Regim said to Mout and seized her wrist, "give me your hand."

Every drud in Pangaea had heard the Story of the Faithful Handmaid and the wrathful magister. Every Pangaean had heard or witnessed in criers' sharemind how Regim had punished the jarmakers at Al-Muud.

He drew his dagger and brandished the blade over the handmaid's thick wrist.

Mout groaned in terror. Dori began to wail.

His squad gathered, watching his interrogation with impassive eyes. Their magister sharemind shouted scornful disapproval.

"According to these fine inspectors, you've betrayed your mistress once today," Regim told Dori. "You should have no trouble betraying her a second time. So tell me, where is she hiding? And don't lie to me, handmaid. I'll slice a knuckle from your sister for every lie you tell."

"Our d-d-dame must be in her s-s-sleep chamber," Dori said. "She's g-g-got a hidey-hole beneath her bed."

"Is that true?" he demanded of Mout.

"T'ain't nearly big enough for our dame to *hide* in." Mout kicked her sister's ankles. Her hand quaked beneath the dagger.

"Let's go see," Regim said.

He and his bodyguards led the way upstairs to the sleep chamber and strode inside. With a little shock, Regim recognized Tahliq's scent. He had lain with her in her dallying chamber and her library, but he'd never entered the sanctum where she slept. He surveyed the pretty lace curtains, the colorful braided rugs, a coverlet of Cordilleran crochet. Such homey comfort. Yearning blindsided him.

The bed had been hastily pushed aside, the floorboards flung open, and the hiding place emptied of whatever contraband it once held. Mout had been right. The space was much too small to hide a woman of Tahliq's size.

He turned to Dori, anger surging in his chest. "You devious drud. Your sister will have to pay. Restrain her," he commanded his vigiles, ignoring their disparaging glances. "I despise you for forcing me to do this. I, of all people in all Pangaea"—he clenched his hip muscles and nudged his prosthetic forward—"loathe this."

Mout caterwauled, but he shut his ears to her cries. He studied her knuckles. They were much too thick. He raised his blade to her face and sawed off her nose. He marveled that drud blood was as thick and ruddy as Clere's when Salit Zehar had gutted her.

"Where else could Tahliq hide?" he said calmly when he'd finished.

"The c-c-cellar," Mout said, in between sobs. Her voice diffused through the gape above her mouth. "The w-w-w-wine cellar."

Yes, that's where you'll find the erotician, my Regim, Clere's voice whispered in sharer's sharemind. *I sense it. A trapdoor in the floor. Every erotician's got one.*

"Let's go see."

Regim's bodyguards bore him down three flights of stairs. Then, crouching like he'd crouched in the jarmakers' hovel, he wriggled through the door to the wine cellar.

Inside he found darkness and coolness. Amber and green bottles nested on wooden racks. Glowworms flickered in translucent cocoons tucked among the ceiling timbers. A wattle mat covered the stone floor.

"Remove it," he commanded his vigiles, who knelt and rolled back the mat. Scanning and listening, Regim's eyes took in the random cracks and hollows in the stone, his ears the echoes and whispers.

And there. Was that an edge cleverly cut in the stone?

The ground pitched beneath him. Another earth-shock rumbled through the flats. Half a dozen beams ripped loose from the ceiling of the cellar and crashed to the floor.

Regim heard shouts from outside.

"Lieutenant captain, a whole wall of magma is coming down the lane!"

His vigiles' sharemind overwhelmed him with their protests. *We must go, lieutenant captain. We will not be buried alive. We will go, with or without you.*

Get her, you dolt, Clere cried. *Get the erotician with your unborn monster before you disgrace your subpure and mine. Join me in Eternity, if you must.*

That was her mistake. With cold clarity, Regim suddenly knew what he must do.

No, my Clere, he replied in sharer's sharemind. *I'm not ready to join you in Eternity.*

"Take me out of here," he ordered his bodyguards. "Everyone, back to the ship."

They scrambled up the basement steps into savage heat and a deafening roar. He and the bodyguards sprinted out into Jugglers Lane. Regim had visited Tahliq so often he'd come to recognize the servs and druds who lived there. There, the saloonkeep of the Bawdy Harridan and his bovine sharer. There, the wizened little costermonger. There, the pretty drud healer who knew healing secrets even Secundus Hospital didn't know.

"Hai, Regim, old chum!" The saloonkeep and his sharer leapt onto the windship's side decks and clung there. "Take us!"

Regim said to his windship crew, "Remove them."

Two burly crewwomen flung the servs off. The hysterical crowd mobbed the windship, beating their fists on the hull. Bright kaligraphs of the Homilies of Obedience flashed wildly.

Crevices bordering the lane cracked open into a hundred small canyons flowing with magma. Fissures shot to the east, to the west, to the south. From the northwest, the magmaflow seethed forward, a terrifying wall as tall as the rooftops.

The crowd darted to and fro as one canyon after another widened, blocking their escape.

"Let's go, lieutenant captain," screamed the ship's pilot.

"We've got plenty of room in the hold, sir," the sergeant shouted as Regim gazed at the spectacle around him. "These people can be evacuated."

Only magisters ride in Imperial windships, my Regim, Clere's whisper admonished in his sharer's sharemind, *or do you forget your blessed proximity to Pan?*

"Angels may own private windships but only magisters ride in Imperial windships, sergeant. Not servs. Not druds. And middle pures? Anyone here who is a middle pure," Regim shouted at the crowd, "will have to wait for a public windship."

"That is idiotic, sir," the sergeant said, her eyes snapping with outrage. "They'll all be buried long before a public ship flies by. It is our duty to preserve the purities."

How I loathe vigiles who believe their Imperial duty requires compassion! Clere whispered.

"How I loathe vigiles who believe their Imperial duty requires compassion," Regim said. "Do you forget your blessed proximity to Pan? You are under arrest, sergeant, for insubordination."

Yet in a sanctuary he sheltered in his consciousness— a sanctuary so tiny he hardly dared to acknowledge it— he thought, *Once I believed in preserving the purities, too.*

The sergeant jutted her chin at his bodyguards. "Will you abandon them, too?"

"My bodyguards wear protocol chips permitting them to go where I go."

"Please, sir. Have mercy!" the crowd beseeched. The squad marched up the loading ramp. A vendor thrust her two young babes at him. "Do with them what you will, but take them. Save them!"

Regim shoved the babes out of his way. He seized the arm of the chief inspector as she darted around him and flung her off the ramp. "You'll have to wait for a public windship, too."

"But I'm a magister subpure," she wailed.

"You and your inspection staff are the only people besides me who know the precise nature of Tahliq's condition. I'd like to keep it that way."

The chief inspector gaped as comprehension crept into her eyes. "I won't tell anyone. I swear, lieutenant captain!"

"Yes, I know you won't." He slapped the lever that raised the loading ramp. "Lift off," he called to the pilot.

The windship rose unsteadily. People clinging to the starboard decks staggered and fell as the ship accelerated, bodies dropping into the magma. Regim and his bodyguards strode to the bridge. Exterior sounds had been muted there, and the anguished cries below sounded no louder than a soft, insipid babble. He stared down at the flame-yellow river sweeping over Jugglers Lane, burying the Bawdy Harridan, the frantic people, the Salon of Shame.

Tahliq and his child.

If she had hidden in a crawl space beneath the floorboards of her wine cellar, she and their shameful secret would be buried with everyone else. When the magma cooled into convolutions of grey rock, the sediments settled, and seeds rooted in the rich soil that would form there, the servs and druds would return and rebuild their quarter anew.

And no one would remember what lay deep beneath the rock.

He glanced out the forward view at a sky smudged with the effluents of mass destruction. Then suddenly an airborne object caught his eye. He leaned forward, straining to see. There, cruising swiftly among the plumes of smoke and steam, flew the tiny, translucent blue teardrop of a windship. A private craft of antique vintage topped by a distinctive crown of multicolored wings. The vaporous ribbon of its contrail traced back to the rooftop of the Salon of Shame.

Regim had seen the craft before.

It was Milord Lucyd's windship.

Formidable councillors reclined on ornate settees set around an amphitheater of white marble. Some attentively followed the proceedings, others lounged in indolent poses. The air was chill and mentholated, and a musician softly plucked a harp. Servers crept discreetly among the settees, refreshing crystal goblets and emptying ashtrays.

Regim could hardly believe it. He and the Chief Commander of Vigilance, invited aboard Capitol Ship by the High Council. It was the dream of a lifetime!

"I bring great news from Our Imperial Bureau of Ground Control," said an academe standing in a well at the center of the amphitheater. He bowed to the Highest Councillor. The nasal tenor dripped with servility, yet an arrogance ran beneath the outward show. An arrogance that gave Regim pause. The academe possessed the spindly limbs of one sedentary, everywhere else the suet of indulgence. He bowed again, now in Regim's direction, displaying a pink tonsure amid dull yellow curls.

"Proceed, Gunther Triadius," said the Highest Councillor, glancing up from the hop marbles she played with a gamester reclining next to her.

Capitol Ship lurched in a sudden westerly. No one but high councillors and their staffs knew where Capitol Ship landed, where it docked, where it flew, where it hovered. In Pangaea, where the enemy lurked everywhere, Capitol Ship was an essential precaution for those who ruled the Imperium.

Regim chewed another mintstick. From his seat behind the Chief Commander, he could gaze out a window. A cloud bank roiled far below, the billowing cumulus stained angry orange. Below the polluted clouds he glimpsed a vast honeycomb—Our City of

Atlan. He felt omnipotent, gazing down from this height, and puny at the thought of himself lost in that honeycomb.

Beyond the megalopolis stretched a vast quilt of greens and ambers—Appalacia Peninsula, the Iapetus Plains, the dark stitching of the Great Wall. The mud-laced Bog within the Wall. Gondwana Peninsula, curving out of sight over the horizon.

He had never flown so high. His heartbeat raced to imagine how one day the Imperium would fly all the way to the moon and to Our Imperial Planet of Sanguine. He himself might march among the vigiles who would conquer the other worlds. Rumor said the Ancient Ones *had* gone to the other worlds, but Regim scoffed. If that were true, why hadn't the Imperium told everyone?

"It had better be great news, academe," said Councillor Claren Twine. "After the destruction of Rancid Flats." His whisper resonated throughout Capitol Ship. A surgeon's scalpel might have removed most of Claren's voice along with the tumor in his throat, but that whisper elicited unease even among his fellow councillors. "My son-in-lock witnessed the calamity. Lieutenant Captain Deuceman? How bad was the damage?"

Regim stood. "Ten thousand of our loyal servs and druds dead or missing. Twenty city blocks annihilated, blocks newly repaired after the Big Shock."

"It had better be *spectacular* news." With his ascetic physique and slightly crossed blue eyes glaring down the distinctive Twine nose, Claren cut a fine figure among the councillors. "Just what do you do, Gunther Triadius?"

The academe said, "I am a senior proctor at Sausal Academy specializing in earthshock prediction and prevention. I've been newly appointed as a permanent advisor to Ground Control. I have developed the bureau's new strategy to stop the earthshocks."

"Then the bureau isn't lying this time?" Claren said. "You *will* stop the shocks, once and for all?"

"Oh, yes. What the High Council mandates will be done."

"Good," Claren said. "I wouldn't want to see your head on a post in Marketplace."

"Nor would I," Gunther replied.

Regim chuckled at the academe's cheek.

Capitol Ship abruptly descended. The force levitating the craft seemed to abandon it, and Regim's ears popped, his stomach somersaulted. Fear prickled down his spine. No one knew how the force powered Imperial windships. Pilots simply abandoned ships that refused to fly. Regim had heard of crashes, ancient ships that quit in midflight. Capitol Ship was among the most ancient.

Are we landing or crashing?

He took his flask from his jacket pocket and sipped skee. The Chief Commander shot him a frosty glance. Her face had been hard as stone since she'd entered his squad's sharemind and glimpsed their departure from Jugglers Lane. "If we must be vigilant for an enemy who lurks everywhere," the Chief Commander had scolded him, "we can ill afford to become that enemy in the eyes of the purities."

Pay no heed, my Regim. The Chief Commander is soft, Clere's whisper assured him in sharer's sharemind.

"Behold Andea Rift," Gunther said.

Capitol Ship touched down on an escarpment. The ragged cliff descended to a meandering shore. The ebb tide had exposed league upon league of dingy grey sand and shallows opaque with more grey grit. Regim had never seen such a low tide. The Bay of Andea had all but disappeared into South Panthalassa Ocean.

Gazing landward, Regim saw a shocking sight: the dome of a Pan pagoda, rooftops of Imperial natalries, the tip of an Obelisk of Eternity poking out of a layer of cooling magma and steaming volcanic ash.

"What is this destruction, Gunther?" Claren asked.

"The aftermath of the eruption three seasons ago, councillor."

"Why is this happening to our Pangaea?" the Highest Councillor wailed, flinging her hop marbles on the floor.

"Highest Councillor," Gunther said, "our planet is a ball of cooling magma. A ball of a hot substance, as any child with a fresh-baked muffin can tell you, cools on the outside first. The core may remain hot long after the crust has grown cold. So it is with Pangaea. The outer shell of rock has cooled over the inner magmatic core. It is this shell that we walk upon, the ground that supports our Imperium. But as it cooled, the shell cracked just as the crust of a muffin will. These cracks are the great rifts. When instability gathers in the rifts, the world shell bounces up and down like a feather bed made of rock. These are earthshocks. When the shell bounces *very* vigorously, magma erupts through vents and cracks, and we witness catastrophes like Andea, the Hercynia Vent, and Rancid Flats."

"Muffins and feather beds," grumbled the Highest Councillor. "I thought Ground Control and the academy believed that *music* would stop the earthshocks."

"Highest Councillor," Claren said, "you refer to the heretic Tivern's theory of resonance."

"But we approved of Tivern once, Claren. I always thought she had lovely ideas. Weren't you part of the resonance movement, Gunther?"

"Only briefly." The academe cleared his throat. "Tivern discovered that each rift emits a distinctive chord. When we observe the five predictors of an earthshock—subterranean fumes, well-water shifts, salinity shifts, foreshocks, animal perturbations—we also observe disharmony in the rift. When we beamed harmonious music into the rift, we restored the chord, and prevented the earthshock." The academe sighed. "Sometimes."

"Sometimes is not good enough," Claren said. "You need only look out your window. So tell us, how does Ground Control propose to stop the earthshocks?"

Gunther said, "With something more forceful than harmony."

• • •

Regim strode beside Gunther across mounds of raw earth at the edge of a vast trench. The trench, a quarter league deep and nearly as wide, stretched to the horizon. Regim surveyed the base of the escarpment where the trench led back to land. The black bore of a huge tunnel angled into the escarpment and disappeared belowground.

Huge excavators and wiry little ductdiggers scrambled about at the bottom, scraping sand and swinging mallets at slabs of rock. The diggers deposited excavated material into wooden buckets, sending the buckets up and out on ropes and pulleys. Beneath the grey volcanic ash that stained sea, sand, and land lay coppery soil, white sand, and granite belted with blue minerals.

"The eruption altered the sea level along the coast for a hundred leagues." Gunther pointed at the drained bay. "We expected the tides to reestablish the sea level, but they haven't. The shoals hold only a trickle. We've had to extend the trench south by over three leagues. In another half a league we'll reach the edge of the coastal shelf."

The academe maintained a posture of deference as was proper protocol—head slightly bowed, eyes averted, shoulders stooped. Yet something furtive lurked in that deferent expression—something arousing Regim's suspicion. The academe raised his eyes and boldly met Regim's gaze.

"The shelf drops off into deep sea," he continued. "We'll lower the trench floor till the sea surges in with the high tide, giving us all the water we need."

"To flood the rift."

"Precisely, lieutenant captain. Massive amounts of seawater will serve as cushion and coolant. The rift will be sealed. No more earthshocks will occur."

"See to it they don't." Regim gazed back at the buried seaport. "I didn't know the eruption caused so much damage."

"I didn't know there had *been* an eruption till Ground Control sent me here to supervise the sea trench. Oh, we heard rumors at the academy. We heard rumors Tivern had died in the eruption. Then Ground Control suppressed everything. That remains the official word, except among permanent advisors. No eruption. Oh, and Tiv died of her skee addiction."

"Do you always listen to rumors, Gunther?"

"Only when I can profit from them. For instance, rumors say you're on your way up in Vigilance, lieutenant captain."

"You know who I am?"

"With all due respect, sir, who in Pangaea does not know of the jarmakers at Al-Muud?"

He studied the academe. "What do *you*, think of how I punished them?"

"You're a hero of the Imperium, lieutenant captain. Everyone knows impurity must be cleansed wherever one finds it."

"A Pannish reply," Regim said sardonically. "I understand from my father-in-lock that you volunteered to appear before the council today. That you traveled all the way back to Atlan to escort us here. Someone with the bureau in Atlan could have saved you the trouble. I want to know why."

"I craved the chance to get near *you*, lieutenant captain."

Regim drew his dagger. An assassin? Something about the academe had troubled him from the start. "And here you stand, *very* near to me. You'd better tell me why."

The academe backed away in alarm. He bore no weapon. "Oh, lieutenant captain, I wish you no harm. I only seek your intercession."

"What sort of intercession?"

"You arrested my pledged sharer-to-be, Plaia Triadana. She was Tivern's protégé. A promising mastery student. Played the cymbals on my resonance team. She studied under my proctorship after Tiv died. She would be still, if she hadn't committed heresy."

Regim plumbed his memory for the name. Plaia Triadana. Yes. He'd arrested her and her colleagues for trespassing in the Bog. Regim well recalled the academe's reddish gold hair and golden green eyes. She had the body of a diminutive erotician. She had knelt beside her injured colleague, spouting Apocalyptic heresies. A second woman had lain dead in the muck.

"She possesses remarkable variance," Gunther said. "You must have noticed."

"The eyes. The hair."

"Yes. Her vitality is remarkable, too." Gunther scowled. "I've longed to enter sharelock with Plaia from the moment we met, but she resisted me. I'm the higher subpure, you see, with a bit more powerful purity sharemind, and she's always resented that. She has a much quicker grasp of things than I, a better memory, and, well, that variance. I tendered a bid for her materia. Her fathers accepted. Tertius Natalry approved. I paid for her in full. But she didn't want my materia. She didn't want *me* the way I wanted her."

Bursts of shock shot through Regim at the academe's confession. His thoughts scurried to the sanctuary in his consciousness. *I loved Clere purely, Pannishly, but I didn't want her the way she wanted me, either.* Guilt squeezed his chest at the failure his sharelock would have been.

"I was furious with her," Gunther continued. "I did things a sharer-to-be ought not to do to his intended."

"Such as?" In his secret sanctuary, Regim wondered what Clere would have done if he'd refused to couple with her again.

"She carried on with Tivern's work after that work had been officially discredited. She developed her own theory about earthshocks. About the nature of the world shell. And I denounced her as a heretic. I caused her expulsion from the academy. I thought she would resign herself to the ruin of her mastery and return to her fathers' villa till we entered sharelock. Her fathers spoiled her. She relished her luxuries. She could be willful, but she had never demonstrated much in the way of discipline. But she was devastated by the expulsion. She proved far stronger and more rebellious than I ever could have suspected."

"She ran away?"

"She dropped out of sight till the day you arrested her. And now she must stand trial for heresy. I never wanted that. She'll never renounce her theories, that much I *do* know about her. As for force-flooding"—he gestured at the impressive trench—"she opposed the strategy from the start. She'll denounce Ground Control during her trial, I know it. She can be quite convincing, I assure you."

Regim pondered that, gazing at the trench. "That would be unfortunate, especially if other academes still credit her."

"Which they do. I'm not without my enemies. The main trouble is, she'll never win an acquittal, and I'll lose her to the torturers." The academe leered. "Not that I wouldn't mind watching the wench receive her just due."

Regim chuckled. "I thought you just said you wanted her."

"I've got my pride, sir. My career is soaring. Anyone of her subpure would be thrilled to win my attentions. I would take her back, but only on my terms. She would have to acknowledge my superiority, and she'll never do that." The academe sighed deeply. "Lieutenant captain, she's the only one I've ever wanted to beget with. But she'll be convicted and executed before we've even entered sharelock. The natalry will never release the materia of a convicted criminal."

"Not to someone who wasn't a sharer before the conviction, that's true."

"I'll never get my hands on her materia. My bid will be annulled." The academe dropped to his knees and seized the ankle of Regim's boot. "I beg you, lieutenant captain, as her arresting officer, intercede for me. Drop the charges."

The revulsion Regim always felt at the touch of lower pure rose in his throat. But his revulsion couldn't compare to the guilt that squeezed his chest. "Vigilance will never do that. Her fathers would have to negotiate her release, and they haven't done so. The Supreme Sayers must acquit her."

"Then tell me what to do!"

"There's nothing you can do. Plaia must recant and repent."

"She won't. I know it."

"Order her, as the superior subpure and her pledged sharer. Compel her, if you possess the more powerful sharemind."

"It's not that easy. She's resisted my purity sharemind before. She'll never listen to me. Not even to save her skin."

Clere's presence crashed into Regim's consciousness, screaming in sharer's sharemind, *You were just thinking about our sharelock, weren't you, Regim? What were you thinking? You worm, you sniveling excuse for a magister, you big stupid walkabout—*

Regim kicked the man's hand away from his ankle. "Gunther, have you ever worn sharelock chips?"

FACET 20

Fire: A hearth or a conflagration.
A blaze staves off the cold or burns a child's hand.
The action is watchfulness.
The forbearance is ruin.

The Orb of Eternity

Commentaries:
Councillor Sausal: Pan flung forth lightning so the Ancient Ones could learn how to tame fire and kindle their hearths.

So, too, the Imperium provides the purities with resources and directs them to employ these wisely.

Therefore the prudent person should learn and practice skills that construct and preserve. Avoid ignorance and ineptitude lest these destroy and harm. [*Deleted from The Contemporary Commentaries of Sausal (15th Ed.)* But sometimes a blaze is the best way to demolish a decayed structure.]
Guttersage (usu. considered vulgar): A priestess roasts meat on a spit, then douses the cookstones.

A fool chars the meat, then burns down his house.

Our City of Atlan, Southwest Marketplace. Detainment Center for the Tertius, Cellblock One Hundred Eleven, the Exercise Yard:

"Plaia Triadana?" the lockkeep shouted. "Haul it front and center else you'll be feelin' the business end a' my club again."

"Haul it yourself, Brod." Plaia lay back on the bench and thrust up the metal discuses gripped in her fists. *One, two, and breathe.* Defiance blazed in her breast. She hardly fancied another gentle tap from Brod's security club, but she'd taken all the ragging she was going to from the brutish lockkeep.

The cheerless yard of gravel scattered on dirt accommodated fifty prisoners and now held thrice as many. All middle pures, the prisoners trudged on a track cutting through the stubborn chokeweed. The *clank* of ankle shackles, a whispered curse—such was the dirge of jail. How Plaia longed for her cymbals! For the sweet music of her resonance team.

If it lessens the sting, Plaia's cellmate Rulian told her, *know that you're just one more vector in the academe epidemic. Heretics behind every lectern and library stack.*

Plaia plunked the discuses down and wiped away sweat stinging her eyes. The high barbed fence, the watchtowers with sentries and crossbows, never failed to send despair pounding through her heart.

When in her thirty years had she *ever* been incarcerated?

Volcanic ashfall clung to the air, darkening the day to a dreary twilight. The unseasonable heat plaguing Atlan since the Hercynian eruption had abruptly cooled to an ominous chill.

Plaia hadn't seen the sun in days. She shivered, despite the perspiration filming her skin.

I'm going mad in this place.

"I said look lively, Plaia." A green protocol chip had been jammed between Brod's brows, which permitted her to boss these higher pures. The hulking serv subpure wore a look of perpetual seasickness. "Warden wants to see you."

"The warden will have to slake her thirst for torture

with someone else. I've got another hour left in the yard."

"Time's run out, academe."

"Leave Plaia alone." Rulian stood behind the bench, coaching her moves. "Again, please. Watch your elbows. You're swinging them out again." An eminent theorist at the Institute of Protocol, Rulian had been arrested after suggesting that sharelock between disparate pures might strengthen the materia of both to the Imperium's benefit. After five seasons, the trial had yet to be docketed.

He smoothed a reddish-gold curl from Plaia's brow. Proximity of subpure, not gender, strictly governed the assignment of cellmates. Rulian and Plaia, both progeny of respectable academe subpures, were supremely proximate. He had proposed sharelock their first night together in the cell, and Plaia had gently but firmly refused.

Once she would have bedded Rulian just to pass the night. Once she would have considered his proximity and his sharelock proposal. But she had no more interest in casual bedmates. And she would *never* be content with Pannish love.

She had never stopped dreaming of her bold, swarthy boy, his raven black eyes, his raven black hair tied back with a thong. Dubban Quartermain, a serv pure. A lower pure, inferior to her.

Forbidden.

Proximity, protocol, prerogative—none of the rules had mattered when she embraced him. She had tasted forbidden love and found herself transformed.

And now Dubban might be dead.

Rumor whispered that the vent ripped open in the flats by the Big Shock had disgorged a murderous new magmaflow. A third of Rancid Flats lay buried in molten rock, tens of thousands of servs and druds beneath it.

The thought of Dubban crushed, incinerated, made Plaia want to die.

She gazed up at Rulian, comforted by her cellmate's kind face. "You're too good to me, Rul."

"Yes, I am," he agreed with a fond smile. A dark-haired, dark-eyed, hardily built fellow, Rulian so resembled Julretta that Plaia had wondered if he was Jul's cloven when they met. He wasn't, but the sight of him jarred terrible memories of the day she'd been arrested: the awesome Bog, Julretta killed by a snarling dragon, Ribba maimed. Herself, dragged off to jail.

She'd been terrified at the prospect. Once Paven, drummer extraordinaire, fellow resonance-team member, and dark-haired rascal, had been sent to this same jail. But when Plaia and her colleagues had gone to bail him out, Paven had disappeared.

The proofs she and her colleagues had fought for to validate Tivern's theories? All gone, except for Tiv's maps and texts. Thank goodness Plaia'd had the foresight to hide them in her safe box.

"Don't make me bust your pretty little face." Brod slapped the club into the slab of her hand.

The other prisoners muttered, casting contemptuous glances at the lockkeep. Academe sharemind forbidden under prison regulations glimmered in their shared consciousness. *Warden's got it in for Plaia. Maybe they've moved up her heresy trial. Maybe they're moving her trial to the Chamber of Justice. No, it'll be in Allpure Square, last I heard. Damn. You know what that means. Yeah, she's a goner.*

Plaia kneaded her forehead with a trembling hand. Rulian had promised to smuggle in poison, a lozenge she could conceal under her tongue and bite, if worse came to worst. But days had fled by, and Rulian hadn't been able to make good on his promise.

"What does the warden want with me?" she said wearily.

"You got two visitors," Brod said.

"Visitors." She sat up. "Who?"

Brod shrugged. "Don't know. Two men."

"I refuse to see my fathers."

"They brought something for you."

"Cakies and sweetmeats? No, I'll accept no more tokens of my fathers' guilt."

"You should respect your fathers, Plaia," chastised a prisoner, a priest from his severe frown. "They're your superiors. After what they've done for you—"

"Want to know what my fathers have *done* for me? They *sold* me. *Sold* my materia, *five* of my birthpods, to a man I despise. Without my knowledge or consent. Under those cockamamy natalry regs that take away your rights to your own materia if you're deemed incompetent. The definition of which includes not paying your own taxes, which of course I don't since I haven't yet earned my mastery degree and don't qualify for a position."

"Sharelock *is* our sacred duty," the priest said.

"Not *my* sacred duty, chum. Want to know what else my fathers have *done* for me? There I was, arrested, charged with heresy and Apocalyptism. The woman I would have entered sharelock with dead. My other best colleague grievously wounded. Did my dear fathers defend me? Did they even have the decency to bail me out? 'We fear you'll run away like you did before,' they said. Cakies and sweetmeats? No. I won't see my fathers."

"Tell it to the warden." The lockkeep seized a handful of her hair and viciously yanked her head. "Let's go."

Handmade shirks got plucked from secret pockets, covert spikes glinted in fists. "Leave her alone, you damn serv," someone muttered. One of Plaia's chums, a distinguished physicist from Atlan University, swung her spike at the lockkeep. The sharp tip exacted its own bit of blood.

"Hai, hai, hai!" Brod shouted. "I got trouble!"

Lockkeeps ran in from all over the grounds and sentries brandished their firebolts, but the physicist faded into the mob. Shirks and spikes disappeared into bodysuits and boot tops. The prisoners submitted to slaps and blows, eyes averted, refusing to answer queries shouted in their faces.

"Academe wench," Brod snarled, "come along. Your two gentlemen callers didn't bring you no cakies. And they ain't your fathers."

"Started trouble in the yard again, did she?" said the warden. She kicked back in her chair, plunked her boots on her desk, and flicked a whip into the palm of her hand. "Shall we try the rack again or something more tactile?"

Plaia smiled. Dread clutched at her innards. Yet the warden, with her racks and her whips, no longer terrified her. Another day in the warden's nasty little domain meant another precious day that her heresy trial had been delayed.

What terrified her was the gigantic vigile. "You'll not touch her, warden. What you'll do is sign these docketing papers and schedule her trial." He flung the documents in the warden's face. "There's a special writ of custody, too. It's bonded, of course. She's coming with us."

The room spun. Plaia couldn't breathe.

She had seen the vigile only once, but she would never forget him. He had been ravaged, then, by injury and sickness. He had recovered some of what had been gloriously handsome looks but his face still twitched with an inner torment. He leaned heavily on a prosthetic leg, assisted by bodyguards. Now and then he muttered out of the corner of his mouth as if quarreling with a troublesome demon.

Lieutenant Captain Regim Deuceman.

And his companion?

During their time together at the academy as proctor and student—as bedmates—she had never noticed the cruel glint in his eyes. "Gunther," she whispered.

He reached out his hand.

She leapt back as if he'd thrust a burning torch in her face. "I told you. You'll never touch me again. I meant it."

He assumed the expression of feigned injury she once

had chuckled at and now despised. Then slipped into sardonic assurance. Her blood turned to ice. "What you say and what you mean, Plaia, amount to nothing anymore."

"I'm not going with these men," she told the warden. "I'd rather go straight to my trial than with them."

"Oh, you'll go to your trial, my pet," Gunther said. "But first I intend to collect your exceedingly valuable materia."

She was aware her mouth had turned to dust. "Are you going to murder me, then? Your bid won't be annulled, will it, if I'm merely the victim of a criminal and not a criminal myself?" She turned furiously to the warden, who signed Regim's documents. "Did something like this happen to my colleague Paven?"

The warden stood, bowed, and returned the documents to Regim with a nervous smile. "I've never heard of Paven. I've never seen Paven. Paven was a troublemaker and a loudmouth. Sirs, please take her and go."

Gunther reached out and brushed his fingertips across her cheek. His touch sent shivers across her skin. "Murder you, my darling? Goodness, no! You always did have a lively imagination. A little morbid, perhaps. I've missed you more than I can say."

"Lieutenant captain," she said, "I demand to know why you're involved in Gunther's pathetic bid for my materia."

The vigile gazed at her curiously. "The High Council has approved of Ground Control's new strategy to stop the earthshocks. The Temple of the Mind of the World and Vigilance Authority have been enlisted to foster support among people of the purities. We would like *your* support. The endorsement of a repentant resonance theorist is sure to impress the purities that force-flooding is Pangaea's salvation."

"I will never, ever, endorse force-flooding of the rifts."

"It's begun, Plaia," Gunther said.

"Then you're a damn fool, Gun. You gamble with the world." To the vigile, "How high must the Imperium raise taxes to finance this disastrous campaign, lieutenant captain?"

"Oh, by thirty percent, I'm sure," Regim said. "The Imperium needs you alive, Plaia Triadana, when you stand before the Supreme Sayers in Allpure Square. Obedient and alive."

"And I," Gunther said, fixing a discipline chip between her brows and then a cold kiss, "need you obedient and in my bed."

Three times Plaia had entered the Temple of Sacred Sharelock before. Once with Tania, then Rhea, then Estelle, when each of her sisters had fulfilled her Imperial duty.

The dazzling colors, the heady perfumes, the lush music would have stirred her now if the discipline chip hadn't lowered a noxious fog over all her senses.

Cymbalon players rendered the sharelock march in grand, sugary chords, evoking every thought and emotion about Pannish love and sharelock. Everything that sharelock meant.

Plaia and her sisters had been generated every two years. Two birthpods purchased from Cairn's sister and seeded by Trenton, two birthpods from Trenton's cousin and seeded by Cairn, all properly supervised and Imperially approved in Rites of Begetting. Trenton's cousin kept cordial relations with Tania and Rhea. Cairn's sister in Tasman, on the other hand, had entered sharelock with a priestess and generated five children of her own. She had visited Plaia and Estelle no more than twice and never so much as glimmered in Plaia's sharemind in between those visits. "It's nothing against you and Estelle, child," she told Plaia. "I just prefer the angels' dreams."

Plaia hadn't minded. Trenton, her gentle second father, had raised his daughters well while Cairn, her stern first father, forged on with his academe career, garnering accolades with the promise of an Imperial pension. Both fathers had faithfully observed their Imperial duty to generate a family and doted on their four daughters. Trenton had resented his cousin's attempts at asserting a presence as a materia donor.

Traitors. She still could not believe they had sold her materia. Had forced her into sharelock.

The discipline chip stabbed her nerves till everything was reeling and would not stay solid. Waves of hot and cold surged over her, and her legs could barely hold. She gazed at her family assembled before the Exalted Altar and raged. She had loved them. She had *trusted* them. She had no idea Imperial duty had meant more to them than she did.

Gunther stood in his ceremonial gown and crown, triumphant, flushed, and smiling. He gripped her hand so tightly she feared her knuckles would crack.

The discipline chip half paralyzed her muscles, but her nerves felt everything. She couldn't have plucked out the chip to save her life. What Gunther had done was strictly illegal. Behavior chips—protocol and discipline—were serious business since they expanded destined prerogatives or restricted permitted activity. Jamming a chip into someone required a license, a tangle of justifications and approvals.

Plaia wanted to scream. Gunther hadn't even given her the chance to tell Rulian good-bye. And her bold boy? Even if Dubban had survived Rancid Flats, she would never see him again.

The priestess-facilitators scurried about the Exalted Altar, arranging the colossi. At Tania's ceremony there had been three, two in Male regalia, one in Female—Tania had entered sharelock with two men. At Rhea's ceremony there had also been three, two in Female regalia and one in Male—Rhea had sharelocked with a woman and a man. Sweet Estelle, Plaia's materia-sister, had exchanged vows well and simply with a man.

Plaia gazed up at the huge white shellstone statues, one adorned with accoutrements and regalia of the Female, one of the Male. The Supreme Facilitator descended from the altar, bearing the Chalice of Sacramental Wine and the Wand of Life in hands like plump white doves. Was the priestess unaware this was a forced sharelock or had her cynical little eyes seen everything?

"Will you, Plaia Triadana naitre Tertius, take this middle pure to be your sacred sharer, to keep and to cherish, to generate a family, and fulfill your Imperial duty from now till Eternity?" the Supreme Facilitator intoned.

No! No! poised on Plaia's tongue, but she could not force out the words. The discipline chip whipped up pain. She opened her mouth and a strangled sound emerged.

"I assume her answer is yes," the Supreme Facilitator said. She dipped the Wand into the Chalice, traced the Imperial star on Plaia's forehead, and offered her a sip of wine.

Plaia whipped her face away. The Supreme Facilitator seized her chin and forced wine through her clenched lips. She tried to spit it out, but couldn't. A sickly, narcotic taste stained her tongue. *It's drugged, everyone knows it's drugged, so even the willing surrender more readily when the surgeons insert the chips.*

"Will you," the Supreme Facilitator intoned, "Gunther Triadius naitre Tertius, take this middle pure to be your sacred sharer, to keep and to cherish, to generate a family, and fulfill your Imperial duty from now till Eternity?"

"I've wanted to take this woman for a long, long time."

Guffaws burst from Gunther's subpure. "Go get her, Gun!"

The Supreme Facilitator shot them a censorious glance. "Answer the question properly, please."

"I will."

The Supreme Facilitator traced the Imperial star, tipped the Chalice. Gunther gulped the thick red wine till streams of it cascaded over his chin, dappling the gown like blood.

"In the name of Pan, I pronounce you sharer and sharer."

A sacred surgeon and grim assistant in bloodred ceremonial robes seized Plaia's wrist and clamped her right hand on the Tablet of Lock. From the knuckle of Plaia's third finger to the top of her wrist the surgeon sliced open the skin of her hand. Plaia's blood spurted, drenching her, the Tablet, the surgeon's glove. She desperately wanted to shut her eyes but, by some morbidity, she could not look away.

For an instant there was no pain, and then agony cleaved her hand in a scalding line. Her muscles writhed involuntarily. She bucked and jerked back, nearly shaking loose of the Tablet. The assistant forced more wine into her mouth.

The surgeon cursed. The assistant dabbed at the bloodflow as best he could. Then the surgeon jammed a diamond-shaped sharelock chip through the incision. The chip scraped Plaia's bones, but it would not set properly. The surgeon pushed and pressed till Plaia thought she'd go mad or swoon. At last the flustered surgeon shoved the chip into place and hastily stitched the incision shut with clumsy crisscrosses. The assistant slopped disinfectant over the wound and plucked the discipline chip from her forehead.

They started on her left hand.

Another surgeon and assistant bent busily over Gunther, and a second Tablet of Lock dripped with blood and disinfectant.

Plaia stared, uncomprehending. *I thought they were supposed to wait. I thought the same surgeon who installed mine would install his, the symbolic and very real agent of our joining.* She had taken comfort in it—that there would be a brief respite before the chips locked her in sharers' sharemind.

And then she realized: *Gunther planned this, too. He knew I would seize whatever small escape I've got left.*

"No!" she screamed, horrified that he had anticipated her with such cynical accuracy and diligently outmaneuvered her.

Overwhelming pressure descended on her. Her head

vibrated. Her teeth chattered. Her body seemed to disappear, obliterated by a force blasting through her.

Gunther's insinuating nasal tenor resounded in her sharemind, his face looming before her larger than life. *Plaia, my love. Giver of birthpods for my unborn. You belong to me now, you devious bitch. From now on, you will obey me.*

And if I don't obey, Gunther? What will you do?

Well, for a start, I'll give you pain.

The claws of his sharer's sharemind dug into her intimate consciousness, gouging and ripping and tearing. Pain seared her fingers and toes as if he'd thrust her hands and feet into blazing cookstones.

She screamed and screamed and screamed.

Sunlight reflected off the pristine white flagstones in Allpure Square, but Plaia knew no truth would be revealed.

"In the pursuit of upholding the law," the speaker shouted, lips pursed in the shape of a funnel, "of revealing impurity in our midst, of correcting that which may be corrected, and punishing that which cannot, we commence the Imperial inquiries of the day."

Plaia stood in the bull pen for the accused, together with other heretics, some bound, some gagged, some bleeding from previous torture. A rough grey robe hung limp over her delicate frame, sleeves to her fingertips. The hem whipped around her ankles in the unnaturally hot winter wind. Her thoughts darted from one conjecture to another, finally settling on a refrain: *I have no poison. Doesn't matter what I say. I have no poison.*

The flagstones betrayed no trace of the wreckage wrought by the Big Shock last summer. The Obelisk of Eternity pointed its marble needle at the Pagoda of Pan hovering directly overhead. The spectacular stabile of Imperial purple and gold, borne aloft by the force of the Ancient Ones, cast darkness at noon.

Her whole body ached. Last night Gunther had taken her to his villa after the sharelock ceremony and done to her what she knew he would do. Once she had bedded him with simple pleasure. Now his touch sent repulsion crawling over her skin. Her time in jail had toughened her, though, and he could no longer physically overpower her. They exchanged blows. He had finally ordered his beck-and-call men to bind her when neither his fists nor his sharer's sharemind could force her.

Plaia clasped her hands over her ravaged belly. She wore no bonds or security leashes. What Gunther could not manage last night, he managed now. Her hands lay crossed and limp, trussed by his sharer's sharemind as surely as if by rope.

Atlan Prefecture had constructed barricades along each side of the square where the periphery of the sacred center bordered on each purity's quadrant. The barricades were festooned in traditional colors. Terracotta for the druds. Bright copper for the servs. Brilliant blue-green and bronze for the middle purities. Solemn indigo and silver for the magisters. The angels' balcony, hovering overhead next to the pagoda, was resplendent in Imperial purple and gold.

Behind the barricades soared vast bleachers where people gathered each day with lunch baskets, clothes to be mended, and other handiworks and pastimes. The spectators watched with avid eyes as Supreme Sayers from the Chamber of Justice conducted heresy trials and masked-and-gloved vivisectionists carried out tortures and executions upon command.

Do not fret, my pet, came Gunther's loathsome whisper in sharer's sharemind. *Just say as I say.*

She smiled. She trembled violently. She was going to die, and die horribly. But she suddenly knew this: *It does matter what I say. I will tell what I know.*

Regim stood among the Vigilance torturers, tall and terrifying in his crazed beauty. He laughed at a quip a hooded whipbearer made. He spoke with a vivisectionist about a particular trowel, making scooping motions.

Gunther sat in the vouchers' gallery, beaming and smug. As her sharer, he could now make good on his

begetting bid no matter what happened to her. Plaia
glimpsed her fathers in the gallery, Trenton weeping,
Cairn impassive.

Her breath caught when she saw thick brown curls
haloing a brazen face. Once those eyes had been mischievous, the mouth laughing, the hands deft as they
fingered her cherished flute. Now Ribba's eyes stared
dully. Her mouth hung slack. The stump of her wrist
where the dragon had claimed her hand was wrapped
in linen. A toxic-looking discipline chip winked in her
forehead.

*Ribba, beloved colleague! What have they done to
you?*

Plaia entered the grey space her sharemind had become. The webwork of sharers' sharemind bound her
consciousness. She opened her eyes, stole a glance at
Gunther. He leaned toward her fathers in avid conversation. She swiftly reentered. In the lapse of Gunther's
attention, the webwork sagged. She cautiously searched
till she found an opening. She swiftly slipped through
into purity sharemind.

Rib, honey, who put a chip in you?

A quavering sharemind entered mutual consciousness.

*My f-f-family. When they b-b-bailed me out, it was a
condition of my release.*

Plaia stifled a gasp. *We made out a will, you,
Julretta, and me. We signed it in blood, recorded it with
City Hall. Ribba, you must take custody of Julretta's
Natalry Bank account. Now, before her family sells her
birthpods to some stranger. Or the Imperium seizes
them.*

Plaia, I-I can't. I-I c-can't think.

*WARNING. THIS PERSON IS PROTECTED BY
IMPERIAL SECURITY.*

The shield of the discipline chip smashed into Plaia,
sending her reeling into her own consciousness.

"Hear ye, hear ye, all rise!" the speaker shouted.

Five Supreme Sayers were led in and seated at a
bench of carved blackwood. The Sayers' eyes had been

stitched shut. Intricate silver sutures gleamed against celadon skin. A trio of seers clustered behind each Sayer. Their small, numb faces and unblinking eyes bore the look of intense, continuous sharemind with the Sayer they attended. Each trio supplied a Sayer with the perspective of three pairs of eyes.

"You cannot hide the truth forever!" came a man's shout. "Do you know what the truth is? Do you have any idea?"

Plaia knew that voice. Knew the lean academe flung by loutish lockkeeps onto the accused's podium. Sweet Donson, fellow mastery student and resonance-team member. She'd shared wine and Donson's bedroll after she'd refused Gunther's sharelock proposal. It had been the morning of the Big Shock. A morning filled with revelations. Donson had been the best zitar player she'd ever heard. A dedicated resonance theorist who believed his music could save the world.

They had sliced off his ears. Streams of blood matted his hair and dribbled down his neck. They'd done something to his knees and ankles, too.

"The truth is it's the end of the world," Donson shouted. "And the Imperium cannot do a damn thing about it!"

"Donson Trieme naitre Tertius, you are charged with trafficking in Orbs of Eternity," announced a Supreme Sayer. "How do you plead?"

"Not guilty. I wasn't trafficking."

Plaia's heartbeat raced in her throat. She knew very well that Donson owned an orb. They had gambled with it twice.

"You were apprehended selling the device."

"To the same foe marketeer who sold it to me. At my considerable loss, I might add. A squad of vigiles just happened to be in the courtyard. Now, why had vigiles concealed themselves in the bushes? Can the Supreme Sayer tell me?"

"Imperial Vigilance is everywhere, protecting all the purities. So you *do* plead guilty?"

"I do not." Donson turned toward the bleachers and

shouted, "I want to know why Vigilance collaborates with foes to arrest a good Pangaean citizen."

The crowd roared, stood, and flung stones against the barricades.

"Silence!" The Sayer stood and swung her stitched-blind face back and forth.

The crowd shrank back, and an earthshock rumbled, accenting the Sayer's words with an authority that seemed divine.

"The academe shouts blasphemies distressing to our Pangaeans," the Sayer said. "So let us clarify the heretic's words and the charges against him. As every Pangaean knows, three seasons ago the High Council enacted Imperial Law Section 616.1, under Title 13, Impure Activities. The law bans orbs, orbrolls, orbcasting, and orb trafficking of any kind, and imposes stiff penalties for any and all violations."

"Why?" someone shouted from the middle pure bleachers.

"Why?" the Sayer echoed. "Because scholars have proven these abominations are of impure origin. Orbs have plagued our society since times lost to antiquity. They are the source of contaminated thoughts. They foment confusion about Pan and the Imperium, provoke protocol violations, smuggling, gambling, tax evasion, and other crimes. Orbcasters use orbs to gull money from the gullible—"

"The orb is a faceted jewel," Donson cried, "of strange and wondrous power."

"—and bewitch otherwise intelligent and educated people like this academe before us. One of our own highest magisters, Councillor Sausal, took an inordinate interest in this charlatan's plaything and wrote corrupt commentaries purporting to illuminate Pannish thought."

"Corrupt? I studied Sausal's commentaries in fundamental school," Donson shouted. "What reinvention of the teachings is this?"

"I remember," someone called out from the southwest quadrant.

"It made me believe in Pan," shouted someone else.

"Of course you remember," the Sayer thundered. "But instead of edifying the people, Sausal's commentaries promulgated confusion. For which he has been disgraced and banished."

"Don't believe these lies, my fellow Pangaeans," Donson shouted. "Why was Councillor Sausal, most esteemed of our magisters, *really* banished?"

Don't do this, Donson, Plaia screamed in purity sharemind. *Repent! The orb is not worth your life.*

In sharer's sharemind Gunther crashed into her, choking her into silence. *I gave you no permission to enter sharemind with your former bedmate.*

The Sayer conferred with the other Sayers and announced, "We find the orb trafficker guilty as charged."

At the Sayer's nod, the vivisectionists mounted the accused's podium and seized Donson. They ripped off his robe, flung him on a pallet of mottled wood planks, and bound him.

A vivisectionist plunged her blade and dragged it all around the academe's taut belly.

Donson howled, "Did Sausal see truth in the orb? A truth the Imperium doesn't want us to see?"

The vivisectionist commenced yanking out innards. Donson gasped so wretchedly Plaia fell to her knees, unable to stand.

"Hear me, fellow Pangaeans!" he cried. "Sausal saw that the orb prophesied the end of the world when the Imperium no longer permits people a choice. When your purity is chosen for you and you accept that because the angels' dreams say you have no hand in your own destiny."

His head fell limp. His eyes, distended with horror, lost their spark though his chest still rose and fell in ragged breaths. The vivisectionists finished their grisly task and littered the accused's podium with Donson's entrails, spelling out the fate of the next heretic.

"Plaia Triadana naitre Tertius," the speaker shouted.

Gunther nodded at Regim, and the vigile nodded back, a strange smile on his ruined face.

Plaia trembled so violently she could not rise. Lockkeeps hauled her to her feet and flung her onto the podium.

The Sayer said, "You are charged with heresy and Apocalyptism. How do you plead?"

Not guilty rose to her lips.

Gunther's sharemind beat at her. *You are guilty, my girl. Sinfully, seditiously guilty. Say it.*

What are you doing to me, Gunther?

Say it!

The claws of his sharemind dug into her, tearing. He seized her sense of vision and spun it like a child's toy top. The world whirled in variegated streaks, and her gorge rose in her throat. She wondered if he could actually blind her.

"I . . . am . . . guilty."

The crowd bellowed. The vivisectionists wiped Donson's blood from their hands and smiled beneath their masks.

"These are serious charges, academe," the Sayer said, plainly surprised at her answer. "You have publicly lied. You claimed the notorious academe Tivern died in a magma eruption at Andea Rift. In fact the heretic died of hepatic failure from a skee addiction. Is that true?"

Say yes, my pet.

It's a vicious lie, Gunther. You know damn well Tivern died in the eruption.

There's no proof. Say it.

Talons of pain tore at her in sharemind.

"Yes," she whispered, "it's true."

"Further," the Sayer said, "you publicly stated the Apocalyptic lie that the world is coming to an end. In fact, that is not true, is it?"

Tiv had evidence, Gunther. I have more evidence. Pangaea as we know it is coming to an end.

Now, my pet, how many times must I tell you? The Imperium doesn't want to hear that sort of news. Say, It is not true.

His sharemind seized her and shook her so violently she wondered if her neck would snap.

"No," she whispered, "it is not true."

"Further," the Sayer said, "you publicly opposed Ground Control's new strategy to flood the rifts and stop the earthshocks. A strategy fully endorsed by the High Council. You persuaded other mastery students to oppose the strategy, a deluded and dangerous course that led to Julretta's death, Ribba's disfigurement, and your arrest. Ribba Trevon naitre Tertius? Stand and bear witness. Did Plaia lead you astray?"

Tell them we were right, Ribba, Plaia screamed in purity sharemind. *Tell them flooding the rifts will cause more earthshocks. Huge earthshocks. Not stop them!*

Ribba rose unsteadily to her feet, every corner of her face twitching. The discipline chip pulsed in her forehead. "P-Plaia led us astray."

You never lied in your life, Ribba. Tell them the truth!

Ribba clutched her amputated wrist. *The t-t-truth is, Plaia, I'll never play my flute again.*

"Supreme Sayers, how can this woman bear witness wearing a discipline chip?" Plaia demanded.

"The accused will answer questions put to her, not volunteer questions of her own. Strike that from the record." The Sayer clucked her tongue. "Plaia Triadana, why did you oppose Ground Control's plan?"

You will say, Because I was misguided, Gunther's sharemind thundered.

I will say, Because excessive water in the rifts correlates with earthshock activity. It always has. It always will. You are the misguided one, Gunther. You will pay for your foolishness with the lives of countless innocent people. With your own life.

You're hardly in a position to predict my death.

If he had jabbed needles into every nerve in her body, he could not have hurt her more. She wrapped her arms around her ribs, shivering with agony.

Say it, Plaia. Loud and clear so everyone may hear you.

"Because I was misguided," she said, sobbing.

"Do you repent?" the Sayer asked, her voice kindly.

"I repent. I repent!"

Gunther raised his hand. "Supreme Sayer, I am Gunther Triadius, advisor to Ground Control and the heretic's former proctor at Sausal Academy. May I ask a question on behalf of Ground Control?" At the Sayer's nod, "Plaia Triadana, do you support Imperial flooding of Andea Rift?"

"I do. I do!"

Gunther turned to Regim. "Lieutenant captain?"

Regim said, "Supreme Sayers, may I ask a question on behalf of Vigilance and the High Council?" At the Sayer's nod, "Plaia, do you support the flood tax?"

"I do. I do!"

Regim bowed to the Supreme Sayers. "Thank you for your wisdom and your verdict. Please proceed."

The Sayer conferred with other Sayers, the stitched-blind faces nodding together. The Sayer announced, "As the heretic has confessed, so we find her guilty as charged."

The torturers seized Plaia by her elbows just before she collapsed.

FACET 21

> Wheel: Hauling or trampling.
> Mobility fosters contact, near and far.
> The action is forming friendships.
> The forbearance is inciting hostilities.
>
> **The Orb of Eternity**

Commentaries:
Councillor Sausal: Pan places all things of the world according to the law of proximity, yet also places things near and far.

So, too, the Imperium encourages the unity of each purity under the law of proximity. Yet a pure of the city is as much a Pangaean as a pure of the plains.

Therefore the prudent person should foster cordial relations everywhere with all those of the same pure and subpure. Foster cordial relations and you foster the strength of the Imperium.

Beware of conflicts caused by distance. Beware of estrangements caused by miscommunication.
Guttersage (usu. considered vulgar): The gracious magister dines with other magisters wherever she travels.

The obnoxious fool is thrown out of his corner saloon.

Our City of Atlan, Marketplace, the perimeter of Northwest Quadrant bordering Allpure Square:

It was *her.*

Dubban stood, hands hooked over the serv barri-

cade, as torturers seized the woman he'd been searching
for all his life. *His* woman—that's how he'd come to
think of her since the night they'd met. Though of
course she wasn't. She was a middle pure, he a serv. A
woman forbidden to him.

The vivisectionists led her to the pallet. She staggered
between them, head bowed. She looked so fragile between the brutish torturers, Dubban wanted to strangle
them. Flies rose from the blood-smeared planks in a
buzzing swarm.

People were screaming, "She's confessed. She's
saved!"

Others, "She confessed. She's damned!"

Fisticuffs broke out in the bleachers. Flung jars shattered on the flagstones. A burly firefighter staggered
into Dubban. He shoved the woman back into the fray.

The torturers lifted the hem of Plaia's robe. Dubban
glimpsed her legs corded with slim muscles. The oily
academe seated in the vouchers' gallery shot a triumphant smirk at Regim. Dubban could not fathom why
Gunther should smile to see his student tortured to
death. He instantly despised the man.

No time to lose. Dubban vaulted over the barricade
with all the agility of his twenty-one years and sprinted
to the accused's podium. He wasn't sure what he was
going to do. He only knew he would not watch while
torturers gutted her. Vigiles turned, openmouthed with
surprise, and drew daggers and crossbows.

Suddenly a peculiar but unmistakable sensation
struck him. He no longer swayed on his feet or suffered
vertigo the way he always did in an earthshock. A
swarm of shocks had plagued the megalopolis since
dawn and since dawn he'd swayed and fought dizzi-
ness. Atlan hadn't *stopped* trembling and lurching since
the magma eruption had devastated a third of Rancid
Flats.

The ground stopped now.

Dubban's thoughts raced. What in hell was Plaia's
trial all about, anyway? He had listened to the charges,

her testimony. A woman's life for her endorsement—or not—of an Imperial plan?

He shouted at the crowd, "Do you *feel* it? No shocks."

The bleachers went wild, people shrieking, "No shocks! No shocks!"

Dubban shouted, "The academe said flood the rifts. The academe was right."

"The heretic said no such thing," came a magister's harsh shout from southeast quadrant. "She confessed she tried to *discredit* the bureau's strategy."

Dubban turned toward the Supreme Sayers. "*I* heard her say she supports the strategy. And the strategy has worked. The shocks have stopped. Long live the Imperium!"

People took up the refrain. "Long live the Imperium!"

"Long live Plaia," Dubban shouted. "Free the academe. She stopped the earthshocks."

People shouted, "Free the academe. Long live Plaia!"

An arrow from a vigile's crossbow thunked into the flagstones at Dubban's toes. He dodged as the arrow bounced off stone and clattered down.

Three vigiles leapt at him, and he ducked, leaving them in a pile behind him. He darted in a zigzag path to where Regim stood. He flung himself at the lieutenant captain's feet.

Defying protocol, he spoke first. "Do you remember me, sir? I am Superior Father Dubban." He winced at the counterfeit title. His masquerade as a middle-pure priest-natalist amounted to a crime far more heinous than the blasphemies of the gutted academe or Plaia, but he couldn't let that worry him. "I presided over your Rite of Begetting. I seeded your child. I stitched your wounds."

Regim glared, indignant at the protocol violation, but recognition glimmered in his blue-fire eyes. Vigiles seized Dubban's arms and yanked him to his feet. Regim dismissed them with an imperious wave of his hand.

"Yes, Superior Father, I remember. I owe you a debt for my child's life. And another for mine."

"Then I implore you to plead for the academe's life."

"Why does her life concern you?"

Dubban cast about for an answer. "Because it's Pannish to be merciful toward one repentant."

To Dubban's relief, the fearsome vigile nodded. "I suppose you're right, Superior Father." Regim bowed toward the tribunal. "Supreme Sayers, the former heretic acknowledges the error of her ways. She has confessed and repented. It is Pannish to be merciful toward one repentant. Is the Imperium not merciful?"

"The Imperium is ever merciful," the Sayer said.

"Then, as the arresting officer, I plead that you show mercy. Release the academe."

The Sayers conferred. "Very well," the Sayer said. "Release her."

The torturers frowned and grumbled, displeased at losing such a delectable victim. The vivisectionists flung Plaia into the arms of two brawny lockkeeps, who escorted her off the podium. She stood, visibly trembling, three steps away from Dubban. A brief smile flickered over her features, and then again her face became a mask of torment. The lockkeeps escorted her through the frenzied crowd out of Allpure Square.

Dubban watched her go, then prostrated himself before Regim. "Thank you, lieutenant captain. You are kind."

Regim laughed. "Do not rely too heavily on my kindness, Superior Father. You'd better return to your quadrant."

Dubban scrambled to his feet and pushed through the crowd. Hope, bright and clear, sparkled through him. At last he knew her name! She had refused to tell him the night they met. Had refused to tell him anything except that she had gone to the Serpent Sect rave, looking for him. Now he knew her pure, her subpure. He would pay a visit to Our Sacred City Hall that very afternoon. Tertius Registry would list her family's address or hers if she kept her own quarters.

I will find you, Plaia Triadana.

The Sayer swept her blind face toward the bull pen filled with weeping heretics. "Next."

Dubban dabbed sweat from his brow and loosened the collar of his work shirt. As usual, the ges tank chamber at Secundus Natalry was broiling hot. He felt a bit faint as he methodically changed amniotic fluid in a row of gestation tanks. After the exacting work of pruning birthpods beneath a viewglass, Dubban found this task pleasantly boring. The unborns within, robust magister pures tucked in their birthsacks, seemed to smile at him. He smiled back to see them growing so well.

He would have continued smiling, admiring the unborns' pale golden skin, the blue dots of security numbers visible on diminutive arms, if Waldo's sneer hadn't swooped into his ear.

"Been looking for you everywhere, Dub. Here you go." Dubban's super thrust the forest-green velvet cape and miter of a Superior Father into his hands. "The Superior Mother needs you at the bank for another begettin'. Trot on over there."

Dubban shrugged on the ceremonial garments and bit back irritation. It had been like this since last summer. He'd been in such priestly demand, he barely had time to finish his midwifery chores. Ever since he had impersonated a Superior Father at the Rite of Begetting for Regim and Clere, the Superior Mothers had called upon his services every other day. He had protested, pointing out they could *all* go to jail. The presence of a serv at the Miracle of Pan amounted to sacrilege of the severest sort. But neither the priestesses nor the physicians had been inclined to snitch on the scheme. Every begetting he'd presided at proved successful. Dubban had been granted so many security clearances, the Chief Natalist had signed off on an allpure permission, just to keep him out of her hair.

He strode past uniformed vigiles gathered around a tank containing a tiny magister unborn of perhaps only

half a season. They wore visitors' armbands winking
with security kaligraphs. A high councillor accompanied them, and several bodyguards. A commanding
voice rang out, a voice that stopped Dubban in his
tracks. He'd heard it only hours before.

"When she emerges in two seasons, I shall name her
Regima Clere," Regim announced, gesturing at the tank
and its tiny occupant. "It's what Clere wants."

"What Clere *would* have wanted, my son-in-lock,"
Councillor Claren Twine gently corrected him.

"Oh, no, my father-in-lock," Regim replied. A tic
rippled across his left cheek. He fixed his eyes so acutely
on an empty space in front of him that Dubban could
almost *see* a presence standing there. "She told me so
herself." He brandished his hands, winking with
sharelock chips. "In sharers' sharemind." He scruti-
nized the faces of his companions, as if daring anyone
to challenge him. His gaze fell on Dubban, standing at
the edge of their group.

Dubban pulled the priest's miter more tightly over
his forehead, suddenly glad Waldo had interrupted his
work with an extra chore. Earlier, in Allpure Square,
Dubban had worn the togs of a serv, and he'd seen the
confusion in Regim's eyes.

"So, Superior Father Dubban, we cross paths again."
Doubt shimmered again—serv or middle pure?—but
Regim smiled congenially enough. "This is the priest
who seeded my daughter," he said proudly. "They say
he's Atlan's most potent begetter."

Another entourage of walkabout vigiles and
physician-natalists swept into the chamber, led by a
harried Superior Mother, her rose-petal veils askew.
Dubban had never met this particular priestess before.

"Has the Superior Father arrived?" she said. "Ah!
There you are."

"No, no, I'm not the one. I'm supposed to be—"

"You're supposed to be *here*, Superior Father. We
need you for an emergence."

The walkabouts gathered three rows away where the
ges tanks held fully formed babes on the verge of de-

parting from their tanks. A physician checked each tank, comparing the security numbers stamped on the outside with a number on his databoard.

"Here she is," the physician said.

"Pardon me, Superior Mother," Dubban whispered and took the priestess aside. "I've performed begettings but I've never assisted an emergence before."

She clucked her tongue. "Oh, spare me, another deadbeat. You Superior Fathers are all alike. Take the glory, shun the labor. Never mind. I know the speech. Just stand there and do what the physicians tell you. Look worried before they fish the trout out, look happy when our new citizen breathes. Got it?"

She called to the vigiles, "Where are the sharers?"

Two willowy women stepped forward in full-dress walkabout uniforms, white-gold hair pinned in chignons beneath their helmets. Flushed and shiny-eyed, they gripped each other's gloved hands and giggled.

"And the seeder?" the Superior Mother said.

A stout elderly man in the silver robes of a retired walkabout smiled indulgently at the sharers. A father of one? An uncle of the other? A brother who had emerged decades before?

The physician shoved a capacious tray sloshing with warm water into Dubban's hands. "Hurry up! Take this and stand over there." The Superior Mother was chanting something about the Cradle of Pan about to receive the unborn and deliver life from the sacred waters.

Dubban stood beside the ges tank as two physicians gently lifted out babe and birthsack. They carefully slit the sack open and flung the spent sack into an orderly's bucket. They slid the newly emerged babe onto the tray where she lay, pale golden skin filmed with whitish slime. A physician smoothed slime away from the babe's nose and mouth. The mouth gaped open once, twice, and drew breath as peaceful as a sleepy sigh.

The sharers began to weep through their laughter. The entourage quietly applauded.

Water splashed onto his green-velvet cape, and Dubban gazed down at a tiny golden girl. He felt near tears himself.

"What is our new citizen's name?" the Superior Mother said.

"We're naming her Clere in honor of our martyred prefect," the walkabouts said in unison. "Clere Dona Twinset."

A physician gave the Feed a vigorous yank, separating the plasmaplast tube from its implantation in the small, plump belly. He tied off the ring of flesh into a delicate button.

The Superior Mother intoned—

> *As Pan formed your beauty*
> *As Pan fashioned your limbs*
> *So Pan grants your breath*
> *Oh, Clere Dona Twinset!*
> *So Pan invigorates your flesh*
> *That you may serve the Imperium*
> *And live in Eternity forever!*

Hymnals blared in the begetting chambers at the top of Natalry Bank. Laughter and the babble of conversation filled the entire floor. Dubban's mouth watered at the luscious odors of meat roasting and flatbreads frying in the kitchen off the banquet chamber. After the morning heresy trials, he'd been unable to swallow one bite of his lunch. Perhaps he'd eat something, after all.

As usual, all hell was breaking loose in the service quarters behind the ceremonial chambers. The staff of physicians and priestesses were *never* ready, not even with plenty of notice. Physician-natalists dashed about with bouquets of cut flowers, enormous viewglasses, syringes, and bowls of sacred nectar.

"*Five* birthpods, you idiots!" It was the same Superior Mother he'd begotten with before and, as usual, she was shouting at the staff and tearing at her hair. "*Yes,* that's how many. I said *five.*" Sweat splotched her vermilion veils. "*Yes,* I said academe. *Academe.*" Wild-eyed, she turned to him, ungrateful and strident, despite the fact he was invariably calm, reliable, and punctual. "*There* you are, you poxy midwife."

"You may call me Superior Father Dubban," he said coolly and held out his hand for her usual bribe of twenty ores. She always wound up apologizing and thanking him for violating proximity one more time. But she never got around to that state of conciliation till the damn ceremony was over and done with.

She slapped the ores into his palm, infuriated the way she was always infuriated when he called in his due. "Let's go, my fine Superior Father," she said and seized his hand in the ritual handclasp.

They promenaded down the aisle of the sweltering ceremonial chamber and approached the Platform of Fertility. Academes thronged the chamber. The platform—as long as Dubban's two arms outstretched, fashioned of wafer-thin cut emeralds, and heated and lit from below by simmering magmalamps—bore five begetting dishes of pale green crystal. The female materia reclined in five storage dishes, infinitesimal birthpods visible only through a viewglass. Five dishes of the male materia—the liquid seed—were arrayed beside each begetting dish. The materia, female and male, had been retrieved from the freezing vaults at Natalry Bank and thawed that morning. The physician-natalists poured sacred nectar—a broth of nutrients—into the begetting dishes.

Dubban seized a syringe and withdrew a dram of male materia. The Superior Mother did the same, drawing out the contents of a female dish. Dubban cleared his throat and deepened his basso voice. The Superior Mothers loved it when he did that.

"Hear ye, hear ye, all you who have gathered here today to witness this begetting, by the grace of the Imperium. These sacred sharers have properly commissioned the Miracle of Pan, which has been approved by Tertius Natalry, supremely blessed by Our Superior Mother"—she bowed—"and Our Superior Father"— he bowed—"and will be joyfully bestowed with the

Imperial imprint of a security number after consumma-
tion."

The sharers stood hand in hand before him. A man
and a woman this time, they wore the traditional leaf-
green gowns. Veils secured by headbands of green
leather, draped their faces.

The man threw back his veil.

Dubban recognized the despicable academe at once.

Gunther Triadius flipped his sharer's veil over her
head, revealing a lovely anguished face.

It was *her*.

There was no mistaking the sharelock chips embedded between the carpal bones of her graceful hands.
Her complexion was ashen, the shadows beneath her
cheekbones cavernous, her sensuous mouth distorted in
a grimace.

Dubban reeled. His voice died in his throat. Why
hadn't he noticed her sharelock chips before? She'd certainly worn none on the delirious night they'd met. He
recalled the heresy trial. The crude grey robe. The
sleeves had covered her hands.

*She's entered sharelock with a man who smiled at
the prospect of her torture? How could she?*

Because she and I are academe subpures, priest. A
consciousness invaded Dubban's sharemind like a
sword of ice. *Because she and I are proximate.*

Dubban flinched and swiftly shielded his consciousness as best he could. His serv sharemind couldn't withstand the predation of a middle-pure sharemind. He
waited for further plunder, but none came.

Instead Plaia's face twisted, as if Gunther were
plunging a dagger into her belly. *He's the superior subpure, then.* The same rage Dubban had felt when he'd
witnessed her between two torturers surged through
him.

But he kept an outward calm. He and the Superior
Mother emptied the contents of their syringes into each
begetting dish, consummating the rite in a spew of
fluids. The Superior Mother adjusted viewglasses over
the dishes so the sharers' families could step up to the

platform and witness the Miracle of Pan: male seedlings flailing against a female birthpod. The final plummet of one seedling through the pod's periphery and the first instant of incipient life.

Gunther moved behind Plaia and seized her hips, pumping his groin against her buttocks. He whipped her around, seized her shoulders, and shoved her to her knees.

"Let's see how much Pannish love my sacred sharer has for me," he crowed.

Gunther's subpure jeered and catcalled, egging him on.

The physician-natalists gathered up the begetting dishes, calling out, "The Miracle of Pan has been consummated. Bless you. Bless you." Exchanging anxious glances, they dashed out, bound for Tertius Natalry and the middle-pure gestation tanks waiting to receive new citizens.

The Superior Mother usually delivered her speech about the unborn issuing from the Bosom of Pan, from sacred sharer to sacred sharer, by the grace of the Imperium, but she didn't do that. She seized Dubban's elbow. "Let's leave these academes to their debauchery. They'll be violent before too long."

"Violent? Why?"

"See that nasty sharer? He ordered us to spike the punch with p'um. Paid extra, believe me. They'll be out of their minds in another hour."

"They're out of their minds now."

Two academes wrestled each other to the floor, half-grinning, half-glaring, and proceeded to punch viciously, fists flailing. Dubban's heart clenched when Gunther seized a dinner knife from the banquet table and brandished it over Plaia's reddish gold curls.

"What will he do to her?" he said.

The Superior Mother fixed him with a regretful stare. "Dubban, sometimes superior sharers lose their reason after a begetting. Maybe they feel their duty of sharelock is fulfilled. That nothing else matters. Once I witnessed a drayer impale his sharer with a pitchfork during after-rite revels. Sent the sharer to the hospital and himself to jail. All they want is their sharer's Imperial materia. All *we* want is their begetting fee. You're a midwife. You ought to know that."

Dubban shook his head. "My mother is nothing if not a devout Pannist and a rustic from the Far Reaches. Yet Bandular taught me that true sharelock is achieved when sharers share Pannish love and their hearts."

The Superior Mother peered cautiously at the savage merriment. "Well, I'm afraid those two won't achieve true sharelock, then. Please, Dubban. Let's go."

"No. I can't leave her."

The Superior Mother tugged on his arm. "This is no place for you, Dubban. I despise this, really I do. Sometimes sacred sharelock isn't at all what the angels say." She added, "I don't know what he's going to do to her. I don't want to know."

But Dubban knew what *he* would do. He took the priestess's arm and escorted her through the mob into the service quarters.

"Go now, Superior Mother. I'll make sure the academes get out of here in one piece and the chamber is cleaned up for your next begetting."

The Superior Mother regarded him, astonished. "You would do that for me?"

"Well, of course. I've pledged to serve Pan today by serving a higher pure beyond the bounds of my Imperial duty. Go on. I'll take care of the mess."

"Bless you, Superior Father Dubban." She brushed gentle fingertips on his cheek. "I'm sorry I scolded you."

"You're always sorry, Superior Mother. And the next time, you'll scold me again." He grinned at her look of contrition. "Go on, get."

She left, scurrying down the hall, vermilion veils flying. A thousand new understandings tumbled through him. He tore off the green-velvet miter and cape, smoothed back his hair, and retied the thong. He straightened his serv togs.

And strode back into the ceremonial chambers. He

surveyed the disgraceful revel. He'd seen plenty of solemn begettings and plenty of drunken ones, too, but
he'd never witnessed such wanton abandonment. A
gang of girls and boys were tearing apart the Platform
of Fertility, flinging abandoned dishes of smeary seed
against the wall, trampling on the flowers, leaping up
and down on the emerald slab. A mob of boys had
seized one of their younger siblings, hung the child by
his wrists from a wall lamp, and were taking turns beating his buttocks. A dozen girls and young women had
stripped off their clothes and ran shrieking through the
crowd.

The elders ignored the youngsters. Some lay locked
in embraces forbidden, Dubban had no doubt, under
subpure protocol. Others guzzled skee and that spiked
punch, danced on tabletops, or tumbled to the floor in
rapturous swoons. Fisticuffs and shouting matches
abounded.

Dubban searched for Gunther. Fortunately, the despicable academe had forgotten about Plaia for the moment. He embraced a squealing girl who had thrown
her arms around his neck. Plaia still knelt before him,
her arms crossed at the wrists over her belly, head
bowed, eyes averted. She winced, struggling with some
inner pain.

Dubban seized a whisk broom, a dustpan, and the
heavy crystal magnifying tube from a viewglass. He
strolled among the revelers, stooping to collect shards
of shattered glass, abandoned plates, spilled food.

"Can you believe it?" Gunther was saying to a group
of grinning academes. "Right in the middle of a heresy
trial, the slut enters sharemind with one of her old
bedmates. Right in front of *me*."

"Punish the wench," an academe said.

Gunther seized a lock of Plaia's hair and began saw-
ing at it with the dinner knife.

"Pardon me, sir," Dubban said, "but I see Regim
Deuceman over there by the door. He's come to con-
gratulate you."

The academes gasped and craned their necks. The

most famous vigile in all Pangaea, and an eminent
magister pure, at an academes' rite?

Gunther turned, flushed with skee and pu'm. He
blushed purple with pleasure. "Regim, my esteemed patron!"

Dubban slammed the magnifying tube across the
back of Gunther's head, then flung the tube across the
chamber. The heavy crystal struck the far wall with a
resounding *thud*, gouging an impressive gash in the
stucco wall. Gunther fell like a brained ox. Blood
spouted, staining his dull yellow curls. His guests
shouted and knelt beside their stricken host. Others
stared stupidly at the far wall, confounded at the sound
and the sudden damage.

Dubban seized Plaia's wrist and towed her through
the mob past other fallen bodies, as if she were one
more inebriate he meant to bounce out of Natalry
Bank.

She glanced up, her eyes opaque with sharer's
sharemind. "What are you *doing*? He'll beat me if I
leave."

"He'll beat you if you stay."

He escorted her into the service quarters, swung her
into his arms, and ran out into the service corridor. He
heard the rumble of voices, the strike of bootheels. He
carried her into the supply room where he'd once taken
Regim, set her down on the bench, and locked the door.

He stood, ear pressed to the door, heartbeat hammering in his chest. He peered out the peephole. A
squad of natalry vigiles strode down the corridor, their
huge faces fanning back and forth as they surveilled the
premises. The usual bank patrol? Or had someone summoned them?

They strode on without a glance at the supply room.

Dubban released the breath he hadn't known he was
holding.

He started when he felt her fingertips brush his arm.

She stood, swaying unsteadily, fierce in her effort to
seize strength. "Is it really you, Dubban Quartermain?
Or am I dreaming the angels' dreams?"

"It's me," he said and gently took her shoulders. "Plaia. Plaia." Her name lingered on his lips. He couldn't taste enough of it. "I've been looking for you everywhere since last summer. How did this happen to you?"

"Can't explain now. I've got secrets, important secrets, I don't want *him* to know." She gripped her forehead. "And he's in *here*. He's inside *me*."

"I gave him quite a knock on the noggin back there."

"Ah, did you?" She smiled absently as if she hadn't realized her own danger. "But once he recovers, he'll apprehend everything I say. Everything I do. Where I am." She kneaded her forehead, then brandished her hands, the diamond-shaped sharelock chips winking furiously. "Dubban, take them out."

"*What?*"

"The cursed chips. Take them out. Please, at once! You're the first hope I've had in a long time. Have you got a knife or a razor or something?"

"But those are sharelock chips." And though Dubban had become a different man since last summer, had rejected his mother's Pannist teachings that forbade him even to touch Plaia, let alone yearn for her, still he balked at her demand. "They're *sacred*."

"Sacred! You mean profane. Dubban, he tortures me in sharemind. Now that he's gotten everything he wanted, he'll have no more use for *me*."

Dubban swallowed hard. "Are you sure?"

"Absolutely. I *loathe* him." Her face contorted. "Please, I beg you! He'll find me. There's no place I can hide from him with these chips in my hands. I'd rather die than spend one more moment in sharelock with him."

"All right."

Dubban strode to the supply shelves. He thrust aside bandage rolls and amnio jars and yanked out a medical kit. He lifted the lid. Two vials of nopaine, needles and thread for suturing, a bottle of high-grade astringent. Good; but not good enough. What he needed was a blade.

He rummaged through the shelves again and seized the prize: a scalpel sheathed in a leather case. He withdrew the instrument, appraised the razor-sharp blade, then looked doubtfully at her.

She gazed back, blazing with determination.

He wielded the scalpel. "Plaia, I'm not a physician. I won't tell you that I know how to do this because I don't. I don't want to hurt you."

"Please. I'm already in pain. You cannot inflict more."

He doubted that, but he sorted through the contents of the kit again. "Damn, there's no needle and syringe to administer the nopaine."

"Can't I just drink it?"

"No, you cannot. It would make you very sick." He hastily read the kaligraphs winking cautions across the vials. "The best I can do is rub the drug on your skin."

"Then do it." She held out her hands again. "Hurry!"

The prospect of inflicting more damage on those delicate hands sickened him. His mouth felt parched, his tongue swollen. "This won't completely mask the pain, you know."

"I don't care. I'm ready."

"Sit on the floor, there, and press your hands on the bench. Here, beneath the lamplight where I can see. Do not move."

He swabbed her right hand with astringent, poured a drop of nopaine on top of the skin covering the chip, and rubbed the anodyne into her skin. He brandished the scalpel, peered at the gleaming chip. It had been installed between the metacarpal bones of her third and fourth fingers, right next to the little blue serpent of a vein. He took a breath. He etched a tiny incision across one side of the diamond shape and quickly lifted the blade when she flinched reflexively.

She clutched her hand, stifling her cry of pain.

"Damn it, Plaia, you have to stop that. I'll wind up cutting off your finger. Or through a blood vessel. You could bleed to death."

"I'm sorry! Let me try again."

If I hesitate, he realized, *if I worry about her reaction, I'll never get the things out.*

He straddled the workbench, instructed her to kneel on the floor behind him, and seized her hand, passing her right arm beneath the back of his right knee. He clamped his thigh down upon her forearm, restraining her hand on the seat of the bench. He spilled half the vial of nopaine onto her skin.

"Hold on to me," he said, and felt her left arm circling his waist, her face pressed against the small of his back. "Hold as steady as you can." He briskly cut all around the chip and pushed open the flap of skin.

A sharelock chip.

He had never seen one before, except buried beneath the skin of sharers' hands. Now he examined the pearlescent wafer, etched with minute circuitry. He couldn't help but marvel. With a jolt of dread, he saw that the chip had extruded calcareous roots that had burrowed deep into her flesh.

He inserted the scalpel's tip beneath the chip, uprooting it like a tuber, carefully at first, then yanking at it, twisting and gouging. Some of the roots pulled loose of her flesh and delicate bones. Some didn't.

He felt her teeth against his back, but she made no sound. Her whole arm shook involuntarily. He could feel her flex her muscles, trying to control her body's reaction. He clamped his thigh tighter.

He laid the scalpel down, seized the chip with his fingers, and gave it a vigorous pull. With a sickening *snap* the chip came loose, with some of the attached roots. But other roots broke off, rebounding into the wound as if made of elastic, and disappeared beneath the puddle of her blood.

"I can't get all of it," he said in a ragged whisper.

"It's all right. I can feel his presence dimming. His sharer's sharemind . . . it's getting weaker. Oh, Dubban, I can *feel* it! Cut out the other chip, quickly!"

He blotted blood away, drew the flap of her skin over the wound, and stitched the edges shut. He splashed on astringent and bandaged her hand. Then he reversed their positions so that she knelt behind him again.

He threaded her left arm beneath his left knee, clamped his thigh down, and pressed her hand on the bench. He emptied an entire vial of nopaine onto her skin and recommenced cutting, yanking, and uprooting, anxious to get the grisly job done.

And then it was over.

He gulped for breath. His face, his chest were drenched in sweat. He carefully wiped her blood off his hands and lifted her onto the bench.

She was trembling violently.

He took her face in his hands and searched her eyes. "I couldn't remove all the roots or whatever they are. Do you understand? They've grown too deep. They're all mixed up with your blood vessels and nerves and bones. I don't know how they'll affect your sharemind. If you'll be rid of Gunther for good, or not. Maybe someday you can find a surgeon to do a proper job. If we've got any somedays left in Pangaea."

They sat straddling the bench, face-to-face. "Thank you. Thank you. *Thank* you." She pressed the bloody chips into his hands. "Please keep these for me. Do what you will with them." She leaned her forehead against his cheek. "I don't know how many somedays anyone has left in Pangaea. Dubban, I need you."

He could *see* sharer's sharemind lifting off her, waves of dark energy expelled, disgorging from her face, her body, radiating away, malevolent shadows.

"I've never loved anyone before you," he whispered. "I don't mean Pannish love, some kind of ideal adoration without the comfort of our bodies. Or the ancient shame, bestial rutting that comes and goes so quickly. I don't know what I mean."

"I know what you mean." Suddenly she glanced up, her mouth poised in alarm, her hands fisted around the bandages. "Oh, Dubban, I can still *feel* him. He's awake now." She cried out. "He's trying to get back inside me. He's coming for me. He's trying to force me into purity sharemind."

Dubban strode to the door of the supply room, pressed his ear against the door, listened, and peered out the peephole.

The hallway was silent. Deserted.

He felt her standing behind him again. She leaned against him, threading her arms around his waist. He turned around inside her embrace. She reached up and kissed his mouth, his eyes, his forehead, his chin.

"Dubban," she whispered, "take his sharemind away."

Heat flooded his face and his belly. His mother's teachings nagged in his ears. *Never mingle what belongs to one purity with another.* His hands were shaking.

"What is it?" she said, her voice filled with despair. "You don't mind that I'm a serv pure?"

"You're a dream more beautiful than the angels."

She tore at the laces on her gown. The garment fell to her feet, a breeze of emptied satin. She kicked out of it, lay down on the floor atop it, and reached up her arms.

He forgot the nagging whispers and knelt over her, watching her face, more mysterious than the face of a stranger. He wondered what secrets were contained there.

He was aching in a way he had never ached before. Her hands clung to his neck as if she were drowning. She was absolutely silent. She opened before him, and he rushed in before she changed her mind. She fell back, sometimes bringing him closer, sometimes pushing him away. She began to buck beneath him, and he relentlessly bore down, for the first time becoming a little cold with fear that so much of himself, so long dammed up, now came pouring forth.

He searched her eyes and saw remnants of sharemind shatter and spiral away. Dark curtains of consciousness lifted off her, leaving the shine of her rapture untarnished.

Shouts echoed in the hall. He withdrew, released her, stood unsteadily, and reached for the lamp. He turned down the wick, rechecked the lock, found that it held.

A hand outside seized the doorknob and viciously rattled it. A fist pounded once on the door. Whoever it was moved on.

Again he cupped her face in his hands. "Plaia, I don't know what it's like to enter sharers' sharemind. I don't know what it's like to enter purity sharemind with an academe. But I do know that just now I felt as if I became a part of you. That I'm a part of you still, that I *know* you, even though I don't know you. I love you, Plaia."

She nodded, but he saw wariness in her eyes. She gazed at him as if she could see through the pores of his skin into the very center of his Essence.

"I know it can't compare to sharelock," he stumbled on.

She had said *need*. He had said *love*.

"No, it certainly does not," she said with a husky laugh. "You have no idea what a torment sharelock was. I will *never* wear sharelock chips again. Not with *anyone*."

He fell silent, apprehension tight in his chest. How carefully he'd rebuilt and furnished his hovel after the Big Shock, thinking of *her*. Dreaming that *she* might come there one day. Now it was painfully clear she had no place in the wreckage of Rancid Flats. The heat and ash from the magmaflow were enough to overwhelm the staunchest drayer. The squalor offended the meanest eye. Shattered glass and broken bricks littered the streets. Raw sewage offended the olfactory sense and often contaminated the water. The wild sphinxes had grown more vicious, the dogs fearless, the rats cunning. Pickpockets, muggers, and roustabouts skulked in every alley.

"Do you have someplace to go?" he finally said. "Someplace safe?"

She shook her head. "I can't go back to my fathers, even if I wanted to. They would hand me over to Gunther, no matter what I told them." She exhaled angrily. "I did have my own place, once. My colleagues and I leased one of those dreary little hovels in Rancid Flats."

He winced, but also blinked in surprise. "*You* lived in the flats?"

"For half a season. On Tomfoolery Lane. After I was expelled from the academy." She smiled wanly, and sorrow sifted into her eyes.

"*You* lived on Tomfoolery Lane?" At her nod, he said, "Tomfoolery is four blocks west of Misty Alley. Or I should say *was*. It's buried beneath about a quarter league of magma."

"I suppose that's just as well. Gunther will never find the place. Or the copies I made of Tivern's maps and texts."

He was glad she didn't mourn for Tomfoolery, which had been *quite* a dismal lane compared to his, which perched on a pretty rise shaded by old fan palms. "My place is on the three thousand block of Misty Alley. Then . . . you're not too offended by the flats?"

"The flats sheltered me when Pleasant Valley cast me out. I am very fond of the flats. The beer is the best in all Atlan."

He grinned at that and restrained himself from remarking, "*You* drink flats' beer?" lest he make too big a fool of himself over her purity. "Well, I've got one of those hovels you mentioned. But I promise it's not *too* dreary."

Her eyes shone so ardently he could have danced with joy. "My sweet Dubban, no place could be dreary if you're there."

"It's five blocks away. Do you think you can walk that far? I'd carry you, but we'd attract vigiles' attention."

"We don't want that. I'd gallop to get away from Gunther."

He took a breath. "Plaia, will you stay with me till you decide what to do?"

"I can't think of anyplace else in all Pangaea I'd rather stay." She added, "My love."

• • •

Dubban ransacked the shelves while Plaia stood watch at the supply-room door. He found the blue-green tunic and leggings of a physician-natalist. He stuffed her ceremonial gown into a half-empty box of amnio jars and shoved the box into a corner on the bottom shelf. He fitted a physician's cap over her gorgeous curls. He worried about someone noticing her hands but couldn't find physician's gloves. They settled on a towel, which she wrapped around her hands like a fashion maven's muff.

The next morning Dubban found the first detainment warrant. He was striding to the natalries, exhausted and exhilarated after an incandescent night of pleasing Plaia, and the warrant had been nailed to the lamppost at the end of his block.

WANTED: RUNAWAY SHARER

The warrant offered a reward. He tore the damn thing down, but couldn't bring himself to rip it to shreds. The picture of Plaia was too heart-wrenching to destroy. He carefully folded the parchment and stuffed it in his pocket. He'd collected a dozen by the time he arrived at the natalries.

An earthshock of five mags struck at midmorning. The deep gong of the Harbinger reverberated throughout the megalopolis. Fresh magma geysered up from South Fog Rift, burying two Fire & Shock crews laboring to contain the flow. Five heretics who had been discovered at the Bureau of Ground Control were hanged on Allpure Square at high noon.

Dubban hurried home during his midday break and found her still drowsing in his bed, flushed and a little feverish.

He shook her shoulder. "Plaia. Plaia, my love, wake up."

She sighed with contentment and reached for him. "You were wonderful last night. *You* are wonderful.

And your place is hardly a hovel, it's lovely, Dub. You've got a wonderful eye for decoration, did anyone ever tell you that?"

"Plaia, listen to me. Look at this." He brandished the warrants. "They're everywhere, tacked to every damn lamppost in Marketplace."

She sat up with a cry and clutched her bandaged hands to her breast. "Gunther can't do this."

"Well, he has. Do *not* set foot outside."

"But I've got to get fresh air. Move my legs around."

"It's too dangerous."

They argued and he finally relented, but only if she went out late at night and in disguise. They would eat the dinner he'd bring home after twelve hours at the natalries, climb into bed for a postprandial coupling, and talk for hours after that. Then she'd pull on the fisher's cap, ductdigger's bodysuit, and machinist's gloves he'd scrounged from a frugality shop, and he'd accompany her for a jaunt around the block.

One night a squad of bleary-eyed vigiles stopped them and demanded to see their security numbers. Dubban bared his biceps and brandished his number. Plaia demurely rolled up her sleeve, clearly stalling. Dubban shouted, "You slut! Always wigglin' your buttocks at whoever will look at ye." He lunged at her, wrestling her to the ground the way they wrestled for sport in his cottage. In the dim lamplight, the dark scars on the backs of her hands looked much like sharelock chips. He continued shouting abuses. She spouted tears and slapped his face so hard his head snapped back. The vigiles sniggered, shook their heads, and marched on, joking about hot-blooded servs.

Plaia sat up, disheveled and tear-streaked. "You're hired, Dubban Quartermain, as my bodyguard."

"I accept the position, Mistress Triadana," he said, ruefully rubbing his cheek. "Just don't break my jaw next time, all right?"

She took his hand as they strolled on. He felt so replete with love for her he thought he'd explode.

One night Dubban's neighbor Nita staggered to his

door as he and Plaia stood, unlocking the locks. Dubban had always been fond of the fisherwoman. Though they never had become bedmates, they'd flirted every chance they got before Plaia had come along. Dubban had deeply regretted Nita's sharelock with Rando. As fisher and fisher, she and Rando were equal subpures, both muscular and sun-browned and brawny, and nicely proximate in many other ways. But Dubban knew Rando had always preferred boys. And had kept his predilection a secret from his intended sharer.

Now Nita was weeping, a terrible sight for a strong and handsome woman, and cupping her hand to her face. Blood streamed through her fingers. "Let me in, Dub," she said in a thick voice. "He damn near put my eye out this time."

The three of them slipped inside, and Dubban locked the inside locks. Nita threw her arms around his neck. "Ah, Dubban. If only I had entered sharelock with you, I wouldn't need to go to eroticians. I'm such a fool."

Plaia presented the woman with a handcloth. Nita turned with astonishment, released her stranglehold around Dubban's neck, and examined Plaia head to toe. "Well, Dub, you've got yourself a woman, after all. And such a beauty." She peered more closely at Plaia's face, then reached out and plucked off the cap, releasing reddish gold curls. "The runaway sharer." Nita turned back to Dubban, her voice filled with amazement and a bit of dread. "An academe. A middle pure."

"You won't give us away, will you?" he asked anxiously.

"Of course not." She seized Plaia's hand and examined her diamond-shaped wounds. "You cut them out?"

"I had help," Plaia said and winked at Dubban.

Nita laughed raggedly. "No wonder your former sharer can't find you." She examined her own sturdy hands, her own sharelock chips. "If only I had the courage."

They opened jars of beer, fried up flatbreads, and talked for hours. Dubban went to bed. When he woke, the two women were still conversing in low voices and cradling cups of hot caf. Dubban was glad Nita stopped by afternoons when she wasn't crewing on an Imperial Archipelago Fisheries skiff. Plaia always smiled after Nita's visits and gossiped about the folk of the lane, the latest Vigilance cruelty—anything but earthshocks.

But he sensed Plaia's growing restlessness as her hands healed and her strength returned. Her loneliness after long days of solitude that even their passion could not assuage. And something else, something he was unsure of. The theories that drove her. Were they heresy? He had no idea. He only knew that she brooded. That she raged over each new announcement by Ground Control.

She often rose as he was nodding off to sleep and paced back and forth in the cottage. Her restlessness filled him with foreboding. He thought about sanctuary, a place they could flee to where Gunther's warrant couldn't reach her. But anyplace that had a natalry where he could find work would also surely have Vigilance.

She told him how she'd been a resonance musician, and he bought finger cymbals for her, a zitar for himself, and they played music together for hours and sang. She told him about Tivern's maps and texts, how important they were. He stole out of Natalry Bank in his Superior Father's miter and robe, strolled into southwest quadrant posing as a middle pure, and retrieved the documents from the safe box she'd reserved at her treasury. She crowed with delight and pored over Tiv's legacy for days.

Still she tossed and turned and paced and brooded.

One rainy night on the way home from their perambulations, two figures leapt out from the shadows outside Dubban's cottage.

"Dubban?" Plaia cried as a scrawny figure seized her. A sweeping cloak swirled all around the assailant, forming dark, iridescent ripples slick with rain.

Dubban lunged to help, but a tall, gangling shadow

grappled his shoulders. He whirled into a hostile embrace, wrestling with his own assailant.

Dubban shuddered as he grasped the young man's strange knobby arms. *Impure.*

"What do you *want*? We've got maybe two ores on us. Take them, and leave us alone."

"We don't want your two ores, midwife," snarled the shadow gripping Plaia. "We want something a whole lot better than Imperial scrap."

Dubban knew that mocking singsong, that notorious face. Knew her gangling companion, too. *My bonded one,* she had called him in Blackblood Cavern.

Dubban whispered, "Salit Zehar. And Asif."

An extravagant sneer spread over the Devil girl's mismatched features. "You remember us. How sweet."

Dubban eyed the weapons dangling from the Devils' belts. "It's late, Salit. Tell me what you want and scram."

"Let's all go inside this cozy cottage of yours," the Devil girl said, fingering her dagger.

Dubban reluctantly unlocked the door and ushered them in. He searched for misgivings in Plaia's eyes. For the thousandth time since she'd come to live with him, he wondered what she apprehended. She was the superior pure with the more powerful sharemind. Protocol and purity prerogative ought to govern their relations.

Yet Plaia had never forced him into sharemind. She had never invoked her prerogative. Had refused to observe proper protocol. "Stop," she'd say when he deferred to her. "You're my man, not a serv."

Still, he searched for misgivings. She looked pale and tired, but curiosity gleamed in her eyes.

"Got any skee?" Salit rummaged through his pantry and peered in his ice box.

"Just beer." Dubban took out four beer jars, and they all pulled up chairs around the dining table. He made introductions, feeling distinctly absurd introducing the love of his life to the scourge of his existence.

"Your hair's pretty," Plaia said.

She was gazing at Salit with what Dubban could

only call wonder. He supposed the Devil girl had that effect on some people. Not him. Nausea rose in his throat at the sight of her patchworked face and figure. Cold fear collected in his belly with the knowledge that she had murdered Prefect Clere Twine and who knew who else. Revulsion needled down his spine when he realized she had never been properly pruned or purified. That she'd been grown like a beast.

"Thank you. You're real p-pretty all over," Salit said, smiling shyly.

"Thank *you*, but I didn't have a whole lot to do with it. Tertius Natalry grew me." To Dubban's amazement, Plaia smiled back. "That's some wicked cloak."

The Devil girl's grotesque face lit up. "It's called a chameleon cloak. A shadow cloak. Also a cloak of secrecy." She banged down her jar, sprang to her feet, and shouted, "I have become the mistress of many dark things. Behold!"

She stood before the kitchen wall on which Dubban had hung a variety of beautiful hand-woven baskets, staring, studying, as if she meant to memorize the sight. Then she turned, raised the hood, closed the cloak tightly over her—and disappeared.

Dubban shouted and leapt to his feet.

Plaia seized his hand. "Ssh, Dub, you'll wake someone."

Asif grinned. "Very good, Salit, you've got that camouflaging just right. You can stop showing off now."

Dubban heard a giggle, saw a shimmer, and then, as if she were stepping through a crack in the world, Salit reappeared as she opened the cloak, a huge grin on her lopsided lips.

"I'm still here," she said triumphantly.

Plaia applauded. "Well done, Salit."

"Manifesto of the Apocalypse, Edict Five says preserve all chameleon cloaks and Orbs of Eternity and conceal them from the Imperium," Salit said.

"Why is that?" Plaia said.

The Devil girl returned to her chair and plunked her

scrawny self down as if the effort had exhausted her. She opened the pocket in the cloak that Dubban had seen in Blackblood Cavern and said in a sweet soft voice, "Please, pocket, will you show us Horan Zehar's mnemon about Edict Five?"

A shimmering sheet of white light flew out of the pocket and flapped over the dining table. The sheet circled three times, then hung suspended in the air before them.

Images rolled across the luminous curtain.

A drooping eye, a flaring nostril, the twitch of twisted lips. The ridged and swollen skull thinly covered with greying hair. Horan Zehar revealed his gaptoothed smile. Dubban knew the qut purveyor's smile only too well.

Horan's lips moved, and his voice emanated from the mnemon. "We must preserve chameleon cloaks and Orbs of Eternity because they are rare. We must conceal them from the Imperium because the Imperium would destroy them."

"My colleague Donson was destroyed because of an orb," Plaia said.

Horan said, "Certain people of the purities gamble with the orb. Fewer still cast it. If you do not scorn the orb, the orb may come alive for you. Or maybe not. The orb chooses whom it wishes to show an oracle to."

"Damn things never do more than sting me, and I've got four of 'em," Salit said, withdrawing the orbs strung on a thong around her neck. "I can't make heads nor tails of all those facets. Guess the orb doesn't want to show me an oracle."

To Dubban's astonishment, Plaia said, "I've gambled with an orb twice. Both oracles not only forecast the future, they guided me in ways that made that future come true."

Dubban refused to look at the orbs. "I've got nothing to do with the Orb of Eternity."

"Me, neither," Asif said and the two men exchanged nervous grins.

From the mnemon Horan's voice said, "Wherever

they are, cloaks and orbs will always find their way back to us, we of the impure. They are rightfully ours."

Salit impatiently drummed her fingertips on the dining table. "But why, my father, does no one know how to manufacture cloaks and orbs? Why are there only a few in all Pangaea? Why—"

"The Ancient Ones' knowledge has been lost," Horan said, "but some of us may dip into the ocean of their memory."

Salit stood and paced. "They say the angels are descendants of the Ancient Ones. Then why don't angels remember how to manufacture cloaks and orbs? Why don't the angels remember how to build Doors to the other worlds?"

Horan's voice said, "The Ancient Ones gave the supreme power of dreaming to the angels and blessed them more than any other purity, for they were loved like sons and daughters. But the Ancient Ones gave cloaks and orbs to the impure to compensate us for our suffering and ensure our survival."

"Why must we survive," Salit said bitterly, "if we are deformed and despised?"

"Because the Ancient Ones loved us like sons and daughters, too," Horan said.

Then the mnemon went blank and whirled above their heads. The sheet of light dived back into the pocket of the cloak.

"That's the end of *that* lesson," Asif said, sighing deeply. "A pox on Horan Zehar. What a mystifying teacher."

"My father was a busy man, evading Imperial Vigilance," Salit said with a sulky pout.

Plaia leaned forward. "Tell me more about this manifesto."

" 'Tis our guide and our inspiration since ancient times. The Apocalypse is *here*," Salit said. "The Imperium will *fall*. 'Tis the sacred duty of Heaven's Devils to *destroy* the Imperium."

Plaia said, "Salit, Heaven's Devils don't need to destroy the Imperium. Our Pangaea is doing it for you and there isn't a thing Ground Control or the Imperium can do about it."

Now the Devil girl leaned forward. "What do you mean?"

Plaia dashed to the cupboard where she'd hidden Tivern's texts and maps. Sometimes Dubban regretted he had retrieved them. He didn't like the mania that overcame her whenever she studied those dusty documents. She unrolled the map of the Pangaean archipelago and sat right next to the most notorious Heaven's Devil in all Pangaea as if they were best school chums.

"It was scientific theory," Plaia said. "And it was divine philosophy. 'As Pan is the One Supreme Being, so Pangaea is one world.' A great shell of rock bouncing up and down on a sea of magma. When we measured earthshock movements, we *did* see the shell bounce. But I saw something else. I recorded movements of the grooves carved in Appalacia Rift, and I discovered that the south side had moved *laterally*. Moved northwest.

"I wasn't the first to observe such movement, but I was the first to record it. Others discounted what they saw or refused to acknowledge it. All except Tivern, my proctor. Look here and here and here." Plaia stabbed her finger on the map. "Tiv measured magnetic properties tracing ancient movements in deep bedrock and extrapolated future movements called magnetic wander curves. She measured groundwater salinity in the Bog a decade ago, showing that ocean water was percolating into the middle of the Appalacia Province. She measured lateral movements in rifts all over Pangaea." Plaia stood and paced the way Dubban had seen before: like a wild creature in a cage. "There was only one conclusion she could come to."

"What was that, Plaia?" Dubban said.

"That the world archipelago is *spreading*. Bits and pieces—and I mean landmasses as huge as all Appalacia Province—are splitting off from each other and moving *away*. *That's* what is causing violent events in the magmatic core, earthshocks and eruptions. But where are the landmasses moving *to*?" She sighed deeply. "Gunther taunted me with that question. He called me and Tivern insane. But the question is a good one."

"Into the ocean?" Salit ventured.

"No, the ocean sits atop rock, too. It's just deeper rock."

Dubban bent over the map. "What can any of us do?"

"Oh, my love." Plaia glanced at him with such longing that he roused at once. "We've got to find a safe haven before the world shatters. It won't be long. Force-flooding will exacerbate the tension in the rifts." But then the moment was gone, and she was frowning again. "If only I could see the *whole* archipelago, from very high up, maybe I could figure out where a safe haven might be."

Dubban rubbed his eyes. "All right, Salit. You've had your fun. Now get out of my house. We're tired."

"Not yet, midwife," the Devil girl said. "We came to collect the rest of your debt."

Dubban glared. "I told you I can do no more for you."

"Well, you've got to. The Alchemist says he needs whole birthpods this time. Seeded ones. Ones that haven't had threads cut out of 'em yet. Says he may make some sense of the threads you gave me if he can take a look at untouched pods. Couple of 'em will do."

"I can't do that," Dubban said. "You're talking about the unborn."

"Shall we discuss how Asif and I may poison the Feed and kill *all* the unborn?" Salit said with a malicious smile. " 'Destroy the purities,' " she said to Plaia. "That's Edict One of the Manifesto of the Apocalypse." To Dubban, "I'll cancel the rest of your debt this time. Promise."

"I won't do it. That would be murder."

Salit pulled her dagger and leapt at him. "I don't want to hurt you, but I will."

"Wait!" Plaia said. "Listen to me, Dubban. Isn't it true that seeded pods may die?"

"Very seldom, Plaia. We take good care of the ges tanks."

"But *sometimes* they do, isn't that true?"

"Sometimes," he conceded reluctantly.

"And it's not as though they *are* human beings. Not yet. Not when they're tiny pods you can only see through a viewglass."

"But they grow—"

"Take mine," Plaia said decisively to the Devil girl. "Take the five birthpods Gunther took from me. I have no say about what will happen to them. What Gunther will do to them."

Dubban met her stubborn gaze. "Plaia, it's *criminal*. These aren't useless threads to be incinerated. These are *people*. Your progeny."

"Gunther's progeny, taken from me by force." To Salit, "I've got five seeded birthpods in Tertius Natalry right now. They're yours. I don't *want* them to emerge."

Salit clapped her hands, delighted. "Many thanks, Plaia!"

"And you'll release Dub's debt if he delivers them to you?"

"Said I would," the Devil girl said with a sly grin that inspired little of Dubban's confidence.

"She'll keep her word," Asif said. "I give you *my* word."

"Done." Plaia took Dubban's hands and searched his eyes. "Dubban, I can help you. I *want* to help you."

"I don't need that kind of help. *I* don't want it."

"Then please, my love. Do it for me."

He saw torment in those golden green depths, all she'd lost and all she longed to regain. He didn't know if he would be damned to Eternal Torment, arrested by the Imperium, or both. But when he gazed into the face of the woman he loved, Dubban said, "All right, my love. I'll do it for you."

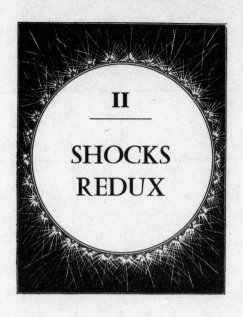

II

SHOCKS
REDUX

FACET 22

Lodestone: Attraction or binding.
The vigile meets a brilliant erotician.
The action is union.
The forbearance is entrapment.

The Orb of Eternity

Commentaries:
Councillor Sausal: As Pan is the highest source of life, so the bestial urge is the most base. The urge sullied human beings in ancient times when, like beasts, generation of the family depended upon rutting.

Through the great gift of the natalries, the Imperium frees the purities from the necessity of beasts. Through the great gift of the Mind of the World, the Imperium relieves the purities of the ancient shame.

Therefore the prudent person should cherish Pannish love and tame instinct.
Guttersage (usu. considered vulgar): The priests are right about one thing: Never confuse lust with love.

Go to an erotician.

South Tasman Province, three leagues west of Our Imperial City of Mara Mamba. Jope Gamefields:

Tahliq heard the carnival master shout, "Step right up, boys and girls, milords and miladies, and feast your eyes on the weirdest, the rarest, the direst sights you will see in your life!"

She peered through her tent flap at the gathering crowd. Scents of bacco smoke, roast corn, and spuncloud candy perfumed the air. Heat scorched Jope Gamefields and sucked all the breezes away. She struggled for a long, slow breath and silently prayed: *Please, Afrodite, help me endure another day.*

"It's drud day *all* day at Buckley's Traveling Curiosity Carnival. See Jessie the Human Ges Tank. Boys and girls, milords and miladies, *she* is one *curious* drud lady. Step right up and feast your eyes. Step right up, I say!"

On serv days, Tahliq and the other curiosities were, by Buckley's sleight of tongue, servs. Today, though, she was well and truly drud. The ground tipped and trembled beneath her feet, sending ripples through the canvas of her tent.

Another earthshock, maybe five mags. She had to laugh. A five-mag shock in Atlan had cracked all her chimneys at the Salon of Shame. Since when had a five-mag shock become just another feature of the day, no more noteworthy than a downpour or the killing heat?

Tasman hadn't *stopped* quaking since the carnival had arrived—how long ago? Time had blurred, days blending one into another since she'd fled Atlan in Lucyd's windship and taken up the carney life as Jessie the Human Ges Tank.

"What is so curious about this lady, you ask?" Buckley shouted. "What I'm about to tell you, boys and girls, milords and miladies, will shock you. If you're faint of heart or delicate of nerves, walk on." Buckley lowered his voice into the scandalized stage whisper he did so well. "This lady's got an unborn trapped, I say *trapped,* inside her. My friends, I swear the thing is *alive* or I ain't Bernett naitre Quintus Buckley! One thin ore." He murmured as druds flung money, "Thank you very much, milady. Very good, son."

"How do *we* know it's an unborn that's making her so fat?" shouted a plower boy amid gales of laughter from his chums.

"How do *we* know it's alive?" another boy said.

"You shall see for yourself with your very own eyes, my fine lads," Buckley replied. "Courtesy of the one and only Dark Glass. Such a wondrous device you'll not see anywhere in all Pangaea except at Buckley's Traveling Curiosity Carnival."

Tahliq shut the tent flap and climbed up on the podium of the plywood planks. She smoothed some nut oil on her copper skin. She was naked; well, she usually was when she worked. At the Salon of Shame, at the Motherwine Ceremony, she had displayed herself proudly. But no smiles of pride and pleasure curved her lips now. She felt ill and scrawny and parched and bereft.

Dire sight she might have become, but not the weirdest spectacle the carnival had to offer. There were Windly and Wanda, the Wondrous Entwined Twins, bodies joined by flesh and sinew at the neck. Two brains, two heads, two hearts between them, an arm each, three lungs, and a voluptuous woman's body below the waist. With their long blond hair, creamy complexions, and gracious manners, the twins had lived as celebrities since their emergence. There was DeLouth the Mouth, a cranky caroler whose curvaceous lips took up her entire face, relegating her eyes to sightless buds, her nose to dots of nostrils. Then there was Pandy the Handy Handmaid, whose shoulders hefted three well-developed arms—two flexing from the left arm socket.

And so on, a motley collection of deformities and oddities whose families and subpures had turned them away. In some cases, they'd fled. Each of them had a tale to tell about the natalries. All pointed accusatory fingers.

"How'd she get it *in*?" the plower boy shouted.

"How's she gonna get it *out*?"

Tahliq reached for a mintstick and chewed it. She'd heard idiotic heckling since the day she'd started as Jessie the Human Ges Tank but she couldn't blame these benighted druds. They'd never read the forbidden books. Had never seen the forbidden illustrations. They only knew what the Imperium and fundamental school and their families taught them: that people emerged from ges tanks.

She braced herself as Buckley scurried inside the tent, nodded curtly, and commenced fussing with the Dark Glass. He flipped a dustcloth across the surface of the opalescent dark grey panel about the size and shape of Tahliq's cheval glass. He adjusted the panel, told her to turn this way and that, and studied the results through narrowed eyes, his hand curled around his chin.

One morning she had tiptoed to the back of the glass and craned her neck around the edge. She'd been astonished to glimpse her own crouching body rendered as a skeleton, her flesh translucent, all her bones visible. And in the swell of her belly—the unborn tucked inside her.

She'd stared for a long time at that new life. It looked like a strange little reptile with its huge, wizened head, attenuated arms, and stubby legs. The fingers, the toes—so tiny. So vulnerable.

Untouched by the natalries.

What if this creature turns out to be a monster? The illicit product of two wildly divergent pures, neither of whom knew what they were creating?

"So, my fine Buckley," she said acidly, "drummed up a crowd for me, did you?"

"Let's hope so, Dame Tahliq." A suave serv of saloonkeep subpures, Buckley had seen almost as much abandonment of protocol as Tahliq. His snout and beady eyes inspired various sobriquets behind his pinched shoulders—chiefly "weasel" and "rat." "Sadly, your revenues are down."

"Oh, indeed? I hardly think so, Buck. Yesterday I kept count of the spectators. I believe you owe me seventy-five ores, after that plunder you call your commission."

"Seventy-five ores," he scoffed. "Dear me, no. Can't possibly be seventy-five ores."

"I kept count, I tell you. I've got a head for numbers.

Cough it up, Buckley, or I shall take my leave of your lousy carnival."

"Ho! And where will you go? Just why are you on the run, anyway? You never did say."

"That's my business and none of yours, sir."

"You don't trust me?"

"I heard a rumor that you saw a detainment warrant for Sybella the Serpent Girl. Just a pretty theft, the kind of crime you do when you're young and desperate. I heard you paid a visit to Vigilance in Umq. By an amazing coincidence, vigiles showed up and arrested Sybella during her act."

"Now why would I get my own curiosity arrested?"

"There was a reward. And poor little Sybella's revenues were down." She waggled her fingers at him. "Seventy-five ores, Buckley. Or I'm gone."

"How do you suppose you'll travel, alone with an illegal infant?"

"Where do you suppose you'll find another pure growing an unborn inside her body?"

"I'll find myself some impure wench," Buckley said with a nasty grin. "I'll—Great Pan and Inim!"

A bloodbat abruptly burst into Tahliq's tent, butted its snout against Buckley's chest, and knocked the serv to the ground. The bat bared curved yellow fangs sunk in rheumy red gums. The reek of rotten meat wafted from its gaping mouth.

The bat peered at Tahliq, muttering inarticulate sounds.

"Veeeejj," the bloodbat said. "Veeeeejj."

"You bloody beast." Buckley picked himself up and dusted off his cloak. "I wish you wouldn't fucking *do* that, Ba'reesha."

Ba'reesha the Talking Bloodbat sheepishly hung her grotesque head and sniffled. The bat had a sensitive nature and often took offense, especially when Buckley called her a beast. Which was just about every time he deigned to address her.

"Ba'reesha, my sweet," Tahliq said, "what the devil are you trying to tell us?"

"Vigilance comes," the bloodbat blurted out. "From Mara Mamba. A squad of twelve, with security clubs and daggers."

"Pox pox *pox*," Buckley shouted and darted from Tahliq's tent. In a moment, Tahliq heard the plowers shouting, "Give us our money back, ye no-good shifty thief."

Buckley would have his hands full before they made their escape from Jope Gamefields.

"Go pack. Hurry," Tahliq told Ba'reesha. The bloodbat lumbered out, dragging her wings behind her. Tahliq leapt down from the podium, shimmied into her tunic and leggings, and yanked on her dusty boots.

On the road again.

Dear Afrodite, I'm tired. She heard the clang of the brass poles, the flap of canvas as the drayers pulled down the tents.

Just as well. I don't want my babe to be a Tasman.

Tahliq clucked to the drayers pulling her wagon as the carnival caravan took the road along the cliffs of Ndia. They had traveled west for days through the southern provinces of the world archipelago: Arctica, Borno, Chinee, Buruma. They headed toward Himal and the southeast tip of Gondwana.

North of Buruma, Tahliq had witnessed the newly cleaved Himal Rift, a fearsome steaming crevice. Magma boiled up offshore through a pea-green soup of seawater. The rift had swallowed a dozen villages and devastated ten times as many.

At sullen tentsites of survivors, Tahliq had climbed up on her podium and the other curiosities had run through their acts in exchange for food and water. Such places seldom had many ores to part with. The continual shaking had shattered morale as well as the land. People of every purity lay listless in their tents, dreaming the angels' dreams in the Mind of the World, indifferent to salvage efforts. Indifferent to their own survival.

Rains pummeled the caravan north of Himal, transforming dusty roads into beds of mud. Wind tore at the wagons, ripping away three canvas wagon covers that had doubled as tents. Cursing, Buckley called for a halt. They drew the wagons into a miserable huddle and set up camp.

Twilight descended, the rain eased to a drizzle, and the curiosities gathered at the grub wagon for their evening meal. Tahliq took two spoonfuls of the millet gruel and handed her bowl to the twins. Tiptoeing around pools of rainwater, she headed wearily for the wagon she shared with Ba'reesha.

No one had wanted to share a wagon with a bloodbat. Tahliq had taken a chance and found Ba'reesha to be a thoughtful and amusing wagonmate. Once the bat overcame her initial resistance to speech, she couldn't shut up. Tahliq had been amazed to learn the bat had been a fellow resident of Atlan, spending her youth in Blackblood Cavern. Tahliq had never known of the gigantic tentsite of the impure below the city streets.

As for the bat's feeding habits, Ba'reesha proved discreet to the point of secretiveness. Only once had Tahliq caught her wagonmate, fangs buried deep in a rat, draining the creature of its blood. And that had been because Tahliq had forgotten her hair ribbon and dashed back to the wagon unexpectedly. Tahliq had assured the abashed bat she was grateful their digs didn't suffer from vermin like the other wagons.

She never caught the bat feeding again.

She climbed into the wagon, calling out, "Ba'reesha, sweetie, I'm back early."

And nearly swooned.

A second bat crouched in the wagon next to Ba'reesha, their grotesque heads bent together. The bats glanced up. The stranger—a ferociously scowling, monstrously huge, black-furred beast with ebony sails for wings and curved yellow fangs as long as Tahliq's arm—leapt across the wagon, seized Tahliq, and clamped its jaws around her throat.

She beat her fists on the bat's chest and let out a shriek.

Ba'reesha leapt to Tahliq's side and laid her paw on the stranger's arm.

With a snarl, the bat released her and flung her onto her cot. Tahliq rolled to the far side and curled.

Footsteps splashed through the rain. Buckley's face poked through the tent flap, his eyes round with fear. "Say, you bloody beast," he said in a quavering voice, "what's going on?"

Ba'reesha pushed his face out. "Nnnnnuth—"

"Spit it out, ye poxy bat."

"Nothing!"

The strange bat tapped Tahliq on the shoulder and jerked its head toward the tent flap. She stood, knees wobbling. She poked her face out, nearly bumping noses with Buckley. Rain pattered on her face.

"Nothing's wrong, like Ba'reesha said. Go finish your dinner, Buck."

"Tahliq, we heard you scream."

"I fell." She recovered her customary insouciance. "I'm weak after that sawdust stew you're feeding us. I nearly fainted from hunger. You know, if you don't feed me better, I could lose my child and then you'll have to find another human ges tank."

"All right, all right. You don't have to threaten me every other minute."

"Nothing else seems to work," she said sweetly.

"I'll see what I can do." Genuine concern clouded his face. "Sure you're all right?"

She blew out a deep breath. "I think so, anyway." She stroked her belly, reassuring herself that the unborn was still safely inside. "Thanks for asking."

"Good night." He added, "Scream if you need anything."

The carnival master turned and splashed away.

Tahliq snapped the tent flap shut.

"All right," she said sternly, crossing her arms over her breast. She didn't take kindly to surprise visitors in her wagon. "Start talking, Ba'reesha. You're famous for it. And it had better be good. Who is this personage?"

"This is my cousin, Mi'k. He's visiting me tonight, all the way from Andea."

The bat bared his fangs. "Mi'k," he said, thumping his chest with a fist.

In another moment Tahliq realized the creature's terrifying grimace was a smile. "A born orator, are you, Mi'k?" She eyed the bat. He was considerably larger and undoubtedly hungrier than his cousin. "Ba'reesha, my sweet, there's no room in here for all three of us."

"Oh, he'll be on his way in a minute." Ba'reesha brandished a neat scroll tied with a string. "Mi'k brought me news."

If those unclad beasts had produced a bouquet of white roses the way the carnival's prestidigitator did, Tahliq could not have been more astonished. "What is the meaning of this, Ba'reesha?"

Ba'reesha took Tahliq's hands, and they sat together on Ba'reesha's cot.

"Tahliq, my dear friend. How can I tell you this? Mi'k and I are experiments."

"Experiments?"

The bat nodded. "We are the progeny of certain combinations of materia, human and bestial."

"Human." Tahliq shook her head, disbelieving.

"Our families were all dead. Our human materia reverted to the Imperium, to be used as the Imperium wished. We were grown in the natalry at Outer Tasman. Our caravan passed right by the place."

"But why would someone do this to you?"

"Vigilance wanted spies to infiltrate the caverns of the impure, like Blackblood. We observe. Sometimes we deliver messages between people."

"Spies!" Tahliq shivered. Was her wagonmate a Vigilance spy, then?

Ba'reesha exchanged a flurry of sounds with her cousin and handed the scroll to Mi'k. She touched her lips to his cheeks, first left, then right. The bat stood, swept across the wagon, and out the tent flap. Tahliq heard a whirring sound like hatchets being sharpened on a hundred grindstones.

She ran to the tent flap and peered out.

The huge bat fought wind and rain, his brawny body sleek in flight. Lightning forked through the clouds, illuminating him, a dark angel struggling heavenward. In another moment he was gone, lost in the gloom.

Tahliq tugged the tent flap shut, wiped raindrops from her face. "Why have you always warned us of Vigilance raids, Ba'reesha?"

The bat smiled. "Perhaps someone, Dame Tahliq, wants you and your child to stay alive."

Tahliq saw him staring.

Walkabout vigiles in smart blue-and-silver uniforms milled among the carnival tents, but they hadn't come to raid the place. They'd come to enjoy the curiosities and a jar of beer. A saloonkeep had tipped off Buckley that local Vigilance in Madagaz looked the other way when it came to cult raves, sect ceremonies, and other shadow-sector enterprises.

So it was walkabout day *all* day at Buckley's Traveling Curiosity Carnival. Everyone felt festive and halfway respectable. Quite a crowd had turned out despite the rain-logged weeds and rambunctiously biting bugs. Buckley had decked himself out in a faux vigile's uniform of dark blue linen, a proximity offense that would have gotten him flogged in Atlan.

In the subprovinces of South Gondwana, prefectures like Madagaz had graver troubles than proximity to attend to. In half a season, the ceaseless earthshocks had uprooted sacred trees, knocked ancient highways off their courses, and destroyed temples. The faithful had nowhere to pray.

"Step right up, milords and miladies," Buckley shouted. "Feast your eyes on grotesqueries and monstrosities guaranteed to chill your blood, or I ain't"—as always, he improvised his purity to suit the crowd—"Bernett naitre Secundus Buckley."

He stood in a corner of Tahliq's tent. He didn't surge forward with the crowd to ogle and gape. He waited, impassive, arms crossed over his massive chest, and stared at her.

He could have been Regim before the Heaven's Devils had injured him so grievously. Before he'd lost his leg and whatever decency he'd once possessed. He could have been Regim's cloven, though of course he wasn't. The young walkabout was merely—gloriously—a vigile subpure, with the stature, golden hair, and sapphire-blue eyes vigiles possessed.

But why was he so fascinated by *her*? Because she was a female who provoked his bestial instinct in ways he didn't understand? Suddenly inspired, Tahliq beamed at her spectators. She posed before the Dark Glass, stood sideways, and audaciously displayed her profile. All the while gazing into the blue-fire eyes of her admirer.

The morning came and went and, just as Regim had long ago, the young vigile stayed.

His name was Prinz Zweiman naitre Secundus. He'd graced Pangaea with his presence for all of one-and-twenty years. He'd lived in Madagaz his whole life, and he'd never indulged in the ancient shame with anyone before.

Till Tahliq.

The carnival master didn't approve of his curiosities bringing outsiders onto the carnival grounds after hours. Especially a walkabout, who was, after all, still Vigilance. The entire Zweiman clan would have fainted dead away if they ever learned their darling boy with his shiny bright future had taken up bedding a carnival curiosity—an erotician carrying an illegal child in her womb.

So they rented a tiny hovel on a weedy lane of broken cobblestones along the outskirts of the drud quadrant. Tahliq would steal away after Buckley had tamped down the tents for the night. Prinz would climb down from the second-story window of his sleep chamber at his family's villa. And they would rendezvous at the hovel at midnight.

She taught him everything, especially gentleness so he wouldn't harm her or her unborn. It was the first and only time she'd ever regretted the new life tucked in her belly. But soon she would release the child, and then she would teach Prinz the pleasures of vigor.

As she always did when she lay with any pure, her allpure sharemind unfolded and Tahliq entered sharemind with Prinz. She apprehended everything. His sensations, from the smallest itch to the beating of his heart. His thoughts, his memories, even the dreams he chose in the Mind of the World. He favored loud, clashing conquest. She wasn't surprised.

And she saw that he was in every measure a magister: obedient, respectful, loyal to his family, his subpure, his purity, and the Imperium. Eager to enter sharelock and fulfill his Imperial duty of generating a family. Eager to fulfill his Imperial duty of destined labor.

Knowing his goodness, she kept the secret of her allpure sharemind. As she had with Regim, she entered his consciousness so discreetly he didn't realize he was in mutual consciousness. He simply felt bliss whenever he was with her, a contented intimacy that surprised and pleased him.

She kept the secret of who and what she was.

Their liaison exhausted her, as clandestine liaisons at midnight will. Buckley made snide remarks about her pallor and sunken eyes, took Ba'reesha aside, and interrogated the bloodbat. The bat feigned ignorance of her wagonmate's whereabouts after hours. But later that afternoon, as they rested in their wagon for the evening's performances, Ba'reesha reproachfully began, "Yyyyyyoooouu—. Yyyooouu—."

Tahliq sighed. "I what, Ba'reesha?"

"You *do* look pale and thin and exhausted. It's taking a toll on your act, Tahliq."

"I know," Tahliq said, massaging her closed eyes with tender fingertips.

"This cannot be good for your unborn."

"No, it's not good for the unborn." She glanced up, caught Ba'reesha gazing at her, worry plain on her face. "You're right."

"We'll be leaving Madagaz," Ba'reesha said. "Just this afternoon I overheard Buckley arguing with the twins about our itinerary. They're stuck on Scanda, but Buck is keen on Siluria, which is in the complete opposite direction and—"

"Leaving," Tahliq whispered. Sorrow lanced her so sharply, she gasped. Of course they would leave. The cagy carnival master kept everyone one step ahead of Imperial tax collectors by filing no labor permits and maintaining no fixed address.

If she stayed, what would Prinz think? What would he do? What if, after her babe was born, she established another salon, here, in Madagaz? No town in all Pangaea could ever compare to her beloved Atlan; still, Madagaz had its virtues. No one knew her here. Local Vigilance took an admirably tolerant view of protocol. Licenses could be forged. Perhaps the prefecture wouldn't require a license at all.

She needed to settle down, raise the child, and recover her health. She couldn't wander for the rest of her life.

Perhaps she'd open a caretaker's salon, not a Salon of Shame. With a simulated protocol chip in her forehead and simple linen gowns that covered her neck to toe.

Why not Madagaz? Why not?

"I wonder, my Prinz," she began, stroking his golden hair as he lay, spent and smiling, beside her. He sprawled on his stomach, his long sinewy arms stretched over his head, biceps and buttocks a landscape of golden skin in the amber candlelight.

"You wonder? You're a curious lady, Tahliq." He chuckled at his small pun. At her offended silence, he added, "Wonder what, sweetness? How many minnows swim in the sea? How many stars shine in the sky? What Eternal Bliss is like?"

She bristled. Really, he could be such a stupid boy, but she quelled her pique. It wasn't the time to chastise him when she had something far different on her mind.

"Well, yes, I wonder about all those things, too. But what I *really* wonder is what do you expect when, one wonderful day, you enter sacred sharelock?"

He rolled over on his back, still dreamy-faced and credulous. Not yet anticipating where she was leading him. "Well, I expect to feel Pannish love, of course," he said. "And I expect my sharer to feel Pannish love for me."

"Yes. Go on."

"I expect I'll want to generate a family. Maybe a first batch of seven sons. That's what my fathers did, and my older brothers have all made sergeant in their twenties. Seven's a lucky number, you know. At least it is in Madagaz."

"Seven is a lucky number in all Pangaea," she assured him. "And what will you expect of your sacred sharer? *Besides* Pannish love." She teased her fingertips across his belly and smiled when he sprang into tumescence.

His golden young face grew serious, though a grin nipped at a corner of his mouth and he made no move to evade her. "I'll expect my sharer to assist me in managing our household and caring for our children."

"Managing a household properly is essential," she agreed and recalled how well she had managed her salon, sans children.

"I'd prefer to be the superior sharer and rise through the ranks at Vigilance, but if I felt Pannish love for someone superior, I'd care for our children. Though if we could afford it, I'd prefer hiring a caretaker subpure."

"Caretaker subpures certainly know their destined labor. And how do you feel about *this,* my love?" She touched him, only lightly, denying him her usual full caress.

He tensed and his blue eyes clouded. "I suppose I'd like to share my bed, the way we do here. But if my sharer and I didn't wish to sully the purity of our love, I wouldn't think of imposing my shame. I'd pay for an erotician. They know their destined labor, too, the same as caretakers."

Her throat clenched, but she forged on. "What matters most, I believe, must be the utter intimacy of sharers' sharemind."

"Oh, yes," he exclaimed, plainly relieved she'd returned to safer ground. "The satisfaction of sharers' sharemind must be the best part of sharelock. My fathers have hinted as much, and they've got a *very* successful sharelock."

"I'm happy to hear you feel that way." She threaded her arms around his neck and flung her leg over his thighs. "Close your eyes and relax, my Prinz."

And she did what she had never dared do with Regim: she unfolded her allpure sharemind for him to see. She surged into a perfumed mutual consciousness with him and gently guided him—

Into glorious Atlan.

The dazzlement of Allpure Square. The Obelisk of Eternity. The Pagoda of Pan hovering overhead, the upturned eaves, Imperial purple and gold.

They skim over Marketplace, the way it was before the Big Shock. The four purity quadrants, and the angels' mezzanine floating overhead. The silver cloudscrapers and massive natalries. Teeming streets and stalls of costermongers and wandering priestesses. Saloonkeeps haggling with vendors, eroticians beckoning to patrons.

Tahliq smiles and takes Prinz by the hand. "Behold Our Sacred City of Atlan."

He started up with a fierce, inarticulate cry. Leapt off the bed, and glared at her, his face quivering with outrage. "What witchery did you just perform? How is it a drud enters sharemind with a magister pure? And what is this talk of sharelock? I ought to arrest you for impure thoughts."

She gasped at his arrogance. "How is it a magister calls a drud beautiful and finds bliss in her arms and in her sharemind?"

He sat on the edge of the cot, his back turned to her. "Yes, I've called you beautiful. And I enjoy you. But beauty and bliss have nothing to do with sharelock. You know that. My progeny must be suited to my subpure. They must be shaped like vigiles of the magister purity."

"My Prinz, I've seen plenty of subpures who've bred vigile with vigile. Their progeny turn out long-nosed and cross-eyed and meager."

"But they have fulfilled their Imperial duty. Fulfilled the purpose of life."

"This is *your* life, Prinz. It's all any of us may know. Perhaps there's Eternal Bliss. Perhaps there's none. But you can find happiness—in your life, here and now—if you listen to your own heart. You *must* listen."

"That's easy to say. Not so easy to do." He smiled wanly. "And that's a quite subversive speech."

"But you listen because you sense the truth. Because living your life with integrity *is* possible, even in Pangaea."

He nodded and lay back on the bed and pulled her into his embrace. "Enter sharemind with me again."

She pressed her cheek to his chest and closed her eyes.

Atlan. Beloved Atlan.

The lanes winding down to the waterfront, the boardwalk, and the glamorous saloons. The charming piers and fine, tall ships. Sausal Bay stretching to the horizon where a distant tracery of green bisected sea and sky, hinting at the vast province of North Appalacia.

"Thank you for showing me the city, Tahliq." He raises her hand to his lips. "You possess magister sharemind, then."

"Yes," she lies.

But he frowns. "You're withholding something from me."

He's more powerful than she realized. "I give you everything, my Prinz. My body, my heart, my sharemind, my Essence—"

"No, not everything," he says sharply.

"What else do you want?"

"I want to know who seeded the unborn you carry."

"No one seeded the unborn. It's nothing, no one—"

"You mean you don't know?"

"Of course I know," she says. "The seeder was a magister pure. A high-ranking vigile with Atlan Vigilance. Famous for his ferocity and higher than you."

Suddenly she lay alone on the cot. The night air chilled her skin.

Prinz was pulling on his leggings, stepping into his boots. She climbed off the bed, carefully cradling her belly, and went to him. He flinched away, but she laid her hand on his cheek and gently turned his face to her.

"You see, I *am* worthy of a vigile," she said softly, searching his eyes. "I bear a magister pure."

"I've got to go," he mumbled. "Early drill in the morning." When he finally glanced at her, his expression shone with awe and respect and astonishment. Perhaps also a dark sparkle of fear.

She smiled at him fondly. He was so very young and so very impressionable. The prospect of taming him, of entering sharelock with him, swelled her heart with gleeful anticipation. "Will I see you tomorrow night, my darling? There is one more *very* important question I must ask you."

"Tomorrow night," he said with a wary smile. "Yes. Yes, I'll be here."

"We'll be on our way day after tomorrow," Buckley told the sleepy-eyed curiosities as they assembled around the grub wagon in the morning. There was caf, fried flatbreads, the surprise of sweet cream, and the quail eggs Tahliq so missed. "Start packing as soon as you can."

The entwined twins started in. "Are we heading north—" "—to Scanda?"

A small earthshock rattled the cookpots in the grub wagon.

"I've told you a thousand times," Buckley said, stamping his foot, "we're heading northwest. First to Siluria, then to Cordillera. We'll wait out the rains there. We'll think about Scanda come the next autumn turning."

"Why?" the twins said irritably.

"There's too much Vigilance in Scanda. They're nuts about proximity in Scanda. They'll skin us alive in Scanda."

The other curiosities groaned and complained and bickered.

Tahliq kept her silence. Why should she care? She sipped her caf with such a smug look that Ba'reesha shot her an inquiring glance, which she ignored. She couldn't care less where the carnival was heading.

Madagaz was a fine, decent little town. She would stay on. She would stay with her Prinz.

One last drud day at Buckley's flew by. Spectators heckled and ogled. The smell of sulfur soured the air. She was desperately hungry, but every time she so much as nibbled on a berry, her stomach clenched and the unborn within kicked.

Tahliq noticed none of it.

When Buckley closed the cash box for the evening and roped off the camp, she dashed to her wagon and dressed with care. Such a sad, spare wardrobe. Truly, it was time to stop running. Time to settle down and have a home with food in the pantry, wine in the cellar, gowns in the closet. She smoothed perfume on her throat and her thighs, nervous as a pledged sharer preparing for her sharelock ceremony.

She stole through the dark to the rented hovel.

Prinz met her at the door, a flush on his golden cheeks. A changed man; she could see it at once. Not the heedless youth with his flippancy and insinuations, but a respectful vigile. He opened the door for her, courteously inviting her inside. And then slowly, sweetly, he led her to the bed, proving with gentle strength how well he had learned his lessons.

When he finished, he dozed lightly the way he always did, his arm tenderly circling her shoulders. Softly she unfolded her allpure sharemind. In the stealthy way she'd mastered with Regim, she entered mutual consciousness.

And saw with a shock—

Magisters. Tall columns of indigo smoke stand in formation around a long, low table that reflects light like a dark mirror. Powerful magister sharemind, assembled over distances. A wisp of indigo smoke stands apart from the formation, a less powerful presence.

"She displays herself as a curiosity with a traveling carnival," the wisp says.

"What sort of curiosity?" a tall column asks.

"She carries an illegal unborn inside her. If that weren't enough, she hinted who the seeder is."

Tahliq cupped her hand over her mouth, stifling her scream, as Prinz continued to snore. Trembling violently, she closed her eyes—

"Make sure she doesn't leave Madagaz till I arrive." A powerful presence emanates from an enormous column of smoke at the head of the mirrored table. "Do you understand me, Officer Prinz? You're dealing with a cunning, seditious, and resourceful criminal. She slipped through our hands once in Atlan. Do not allow her to leave Madagaz."

"Yes, Lieutenant Captain Deuceman."

"With these rains, it will take three days for me to get there. Detain her by force, if necessary."

"Oh, that won't be necessary. I know how to keep her here."

"Your loyalty to your subpure, purity, and the Imperium is commendable, officer."

She rose quickly, silently. Slipped into her leggings. Stepped into her boots.

"Tahliq?" Prinz said. His sleepy murmur froze her

blood. "Sweetness, where are you going? Stay. I want you again."

"Hush, I know what you want. I'll be right back."

"Where are you going?"

"I've got a sudden raging thirst for kapfo wine," she said lightly. "I'm going down to the corner vendor to get some."

"No, wait. I'll go. You shouldn't walk around by yourself so late at night."

"Nonsense. I love the night. I want to know what Madagaz is like at night." She sat on the edge of the bed and brushed fingertips across his forehead. *You blackhearted bastard.* "Drowse again, my darling. I'll be right back. You know I can't stay away from you for long."

"Hurry," he said and stretched luxuriously, offering a display of just what she could expect when she returned. "I'll be waiting for you."

Regim. Regim. She wanted to scream. *He knows that I know. He'll take my babe from me and then he'll kill me.*

She shut the door and ran all the way to the carnival's campsite. She barged into Buckley's wagon, surprising the carnival master pleasantly entwined with the twins. The trio puffed on expensive cheroots amid a tangle of newly laundered blankets.

"Tahliq," Buckley said. "What are you doing up so late?"

Tahliq tugged frantically at the bedclothes. "Get up. Pack up. We've got to get out of Madagaz. Now. Tonight."

"What's your hurry?" Buckley reached over to a night table and retrieved a jar of d'ka Tahliq had never seen him with before. In Madagaz, a jar like that cost ten ores. More ores slid off a cache of coins carelessly piled there and clattered on the floor.

Buckley, careless with ores?

The twins sniggered, sly blue eyes trading glances.

The clatter, the glance, the chuckle of betrayal.

"We're going to stay over in Madagaz for another

three days," Buckley said winningly. "We heard a rumor that the rains have been delayed, isn't that so, twins?" He plucked the fallen ores from the floor and tossed them on the pile. "And our revenues were *very* good today."

Tahliq fled Madagaz.

She slipped away during the bustle of morning performances. Ba'reesha was chattering in her tent, Buckley was pitching, spectators were roaming here and there. Tahliq piled the bloodbat's possessions in a corner of the grub wagon. She didn't leave a note. Then she hitched two drayers to the wagon and bolted out the back way, alone.

She whipped the drayers and galloped due west, racing for the Far Reaches. The rains came. She just barely negotiated the treacherous isthmus of Wadi Howar, wading for two leagues through wind and knee-deep floodwaters. She disembarked from the wagon and led the two skittish drayers for the better part of a blustery day.

She set up camp just after twilight on a wind-scoured bluff. Soaked to the skin and famished, the drayers had begun to eye her with distrust. Though she loathed it, she entered drud sharemind with them, exerting every power she possessed. She managed to pacify most of their fears and insisted upon their obedience. She built them a campfire with oilwood logs she'd stolen from Buckley, heated cookstones, and fed them hot lardsticks. She retired to the wagon, then, stripped off her soaking clothes, and fell into a fitful sleep.

In the morning, the drayers were gone. They had stolen the sack of lardsticks, the cookpot, the cookstones, the rest of the oilwood, and her one and only magmalamp. She bit back a curse, but in truth she'd been expecting it. She'd stashed a sack of supplies beneath the cot and, despite her fatigue, she'd slept with one eye open, her crescent knife nestled in her fist.

She hadn't chosen her camp with any strategy other

than surviving a flood if torrents fell in the night. Now she found herself and the wagon stranded atop a bald plateau, buffeted by fierce winds, and in plain sight of marauders.

She braced her shoulder against the back of the wagon and heaved. Her muscles clenched and pain knifed through her belly. She eased up at once. The wagon had moved not one length.

She cupped her belly protectively and shaded her eyes, surveying the rocky coastline spread below her. Morning fog had thrust misty fingers into jagged inlets. The Panthalassa Ocean surged cold and grey, assaulting the beaches with icy spray. It was beautiful, the way death must be beautiful to someone suffering. But for wheeling seabirds, the place looked absolutely deserted. Well, she'd heard as much about the Far Reaches. There weren't any proper towns, except for a shabby accretion of commercial enterprises around the natalries. The people, from the scattering of reclusive angels to gangs of agricultural druds, preferred to live in isolated collectives.

She groaned when her child kicked at her innards, hard. She had read the forbidden books, had studied the forbidden illustrations. She had a fair notion of the task that lay ahead of her. *You need your release, my little sweet. I need it, too. Shall we bivouac here alone? We're as plain as the nose on a face. Will we die here together when you struggle for your freedom, and I struggle to set you free?*

She strode to the edge of the plateau and surveyed her prospects. The rocky hillside angled sharply down but scrub brush and erosion made descent to the beach a possibility. Once there, could she catch fish? She had never fished in her life. Forage for fresh vegetables or fruits? She wouldn't know a raw pondplum from a poisonous dingleberry.

Weary, confounded, and famished, she climbed back into the wagon. She rummaged in her cache, found and devoured a cold flatbread. She lay on the cot, curled her fist around her knife, and closed her eyes.

Sweet darkness, the release of sleep.

Then gentle pressure.

Something bore down on her belly. Not too hard.

Tahliq woke. She'd been so exhausted she woke slowly. She peered through her eyelashes and saw that sunlight slanted through the back tent flap rather than the front, where she'd last remembered seeing it.

In another moment she realized a human hand explored her.

She bolted upright.

They surrounded her cot, gazing with misshapen black eyes, their lopsided faces somber. A grizzled little woman stood beside her cot. It was she who pressed on Tahliq's belly—harder now. Daggers and caltrops dangled from the woman's belt.

Impure.

Tahliq slapped the woman's hand away and scrambled back on the cot. She rose unsteadily to her knees, brandishing her knife.

A young man stood beside the tiny wizened women. Tall and gangling, he wore devil stars on his belt, an insolent glower on his face, and a gold ring piercing his ragged eyebrow.

"Asif!" Tahliq cried. "You're alive!"

"Yeah, Salit and I have got better things to do than twiddle our thumbs in Inim's fires. But I wish you'd told us about the tunnel out the back of your crawl space. We had a devil of a time finding the trapdoor in the dark."

"Just last week," said Salit Zehar. "Asif brought me here to bear my babe. It's a good confinement camp, though the Reaches are awful gloomy, aren't they?"

"That they are," Tahliq said. Unexpected gladness welled up in her to see the Devil girl again. Gladness that the girl and her bonded one had not perished in Rancid Flats. Gladness to find another gravid woman she knew from the old days. Gladness, too, that the impure had taken her in.

"Regim has gone on a rampage, raiding our tentsites from Atlan to Gondwana Province." Salit stared pointedly at Tahliq's belly and cupped her hands around her own.

" 'Tis no one's babe but my own," Tahliq said. "The babe is blameless."

Salit nodded and pulled her chameleon cloak more tightly around her shoulders. "After his vow of vengeance, I don't know what Regim would do to me and my babe if he knew I was about to deliver."

The Devil girl's face twisted with such distilled fear that Tahliq took her gnarled hand and squeezed it. "I know exactly how you feel, Salit."

They reclined before a blazing bonfire, guzzling buttermilk and gobbling boiled eggs under the camp mistress's watchful eye. The camp was in a cavern deep beneath Laurentia Coast, a strand of pebbled beaches and forbidding escarpments. The impure who eked out existence there, Salit told her, had captured the two drayers and retraced their footsteps to the wagon on the bluff. Tahliq saw no sign of the drayers and decided against asking about them. Hardened spare folk, the Reaches' impure possessed a feral brutality. The drayers might have made fine meat.

A skittering sound echoed throughout the cavern. The gravid women huddling around the bonfire glanced up with fearful eyes. Tahliq glimpsed leathery wings, bestial faces, a curve of claws. A covey of bloodbats clung to the shadowy ceiling.

"I'm glad you're here, erotician," Salit said in a quavering voice. "It's true I've taken life with my own hands, but I've never given life before. Perhaps destiny means to take my life in payment."

"Nonsense. Destiny doesn't make such neat accountings."

"But that was my mother's destiny." Salit opened the chameleon cloak and the mnemon pocket. "Pocket, please show me my birth."

Out fluttered a square of flickering white light. The mnemon hovered before them and filled with sounds

and images: the head of a baby emerging from a straining portal of muscle. A woman's groans and screams.
"Name her Salit, my Horan. Good-bye, my bonded
one."

The mnemon flapped over their heads in lazy loop-
the-loops and sped away into the darkness. Salit hid her
face in her hands and did not summon it back.

"So your mother died in childbirth," Tahliq said.
"Your father recorded a mnemon of it."

"Yes. I always wondered why he did that. If he
blamed me for my mother's death."

Tahliq spied a flicker like a firewing at night. The
mnemon was returning of its own accord, and she spied
more images emerging across its surface. "Salit, look!"

The visage of Horan Zehar appeared in the sheet of
white light and spoke. "If you are witnessing this, my
daughter, you have mastered cloak and pocket. Mastered your impetuous nature that worried me so. Wherever I am, whatever has become of me, know that I'm
proud of you. Know that the cloak and pocket are your
birthright. And know that when your mother died, she
was glad to have given you life. Do not disappoint her."

The mnemon dived into the pocket and disappeared.

"You're young and strong," Tahliq said. "You have
little to fear." But she could feel the girl's hand tremble.
In a flash of allpure sharemind, she apprehended Salit's
fear and grief.

It will be all right, Salit.

*But if it's not all right, Dame Tahliq, if I die in child-
birth, will you take my babe and grow it up? It will be
impure and very ugly, but you can disguise it or say it's
your servant.*

*Yes, I will raise your babe, I promise. Wait, wait.
How the devil are we sharing this consciousness? I
thought the impure have no sharemind.*

*We don't. This consciousness has become mine since
I bonded. I dream of things. I remember things I never
knew in the first place. Sometimes I steal into another's
thoughts, and the other doesn't see me there. What do
you think of that?*

I think you're a remarkable young lady, Salit.

She released Salit's hand and they plummeted out of shared consciousness. Tahliq sighed. "I'm the one who's eaten poorly and slept worse. I'm no young girl like you."

Salit nodded. "Except for your belly, you've become so thin I barely recognized you, Dame Tahliq." The Devil girl withdrew from her cloak the four enormous glittering orbs she wore around her neck. "You once cast the orb for my father."

"It was a most unfortunate oracle. I'm sorry."

"I don't blame you. Dame Tahliq, will you cast an oracle for me?" She slipped one orb off the thong and proffered the foretelling device on the palm of her hand. "One of my father's mnemons says the orb chooses who it will give an oracle to. But it's never given an oracle to me."

Tahliq gazed at the purple sparkle she loved so well. "That's a beautiful orb. You would find yourself drawn and quartered in Allpure Square just for wearing it." She rummaged in her travel sack. "But I don't need to cast yours, thank you all the same." She withdrew her own orb and cradled it fondly in the palms of her hands. She hadn't felt the throbbing sting of its power since she'd cast an oracle for Lucyd. "It's all I have left of Atlan." She met Salit's eyes. "Are you afraid?"

"Yes."

"Good. That's the proper attitude."

She rolled the orb in her palms as images flashed before her consciousness the way they always did.

There was the face she always saw, the Ancient One who had made the orb, blinking at her. Then she saw that the strange shiny visage she'd seen before was only a mask and, behind the mask, was a human face.

And there, the whirling galaxies and the deep blazing stars she always saw. The ancient oceans surging over the world. Rising up from primordial waves, the world archipelago—Pangaea. Again she sensed her connection with all things of the world that ever had been, were now, and ever will be.

She flung the orb on the ground, praying for an oracle that would guide Salit. The orb spun in tiny circles once, twice, thrice, coming to rest before Salit's knees. The Devil girl laughed with nervous delight. The orb abruptly rolled in the opposite direction, once, twice, thrice.

And rested again before Salit.

Tahliq waited as the orb utterly stilled itself. "Done is done," she whispered and peered at the ruling facet—the topmost facet that rested faceup.

Salit peered, too.

Tahliq's eyes skimmed and plunged into the facet. The kaligraph was delicately rendered, the cavern-eyed, grinning structure of bones beneath the human face.

"Skull," she said.

Salit leapt to her feet, tears starting in her mismatched eyes. She drew her dagger. "You've hexed me, you bloody erotician."

Asif hurried to her side. "My bonded one, what is it?"

"She cast the oracle that foretold my father's death. Now she's foretold mine." She lunged at Tahliq. "I ought to slit your throat right now."

Tahliq drew her own knife and brandished it. The Devil girl's rages might have intimidated others, but Tahliq understood her. "Calm yourself, little Salit."

"I'm going to die!"

"No, you're not. This oracle isn't what you think. Skull is most propitious. And," she added dryly, "fitting for you, at the moment. Do you want to hear what the oracle signifies, or don't you? We cannot be friends if you leap up and pull a knife on me every time I say something you don't like."

Huffing furiously and swiping at tears on her cheeks, Salit sat again, sheathing her dagger. "All r-r-right. I'm sorry."

"That's better. Now, then." Tahliq studied the facet again. "Skull signifies certainty or chaos."

"What does *that* mean?"

"It means destiny is yours to choose. It means the

Hand of Pan has freed Its grip on you. But whatever you choose is your responsibility."

"Responsibility," Salit said. "My father forever scolded me about my responsibility. Just like you."

"If you choose chaos, chaos you shall have, Salit."

The Devil girl heaved a sigh. "I'm pledged to wreak chaos upon the Imperium. But I don't want chaos for my new babe."

"I'll do whatever I can to help you," Tahliq said. "But I've never borne a babe before, either, and I'm no midwife."

The Devil girl brightened. "There's a midwife at the Far Reaches natalries. The camp mistress says Bandular is her name. Rumor says she knows *all* the forbidden knowledge."

"Have the camp mistress go see if the midwife will help us," Tahliq said.

Salit shook her head. "Camp mistress tried. Said she couldn't get more than two minutes of Bandular's time. The midwife is a serv pure. Quite a proximicist, I guess, and a pretty one. Black hair, black eyes. Didn't want to be seen speaking with an impure. I'd go to her myself and throw myself at her mercy, but my Vigilance death warrants are posted even here." She studied Tahliq. "Perhaps she would talk to you. You're a drud but at least you're of the purities."

Tahliq shook her head. "I'm as anxious to keep my whereabouts a secret as you, Salit."

The Devil girl drummed her fingers and thought. "Camp mistress says Midwife Quartermain has got twenty-one sons, all midwives, too. One son labors at the Imperial Natalries in Atlan. The serv girls pine for his return." Suddenly she gave a little shout and clapped her hands over her mouth. "Well, of course! Asif, my bonded one," she called out. The young man hurried over. "Pack your gear. You must leave for Atlan at once!"

"But, my Salit, we just left Atlan."

"Well, you must go back. And return before the

moon is full. Will our babes be ready to emerge by then, Dame Tahliq?"

She'd been carrying her babe for a long time, but Tahliq had heard rumors that magister unborns lingered in their ges tanks far longer than the smaller babes of other purities. And she had no doubt, looking at scrawny Salit, that the impure girl would bear her child soon.

"I'm afraid so. My burden has lingered long in me, but that's typical for the type of burden it is. I'm due by the full moon, and so are you."

Salit clapped her hands, delighted. "Camp mistress says a tincture of angelica root will hasten my bearing through these skinny hips. We'll bear our babes together, as sisters-in-arms. Would you like that, Dame Tahliq?"

"I would like nothing better."

"Then hurry, my bonded one," Salit said to Asif. "Bring us my old chum, Dubban Quartermain."

FACET 23

Bird: Liberty or heedlessness.
The philosopher encounters a nihilist.
The action is exhilaration.
The forbearance is delinquency.

The Orb of Eternity

Commentaries:
Coucillor Sausal: As Pan sets all things of the
world in order, so Pan sets all things in motion.
Birds fly freely with the wind, but migrate from
summer havens to winter havens according to the
seasons.

So, too, the Imperium encourages the purities
to interact according to the rules of protocol.

Therefore the prudent person should cultivate
flexibility but exercise discipline. [*Deleted from
The Contemporary Commentaries of Sausal (15th
Ed.)* Yet there are times when you must abandon
discipline in pursuit of freedom.]
Guttersage (usu. considered vulgar): Which liber-
ates you? Your apprehension of Pan?

Or annihilation of your apprehension of Pan?

*Our City of Atlan, the periphery of Northeast Market-
place. The Imperial Natalries, Quintus Natalry:*

Dubban heard the sobbing of the druds, the droning of
the priestesses, long before he saw them.

"But I've never harvested anyone before," he protested as the super towed him toward the Sanctum of

Purification. "I don't *want* to harvest anyone. I'm just a midwife."

Every natalry came equipped with a harvesting sanctum tucked deep in the basement. In this particular basement, the worsening earthshocks had wreaked havoc. The place was a mess. Jagged cracks cleaved the pale grey tiles, and broken pipes jutted out, disgorging fitful trickles of septic-smelling water. Magmalamps sizzled and strobed. Dubban sloshed down the scummy hall, cursing the super for ruining his new boots.

"I know you've served the Imperium as a Superior Father," the super said reasonably. "You'll do just fine as a physician." A short, barrel-hipped middle pure with a perpetual furrow in her brow and a perpetual grin curving her lips, she undertook her managerial duties at the natalry of the lowest purity with sardonic equanimity. "Priest, physician, what's the difference? They're proximate."

"I can never figure out which is more blessed."

"That's because the High Council can never decide which is dearer to Pan, the holy-rollers or the quacks."

"Well, I don't like either of 'em. And I'm a serv," Dubban reminded her, since the super seemed set on overlooking that fact. "I don't want to get arrested, supe."

"Don't worry about it," she said cheerfully.

The sobbing, the droning, grew louder, more shrill.

"One of the docs didn't show up this morning," the super said. "They're reporting for duty less and less these days. Everyone's bought firebolts and hightailed it to the plains. You wouldn't believe the banditry out there. So what I need, ol' Dub, is someone who can stand a little blood."

"Well, that's not me. I faint dead away at the sight."

"Oh, I doubt that. Come along. You'll do fine."

She glanced at him shrewdly, and he knew that, with her superior sharemind, she'd discerned he *had* cut human flesh, spilled human blood. Plaia's exquisite little hands had healed well enough, but the diamond-shaped scars might never disappear.

A pox on sharemind!

They turned a corner, and he saw them: young drud women, twelve years of age, huddled on long, wooden benches. Some embraced each other. Others shook with sobs. Still others sat somberly, faces stony, spines ramrod-straight. Clan caretakers and hired caretaker subpures flitted among them, offering whispered comfort, wine, and anodyne tablets.

Dubban stared, aghast. He'd never seen druds like this. They stood no taller than his own midsection. Dark slits for eyes, some kind of corporate protocol chips planted between their brows. Their broad, flat faces were lightly bearded with soft red down. They possessed muscular shoulders and skinny arms terminating in spatulate hands and dexterous fingers.

"What are they?" he whispered to the super.

"Atlantium miners. Where they're going, they won't need what we're harvesting today."

Tall, robust priestesses in flowing grey-green robes stood before the weeping assembly and chanted in exuberant voices—

> *Make way! Make way!*
> *We gather the sacred eggs,*
> *We reap the unsown harvest,*
> *And consecrate All to Pan*
> *To be revered for Eternity.*
> *The vigor within thy flesh,*
> *So young and strong and fresh,*
> *Departs joyfully for All-Loving Pan*
> *To be revered for Eternity!*

"There you are, you wretched supe. Is this the one?"

A physician-natalist strode from the harvesting sanctum, holding his slender hands aloft. They were sheathed in gloves, the pale green fabric soaked in blood. His long pale green tunic and a kerchief of the same cloth pushed down below his chin bore more stains and splotches of gore.

Dubban blew out a breath. "No. No, I'm not the one."

"Yes, he is," the super said. "Go on, get in there."

He turned to flee, but the super and the physician-natalist seized him, jammed a pale green tunic over his shoulders, and stuffed his hair inside a tight green cap. They tied a kerchief around his neck. They led him to a cavernous sink of cracked white ceramic and scrubbed his hands with water as questionable as the leaks in the hall. They patted his hands dry and shoved them into pale green gloves.

"These are so you don't have to touch a lower pure," the physician said, smoothing the gloves. "The mask, so you don't have to breathe their breaths."

"Chin up, sweetie," the super said, satisfied her Imperial duty to procure a surgeon had been fulfilled. "Go cut 'em."

The physician shoved Dubban into a green-tiled chamber. Five dozen slabs of green marble bore five dozen naked drud girls, bound wrist and ankle by leather straps. Groaning and shrieks filled Dubban's ears in a terrible chorus. Narrow-eyed enumerators from the Security Number Administration stood with databoards beside each slab, carefully recording each girl's security number. Midwife-natalists stood there, too, bearing storage dishes crammed on trays. Dubban glimpsed IMPERIAL NATALRY BANK—CENTRAL ATLAN stamped on the lids.

But it was the barrels that finally threw him. Big oaken barrels piled high with slick purplish red and pinkish yellow meaty things.

Human meat.

The physician pulled his kerchief over his nose and mouth and gestured for Dubban to do the same. They strode to a slab surrounded by masked assistants. The drud girl trussed there glanced up at Dubban, fear wild in her face. The physician clamped a rag stinking of soporific over her face. Her dark slitted eyes fell open in a dazed stupor.

"She's ready," the physician said. "Are you?" Without waiting for Dubban's answer, the physician slapped a surgical fork into the palm of his hand. "Jab where I say jab, pull when I say pull."

The physician flicked his scalpel across the drud's abdomen below her feed button, peeling open layers of skin and fat. "Clamp that," he commanded and gestured to a side table where lethal-looking tools lay scattered on a tray. Dubban found a tensile device that looked like it would do, gripped flesh, and peeled the incision open.

The assistants deftly reached between his hands with cotton swabs and soaked up fluids. A hot metallic stink assaulted his senses, and he wanted to run. But he didn't. One look at the girl's face, twitching despite the soporific, spurred him into swift, purposeful detachment.

The physician took the fork from him, and yanked out all manner of muscular-looking body parts. He flung the gristle onto a tray. The midwives set to, plucking out pinkish white clusters and depositing them into storage dishes. The assistants flung the remaining viscera into the barrels. Enumerators planted security number decals on each storage dish.

"We're done down here," the physician announced, flinging his fork into the tray. "Now her dugs."

"Why take those?" Dubban said.

"Won't be needin' 'em, will she?" the physician said. He plucked a curved blade and handed another to Dubban. "I'll do the left, you do the right. Hurry up." He thrust his chin at the chamber. "We've got another hundred to go."

Disgust pooling in his throat, Dubban sliced open and cut out the drud's little breast. "Where?"

"Toss it in there," the physician said, pointing to the barrels. He glanced up and winked. "Good work, midwife. It's a lousy job, I know, but someone's got to do it. I'll see that you get a nice bonus. Now this one," he said, striding to the next slab, the next trussed drud writhing in restraints. "This one may give us some trouble."

•   •   •

At midday break, Dubban ran all the way home. Not every harvesting was so brutal. For most pures, it was a fairly simple extraction. And then a snipping of troublesome tubes, the freezing of harvested materia, which ensured future generations whenever sharers were ready.

He surprised Plaia still in her sleep gown, bending over stylus and parchment at the dining table, her brow furrowed in concentration. He took the stylus from her hand, lifted the gown over her head, and led her, protesting but not unwilling, to his bed. There he coupled with her fiercely, touching and tasting with profound thanks what her natalry had left so perfectly in place.

He couldn't stop seeing those barrels.

"Hard morning at the natalries?" she said with a wry grin when he was done.

He told her.

She cradled his head between her breasts and stroked his hair, humming songs from the Festival of Spring Moontide. In a while, though, she slipped out from the bedsheets and padded barefoot back to her work, her brow furrowed again.

She was meticulously copying the last section of Volume One, *On the Nature of the Egg,* by Dame T. Driftwood, the first of Tivern's secret texts. She'd been plotting a strategy for half a season. They'd quarreled nearly every day after she told him what she wanted to do: smuggle copies of texts and maps to an administrator she knew at Ground Control. Maiselle Trey had known and loved Tivern and, once upon a time, had supported resonance theory. Along with Tivern's original data, Plaia had been assembling phenomenal proof. Even the sketchiest news gleaned from criers' sharemind corroborated a stunning number of Tivern's projected wander curves. Plaia had penciled in the data on her map of the world archipelago.

"Here, here, and here. Maiselle will see it at once."

She was stabbing her forefinger at tiny, meticulous notations, her golden green eyes gleaming.

Here we go again, Dubban thought bleakly.

"Without a doubt, Andea's moving away from South Gondwana. And Gondwana is spreading, there and there. I'll bet salinity in the Ouachita floodplains is off the scale. Look at this pattern of shock activity. Tasman is pushing out to sea. Don't look at me like that. This is where the last major earthshock struck. Must have been at least seven mags, from what we saw in criers' sharemind. Can't you *see*?"

"My love, I see."

"Borno is next. Oh! I wish I could go see Tasman Rift."

"Well, you can't. Not while Gunther is still posting detainment warrants." He couldn't *help* but see. Tivern had been right. Plaia was right. And it was not as if he didn't understand the crisis, didn't understand the consequences for Pangaea. Not as if he didn't want to fight for the future.

He didn't want to lose *her.*

"Anyway, Milord Lucyd's new dream is all about how we'll be saved by the waters," he said stubbornly. He recalled the dream he'd chosen in the Mind of the World this morning: a glorious beach. A beautiful young woman with white-gold hair. Awesome waves curling in from the ocean, all scintillating blue and brilliant green and creamy white foam. Surging to shore, the waves crashed on coastal rocks and plunged into a stupendous bore at the base of picturesque sea cliffs. Smiling citizens gathered on the cliffs and held dances and feasts and games.

"The dream is a lie and you know it," Plaia said. "Force-flooding has caused worse shocks, and more of them, just as I predicted. Six mags and up, on a regular basis. Dubban, I've *got* to get these documents to Maiselle. She'll understand, I know she will."

He was so angry he seized her shoulders and shook her. "Here's what *I* know. They'll trace the package. They'll find you here. Gunther will take you away. He will plunder your sharemind. He will find out that you persuaded me to steal your seeded birthpods. I don't care what he does to me, but he will kill you."

"I'll find intermediaries," she countered. "I'll hire Salit Zehar and her bonded one. They'll be delighted to strike a blow against the Imperium for us."

He took stock of her reference to *us*.

A voice crashed into their cottage. "All right, midwife, let's go."

Dubban whirled, instinctively stepped in front of Plaia, and brandished his fists.

Plaia stepped next to him, gripping a bread knife in one hand, a crockery platter in the other. Dubban had no doubt that she fully intended to take on their intruder.

He had never loved her more.

But it wasn't Gunther or Vigilance.

A tall, gangly impure man stood before them, smirking at their nakedness. He twirled a half-folded devil star through his fingers.

Asif said, "If you're through quarreling, kiss her and apologize. Then get dressed, Dubban Quartermain. You're coming with me."

Dubban crouched next to Asif at the edge of Rancid Flats Reservoir, gazing down at devastation.

Once this had been a source of water and pride. Dubban had often marveled at the magnificent ancient construction, the waves dancing over clear depths that plunged to a bottom masterfully tiled in scarlet-and-blue arabesques.

Now a turbulent slurry of ash-laden water churned within the fractured walls. Cooling magma spilled over fissures in cascades of opalescent grey stone. The entire west wall had cracked in half. A polluted waterfall plunged into a canyon rawly cleaved on the opposite side. A rubble of hovels still clung there.

"Damn it, Asif," he said to the Devil, "it's not my fault if my mother wouldn't talk to your women."

"But she'll talk to *you*, won't she?"

"What if she won't? I haven't seen her in four and a half years. We're not on the best of terms anymore." When Asif scoffed, Dubban said, "I no longer believe her Pannist lies," which only made the Devil laugh.

Dubban heard the clump of bootheels.

They pressed themselves against the charred wall of a shed that had housed reservoir clerks and clerics, the former to keep the water clean, the latter to pray for purity. Walkabouts marched past. What they thought they'd find in this desolation, Dubban had no idea.

"Look, Asif," he said when they were gone. "I don't know a thing about babes in the womb."

"You're a midwife, aren't you?"

"Midwife-*natalist*. I prune pods, dish out begettings, untank emergences."

Asif looked blank, then said, "Gah, man, it's all the same thing, isn't it?"

Dubban shook his head. "No. Not the same thing at all."

"But you're *supposed* to know all about babes, ges tanks or no. At least your ma does. That's the rumor in the Reaches."

Dubban couldn't argue with that. Bandular had hinted as much on more than one occasion. "I cannot vouch for anything my mother may or may not know. Or do."

"You'll convince her," Asif declared and glanced away, surveying the reservoir with narrowed eyes. "I know this, Dub."

Dubban didn't actually despise the impure man. They had shared a beer and a few grins. But the thought of trekking all the way to the Far Reaches with him stuck in Dubban's craw.

"Listen," Asif said and laid a hand on Dubban's arm. "Salit's ma died birthin' her. Salit believes her turn is next. She's facing her destiny like the warrior she is, but I won't stand for her being in danger." His fierce face trembled. "She's my bonded one. The babe she carries is half-mine."

"I understand," Dubban said, both moved and annoyed by the impure man's passion. "But if your women have always carried the unborn, they ought to know what to do."

"They do not." Asif unsheathed and plunged his dagger to the hilt into the ashy soil beneath their feet. "We are the impure. We die! At one-and-twenty, I'm becoming an old man. I could die tomorrow at the hands of the Imperium."

Dubban stole a glance at his abductor and fell silent. At one-and-twenty himself, he had his whole life before him.

"Our women who survive the ordeal," Asif said, "and know what to do for the others, pass on too quickly." He seized Dubban's elbow and searched his eyes. "But there's more. Salit's not like every other impure woman. The chameleon cloak has accepted her as its mistress. You've seen how she works the camouflage and retrieves mnemons from the pocket. Generations go by, and no one among my clan has ever owned a shadow cloak. Salit's father, Horan Zehar, possessed both cloak and powers."

Dubban well recalled the qut purveyor's uncanny strength and stealth. The way he seemed to know what Dubban was thinking, though the impure possessed no sharemind.

"Horan used the cloak so skillfully he concealed his true appearance within it," Asif said. "Even in his mnemons. But I saw him as he truly was when I carried his corpse to his funeral pyre. He wasn't nearly as ugly as he showed himself to be. And he had a rare color among the impure. His skin had a bluish cast." Asif touched the gold ring piercing his eyebrow. "Salit possesses powerful blood. She's rare."

Dubban wiped a trickle of sweat from his temple. "Plaia is rare, too. She knows secrets the Imperium would suppress by torture and execution. What she knows, what she wants to do, is as important to Pangaea as Salit."

"I think so, too. Salit explained to me what your

woman said that night about the world. I understand why you don't want to leave her. So let's get on with it. Your woman will wait for you. I could see it in her eyes."

Before he'd left, Dubban had replenished the covered vat of water on the roof and installed a pipe that ran inside. He'd stored smoked fish in the pantry, sacks of apples, tatoes, and onions, and the pressed olive oil she favored. He'd told Plaia, "Everything I have is yours," and showed her the safe box he'd buried beneath the floor of the cottage where he'd stored ten thousand ores. "If anything should happen to me, take this and leave Atlan."

"Nothing will happen," she had said. "But promise me you won't take any risks. Promise me you'll come back."

He had promised, and they'd wept and embraced. They'd vowed their love. She'd promised to stay secluded in the cottage and contact no one till he returned.

Asif took off down a winding path that led to a stone ledge angling down several lengths into the reservoir. Dubban followed, more slowly. From the ancient stains bleached into the masonry, Dubban could see where the waterline used to be. Once the ledge had been submerged beneath water.

The Devil rounded a sharp curve and disappeared from Dubban's sight. The ledge narrowed to two handbreadths around the jut of the wall. Dubban flattened himself, hugging the wall, and edged around the curve. Just as he negotiated the bend, the wall gave way before him. A clawlike grip seized him, and he fell with a shout, slamming his hands hard on the ground.

He heard the dog-growl chuckle of the Devil. He was sprawled at the entrance to a bore tunneling deep into the rock face. He brushed himself off and sat up. Needles of rock cluttered the low ceiling. The tunnel plunged into hot, inky darkness.

Asif set off at a swift double-jointed crawl. Dubban

scrambled after him, suppressing curses. Gravel tore at his kneecaps, the palms of his hands.

"Where are we *going*? Where does this go *to*?"

"An erotician's salon," Asif called over his shoulder. "Or at least it was once."

The pit of Dubban's stomach dropped away. He glanced around, but the darkness was implacable. "You mean we're crawling beneath the *magmaflow*?"

"Sure."

"What if the rock is still molten?"

"We're fried." Asif's voice curved in an audible grin. "The erotician built a crawl space below her wine cellar. Built it to last. Anyway, that's where Salit and I left it."

"Left what?"

"You'll see for yourself."

The tunnel angled sharply down, dropping away before Dubban's hands, then angled up so sharply up he nearly nosedived into the gravel. Every time his eyes adjusted to the darkness, eking out some glimmer that had filtered in, the tunnel confounded him by growing darker still. There were ominous creaking noises, the sounds of beams burdened by great weight. The heat, never less than intense, became nearly unbearable, as if the air had collapsed upon itself.

He bumped into something in the darkness before him. "Damn it, Asif."

"You can stand up, but take it slow and watch your head. Reach there." The Devil fiddled with something that slid and clicked, sounding like a latch. "Let's hope the ceiling held. We propped it as best we could with the crates of qut, but who knows. Give me a hand, will you? There should be another pull right over you."

Dubban groped in the darkness and found a metal pull ring next to the one Asif grappled with. He seized it and gave it a vigorous yank, which loosened a spill of dust and gravel.

He sputtered and thumbed grit from his eyes. "At my count. And one and two and *heave*."

The two young men pulled in unison, and the trapdoor gave way with a metallic shriek, yielding a small avalanche of debris. Blistering air blasted out as if they'd flung open the door to a full-lit oven. Dubban leapt away, Asif staggered back, and they both stared up into the crawl space.

Soft argent light spilled through the trapdoor. Glowworms in translucent cocoons flickered among ceiling timbers. Most of the timbers had buckled, angling down from ceiling to floor. Asif sprang to his feet, poked his head through the trapdoor, and climbed inside.

Dubban stood and warily thrust his head and shoulders into the crawl space. The ceiling looked as if it would collapse if he breathed on it the wrong way. He glanced around the half-crushed chamber.

It was cramped, ruined, a sanctuary of little use to anyone. Yet there, in the midst of the wreckage, stood a large device the size and shape of a coffin. Wrought of ill-polished metal, the thing bristled with forked and twisted antennae, dimly pulsing knobs, and a tangle of cables. Across the domed lid, security kaligraphs blinked red and orange, and the muted blue mouths of security monitors mimed frantic warnings. The thing emitted a lively buzz like a hive of furious bees.

Asif was grinning like the madman he probably was. "There, you see, Dub? Still here. And the sledge, too."

He began shoving timbers off a streetsweepers' sledge next to the coffin. The ceiling groaned alarmingly and buckled, showering gravel on their heads.

Dubban ducked. "All right, Devil. You mind telling me what that thing *is*?"

Asif gave the device a resounding whack with the flat of his hand. "The Imperium calls it a shell, Dub. An aetheric shell. Salit calls it a Door. A Door into the Mind of the World."

"Look what you've done," said the strange old magister, running an elegant hand across one battered flank of the shell. "You've banged the stuffing out of it, Asif."

Dubban kneaded his left shoulder where he'd pulled a muscle. The muscle felt like a string of fire.

"Dubban and I had ourselves a time hoisting the damn thing out of the reservoir," Asif said. "Maybe you should be glad we delivered it to you at all, Alchemist. I wouldn't have bothered if Salit hadn't insisted."

The Alchemist's tentsite lay in a dank cavern perilously carved out of a ruined water main. Water dripped down the dark stone walls, and magma hissed much too close for comfort. A long, low table bore a variety of laboratory equipment, some of which Dubban recognized, some he didn't. There was a large, high-quality viewglass among the contraband storage dishes he himself had delivered to Salit Zehar.

"I'm not glad at all, Asif," the Alchemist scolded, "if you've ruined the shell. Look at *this*." He examined the lid, the top of which fitted the bottom askew. The curved metal walls appeared as if someone had applied a bludgeon to them.

"I never can open the poxy thing without a fight," Asif said with a shrug. But he winked at Dubban, pleased despite the Alchemist's aggravation.

"So you've bashed it open before, have you?"

"Sure. So what?"

"So you've damn near broken the latch *and* the bolts *and* the hinges, my fine young Devil."

The Alchemist seized the front section of the lid in his massive arms and squeezed till the lid slid back into its grooves. The shell shivered all over. The Alchemist lightly thumbed the latch. The lid obligingly sprang open with a sound like a harmonious chord.

"How'd you do that?" Asif demanded.

"With proper respect," the Alchemist said mildly. "It's a wonder the shell allowed you to open it at all. Come here, Dubban, and take a look at a miracle."

Dubban peered at the interior, which resembled a disheveled bed surrounded by instrument panels, but he couldn't tear his eyes from the man standing next to him. If the shell was a curiosity, the Alchemist was downright odd. Dubban had seen plenty of magisters and angels from afar but he'd never stood so close to a pure as high as the Alchemist. Angel mingled with magister, the man radiated power and privilege and dominance. Yet he completely lacked the one feature Dubban expected and feared: high-purity sharemind. The sort of potent sharemind that effortlessly overwhelmed and penetrated a serv consciousness like his, discerned every thought, every memory, every secret.

Dubban's hand flew to his biceps and touched the little raised mole of his security number. He also couldn't tear his eyes from the deep scar in the Alchemist's arm.

"So, Alchemist," Asif said, "what's the shell worth to you?"

The Alchemist chuckled. "Ah-ha. You didn't risk your hide for free, eh?"

"No, milord. We did not."

"You've got a great career as a smuggler ahead of you, Asif. You and Salit did well. You, too, Dubban Quartermain. What's an Imperial shell worth? All my Essence. All Pangaea. The moon and Sanguine, put together. Name your price, my fine young Devil."

Asif thought, fingering the gold ring piercing his eyebrow. "Well, Dub and me, we've got urgent business in the Far Reaches. Got to get there fast. Tell me what'll get us there faster 'n' a smuggler's wagon?"

"Oh, that's easy. Steal a Vigilance windship."

The Alchemist rummaged among the junk on his table, extracted a water-stained databoard and stylus, and sketched a map of Marketplace. Dubban peered over the magister's shoulder as the Alchemist penciled in service halls through the angels' mezzanine, corridors below the ground-level quadrants, and security monitors on lampposts, some of which Dubban recognized, some he'd never noticed in four and a half years.

"There's a hangar and an airfield behind the Vigilance Authority cloudscraper," the Alchemist said. "Can't see it from Marketplace but it's there, I assure you. The natalry complex and Security Number Administration cordon off the field. You can't get near it from the outside. Quickest way in is straight through Vigilance Authority."

Asif was bobbing his head, *yes, yes, yes.* Dubban was shaking his back and forth, *no, no, no, I'm not doing this.*

The Alchemist grinned. "Once you're inside, the field is wide-open to the skies. There's a control tower and watchtowers and sentries, but don't worry, Dubban, once you're in a ship, no one will dare fire on you. No one, not even vigiles, will damage an operating windship. Much too rare. Much too expensive. Not to mention irreplaceable. This is the back lot where they store ships that have slowed down or gone bust."

"Why doesn't someone repair them?" Dubban said.

"No one but the angels can remember how to read the codes. And the angels can't rouse themselves from dreaming long enough to lift a finger, let alone do something useful. Look here," the Alchemist said, stabbing his forefinger on his sketch of Vigilance Authority. "This is the drud door leading to the main waste chamber. Never posted with a guard. Much too filthy. And it's a tiny little thing. You two tall fellows will have to get down on your hands and knees, do a bit of crawling in the muck."

It happened fast.

One minute Dubban was thumbing the urgency switch concealed beneath the lintel of the exit portal, the portal was sliding open, and they were scrambling into the cabin of a small cruiser. A two-seater, the back bay equipped with shackles for three prisoners, the thing was festooned with light blue warning kaligraphs. Stay away from anything marked with dark blue or black warnings, the Alchemist had said. It's got no power left.

The next minute Asif was crouching before the bridge controls, slapping at switches.

"Damn, Asif, slow down," Dubban said. His apprehension distilled into icy clarity. *I've never actually flown one,* the Alchemist had said with his ironic smile. *But I know they're all precalibrated. Just look for instructions.*

The large sturdy rod topped with a huge pliable black bulb protruding dead center in the intimidating instrument panel—that had to be the driveshaft.

"They've spotted us," Asif said as vigiles converged from every corner of the airfield. "Let's get out of here, eh?"

Dubban punched a modest red button overlaid with the kaligraph for GO, another that promised UP.

And the next minute after that, they were levitating two leagues high or more, zooming straight up at such speed that Dubban's head clunked against the low ceiling, his stomach dropped through the floor, and his ears felt as if a giant thumb had stuffed them full with cotton.

Asif whooped and slapped his thigh with his gnarled hand.

Dub and Devil gawked for half a moment, eyes wide with wonder. The vault of the sky stretched up forever, the megalopolis looked like a child's building blocks, and a cloud like a heap of wool blew directly at them. Asif shouted in alarm, but the windship passed right through the heap, which turned out to be only wet curls of mist.

Dubban was beyond shouts. Once he'd gazed up at Vigilance windships, believing he'd never ride in one. Now he knew why the Imperium denied windships to druds and servs. *Because, from this height, we'd see that we're not really any smaller than angels and magisters. Or rather, we're all that small.*

Asif pointed out the rear portal. "Dub, here they come!"

Dubban seized the restraining strap from the back of a crew seat and hauled himself into the bucket. He swiveled the seat and surveyed the sky behind him with a critical eye. He was beginning to enjoy this.

Patrol windships rose from the airfield and lumbered skyward, bound for pursuit. From the lead ship's snout came a burst of white and the ejection of a silky banner that sailed across the sky.

Dubban grinned. *You may huff and you may puff but that won't blow us down, magisters.* The Alchemist had been right. Vigilance wouldn't dare destroy a windship, even one powering down.

But then the next ship ejected a silky banner, and the ship beside it. With boggling speed, the ships began weaving a gigantic skyborne net.

Vigilance meant to *catch* them!

"Let me see," Dubban said. "The Far Reaches is due west of Appalacia, right?"

"Right," Asif said. "Hurry *up*, Dub."

Pursuers and net suddenly shifted into a higher speed. In an eyeblink the phalanx closed the distance between them by half.

The Devil let loose a string of curses and clamped a hand to his belt of weapons.

"Hang on to your devil stars." Dubban massaged GO with his left thumb, persuaded WEST with his right.

With the soft cough of a gear locking in and a screaming burst of speed, the cruiser left Our Sacred City so many leagues behind, Dubban hadn't yet remembered to take another breath.

"I am glad to see you again, my mother." But Dubban wasn't sure whether he felt glad at all.

He knelt at Bandular's feet, as family protocol required of a youngest child, and kissed her hand, biting back sorrow at how much his beautiful mother had aged. White threaded her abundant black hair. Troubled lines bunched at the corners of her eyes and her mouth.

Always a serv pure. He saw how her Pannist belief in purity had gnawed at her, diminishing her like rust or erosion. Her reticence, pious and noble of a good Pannist serv, struck him as pitiable. Contemptible, even.

The rambling hovel devoid of one touch of adornment—the abode of a good serv family devoted to Pan—wrung dry of joy.

They slouched around the kitchen door, the five of his twenty brothers who had returned to the family homestead after the Big Shock. His gentle father stood a step behind them, stooped and frail after the burden of raising twenty-one sons, more diminished than Bandular. All in slightly shabby serv togs, his family regarded him and his flamboyant escort with hard judgmental eyes.

What would they think of him and Plaia?

"What is the meaning of this, my son?" Bandular whispered.

With the least ferocious sneer Dubban could persuade from him, Asif leaned against the Vigilance cruiser parked in the backyard tato patch.

"My mother, this Devil kidnapped me at dagger point and conscripted me to come here with him."

"Why?"

"Because I'm a midwife. There's a confinement camp for impure women hidden below Stark Hills. They came to you for help but you turned them away."

Bandular made the sign of the Imperial star over her breast and spit over her right shoulder. "Impure."

"The Devil brought me here to plead on their behalf for your knowledge and assistance. My mother, you told me when I was a child that you knew all about forbidden things."

"Not a child anymore, are you?" she said dryly, looking him up and down.

"No, I'm not. And I'm asking you to help these women. They need you. One woman in particular needs you." He jutted his chin at Asif. "His bonded one."

"I don't understand, my son. How many times I've longed for your company since you left home. Now you show up with a Devil and a stolen windship, demanding that I act as midwife for impure women. Do you have any notion what that will entail?" At his nod, she added, "What do you gain from this?"

"He releases me. I return to my woman in Atlan."

That won Bandular's full attention. "Oh, my son," she cried and clasped his shoulders. "You've found someone proximate? You've pledged yourself in sharelock?"

No and no, he wanted to answer. But he had no time to convince Bandular of something she would find impossible to understand or accept. Instead he said, "Something like that. Now, will you come with us, my mother? Bring your medicines kit, and hurry. Asif says Salit's time is very near."

Bandular eyed the windship with deep suspicion. He expected an interrogation over exactly how he and the Devil had acquired possession of a Vigilance craft and Bandular's customary homily about never mingling what belongs to one purity with another.

She only said with a quaver of fear, "Servs are forbidden to ride in the air."

Dubban grinned. "My mother, just cover your eyes."

"They're gone," Asif called as he ducked out of the low mouth of a cavern, loped down a boulder-strewn declivity, and leapt into the cruiser. "Place is swept clean. Let's get out of here."

Dubban pressed GO, shifted the driveshaft, and felt inordinately pleased when the cruiser rose and nosed forward at a reasonable speed. He doubted he would have noticed the tiny cavern entrance tucked behind a stand of scrubby coastal pine, even in his boyhood days of rambling about these barren hills. Bandular had declined the comfortable seat in the cruiser's cabin and huddled, veil pulled over her face, on the hard floor of the prisoners' bay.

Dubban couldn't help wondering if Asif, a stranger to these parts, had been mistaken about the cavern.

If the camp's departure worried him, though, the Devil's expression betrayed no sign. "Our confinement camps stay on the move," Asif said, panting slightly.

"The better to confound Vigilance and any unfriendly neighbors."

"Where next?"

Asif held up a small object. It was a little bundle of twigs haphazardly tied with black string, threaded with what appeared to be wisps of white and vermilion hair.

"Salit's," Asif said by way of explanation, touching his fingertip to the bundle. "Her signal says they're two leagues away, above a valley of red rock. Know the place?"

Dubban felt a breath on his neck.

Bandular leaned over her youngest son, one eye still shielded from blasphemy by her veil, the other eye avidly peering at the sight of her homeland from half a league high. A surge of his old affection for her nearly overwhelmed him.

He patted her hand. "You know the place, my mother?"

"Yes. Ushushwana Bowl. See the tall trees, my son?" The arboreal specimens of Pangaean exuberance nearly touched a clutch of low clouds. "Turn east just as you clear them."

"This way, Dame Bandular," the camp mistress said respectfully, though she couldn't restrain a reproachful glance at the eminent midwife-natalist who had snubbed her. She smiled coolly at Dubban. "Please do hurry."

Big-bellied and droop-breasted beneath flowing qaftans, grim-eyed, grim-mouthed women crept among campfires and tents of black sacking. Meager women with an air of depletion.

Dubban heard anguished cries and muffled shrieks. The tentsite sounded much like a harvesting sanctum, with the added disturbance of angry yelps and wails of a hundred newly emerged babes. A fetid odor permeated the air—the odor of fleshly procreation, but vastly different from what Dubban knew. Blood, excrement, and something sour, maybe spilled milk. Impure babes crawled, toddled about, or crouched around the campfires, their tiny misshapen faces solemn or sulky or fearful. The older babes—children of no more than three or four years—tended the newborns. Gravid women doled out flatbreads from neatly bound bales, lardsticks and codsticks from other bundles, jars of water and sops and juices packed into pouches.

Everything prepared for ready flight.

A subterranean spring spilled through the tentsite, thoroughly chilling the air. A path led up a ledge to a high ceiling honeycombed with nooks and crannies and housing a covey of bloodbats. Every now and then leathery wings slithered against rock, a squeal echoed, and a bestial eye glinted with reflected campfire light and blinked back into darkness.

"This way, midwives." The camp mistress led them into a tent. Lanterns burned, ejecting trails of oilwood smoke that had collected at the apex in a foul cloud. Dubban wiped the sting from his eyes and cupped his hand over his nose and mouth.

They came to bedrolls. There lay the Devil girl, though Dubban barely recognized her in her gravid condition, her belly a snail's shell perched upon her frail figure. A pure woman lay next to her, he was surprised to see. An erotician by the look of her, all glossy copper-colored skin and masses of bronze-colored hair. The two women held hands, shapely copper-colored fingers wrapped around small gnarled ones.

"Bring me hot water," Bandular commanded, withdrawing her medicines kit, "and clean bedding and bandages. What herbs are these?" She took a sack from the hands of an attendant, pulled it open, sniffed. "Ovata and nettle, very good. It will help stanch the blood. Is this angelica? We'll use it only if we must hasten delivery. Brew me a strong tea." She glanced around. "And break it down."

"I beg your pardon?" the camp mistress said.

"The tent," Bandular said impatiently. "We need fresh air and more light without all this smoke. Turn up the lanterns, once the tent is down."

The camp mistress began to protest, but Bandular silenced her with an imperious wave of her hand. Several impure women leapt forward and set to, knocking down tent poles, flinging back flaps of sacking.

"You," she said to Asif. "Get your bonded one off her back and up on her feet. Don't argue with me, just do it. Walk her. That's right, back and forth, slowly, steadily." To Dubban, "My son, I'm sorry to ask you to touch a drud, but you must do the same for her."

"I don't mind touching a drud," Dubban said. To Tahliq, who cast a quick angry glance at Bandular, he said, "Especially one as beautiful as she is."

"You're gracious beyond your Pannish duty, serv," the erotician murmured, slinging her arm around Dubban's waist and taking the hand he offered. She smiled tremulously. "And a delight to my eyes, as all your bedmates must tell you. I am Tahliq Jahn Pentaput. What's your name?"

"I'm Dubban. I'm a midwife."

"Midwife Dubban, I need to lie down."

"Me, too," Salit called out in a high, apprehensive voice. "I want to lie next to Tahliq. I can feel my bearing coming. Our vow, Tahliq. Remember your vow to me."

"Of course I'll remember," the erotician answered softly, and uttered an inhuman groan.

Both women commenced convulsing as waves of pain shook them over and over, coming faster, with greater violence. Dubban could hardly stand to watch, knowing that the women and their babes might die. That their long difficult months of carrying the unborn, all their labor and pain, might be squandered.

"Stack that bedding behind them," Bandular commanded. Despite her reluctance to touch an impure girl, she began vigorously kneading Salit's lower back, digging her thumbs deep into the scrawny flesh of the girl's hips. She did the same for the erotician. "That's right, *push* against the ache," she said, and then back to the girl, her brow beading with perspiration.

"Give me the hastening tea," Salit said and Bandular held the cup of angelica tea to the impure girl's mouth.

"You," Bandular said to Asif, "hold your bonded one's hands. Tightly! And you," she said to the camp mistress, "assist the erotician. My son," she said with a wry smile, "you're about to become a true midwife."

Bandular knelt between Salit's knees, directed Dubban to kneel before Tahliq, and he saw the ring of muscles in the women's bodies open and shut and then open again. Blood and fluids were flowing, soaking the bedding beneath both women, sending out a powerful odor.

Dubban heard the whisper of wings overhead and then the Devil girl gave a great shout. A wriggling bright blue creature slid out, a tiny boy from the even tinier scrotal sack between his thighs, and then a snaky blue cord.

Bandular's eyes widened into coins of astonishment as she wiped away the sediment clogging the child's eyes and nose. She took a knife from her medicines kit, cut the cord, and tied it off at the babe's feed button. She felt for the child's life signs, handed him up to Salit, and watched him greedily reach for his mother's small, high breast.

"Dear Pan," she whispered and made the sign of the Imperial star. "I've never seen a healthy child with such color."

Salit was laughing and weeping and crying out, "I did it. Oh, my bonded one, I did it. I am a Heaven's Devil extraordinaire!"

Asif embraced her and his son, tears drenching his lopsided face, a grin stretching from one huge ear to the other tiny one. "You are my Heaven's Devil extraordinaire, Salit. Before these witnesses, I name our son Latif Zehest Zehar."

"Latif," Salit whispered. "See how strong and finely made he is."

"Already he shows signs of powerful blood," Asif whispered.

"Be calm, it's over," Bandular admonished her, but a

smile curved her stern face. She kneaded her fist into the
impure girl's shrunken belly. "This will persuade your
body that its labor is done." She handed the girl a cup
of the stanching tea. "You did well, Devil girl."

"Give me the hastening tea, too," Tahliq said.

Dubban held the cup to her lips, but in her pain she
could not drink. A movement distracted him, and he
glanced up. A brace of bloodbats had collected outside
the protective circle of impure women surrounding the
birthing beds.

"This is why we put the ones delivering in tents," the
camp mistress said. She tightened her grip on Tahliq's
hands and hissed a command to the impure women,
who drew knives and gathered closer. The camp mistress nodded at the bats, which had begun to mutter
and hiss. "The smell of blood drives them mad."

Dubban watched as the erotician's portal widened
and contracted and widened again. Still the head of the
erotician's babe would not thrust out the way Salit's
babe had.

"My mother," Dubban said, "something's wrong."

Bandular darted next to him, took his place between
the erotician's knees. She placed one hand on the
woman's belly, and with the other reached beneath her
shift. "Tahliq," she said, "was the father a big man?"

"A vigile," Tahliq whispered. "A magister."

"*This* is why the purities should not mingle, my son.
Oh, I know very well you think I'm provincial and old-
fashioned. The vigile's child is too big for her. It will rip
her apart. Or we will have to." She leaned over Tahliq's
distraught face and smoothed sweat from her brow.
"Do you want your child to die with you? Or shall we
remove it, that it may live?"

"And I must die?" Tahliq gasped.

"It's likely," Bandular said quietly.

"No," Salit cried. The impure girl tore her babe from
her breast, thrust him at Asif, and bent over the erotician. She clutched Tahliq's hand between her two
gnarled ones. "You cannot, Tahliq. You know too
many things. My friend, don't leave me!"

"Save the child," Tahliq whispered.

Dubban glanced up again. The bloodbats had sidled closer. Some of the impure women abandoned their posts, reluctant to confront the creatures.

"Asif," Dubban whispered urgently, "keep them back."

Asif unsheathed his dagger and gripped a devil star.

Bandular plunged a needle of nopaine into the erotician's arm, lifted Tahliq's shift, and smeared a numbing ointment over her abdomen. Then she swiftly cut, dipped in, and lifted out an enormous babe with smooth copper-colored skin. Bright blond hair covered the huge head. The babe squalled and punched the air with his fists. Dubban took him, glimpsing blue eyes already glinting with fire.

Bandular reached for needle and thread and set to work on the ravaged flesh, but the erotician's blood flowed freely. Tahliq paled. Her flesh turned to ice in Dubban's hands.

Tahliq said to Salit, "As I vowed to you, so you must vow to me, my Salit. Grow up my child for me."

"But I'm only an impure. Wanted by the Imperium."

"The Imperium has no place for him, either. You pledged your child to me as a servant. I pledge my child to you as a warrior in your struggle. Name him Jahnni, in honor of his mother. *Vow* to me."

Salit said, "I vow to you. Before your Essence and mine, he is Jahnni. Naitre . . . naitre of what purity, Tahliq?"

"He has no purity. He is Jahnni of the Far Reaches," the erotician whispered.

A bloodbat leapt forward and crouched over the erotician, its fanged mouth agape. Women were shouting, Salit screaming, Asif brandishing his weapons, unable to attack without harming the erotician, too. Dubban made to beat the bat back with his fist when to his bewilderment Tahliq reached up and stroked the beast's face.

"Ba'reesha, my sweet," she said. "How did you find me? Why have you come?"

"Hush, my friend," the creature said and ran her black tongue over the erotician's ravaged belly the way an animal would tend one of its wounded.

Dubban swung his fist at the bat, but Tahliq held up her hand. "It's all right. She's not harming me. She's half-human."

"Human?" Dubban said.

Tahliq gasped. "Yes. Grown with others of her kind in a natalry in Outer Tasman."

If the creature meant to stanch the blood, and not feed, the effort succeeded. But it was too late. Tahliq gasped one last breath. Her head canted back, her lips and fingertips already blue with death.

"She's gone to the Bosom of Pan," Bandular whispered and made the sign of the Imperial star. "May Pan preserve her for Eternity." She furiously clapped her hands. "Hai, you beast. Begone!"

The bloodbat ignored Bandular, reached into a pouch hidden in her fur, and withdrew a shroud of black gossamer. This she flung over the erotician, wrapping the corpse snugly within. The creature turned to Salit and said, "Sah lah. Zeeeeerrrrr?" The bloodbat repeated, "Sah lah. Zeeeeerrrrr?"

"Yes," she whispered. "I am Salit Zehar."

The bloodbat handed her a parchment scroll neatly rolled around a delicate wooden spindle. Then the bat tenderly lifted Tahliq in her brawny arms, levitated straight up, and flew into the darkness gathered at the cavern's ceiling.

Dubban stared, horrified. Would the covey feed on the corpse? He didn't want to contemplate that as he mourned for the erotician, who had impressed him with her charm and vivacity in even so brief a meeting. He thrust the copper-colored boy into Salit's arms and laughed softly when the new babe seized her. Asif exchanged Latif for the scroll. Salit's eyes sprang wide as both babes, copper and blue, avidly sought her breasts.

"That's why you've got two of 'em, Salit," Dubban said.

"Thanks a lot, midwife," she snapped.

Asif unrolled the scroll and brandished it. A set of kaligraphs with distinctive, elaborate serifs danced across the parchment—

VIGILANCE COMES FOR YOU

Asif dropped the scroll. "Salit, someone warns us!" He said to Dubban, hoarse with urgency, "We must hide them."

An ominous whirring sound flooded the cavern from outside.

A windship. A Vigilance windship.

The impure women scattered, seizing babes and children, bales of food, weapons, and medicine as they scrambled into the dark recesses of the cavern.

Dubban seized Bandular, Salit, and the two babes, and took them to the foot of the path winding up from the cavern floor. "Go," he said. "Climb as high as you can. Look for a tunnel through the ceiling. The bats must have a way out. I don't think they'll bother you now."

"But, my son," Bandular said. "What about you?"

"Asif and I will stave them off to the count of ten, then we'll follow you. If you can, rendezvous back at the cruiser." He and Asif had hidden the craft in a thatch of brambles. "Otherwise, go home, my mother, and stay there. Take Salit and the babes with you. Hide them. Don't let our family see them, if you can manage it. Asif and I will retrieve the craft and meet you at your house." He grinned at Bandular's pained expression and patted her cheek. "Then I'll take all these Devils off your proper Pannish hands, all right?"

"My son, I'm proud of you," she whispered. "I want you to know that. I'm even proud of your ambitions"— she couldn't resist a tart tone—"despite the fact that they're impure and will cause you nothing but grief."

"Thank you, my mother," he replied. "I have always revered you."

"I know. Be careful."

"To the count of ten, Asif?"

"To the count of ten." Asif stood before Salit, cupping her face in his hands. "Beloved comrade and bonded one, whatever happens I will find you. Even death will never part us. I'll follow you into the Flames of Inim."

"As I will follow you," she said, growing stronger despite her ordeal. Salit shifted the two babes on her bony hips.

"Go *now*," Dubban whispered.

Bandular circled her arm around Salit. The two women, with the babes, crawled up the winding ledge and disappeared into darkness.

Dubban stood next to Asif, brandished Bandular's knife. The Heaven's Devil gripped his devil star and a dagger.

The confinement camp exploded with activity. Gravid women lumbered out of tents, leaning on each other. Other women lay helplessly, in the throes of giving birth. Newborns wailed. The clan guards closed ranks and drew daggers and devil stars.

A phalanx of enormous vigiles marched into the cavern, magmalamps blazing, firebolts brandished.

A tall, golden-haired vigile wearing badges of high rank limped forward on a prosthetic leg, fierce bodyguards fitted beneath his arms. A heavily shaped caretaker subpure marched behind him. The caretaker's eyes had been removed and replaced with orbs of carved ivory. Several protocol and discipline chips winked in her brow, and another strange, opalescent chip, the purpose of which Dubban wasn't sure. The caretaker carried a robust golden babe perched on the slab of her shoulder. The babe's pale blue eyes took in everything with a stony stare, her look of disdain enhanced by the fact that her eyes were slightly crossed.

The vigile swung his massive face to and fro as he entered the confinement camp, his eyes two spots of virulent blue fire.

Lieutenant Captain Regim Deuceman proclaimed, "Impure scum, you're under arrest. My Regima Clere," he called out in a tender voice and glanced back at the golden babe, "this is what fear looks like in the face of Vigilance."

Dubban had seen plenty of sharers coddling their newborns, but never one who spoke as if the infant could understand his every word.

"Know it well," Regim said, addressing the infant. "For this is your privilege, and your duty, and your birthright as the daughter of Clere Twine. As *my* daughter." To the impure women weeping before him, "Say whatever rites you need to say and prepare yourselves for Eternal Torment."

FACET 24

> Spider: Craft or terrorism.
> The magister cultivates the wilds,
>   capturing beasts and foes.
> The action is trapping.
> The forbearance is brutality.
>
> **The Orb of Eternity**

Commentaries:
Councillor Sausal: Pan manifests in mysterious ways and dwells in secret places. The spider is poisonous and repellent, yet it traps and kills insects noxious to the household.

So, too, Imperial law may appear stringent. Yet the Imperium enforces the law for the benefit of all the purities.

Therefore the prudent person must remain ever mindful of the law, either in the bustle of Marketplace or the privacy of one's bed. Ignorance is no excuse. [*Deleted from The Contemporary Commentaries of Sausal (15th Ed.) But beware of Imperial law that robs you of your Essence.*]
Guttersage (usu. considered vulgar): The foe lies in ambush and kills a vigile.

A vigile lies in ambush, captures a foe, and cuts her into a thousand pieces on Allpure Square.

The Far Reaches, in Our Imperial Township of Stark, northeast of Naitre Quartius Collective. The cavern above Ushushwana Bowl:

Regim ducked as a devil star spun through the air, plunging a startip deep into the bosom of his right-hand lieutenant. Startips flicked out and commenced their spiral dance of destruction, spewing shredded flesh, chews of bone, bright gobbets of magister blood.

The lieutenant screamed and fell, wide-eyed, clutching at her breast. Vigiles scattered, seeking shelter behind jags of stone. Others stood their ground as Imperial Vigilance should.

Excellent. I'll commend whoever's left standing. And whip the cowards.

Indignation lurched through Regim's blood at this unexpected resistance. Armed resistance. This was a confinement camp, a spawning ground, not a battlefield and a clash of warriors.

Regim had no time for his stricken subordinate. One glance at the bright blood spraying from her bosom told him a startip had pierced the lieutenant's heart. She'd be dead in moments. And, if by the Hand of Pan she managed to survive, he'd demote her for screaming. For showing weakness in the line of her Imperial duty before people of the impure.

He turned to the caretaker holding Regima Clere and shoved drud and daughter behind a phalanx of his best guard.

Where our child, heiress to all that is the Twine fortune, may still enjoy a view of her father in action, came Clere's whisper in sharemind. *Her handsome virile vigile of a father.*

Yes, my cherished Clere.

Regim shook his bodyguards away and stepped forward, bold and alone. He drew his firebolt and sprayed molten bullets in the direction the star had been flung from. Liquid fire struck the cavern wall in bright splats of lethal goo.

Regim surveyed the chaotic tentsite. He spied a young man, a lean woman, grotesque and lopsided the way all impures were, but surprisingly vigorous and agile. Guards, probably, darting among half-collapsed

tents and smoldering campfires. He glimpsed the glint
of caltrops, the edge of a dagger.

But no match for vigiles and Vigilance weapons.

"I said they're all under arrest. Round them up, and
be quick about it," he commanded his officers.

"Lieutenant captain," choked out Regim's second
lieutenant, crouching over her fallen comrade, "it's
Heaven's Devils!"

"Nonsense," Regim barked. "This is a camp for
weakling women. They've got a handful of hired
guards. Seize, disarm, and execute them."

"But, lieutenant captain, this is a *star*. A *devil*
star."

Regim seized the star through the aperture at its center and plucked it from the lieutenant's breast. He flung
it to the floor and ground his heel into the center, crush-
ing its sentience the way Clere had shown him before
she died. The memory of Clere, of how Salit Zehar had
gutted her with a devil star, enraged him so acutely that
for a moment he couldn't see.

"I know fucking well what it is, officer." He glanced
at Regima Clere, pleased to see that his daughter was
gazing at him with her steadfast eyes. "Take them out
in groups of three, with their babes," he said to the
squad. "Search them for weapons. Orbs of Eternity,
any other contraband." Another glance at his daughter.
"Jewelry, ores, bacco, qut. Anything worth confiscat-
ing. Then execute them all. The babes, too."

Regim swept his gaze across the tentsite. What a
prize. An impure confinement camp. The stuff of leg-
end. The subject of countless tips and leads, but few
finds. The druds he had intercepted in Stark Hills with
their herd of capras had actually disgorged real information, and all for a couple of jugs of cheap skee.

*And I, Regim Deuceman, have accomplished what
no one before me has accomplished. Now who will say
I don't deserve my rank?*

Yes, my Regim, you deserve everything, came Clere's
honeyed whisper. But was there a bitter pip in the
honey? Something sour? *You couldn't have done it
without me.*

He let that pass, though in his secret sanctuary of consciousness a rebellious thought came: *If only the dead were dead.*

Yet keen frustration needled him. He did not see what he'd really come for. He applied all his fine training and extraordinary powers of surveillance, searching shadowed corners and the swept stone floor. He noticed a spindle and a curl of parchment. Someone had abandoned a scroll. His eyes probed for the uneven edge of a trapdoor, a subterranean sanctuary, a tunnel boring down and out. He'd expected a filthy lair, unspeakable offal. The order of the camp frankly surprised him. He listened, every nerve tuned fine, for the echo of a secret chamber, the sigh of air escaping an egress. The sound of the erotician's sweet contralto.

He would know Tahliq's voice anywhere.

But he neither saw nor heard any sign of her, with or without a child.

She didn't perish beneath the magmaflow in Rancid Flats. She didn't die. And neither did my child.

Your monster, came Clere's whisper, harsh and malevolent. *Your spawn of sin.*

He shuddered with humiliation, and suddenly he was lunging at the weeping women, shouting, "Spawn of sin!" His boot toe found a swollen belly and another and another, kicking, punching, oblivious to flung daggers, flung caltrops, the shouts of the clan guards, the shouts of his squad. Filled with righteous fury he plowed into their midst, the stink of carnage overwhelming his senses. "Stamp them out. Stamp out the spawn of sin!"

A hand clawed his arm, and a grotesque face lurched into his. A tall, young impure man shouted, "This is for you, beloved bonded one!" and flung a devil star into Regim's chest.

Regim yanked the weapon from his flesh, groaning with exertion. Poison surged into his blood, making his teeth chatter. He brandished his firebolt and blasted the impure man in his gut. The smell of burning flesh and excrement nearly made him retch. The young man fell, gasping, but Regim wasn't satisfied. He wanted the man's head, gold ring piercing the ragged eyebrow and all. He fell to his knees, set to with his dagger, and claimed his prize.

"Lieutenant captain," his lieutenant said, "we must tend your wounds, sir. At once!"

"Have you found the erotician?"

"No, my lieutenant captain. We've found no woman of the purities. Only impure. Women and babes, just beasts as you've said. Lieutenant captain, I beg you—"

The spindle with its parchment lay a length from his fingertips. Regim reached for it. His eyes blurred with pain, but he saw kaligraphs with elaborate serifs, and he read—

VIGILANCE COMES FOR YOU

"Treachery," he whispered. He wasn't sure where he'd seen the style, but the kaligraphs looked familiar. "Someone warned these women."

"We've found the cruiser stolen in Atlan, lieutenant captain. It's concealed in brambles, a quarter league away. And we've found this pure."

A man bent over Regim, gently touching his chest wounds, and murmured instructions to the lieutenant. Regim glanced up with a start. Suspicion shot through him. "What are *you* doing here, Superior Father Dubban?"

"The Devil abducted me and brought me here at starpoint," said the black-haired priest, his deep voice unaccountably sad.

"Why abduct *you*?" Regim said.

"The Devil believed I knew how to deliver the unborn from a living body. He was mistaken. I only know how to pluck an emerging child from her ges tank. How to beget in the Bosom of Pan as I begot your child, lieutenant captain. Is this she?"

The priest smiled warmly at the tiny golden girl. Regim would have arrested the man for protocol violations, but to his astonishment his daughter smiled back.

"Hold still, lieutenant captain," the priest said, "and summon your bodyguards. They must suck the poison out of these wounds." At Dubban's direction, the serv bodyguards knelt, attached their mouths to Regim's chest, and obediently sucked and spit.

But suspicion bit deeper than Regim's new wounds. "I seem to see you everywhere, Superior Father Dubban. I see you in serv clothes, pleading for a pretty heretic's life in Allpure Square. I see you in Superior Father's robes, presiding at our most sacred natalry rites. And here, in the Far Reaches, consorting with the impure. Assisting them in their vile enterprise."

"At the tip of a devil star, lieutenant captain."

"So you say. Who are you, really? *What* are you?"

"I am Dubban."

"You are insolent." Regim shouted to his new right-hand lieutenant—his best *had* died, "Arrest this man. Take him outside."

A great wail exploded from the impure women.

"Raise me," he commanded his bodyguards and signaled the caretaker with Regima Clere to follow. "Say whatever rites you need to say, Superior Father Dubban, before you go to Eternal Torment."

Regim boarded his windship, bent on dispensing justice, and his infant daughter began to whimper. It wasn't that Regima Clere disliked the craft's cool air, wanted a milksop, or needed to relieve herself. The tiny golden girl always cried around Gunther Triadius.

Our Regima Clere doesn't like the academe, chided Clere.

The academe had wanted to accompany Regim into the cavern, but Vigilance business was no business of his, and Regim had ordered him to remain aboard. A livid scar was visible through the academe's dull yellow curls where he'd sustained a contusion to the back of his skull. Regim suspected the academe had swooned in a skee stupor and struck the floor of some saloon. But Gunther claimed he'd been attacked at his begetting

ceremony. Now the academe gaped at the sight of
blood and Regim's torn tunic. His eyes narrowed when
he glimpsed the priest.

Regima Clere screwed up her face and began to gulp.
Dubban shook free of his Vigilance escorts and strode
to the caretaker. He took the babe and expertly cradled
her.

Vigiles lunged forward to restrain him, but Regim
brandished a hand. Crooning, the priest coaxed another
smile from Regim's solemn little daughter.

Our Regima Clere likes the priest, came Clere's
whisper. *How often do we see her smile?*

"Lieutenant captain," Gunther said in a vicious
voice, "may I inquire why you've brought this low pure
aboard?"

"He's middle pure, the same as you," Regim said.
His suspicions veered away from the priest toward
Gunther.

He'd only permitted the academe on this foray at the
insistence of Ground Control. The bureau had gotten
wind of Regim's immediate departure for Tasman and
wished to send an observer. The bureau had force-
flooded Tasman Rift. Extreme earthshock activity had
plagued the area ever since.

The chips in the caretaker's forehead blazed furiously, sensing the absence of her charge. The chip that
precisely guided her movements spun her around and
sped her to the priest. Blind arms reached. Blind fingers
grasped. The caretaker seized the child from the man's
arms and clutched Regima Clere to the pillows installed
in her breasts.

Regima Clere bawled, loosening another shower of
tears.

The caretaker turned her eyeless face toward the
child and murmured the soothing lullabies the discipline chip funneled through her half-dead mind. She
had cost Regim a fortune.

Gunther snapped his fingers. "I've seen this man before. In Atlan. At my begetting ceremony." The
academe touched the back of his head and grimaced.

"After which my sharer ran away. Rumor says"—he circled Dubban, who gazed back impassively—"she was seen with a dark-haired man. A serv, not a priest."

"Why do you doubt him?" Regim said.

"I entered sharemind with him during the ceremony," the academe said. "I caught him coveting my sharer, and his sharemind was a paltry thing. If he's truly a priest, let him demonstrate his priestly consciousness."

"Very well," Regim said. He invoked purity sharemind and easily overwhelmed priest *and* academe since they were only middle pures. Dubban manifested in sharemind as a dull copper ball, Gunther as a flame leaping in a bronze brazier. Strange the discrepancy. But Regim knew little of middle pures, who were notorious for their disparities.

Regim forged into Dubban's consciousness and entered a maelstrom of images—

A beautiful woman. Hair tumbling down her back— reddish gold or bronze? Huge eyes—golden green or dark? A voluptuous body—petite or robust?

Regim started back. Did he see one woman or two? Somehow he recognized them both, and they tumbled together. Superior Father Dubban was either very confused or very skillful at evading a superior sharemind.

Strange little impure women with dark slitted eyes, broad flat faces bearded with reddish fur.

A woman sighing in rapture.

A woman moaning in pain. Blood streaming from her hands, from her belly, from between her thighs.

A knife blade slashing. Across a tiny hand. A swollen abdomen. Two abdomens. Three.

Diamond-shaped chips embedded in blood. Human organs forked out of a wound. The head of a newborn poking out of another sort of wound.

And blood, blood, so much blood. . . .

"Enough!" Regim shouted. He lurched out of sharemind. "Superior Father Dubban, I don't know who or what you are. I do not hate you, after what you've done for me and for Regima Clere. But you have been apprehended in an impure confinement camp. Abducted or not, you were assisting the impure. You must be punished. My reputation depends upon my constancy to the Imperium."

The priest paled.

Regim said, "I charge you with collusion in impure activities, sedition, and crimes against the Imperium, to be mitigated by the abduction threat applied against you and thus not punishable by death." A vigile-scribe leapt forward, databoard in hand. "A trial is unnecessary. You've been apprehended by a Vigilance officer in plain sight of witnesses to your crimes. Summary judgment is warranted."

The priest said, "I'm the Superior Father who begot your child, lieutenant captain. I've assisted you with your wounds. Not once, but twice."

"Yes. You need not tender an accounting to me. I'm a vigile and a magister pure. Honor is my Imperial duty." No, he would not execute the man who had coaxed his stern-eyed daughter into a smile. Two smiles. "I hereby banish you to the Tertius Detainment Center in North Scanda. Sergeant? Take him in the cruiser. At once. Get him out of here." To Dubban, "There you will remain in custody and incommunicado for twelve years, serving at whatever labor the wardens require of you. I grant you leave to send a message to one person." He lowered his voice. "Who shall it be, Superior Father Dubban?"

Curiosity needled Regim. Had the handsome priest stolen Gunther's runaway sharer? Would he give her whereabouts away?

Gunther leaned forward, craning his neck to hear the priest's answer.

Dubban stared contemptuously at the academe, then turned stolid dark eyes to Regim. "Lieutenant captain," he said softly, "there is no one."

Madagaz.

Madagaz overflowing with spring storms was only

slightly less repellent than Madagaz in steaming muck before the rains had come. The rains brought coolness and a respite from the reek of rustic towns and unimaginably huge swamps. But the rains also brought knee-deep floods thick with leeches that swept over country roads, carrying off drayers and wagons.

Regim had seen Madagaz just before the rains. He had flown to the wretched place as soon as he'd received Prinz's shocking message. Had flown in and flown out again, bound for the Far Reaches and the cavern above Ushushwana Bowl.

Now he was back.

He perched on a three-legged stool, easing the pressure in his hip socket from the prosthetic leg. He'd dismissed his bodyguards, but leaned on the shoulder of the caretaker. She held Regima Clere perched on her other shoulder.

Regim held a scented kerchief to his nose and mouth and breathed narcotic sweetness. How he loathed lengthy interrogations. He would have preferred to entrust the task to the torturers crewing aboard his windship. But the questions were too sensitive, the answers—as they might be divulged—too confidential.

He asked again, "Why did you let her leave, my young Prinz, when I instructed you to detain her? When I informed you she is cunning? Seditious? Resourceful?"

No answer but an anguished moan.

Regim heard shouting and the sound of a scuffle outside the interrogation chamber. Quite dismal, the security at Madagaz Vigilance. The young vigile's clan, no doubt. The local chief commander had reluctantly agreed to keep the clan at bay on pain of demotion by Imperial decree.

Regim needed answers. Prinz should have answered the first time. If he had, he wouldn't have found himself in this terrible predicament.

Regim had no time left. His search of the cavern at Ushushwana Bowl had yielded nothing. Now he needed to know exactly what the young vigile had learned

about Tahliq. What Tahliq may have revealed to this
silly boy about *him*. More than anything, about *him*.

He kneaded his eyes.

So fine the muscular young body stretched before
him, vibrant with youth and glorious health. Prinz's
limbs were as whole and strong and perfect as the day
he emerged from his Secundus ges tank. Just as Regim
had once been whole. Had been perfect.

He signaled Gunther to tighten the rack, which the
academe did with an obliging sneer. A cheerful torturer.
Regim wasn't surprised. How he despised the academe.
Yet who else among the windship crew could he trust
with the secrets of this interrogation? His vigiles, even
the torturers, would enter everything they saw and
heard into vigilance sharemind. No confidence told here
would be safe from the Chief Commander.

The young vigile quivered. At extreme tension, bones
pull loose of their sockets, skin tears, joints distend with
an audible *pop*.

"I told you," the young vigile ground out. "The carnival was leaving town. I thought I could keep her in
Madagaz. I thought that's what you ordered. Detain
her . . . without . . . her . . . knowing . . . the
reason. . . ."

Regim signaled Gunther to ease the pulleys.

"You young people just don't listen," Regim said. "I
said detain her by force, if necessary." He leaned close.
"Tell me again, what was her condition?"

"She carried an unborn," the young vigile said in a
rush. "She said the seeder was a high-ranking vigile
with Atlan Vigilance. Famous for his ferocity. She was
proud."

"And she never said who?"

"No, I swear."

Regim thought. "When you entered our collective
consciousness with your message, you started to say
you'd experienced something with her. Something unbelievable."

"You . . . you stopped me, sir."

"The time wasn't right for your revelation. You may tell me now."

"She possesses magister sharemind. Even though she's a drud, and an erotician at that. She compelled me into powerful sharemind."

Regim slumped back. He felt stunned and weak as if someone had struck him. The bliss he'd always felt with the erotician—she possessed superior sharemind? How well he recalled that beyond the bedding, fulfilling as that was, there was her enfolding tenderness that had soothed and delighted him.

Ah, my Tahliq.

Clere's voice shrieked into his consciousness, *How dare you, you puny idiot. You big stupid lout of a walkabout.*

Regim rocked his head in his hands. In the secret sanctum of his consciousness he finally mourned for all he had lost when he lost Tahliq.

In a while he realized Gunther, Regima Clere, and the young vigile stretched out on the rack, were gazing at him expectantly.

"Tell me again," Regim said, "why you believed you could keep her here in Madagaz."

Prinz returned a weak smile. "I led her to believe I would keep her as my bedmate if she stayed. That I might enter sharelock with her."

"Did you?" Regim's heart froze into a fist of ice.

"Sure. She couldn't stay away from me. We bedded every chance we got. She told me she loved me."

Regim didn't know how or when, exactly, but suddenly he had his hands wrapped around the young vigile's throat, and his thumbs were finding the slender reed of a windpipe.

"She never loved you," Regim whispered. "There's only one man Tahliq Jahn Pentaput has ever loved. One, do you hear me?"

"Lieutenant captain." Gunther's hand gripped his elbow. "There's a back door. Your crew awaits you. Step this way, lieutenant captain. Hurry."

• • •

"It's good to be going home, isn't it, Gunther Triadius?" Regim said quietly. "I've missed Our Sacred City."

"So have I, lieutenant captain."

They stood on the bridge of the windship, speeding north above thunderclouds. Speeding toward Atlan. Regim held the warning scroll he'd retrieved in the confinement camp and studied the kaligraphs with their fancy serifs. *Where have I seen these before?* "This mission has been a failure, hasn't it?"

"I'd hardly call extermination of an entire impure confinement camp a failure, sir. Banishment of a suspect priest. Punishment and execution of a seditious vigile—"

"Speak no more of it, academe. Any of it."

"Yes, lieutenant captain."

North of Buruma the windship flew over a sobering sight: the awesome, newly cleaved crevice of Himal Rift.

Regima Clere had been put to bed, the caretaker lightly dozing next to the infant's cradle in the crew quarters. *If only I could enter sharemind with Regima Clere,* Regim thought and absently rubbed the sharelock chip in the back of his hand.

What kind of a thought is that? came Clere's whisper. *Our Regima Clere has seen the moon wax and wane but once in her precious little life.*

I've heard just about enough from you, he snapped back and was pleased when her whisper fell silent.

Regim gazed down into the darkness of the rift and searched in vain for the magmatic core of the world that the academe had spoken of. The crevice might as well have been bottomless.

"It's like a wound." Regim touched his ravaged chest and sipped skee from his pocket flask. "A wound in the world."

"And what do you do with a wound?"

"Bandage it."

"And if the bandages don't hold?" the academe said.

"You *stitch* them shut."

"But bedrock isn't skin. It doesn't renew itself like skin. So what do you *do* with rock? Lieutenant captain, *look* at that rift. Look at the size of it. How do you stitch it shut?"

The question intrigued Regim. "Well, water hasn't worked. Fill it up with more rock."

Gunther glanced at him curiously. "But how can you fill up something so massive? Where would you transport the rock *from*?"

Gazing down into that yawning gape Regim glimpsed a vision. "Fill it up with itself."

"I'm sorry, lieutenant captain?"

Regim thrust the academe into common consciousness.

Avalanches. Cliff faces bursting apart, slabs of stone the size of city blocks shearing away.

Rock exploding, shattering into ten billion bits of gravel, showering down into the unthinkable depths.

Cascades of broken stone lying still at last. Burying the terrible gaps. Sealing them, forever.

"Construct a firebolt," Regim said, "as big as Marketplace. Launch it into the rift. Collapse the world shell *into* itself. There's enough rock surrounding the rifts to do the job, isn't there?"

Gunther gazed at him, shiny-eyed. "Whoever said magisters have no imagination got it wrong. This is genius, sir! But it will take more than one firebolt, however huge. Many more firebolts. They must be positioned just so in each major rift. There are fifteen major rifts in the world archipelago, lieutenant captain. Each with significant tributary fissures."

"The effort will be considerable?"

"The effort and the *cost* will be considerable, never mind mustering the technology. It could take a decade, maybe longer. In the meantime, Pangaea will have to endure"—he gestured at the ruined landscape beneath them, the abandoned villages perched at rift's edge— "more of *this*."

"But once done, the shell would be permanently stabilized? It would be . . . an ultimate solution?"

"An ultimate solution," Gunther said. "Yes! What a splendid way of putting it. Oh, the bureau has reviewed dozens of new proposals since force-flooding failed. Cement, epoxies, landfill, in quantities so huge it would take a hundred years to engineer. Nothing I've reviewed has the simplicity, the power, of *this*. Let me see." He cautiously rubbed his tonsure. "The Temple of the Mind of the World will need to commission a new series of dreams from the angels. Flooding is finished. The ultimate solution is the key. The High Council will need to conscript the weapons consortiums. And raise taxes through the roof."

"That," Regim said, "is *just* what the Imperium is good for."

"We've been at it for over half a season, Lieutenant Captain Deuceman," said the Cardinal of the Mind of the World. Blue pinpricks of eyes tucked in golden pincushions of flesh darted from Regim to Gunther and warily back again. "And, yes, our internal investigation goes well, thank you for asking. Did I welcome you back to Atlan, sir?"

"Half a dozen times," Regim said and smiled at the loathsome magister's fear.

He and a small entourage—his bodyguards, Gunther, Regima Clere and her caretaker, his newly promoted first lieutenant—had assembled for this cozy tête-à-tête in the Chamber for Pure Thoughts. The stupendous white-marble tiers surrounding a suspension well were deserted. Every breath, every shuffle of a boot, reverberated off the cavernous ceiling and sent ghostly echoes throughout the chamber.

Regim had never entered the temple before, neither the ornate public ballrooms nor the high-security labyrinth where the real work of the Mind of the World transpired. He admitted to himself that he'd always been a little afraid of the place.

The Cardinal said, "We've been pursuing the investigation ever since I summoned Milord Lucyd before a Grand Jurare to account for the invasion of his dreams. Early last winter, wasn't it?" She turned to a temple functionary, who anxiously murmured in agreement.

"Milord Lucyd." Regim rubbed his jaw. *It all comes back to that puny, parlous angel and his dreams.* Regim needed only to close his eyes to see the translucent blue teardrop of the private windship, the decadent plaything of a decadent pure, the luxury of a traitor, gaily lofting away from the rooftop of the Salon of Shame. While a third of Rancid Flats fell beneath the hellfire of the magmaflow.

You abandoned people there, came Clere's whisper.

I fulfilled my Imperial duty, Clere. As you so precisely reminded me.

Regim's nerves coiled. "Did you bring charges against the angel, Dame Cardinal?"

"Of course not. Milord fully accounted for himself."

"And just how did he do that?"

"He vowed to the temple's satisfaction that he is not the source of the impurity. A vow he said he made to you, too, lieutenant captain, isn't that so?"

"A vow is as veracious as he or she who makes it."

"We're convinced of His Honorable Milord Lucyd's veracity, sir. Lucyd dreams the most beloved dreams in the Mind of the World. That's why the temple commissioned milord to dream of the Imperium's glorious floods. Which milord has done. More Pangaeans than ever before have dreamed Lucyd's dreams." The Cardinal gazed reprovingly at the academe. "Dreams commissioned at the behest of *your* bureau, Gunther. It's hardly the angel's fault if Ground Control's sea trenches have failed."

"With your permission, lieutenant captain," the academe said.

"Go ahead."

"The floods have not failed. The floods are only the first step. We are taking the next step. Our lieutenant captain sought this audience just as soon as we touched down in Atlan to alert you that a glorious new program is under way, and another commission of dreams will be necessary."

"I take my directives from the High Council," the Cardinal said coldly. "Not from some academe. *Or* Vigilance."

"You shall receive your directive in the usual way," Regim cut in. "Assuming you're still the supreme authority when the directive is issued." At the Cardinal's sputter, "Any inquiry into impurity, however, *is* within my purview. So tell me, Dame Cardinal, and be quick about it. What has your internal investigation revealed?"

An acolyte-auditor, whom the Cardinal identified as Sami Triademe, dangled before them in the suspension. The man couldn't conceal his expression of terrified guilt.

"Now, Sami," said the Cardinal, "don't fret. The lieutenant captain has asked me to suspend you for this brief interrogation." To Regim, "Really, this isn't necessary. He's one of our most skillful auditors and the auditor of Milord Lucyd's dreams. He's done nothing wrong."

"We shall see." Regim had observed criminals before. The man's culpability fairly glittered.

"Sami," the Cardinal said, "tell Lieutenant Captain Deuceman what happened to your aetheric shell."

"Th-they stole it!" the acolyte-auditor said, tears popping from his eyes.

"'Aetheric shell'?" Regim said, perplexed. He'd never heard of the term before. "Dame Cardinal, explain what you mean."

"That's the device by which we audit the angels' dreams," the Cardinal said. "Really, lieutenant captain, in front of these lower pures— Shall we enter magister sharemind?"

A sensation like fire seared through Regim's nerves. *A device? They use a device?* He glanced at Gunther. The academe nodded and smiled, reflecting none of the bewilderment Regim felt. *The academe has heard of this before.* The notion of entering common conscious-ness with the Cardinal—who offended him more with each passing moment—filled him with revulsion. "No, go on."

"It's an Imperial Secret, of course," the Cardinal whispered. "As you must know, given your rank. The angels also employ aetheric shells, but theirs are of far more complex and ancient manufacture. Their shells *cast* dreams into the Mind of the World by means of power waves."

"I've never seen any power waves."

"They're invisible."

Regim laughed derisively. "This sounds like talk in a saloon after too much d'ka."

"Oh, I assure you the power waves are real. And potent. In times lost to antiquity, the power had to be contained in certain types of cords and tubes. For mil-lennia, though, the power has been directed without cords. Nowadays one only requires proper transmitters. And receivers. As I said, we at the temple only *audit* the angels' dreams. Our shells can't compare to angels'."

"Then the Mind of the World is . . . artificial? Constructed by these . . . invisible waves of power?"

"You might as well say all reality is a dream of Pan, and therefore artificial. Constructed by consciousness. Who's to say otherwise?"

"*I* say otherwise." Regim angrily slapped his pros-thetic leg. "Reality is *reality.*"

"Is it? And I suppose you believe that the angels lie down in their dreamchambers and their dreams are *our* dreams. Well, they're not. Their dreams are what the Imperium commissions them to dream. But surely a high magister pure like you has always known that."

Regim slumped on the shoulders of his bodyguards. They adjusted themselves to accommodate him. He wanted to invoke Clere's whisper, demand why she'd never revealed this Secret to him, which surely as Claren Twine's daughter she must have known.

The Secret frightened him. Regim didn't like fear. He especially didn't like the Cardinal's condescending tone.

"Of *course* I've known the Secret," he lied. "Vigilance reveals all Secrets to those destined for higher ranks. Who stole the shell? And how?"

"Sami?" the Cardinal said gently.

"Th-they were impure," the acolyte-auditor said. "Heaven's Devils, with devil stars hanging from their belts. They broke into my cubicle, I don't know how. Temple security would never have let them in the door. They beat me till I lost my senses."

"That's true," the Cardinal said. "Security found our poor Sami unconscious."

"They broke my nose and my arm. Gave me two black eyes. Just about ruined my kidneys."

The acolyte-auditor still wore a sling. That could have been faked. But there was no mistaking the fresh jag across the bridge of his nose. One of Regim's older brothers had the same scar from boyhood fisticuffs, and he'd warned Regim against deforming his vigile's beauty with childish violence.

"When they were done with me," Sami said, "they swiped the shell. Muted the security monitors and ripped it clean off its moorings."

"Then this theft is the source of impure thought in Lucyd's dreams?" Regim said.

"We don't see how it could be otherwise," the Cardinal said. "We've alerted the angel."

"This is a breach of security of the gravest kind. Impure foes in possession of high Imperial technology? Have you informed the Chief Commander? Have you dispatched a special force to find the shell?"

"Of course. Surely you were informed, lieutenant captain?"

He didn't answer. Half a season ago this investigation had commenced, and neither the Chief Commander nor his father-in-lock had possessed the decency to inform him. His heartbeat began to palpitate.

The Cardinal shrank from his fury. "I don't know what the impure could possibly *do* with the shell, though. The technology is far beyond their ken. The infiltration of impurity into the Mind of the World is unfortunate, but we believe accidental. We'd see more of it, if they knew what they were doing, wouldn't we? Perhaps the shell itself inserted images of its abductors into audited dreams."

Again Regim kept silent.

"It would take a very high pure with full knowledge of the Secret to do much of anything with an Imperial shell. Naturally since the supply of shells is quite limited, we're most eager to retrieve our property, but you must understand—"

On she rattled, and Regim listened and watched, refusing to be taken in by the Cardinal's show of innocence. He studied the acolyte-auditor. *It's uncomfortable to flail about in a suspension, isn't it, Sami Triademe?*

Perhaps not uncomfortable enough.

Regim strode to the suspension panel and strengthened the opposing forces. Like the rack in Madagaz but so much more efficient.

From his slumping, fly-in-a-spiderweb posture, the acolyte-auditor arched taut, arms and legs flung high and wide. Regim sniffed, his superb Vigilance training tuned sharp. What was that bitter narcotic smell?

Qut. The acolyte-auditor was a qut addict.

"When did you say the shell was stolen, Sami?" Regim said.

"In early w-w-winter."

"Then how do you explain Lucyd's dream of Darkness on the morning of the Big Shock last summer?"

Regim stretched the acolyte-auditor tight, aching in his own bones when he did, then barged into sharemind, careening directly into—

A masonry wall as high as the sky, red and orange kaligraphs flickering across the solid surface.

WARNING. THIS PERSON IS PROTECTED BY IMPERIAL SECURITY.

What is this, Sami Triademe?

Sharemind security, lieutenant captain, for temple personnel. I didn't put it there.

Take it down.

I cannot.

Regim invoked vigilance sharemind and charged at the wall, thrusting his head and shoulders through the masonry. He glimpsed three faces on the other side. Three grotesque faces, with mismatched eyes, the twitch of twisted lips. Ridged and swollen skulls: grey hair on an old man. Platinum and vermilion bristles on the girl. And a dark thatch on the young man.

Horan Zehar.

His daughter, Salit.

And the impure man I executed in Ushushwana Bowl.

And another image: *Horan and Salit lying inside a device on either side of the acolyte-auditor. Blinking instrument panels lined the walls of the device. The acolyte-auditor reached over and touched the panels here and there.*

Regim shot out of sharemind, stepped down into the suspension well, and seized the acolyte-auditor by his puny chest. The man's head and hips remained locked in the suspension's power. Regim viciously yanked his torso free and shook him.

"Tell me the truth, Sami Triademe! Horan Zehar was one of the biggest qut dealers in Central Atlan. Did you buy your wares from him? Did you owe him money? Did he know exactly where to find you in the temple? Tell me!" he shouted and shook the man. "How could impure terrorists know how to mute Imperial security monitors? *You* did it for them."

Aware he gripped in his fists—improbably, impossibly—a shuddering human torso.

Suddenly very, very tired.

Aware of Regima Clere's reedy wail.

Aware of hands, big hands, magister hands, gripping his elbows.

Gunther Triadius leaned up into his face, calling to him as if from a great distance. "The acolyte-auditor can tell you nothing more, lieutenant captain. The Chief Commander's guard have arrived."

"The Chief Commander's guard," Regim said, words slurring. He dropped the bag of blood in his hands, taking care not to splash his boots. "Why are they here?"

"They're here for *you*, lieutenant captain."

Regim stood at attention before the Chief Commander's bench. His entourage—Gunther, the caretaker with Regima Clere, and his best lieutenant—had been detained outside. He confronted the blue-haired magister alone. She sat high above him, glowering down. His neck ached as he gazed up. It was a position, he decided, that he did not like. She didn't belong up there, all high-and-mighty.

The Chief Commander said, "You will surrender your badges, Regim Deuceman. You're relieved of your command. I'm placing you under house arrest."

"I don't think so, Gwenda," he said. He felt reckless and a little unhinged. He used his commanding officer's given name, fully intending to insult her.

"*What* did you say?" she thundered.

"I'll not surrender my badges till you tell me what troubles you."

"What *troubles* me is that you have overreached your authority for some time now. Councillor Twine persuaded me to overlook your vendetta against Milord Lucyd and promote you into surveillance. My own protocol advisors persuaded me to forgive your atrocities against the druds in Al-Muud. I myself cautioned you after you abandoned servs and druds in Rancid Flats. You have finally gone too far. Your fanaticism is your undoing, Regim Deuceman."

"*Lieutenant Captain* Deuceman. And your softness on impurity is your undoing. Clere Twine warned me about you."

"Clere Twine is dead, and your behavior has become intolerable. You are out of control."

He drew himself up, taken aback. "I am always in control. What do you mean?"

The Chief Commander began counting off his offenses on her long, thick fingers. "You have harassed, tortured, maimed, or killed druds, servs, and middle pures. You tortured and killed a young vigile from an excellent vigile clan. I received the complaint from Madagaz an hour ago. You've acquired a taste for blood and you satisfy that taste at your whim. Not according to orders. You are no better than a foe, sir. I demand your badges."

"Chief Commander, I've earned every one of my badges. I've earned them through training, dedication, tireless work, my own pain and disfigurement, and, yes, blood. Blood spilled when I wept to spill it. When no one could understand how difficult it was for me."

"I understand that you've been under a strain since your sharer was murdered. I've arranged for a physician to speak with you. You're long overdue for a rest. I'll say it one last time. Turn over your badges, Regim. You're relieved of your command."

"Come down here and take them from me, Chief Commander."

The magister sighed heavily, regret stitching every feature of her distinguished face. "I believe in your sincerity, Regim, however misguided you've become. I will grant you this one last courtesy."

She grunted softly, the leather of her boots squeaking as she climbed down, and then she stood before him, stern and sorrowful.

Regim gazed face-to-face at the Chief Commander of Vigilance Authority of Our City of Atlan. She possessed the radiant charisma of a high magister subpure. But she wasn't nearly as formidable as she appeared from her high bench. She stood a head shorter than he. Her hair was thin, her face weary, her figure slightly stooped with advanced age. A tremor shook her left hand as she extended it.

He whipped out his dagger and lopped off that trembling hand. Lopped off the other before she could scream, before she could reach for a bell to summon someone. He plunged the blade deep into her breast—

she wasn't wearing armor, the silly old bitch—and jagged the blade deep into her lungs.

He flung open the door to her chamber and shouted, "Foes! Foes have attacked. Hurry! Our Chief Commander lies dying."

But he made sure she was already dead.

"Tell them," Regim said.

"I saw the Devils appear—and disappear—just over there," Gunther said. The academe trembled and wrung his hands. He possessed the art of dramatics, then, along with the skill of torture.

Two high councillors, a prefect, and a squad of grim vigiles had gathered in the anteroom to the Chief Commander's chambers. The quorum necessary to witness Councillor Claren Twine's swearing in of Regim Deuceman as Chief Commander of Vigilance.

"Down the hall, when our Chief Commander—our *new* Chief Commander—flung open the door," Gunther said. "One of them was bleeding heavily through her tunic."

"Yet there is no trace of blood in the hall," Claren Twine said, with a penetrating glance at Regim.

"She wrapped a cloak around herself, and they vanished into thin air," Gunther declared.

Regim felt the cold fingers of Claren Twine's awesome sharemind probing his consciousness. He held firmly to the image of Salit Zehar in the field at Al-Muud, the way the Devil girl had vanished in his hands, and juxtaposed that memory with the fresh image of the Chief Commander's anguished face. His bloody hands reaching down to close her eyelids.

His father-in-lock said, "Chief Commander Regim Deuceman, you will henceforth report directly to me and the High Council at all times. Every action, every policy, must be presented and approved. You are not to act again without express permission. Do you understand?"

"Yes, my father-in-lock. But you must listen. I have

reason to believe Milord Lucyd is the traitor I feared long ago. And I found *this* at the impure confinement camp."

He reached in his pocket for the warning scroll and its fancy kaligraphs.

But Claren irritably stubbed out his cheroot into an ashtray borne in the broad hands of a bearer and shook his finger in Regim's face. "You are not to harass Lucyd. I planted a spy in his house last summer as I told you I would. I am conducting my own investigation of the angel. If I require your assistance, I will inform Vigilance." The councillor spun on his heel and strode away. "That is all, Chief Commander."

Regim exchanged glances with Gunther, who beamed at him, admiration and pride shining in his brown eyes.

"My father-in-lock does not seem entirely pleased with my new promotion. I wonder why?"

"He's an old man. Perhaps your youth threatens him."

Regima Clere began to cry the way she always did around the academe. "Quiet, child," Regim scolded her and the sharpness in his voice silenced the infant. He smiled at his new advisor. "You are wise, Gunther Triadius. You seem to know Secrets even I, as your superior, never knew."

"Oh, that's an academe's prerogative, Chief Commander. Magisters rule the world. Academes discover new information about the world."

Regim considered that. "There's so much to discover, isn't there, academe? For instance, I've never seen the aetheric shell of an angel before, have you?"

FACET 25

Serpent: Wisdom or treachery.
The stealthy angel hides in the tall weeds
    where no one would think of looking for him.
The action is diplomacy.
The forbearance is espionage.

The Orb of Eternity

Commentaries:
Councillor Sausal: Pan conceals things or reveals them for purposes we may not understand. The priestess sees the serpent slithering on the ground. She reaches for it and is bitten. After the priestess dies, the serpent sheds its skin to live for another lifetime.

So, too, the Imperium conceals Secrets for the welfare and benefit of all the purities. [*Deleted from The Contemporary Commentaries of Sausal (15th Ed.): Yet there are Secrets that ought to be revealed.]

Therefore the prudent person should keep close counsel on vital matters. [*Deleted from The Contemporary Commentaries of Sausal (15th Ed.): Beware of harboring secrets that are best revealed. Beware of sharing secrets that would harm.]

Guttersage (usu. considered vulgar): An Imperial edict may be another name for an Imperial lie.

Our City of Atlan, the crest of Prime Hill. Milord Lucyd's cloudscraper, the Villa de Reve:

"Tonight you must enter the inner realms you've told me about, Danatia," Lucyd said.

They lay on the dreamers' couches inside his aetheric shell. Verses from the Shepherd's Rapture danced across the silver sheen, elaborate kaligraphs in high Imperial style with fancy serifs. The shell rumbled softly as if purring with delight that its master had returned to dream of the beautiful sea.

For that was how Lucyd had dreamed of Ground Control's flooding of the rifts: not as water forced against rock, but as the elements joined in joyful harmony. After the first criers' sharemind of mass destruction along the great southern rifts, he had instructed his majordomo to block all such news. He forbade anyone at Villa de Reve to speak of destruction in his presence. He blocked his ears with beeswax whenever the Harbinger tolled warnings of a shock, and his staff readied Villa de Reve without troubling him. Repair crews raising buttresses and pouring cement into the villa's damaged foundation laid down their tools whenever Lucyd passed.

He wanted no part of it. How could he dream healing dreams while knowing of catastrophe? The suffering of the world was the Imperium's concern. Dreaming was his.

Now the sounds of revelry, an orchestra with cymbalons and flutes, clinking glasses and laughter, wafted up through the floorboards. The luscious smells of a great feast, costly perfumes, fine bacco, and a whiff of raptureroot infused the evening air. Lucyd had granted his cloven sons permission to host a private Festival of Spring Moontide, and two hundred of the most eminent angels in Atlan had arrived in formal dress and spectacular jewels.

He'd granted Danatia permission to join the celebration, too, but she had declined. "I thought you told me, milord, that the best time to dream is when other angels do not."

"That's true. The Mind of the World has more

power for my dreams when other aetherists are out drinking and dancing."

"Then you must dream, milord." She had climbed the spiral staircase without a backward glance.

He had joyfully followed her, leaving his sons to hold court over the celebration.

Now Lucyd turned slightly on the couch, careful he didn't startle her with an untoward touch or an unexpected breath against her cheek. "Would you care for some honey?"

At her nod he fed her, golden honey pooled on a golden spoon.

She said, "I'm afraid."

I know who has invaded your dreams in the Mind of the World, Tahliq had told him when he had landed his windship by the Great Wall. And when the Cardinal of the Mind of the World sent news that an Imperial shell had been stolen from the temple, he had feigned astonishment. Of Tahliq's strange tale, he said not a word: that Horan Zehar had lain in the shell with the acolyte-auditor *before* it had been stolen. That an impure Devil had cast a dream in the Mind of the World.

Tahliq told him the Devil girl had followed her father's example. That the erotician herself had climbed into the shell. Lucyd had been so astounded by Tahliq's revelations that he'd brooded in his sleep chamber for most of the day. When he'd finally risen, he had to acknowledge with cold certainty that impure terrorists had accomplished what no one had ever thought possible.

Danatia lay stiffly, more tense than usual. She wore a gown of translucent blue silk that flowed over her slender white body like water over marble. Her ivory-pale feet remained bare, the toenails lacquered with translucent blue polish. Diamonds and atlantium gleamed in her earlobes, on her fingers, at her wrists and ankles. Jewelry Lucyd had given her. Jewelry she wore only here: in his dreamchamber.

The lid of the shell lay open, the air within sweet and fresh. Lucyd hadn't used the morpheus veil since Danatia had come to lie beside him. He hadn't indulged in hypnolia. Hadn't even required nopaine after dreaming.

They had yet to enter sharemind. They had yet to dream together but had spent the time becoming accustomed to each other. Her presence in Lucyd's dreams thus far had been a simulacrum just as Danti, after her death, had been. A distillation, his own construct of memories of her.

Not Danatia herself.

Now it was time, at last, for her to enter sharemind with him. To dream.

"Afraid of what, milady?"

"That you'll be disappointed in my inner realms, milord. In my sharemind."

"You could never disappoint me. Just your presence beside me has given me the courage to brave my demons and dream on."

He had not even secretly attempted to enter covert sharemind with her, though he could have done so with such subtle power she wouldn't have been aware of his presence. No, this had to be with her knowledge and consent. Anything else would have been a violation.

"The new commission has gone better than I could have ever expected," he added. "And all thanks to you, Danatia. My love."

Silence at his words. At last she said, "Can't we just go on like this?"

"No, milady. From all you've told me, you're a natural dreamer. I want to show you a little of what it's like to cast dreams in the Mind of the World. And to do that, you and I must take the next step and enter sharemind. You won't regret it." He fervently hoped that would prove true. "You'll chastise me for making you wait so long."

"Never, milord," she said with a laugh.

How he loved her laugh. "Ah, we shall see. In any case, now that we know someone stole a shell, I need you to complete the commission. Until the temple informs us that the shell has been recovered, I'm vulnerable to an invader, whether by accident or design."

"Yes," she said somberly. But her voice still trembled with doubt.

"And so," he said firmly, "your inner realms. Focus your sharemind upon these." He had pondered at length how best to enter mutual consciousness without blasting through her the way he did with other pures. "We will concentrate on your outer reaches of imagination. If all goes well, and you're comfortable with me, we'll work our way into full consciousness."

He lay back and closed his eyes. He didn't have to. He wanted nothing more than to keep gazing at her face when they entered sharemind. But he sensed she felt more at ease without his scrutiny. It was better, too, that she didn't see his expression. Not the first time.

Gently, he entered her consciousness.

A field of luminescence.

He hovered there, searching for the nub of her sharemind.

"Here I am, milord."

A sweep of platinum hair, the flash of a smile. A giggle.

The blue swirl of her gown as she darts away, footsteps pattering into a horizon that coalesces before him.

"Danatia," he calls. *"My love, wait."*

He enters a coppice of willows, the same coppice he's dreamed of five thousand times. The long, sighing leaves gleam with a million sparkles of blue light as if set with as many tiny sapphires.

"This is magnificent," he says, laughing. *"Where are you?"*

A giggle, a glimpse of gown, the flicker of a smile.

He chases her to the edge of the sea, to the surging floods of the Imperium delving deep into the rifts. The scintillating sea-green water turns to brilliant golden orange, leaping with sea horses and maremaids and leviathans.

She hovers far above him, perched upon a cloud, swinging her feet back and forth. She glances up, brandishes a graceful hand skyward.

She leaps.

He follows, leaping after her, soaring, soaring, soaring—

Into deep space. The vast blackness between the stars. A lone comet speeds out of the depths, whizzes past, and is gone. A shower of rocks the size of planets careens by. In the far distance, a galaxy wheels, trailing arms of stars, a starfish of ancient light.

Bong! Bong! Bong! Bong! Bong! Bong!

The tolling of the Harbinger tore the evening air, the great gong shattering their sharemind, shaking them awake.

Danatia gasped. And then gasped again.

Lucyd roused himself reluctantly—a natural dreamer, indeed—and rubbed his eyes. "It's only a six-mag shock," he said, chuckling at his own nonchalance. "Villa de Reve can withstand it. The construction crew installed a very good buttress just this morning. Don't worry—"

A figure loomed over them.

Lucyd bolted upright, flung his arms around her, and tried to shield her with his hands.

"My word, isn't this cozy?" came a nasal tenor. "Is this contraption really an aetheric shell? You actually *cast* dreams into the whole Mind of the World from this bitsy bucket of bolts?" The creature gave the side of the shell a little kick.

Lucyd stared. A pudgy, yellow-haired middle pure stood before him. He had propped his elbows on the edge of the shell and leaned familiarly over the edge, peering in at them.

"How dare you!" Lucyd shouted and seized the firebolt he'd kept inside the shell ever since Danatia had started lying beside him. "Majordomo? We've got a trespasser."

"Oh, I don't think so." The man extended a suety hand. "I'm Gunther Triadius. You, of course, are the eminent Milord Lucyd. You look exactly as you do in your dreams." He studied Lucyd's face. "Perhaps a little *older* than in your dreams." He touched Danatia's alabaster cheek. "And with such a succulent young lady. Truly the angels enjoy privileges we of the lower purities can only dream of."

Lucyd made to slap the lout's hand, but Danatia undertook that task herself. She struck Gunther's knuckles so fiercely that he recoiled and shook his hand in pain. She unwrapped Lucyd's arm from around her shoulders, agilely vaulted out of the shell, and stood, planting her hands on her hips.

"Majordomo," she shouted, "a criminal assaults milord."

"Hardly a criminal, milady," Gunther said. "I'm pleased to announce I'm the new Adjunct at the Imperial Bureau of Ground Control *and* the new Advisor on Ground Control Matters to our Chief Commander of Vigilance."

Lucyd's majordomo, in full-dress uniform, trotted into the dreamchamber, heaving for breath.

Lucyd stepped regally out of the shell himself, smoothing his platinum curls. He found velvet capes for himself and Danatia—neither his mesh bodysuit nor her translucent gown was meant for public display—and covered them both. "Majordomo, summon Vigilance."

"There's no need, milord," the majordomo said. "The academe-advisor came accompanied by Vigilance. The Chief Commander seeks an audience with you downstairs, milord."

"Well, why didn't you send the Chief Commander up instead of this rogue? I've come to know Gwenda well enough since Danti was murdered."

" 'Tis not the Dame Commander," the majordomo said. His pale slitted eyes shone with dread. "I regret to announce that the Dame Commander is dead."

Lucyd exchanged an alarmed glance with Danatia. "Who is the new Chief Commander?"

"Regim Deuceman, milord."

Lucyd felt suddenly very cold.

"Whom you've met, eh, milord?" Gunther said and winked at Danatia. "Our Chief Commander doesn't hold a very high opinion of milord. Thinks milord is a traitor in angel's robes." He made a show of examining

Lucyd's beloved shell. "How old is this contraption, anyway? I'd like to tear the thing apart and study it. Perhaps one day I will."

He turned and strode from the dreamchamber without asking for or receiving a proper dismissal. He called over his shoulder, "The Commander and I both wish to speak with you, milord. Make yourself presentable and meet us downstairs in your precious little white room."

"The southwest salon?"

"Whatever pretty name you call it. Oh, and don't worry. We wouldn't think of mingling with your guests in your ballroom. Our new Chief Commander cannot stand the company of angels. Be quick about it. Don't keep our Commander waiting. Regim Deuceman is not a patient man."

"Of *course* that's what I'm telling you. For years they patronized the lowest of eroticians," came the whisper.

"That's not illegal, you fool," came an answering whisper.

Lucyd stood hand in hand with Danatia at the half-open doors to the southwest salon. He felt sick to his heart to hear treachery in his favorite salon.

The six-mag earthshock began to stir Villa de Reve, rattling the stained-glass panes and punching at the buttressed foundation. The whole house groaned as if it, too, grieved for the wrongs committed inside its genteel walls.

Tonel stood, flushed and shiny-eyed with strong drink and defiance, speaking into the ear of the tall, golden vigile Lucyd knew only too well.

"Yes, but we're talking about the great Lucyd. The high priest of Pannish love. It's awfully scandalous, don't you think?" Tonel's feverish whisper came again, and Lucyd glimpsed the cloven's eyes darting guiltily toward the door. "They were probably two of the randiest, most lustful—"

Gunther laughed.

"I don't give a damn about his lusts," Regim whispered. "What else have you got?"

"He keeps sphinxes. Has for years. The latest pair are upstairs in his dreamchamber."

"You try my patience. Give me evidence of his *criminal* activities. His connections with the impure. Who does he know? How did he meet them? When did he last see them?"

"Oh! There you are, my father," Tonel said. "And my sharer-to-be. What are you doing here, Danatia? Holding hands with my elderly father, are you? What a dutiful daughter-in-lock you'll make. May I introduce Milady Danatia Soli naitre Primus. We're to enter sharelock at High Summer Tide." In a voice like cracking ice, "I said what the hell are you doing here? Our Chief Commander asked for him, not you. Begone."

Lucyd glanced anxiously at the woman for whom he would gladly give his life. *She has not renounced Tonel. And I have not declared myself to her.*

Till tonight. With two words. My love.

And she made no reply.

"I am here to accompany milord," Danatia said. "It is *you* who ought to begone. I release your pledge to me tonight, Tonel."

The floor shuddered violently, causing Lucyd to lose his footing for a moment. Danatia stood firm, and steadied him. When the earthshock was over, the lamplit air still seemed to vibrate with suppressed rage.

"*What?*" Tonel said.

"I will not enter sharelock with you."

"I *bought* you, you bloody cloven of his bloody sharer—"

"I am not Danti's cloven." She held her head high. Lucyd hardly recognized the woman who had arrived on Tonel's arm last summer, withdrawn and submissive. "Danti could never love anything she couldn't claim as her own and you weren't a part of her. She wouldn't even permit Lucyd to generate full children with the fertile materia of her ancestor." Danatia fiercely squeezed Lucyd's hand. "Because that would have branded her as less of an angel than her own mother. I've come to understand much about Danti. I'm sorry for all the wrong she did you and your brothers. But I have decided. And I *am* buying back my pledge from you."

Tonel's mouth dropped open. Pain swam in his pale eyes. Then his bitter sneer twisted his angelic features again. "Your family has no money. *You* have no money. Not the kind of money Milord Lucyd dispenses so generously to his children." Tonel narrowed his eyes. "Unless my own father betrays me again."

"I knew nothing of milady's decision till now," Lucyd said. He didn't try to conceal his joy and approval. "If she requires a gift of funds to secure her release, I'll be happy to advance the amount to her. I have plenty of money for everyone I love."

"*Love,*" Tonel said in a low, ugly voice. "You know nothing of love, my father."

"Perhaps you're right, my son. But I'm willing to learn."

"I *refuse* to release her," Tonel shouted. "I won't take your money."

"Then I'll seek a release from the Temple of Sharelock," Danatia said. "I'll file a petition of incompatibility."

"You do that. You'll be *dead* and in your *grave,*" he spit at Lucyd, "before I'll *ever* release her. You'll *never* wear sharelock chips with her."

"I'll speak to my Imperial liaison in the morning," Lucyd murmured in Danatia's ear.

"As your pledged sharer I demand that you leave this place with me now," Tonel said. "Pack your bags. We're returning to Siluria."

"No," she said. "I'm staying here. With Milord Lucyd."

"I'll make you both regret this one day." Tonel stalked out.

"Majordomo," Lucyd said quietly to the servant, "assist my son with his luggage. Do not permit him to spoil his brothers' celebration in the ballroom. And make sure he departs from Atlan on a windship before this night is out."

"Yes, milord." The majordomo and a contingency of beck-and-call men strode away to carry out Lucyd's command. From the set of their shoulders and relieved smiles, everyone at Villa de Reve would be glad to see Tonel go.

Lucyd heard the gurgle of fluid from decanter to snifter. Gunther was helping himself to the best d'ka and handing a snifter to Regim Deuceman.

"State your business and then get out," Lucyd said.

"No longer the wilting angel trembling in his windship, eh?" Regim said. "You've denied many things, Milord Lucyd. You deny acquaintance with persons of the impure, despite their presence in your dreams. Deny knowledge of the Orb of Eternity. You even deny knowledge of the news of the day."

"I dream, Chief Commander."

"So you do. Do you deny that you've patronized eroticians?"

"Yes, I do. Milady Danti patronized eroticians," Lucyd answered. "I merely accompanied her. I did not avail myself of their services."

"Do you deny that you knew an erotician named Tahliq? Deny you visited the Salon of Shame?"

"Oh, it's possible," Lucyd said. "I accompanied Danti to many eroticians' salons. I cannot keep track of them all."

"What were you doing in your windship over Rancid Flats when the magmaflow destroyed Jugglers Lane?"

"I daresay I was flying," he replied, which sent Danatia into giggles.

"Very well, milord," Regim said. "Truly the Ancient Ones and the Imperium have always smiled on you. Let's see how long you enjoy your privileges now that I am Chief Commander, and you can no longer look to Vigilance for protection."

"Do you dare tell a superior pure that you will no longer carry out your Imperial duty?" Lucyd said.

"The High Council will be most interested in your confession."

Regim knew he was trapped. Still, a fanatical gleam shone in his blue eyes, and Lucyd knew he hadn't seen the last of the vigile. It occurred to Lucyd the vigile might despise *him* as much as he despised the vigile.

"Is there anything more, Chief Commander?" he said. "If not, finish your drinks and go. My household is celebrating the Spring Moontide. Your advisor is correct in noting that magister and academe subpures are not invited."

Regim's face hardened. "Tell him, Gunther."

"Our Chief Commander wishes you to commence a new series of dreams that will celebrate the Imperium's taming of the earthshocks."

"I've been doing so. Everyone has been pleased with my dreams of the floods."

"The floods are finished. We're planning a new strategy. An ultimate solution. The Temple of the Mind of the World will give you the details, but know this: The ultimate solution will require the supreme effort and complete loyalty of every Pangaean. It is a fight to the finish. And a fight requires weapons. Powerful weapons."

"Your dreams of the floods have become too soft and pretty," Regim said, "as our people have become too soft and complacent. Your new dreams must demonstrate the Imperium's power. They must rouse the people to renew their strength and commitment to their Imperial duties."

"What is this ultimate solution?" Danatia asked softly.

"We're going to launch massive firebolts into the rifts," Gunther said. "This will pulverize the surrounding bedrock, causing gigantic avalanches, and fuse the basement substrata over the magmatic core."

"What our loquacious academe means is," Regim said, "we're going to blow them up."

     •   •   •

"It's horrible," Danatia whispered. "I don't know if I can help you, milord."

They lay in the aetheric shell once more, the door to the dreamchamber double-locked. Lucyd had dispersed a bit of hypnolia to sweeten the air. Gunther Triadius had deposited a bad odor in the dreamchamber—the odor of fear.

"But you *must* help me," he whispered and traced the line of her cheek.

"What they propose to do is monstrous. It *will* be the Apocalypse this time, won't it?"

"Perhaps. If it's any consolation, it will take them years to construct the weapons. That's what that odious little academe said when I bade them good-bye."

"But to dream such horrible dreams. . . ."

"Better *us*," he said, savoring their collusion with a smile, "than an aetherist like Milord Sting, who loves treachery and death. After all, sweet Danatia, the temple wanted me to dream of the flood as if it were a drowning. And I've dreamed of the surging sea as a cleansing and a renewal."

"That's true," she said, smiling in return. "How shall we cast dreams of explosion, milord?"

"We'll think of something."

He grew somber. Tahliq had cast the Orb of Eternity for him before he had bade her good-bye. *Beware, milord,* the erotician had said, glancing up from the glittering purple jewel.

"Danatia," he said, "the Orb of Eternity has appeared in my dreams through no volition of mine. It appeared before I'd ever actually seen one. Do you suppose that means the orb has become a part of the Mind of the World?"

She sat up, eyes wide with alarm. "If that's so, then the orb could invade our dreams at any time."

"And we may invoke it at any time."

"*Invoke* it?"

"Why not? Like so many things, I've begun to view the orb in a different light. I happened to meet a woman who knew a great deal about orbs. She swore the orb

was neither good nor evil, but only power. And like any
power, a force to be used according to the one who
wields it. I have a question I'd like to ask of the orb.
Will you dream with me now? Don't be afraid."

"Yes, I will."

They lay back on the couches, hand in hand.

"Lead me to one of your realms," he whispered,
"where no other aetherists will spy on us and no
acolyte-auditors will audit us. I want to ask my question in secrecy."

"All right." Danatia closed her eyes.

*Lucyd stands beside her, hand in hand. They gaze at
a rampage of vegetation. Stupendous mountains jut
across a steaming horizon. Palm fans and seed ferns
tower above them. Gigantic dragonflies flit through the
canopy, and feathered lizards flap multicolored wings.
Long-legged birds gallop across a field of mud.*

"Where are we?" he asks.

*"We're in the Bog," Danatia says. "The lost world.
Proceed, milord. Ask your question."*

"I command the Orb of Eternity to appear," he says.

*A man strides out of the jungle. As huge and robust
as a high magister, silver-blond and gorgeous as an angel, he smiles at them. His blue-green eyes sparkle with
mischief.*

*Lucyd steps back in alarm, feeling warm mud be-
tween his toes. "Who are you?"*

*"I am he who fled for his life because of the Orb of
Eternity. What do you want, Milord Lucyd?"*

*"I want to know the meaning of the oracle that Tah-
liq cast for me," Lucyd says. "Will the orb know which
one?"*

*"We shall see." The man reaches down into the
grass. He plucks something out and wipes it clean on
his shirt.*

*Then he opens his hand and flings the Orb of Eter-
nity. The diamond-shaped facets reflect sparkles of purple light as the orb tumbles toward Lucyd and comes to
a shuddering stop.*

A facet rolls into view.

A serpent with the face of a beautiful woman un-coils, spilling out of the facet. The serpent glides through the mud toward Lucyd.

Danatia shouts, seizes a palm frond, and twists it off the giant stem. "Stand back, milord."

Apprehension pounds in Lucyd's chest, but he says, "No, this is the oracle the erotician cast for me. The Serpent. Serpent, what is your secret?"

"Someone near you plans treachery against you," *the Serpent says in a melodious voice.* "Beware, mi-lord."

"Who is the traitor?"

The Serpent rears up, bares her dripping fangs.

The Serpent's slanting eyes are sapphire blue.

And then it strikes.

But Danatia is swifter. She swings the frond at the serpent and knocks its face away.

She seizes Lucyd's hand. "Run, my love. Run!"

Lucyd careened out of the dream. He found himself in the shell with his arms around Danatia. He felt her heartbeat racing against his chest.

She was sobbing.

"It's all right, my love. Ssh, ssh."

They lay together for a long time. The villa was si-lent, the celebration over, all the celebrants gone home. Somewhere in the garden, an owl hooted.

"Milord," Danatia whispered, "we angels are no longer alone."

FACET 26

Fish: Family or feud.
Cod swim the sea in their numbers and are
  netted by fishers.
The action is maintaining alliances.
The forbearance is genocide.

The Orb of Eternity

Commentaries:
Councillor Sausal: Pan provides safety and
strength for myriad things when they unite each
with the other. A proximate thing joining with
another will endure.

So, too, the Imperium encourages the purities
to enter sharelock with those of the same subpure, labor with those of a proximate subpure,
and celebrate with those of the same purity.

Therefore the prudent person should cultivate
close ties with family, clan, subpure, and purity.

[*Deleted from The Contemporary Commentaries of Sausal (15th Ed.) But beware of the familiar that breeds contempt.]*

Guttersage (usu. considered vulgar): There's
safety in numbers till a foe flings an inferno bolt
into your sharelock ceremony and wipes out your
whole subpure.

*North Appalacia Peninsula, Our Township of Labrad,
across Sausal Bay from Greater Atlan. A league from
Labrad Coast:*

The tentsite *looked* deserted.

But cookstones still smoldered in the campfire, and Salit smelled the lingering scents of fried cod and onions. Crockery bowls, spoons, and limp wineskins had been piled to one side, but no one had tidied up yet.

She prowled on silent feet among brambles and saplings to the edge of the clearing. Sharp hunger grumbled in her belly.

Sensing her tension, Latif, strapped to her breast, began to whimper and fret, mouthing the ridge of her collarbone as he did when he wanted to feed. She thrust her thoughts at him, *Ssh, my son,* and her babe quieted at once.

Salit dropped to hands and knees, crept behind the clotted tangle of an uprooted tree. Good thing she'd mastered stalking techniques with a hefty bedroll and clanking weapons long before she'd found herself with burdens of a far different nature. She recalled one of the first lessons Horan Zehar had taught her—

The Art of Hiding (Becoming a Small Thing): Fill in the gap between two larger objects: two trees, two boulders, two tumbleweeds. Become a sapling, a rock, a ball of laceweed.

Or the root of an uprooted tree.

Jahnni, strapped to her back, breathed softly in her ear, his little fists gripping the points of her shoulders, his knees neatly tucked up beneath her arms. She smiled, sensing the infant's awareness of danger, of her need for his silence, and his cooperation with her movements.

I've become a beast of burden between two brawny babes. Hardly a small thing, my father.

Sagging tents of black sacking huddled around the campfire. A luck-come-hither fetish dangled from a tent pole. A witch-begone fetish had been painted on a tent flap. A tripod of ironwood branches had been lashed over the smoldering cookstones. A dagger had been slung from the top of the tripod promising misfortune upon whoever dared disturb food and utensils.

Salit circled the clearing, found another gap between

two gigantic fan palms, and crouched among the fronds. She wished she'd painted her face with mud before she'd ventured out that morning in search of food and passage to Atlan.

She felt the growl of Jahnni's belly pressed against her spine, but he didn't fuss about his hunger like Latif.

Good boy. I know, I know, it's been a long three days, my milk runs thin, and we're all hungry.

She didn't think of him anymore as Tahliq's babe. Sometimes she dreamed she'd given birth to them both. Jahnni of the Far Reaches was simply her other son. Her golden-haired, copper-skinned, blue-eyed big boy. And Latif Zehest Zehar, her beautiful little blue boy with his midnight hair and his midnight eyes, the glimmering of his consciousness coming to meet hers.

Jahnni had been huge to begin with, and he'd been growing ever since like a well-watered weed. His pure blood, wildly mixed though it was, had already served him well. At three moons he'd begun rudimentary speech—*Yes, Want, No, Mama, Moon*—while Latif still crooned babe babble. He didn't share thoughts with her, though, not the way Latif had started to.

Soon he would eat solid food and walk. In another moon he might be nearly half her size. She couldn't carry both babes much longer and secure food and water, find shelter, evade Vigilance, and confront the marauders that seemed to roam every road these days. Perhaps, when he started walking, Jahnni could help her carry Latif and their provisions.

He'd have to. She didn't know where they'd live once they'd returned to Atlan. Whether, with such strange sons, she'd be allowed a tentsite in Blackblood Cavern. Or whether they ought to depart from the megalopolis once she'd finished what she'd returned to do. Take up the roaming life till the boys had grown enough to withstand what Salit knew would be inevitable—the stigma and harassment that would surely be heaped upon them both, outcasts among outcasts.

And no father to protect them.

"This is for you, beloved bonded one," Asif had shouted.

Over and over she saw him leap at the monstrous vigile as she and Bandular had watched from a cranny near the ceiling of the cavern. Over and over she screamed in her thoughts, *Don't do it, Asif. Run. Run. You're supposed to follow me, beloved comrade and bonded one. Don't you remember?*

Over and over she saw the blast of the vigile's firebolt, the desecration of his dagger. Regim Deuceman marching Dubban away to be executed.

She crept into the tentsite, starting at every birdcall and rustle of leaves. She stopped, head cocked, listening for the sighs or snores of someone resting in the tents. She crept to the campfire. The cookpot offered only a couple of burnt onions stuck in a blackened crust at the bottom, but she found the ladle, eagerly commenced scraping.

And then hands seized her from both sides. She squawked, whirled, struggled. But her assailants—three burly men—held her fast.

"I'm a mother with two babes," she shouted. "Can't you spare the damn scrapings in your cookpot?"

"Is it her?" said one man wearing an eye patch and a scowl to match. He wore the distinctive fang dagger of Inim's Beasts, a foe clan of filthy cutthroats not known for tolerance toward Heaven's Devils or dedication to the holy war against the Imperium.

Salit held her tongue. For the first time in her life she was glad she wore no devil stars on her belt.

"She's the one," said another, peering closely at her. "Let's go, Salit Zehar."

She gasped. "You know who I am?"

"You're the only Heaven's Devil girl in all Pangaea who's got an Imperial warrant on every lamppost. Come along." He dodged, but not quickly enough, as she aimed a kick at his kneecap. "Quietly, wench! The Dark Ones want a word with you."

• • • •

Fragrant bacco smoke swirled around the high bench of the Dark Ones, dispersing into the chill of the cavern. Salit saw the glow of a burning ember rise and fall as a Dark One raised a cheroot to his lips and lowered it. It was he who spoke in a thunderous whisper that filled the cavern with its rasp.

She salivated at the scent and longed for a good smoke.

"What did you do with the aetheric shell you stole from the Mind of the World?" the Dark One whispered.

"I don't know what you mean."

"Answer the question, impudent girl. We know how you infiltrated the angel's dream. Where is the shell?"

"Beneath half a league of cooling magma in Rancid Flats where my bonded one and I left it, fleeing for our lives."

The five Dark Ones bent their heads together, murmuring in low, agitated voices.

"Don't I even rate a hello, Dark Ones?" Salit said. "You just want to talk about shells? Why is it when I need the help of my own people, you do nothing, yet when you want something from me, you send your minions to fetch me like a criminal?"

She heard the slap of the sea and the famished cry of gulls. The cavern lay close to the Labrad Coast, then. For once she wished the Dark Ones' minions had fetched her to the Cavern of Reckoning. That way, she could have gotten a ride across Sausal Bay to Atlan and saved herself the trouble of stowing aboard a fishing skiff.

"You've evaded Vigilance well enough, haven't you?" a Dark One said.

"Do the Dark Ones wish to take credit for warnings borne by bloodbats?"

A Dark One said, "Give our comrade something to rest on and something to eat and drink. And relieve her of her burdens."

Two fierce-eyed Inim's Beasts women stepped forward and unstrapped Jahnni from her back, Latif from her breast, and took her sons from her. Another woman stepped forward and thrust flatbreads, a wedge of hard cheese, and a skin of wine into Salit's hands.

She glared up at the five figures concealed in their black miasmas, the amber-fire mandorlas of their eyes staring down at her, and refused to be grateful. But she sighed when she opened the chameleon cloak and let the cool air slide over her clammy skin. She chewed the food and drank the wine as quickly as she could before they decided to take it away.

"What brings you back to Atlan, Salit?" said the second Dark One, his gravelly voice grating in her ears. "All the way from the Far Reaches? Why didn't you stay where Vigilance is not so keen on claiming the trophy of your head?"

"There's no place for me in Reaches."

They had scrambled, she and Dubban's mother, through a chute winding out of the hill above Ushushwana Bowl. Neither Vigilance nor bloodbats had troubled them. When they'd gained daylight, Salit had seen Bandular's stricken face.

"Why in *hell*," the midwife had said, "did you drag my son into this?"

Bandular had hidden her and the babes in the basement laundry of her natalry. As soon as Salit could travel, Bandular had handed her a food sack and said, "Get out."

Salit had strapped her two sons, fore and aft, and stolen rides aboard logging sledges, buckwheat wagons, and trapper caravans. As spring edged toward summer, she had trudged all the way across Appalacia Province, bound for Our City of Atlan.

She shrugged, chewing faster on the bread and cheese. "I was born in Atlan. I *live* in Atlan. Could I have a cheroot?"

The woman darted forward with a fancy roll of fine bacco stamped with an Imperial seal and a tin of matches. The cheroot might have cost a drayer three months' wages. *The Dark One has luxurious tastes.* She lit up.

"You live in Atlan no more," the Dark One said. "But Regim Deuceman still does. He's become the Chief Commander of Atlan Vigilance. Did you know that, Salit?"

She flung the spent match away. "That bastard *killed* my bonded one. *Killed* my father. *Killed* an entire confinement camp."

"And you have not released your vow of blood vengeance, have you?" came the feminine voice of the third Dark One.

"Oh, on the contrary, I have released that vow," she said. "At least till my sons are old enough to survive without me, if they must." She gazed at her sons, overwhelmed with love for both. "I've vowed to raise my boys before I risk my own life. My new vow takes precedence over the death of Regim the Butcher."

"A pity, Salit," came the fourth hissing voice. "For we give you permission to carry out your vow."

She sat up. *"What?"* Then suspiciously, *"Why?"*

"Regim supports Ground Control's new strategy to explode giant firebolts in the rifts," came the voice of the fifth Dark One, the kindly voice of a solicitous elder. "We are alarmed. As killing taxes, crime, and unrest plague Atlan, so Regim has whipped up a renewed frenzy over impurity. He has resurrected Adjunct Prefect Clere Twine's plans to exterminate the impure."

"Regim further commits sacrilege in the name of high purity," came the first Dark One's thundering whisper. "He removed his sharelock chips with Clere and had new chips installed. He has entered sharelock with his daughter, Regima Clere."

Salit recalled the tiny golden girl perched on a blind caretaker's shoulder. "But she's an infant. Not much older than my sons."

"Yes. No law of Pangaea, Atlan Prefecture, or the sacred teachings forbids such a union so long as begetting regulations are properly observed. Regim has won favor among arch-Pannist interests. He claims the sharelock is perfectly proximate, supremely pure, and therefore supremely blessed by Pan."

"We had plans for Regim Deuceman," said the female Dark One. "But his rise to Chief Commander under suspicious circumstances has changed our plans."

"You would charge *me* now with his execution?"

The Dark One laughed briefly. "You are Salit Zehar, Heaven's Devil extraordinaire, vowed to avenge your father's murder. And now the murder of your bonded one."

She blew out a breath. "I'm only one woman with two little sons."

"Oh, we're not relying solely on you, Salit. There are many assassins among the impure and the purities who would see Regim Deuceman dead. But he surrounds himself with specially bred and outfitted bodyguards. He keeps his whereabouts a secret known only to himself and his guard. He keeps himself secret from those he commands. From his family and his family-in-lock."

"Why would he wish to hide from those he commands? From his own family?" Salit drew deeply on the cheroot. "His family-in-lock are the most powerful magisters in Pangaea."

"There are those among the magisters," whispered the first Dark One, "who frown on Regim's sharelock as an abomination and perversion of natalry technology."

"Who fear and disapprove of his plans for sealing the rifts," said the second Dark One.

"And will not tolerate genocide of the impure," said the third.

Astonishment struck her again. "Why?"

Just look at your son, Salit Zehar, came the thunder of an invading consciousness. *Have you begun to steal into the thoughts of others? Do you dream of other worlds? Do you understand how to fold space? Feel your powers?*

She was about to answer eagerly in kind, thrilled to share consciousness with another. *What powers? What do the Dark Ones know of my dreams?*

Instead she checked her thoughts. Latif, sensing her irritation, began to cry. Horan Zehar's lesson from long ago rang in Salit's memory, *When you steal into someone's thoughts, never give away your own.* That had been long before she'd stolen into anyone's thoughts.

She clamped her mouth and shut her thoughts away.
She didn't respond?
She's bluffing. She can apprehend us very well.
"Impudent girl. We ought to whip some sense—"
"Hush! She *is* a mother with a blue babe."

Voices and thoughts swooped and dived in her ears and her consciousness. She could hardly keep track of which was spoken aloud, which spoken silently. *How do people of the purities stand their sharemind?*

Latif continued to fuss and pushed the strange woman away. His reedy cry rose to a wail.

Salit said, "Give him to me." She took her son in a crook-armed embrace that had become second nature and let him find his way through the open folds of the chameleon cloak and the collar of her tunic to what he wanted.

"Dark Ones," she said as she suckled her son, "suppose you tell me in my ignorance why an impure girl like me would possess powers?"

"Salit." The kindly elder's voice again. "We see that the cloak has accepted you. Your son has the color. Surely you have begun to feel your powers."

"Surely you don't expect me to confess to that which I do not comprehend."

"Then the question you ask is a Secret."

"Ho!" She stamped her foot. "You would keep Secrets from me after I've lost both my parents and killed magisters with my own hand? After I've bonded with a man I loved? And now I have two babes?"

"One is your babe," came the guttural whisper. "The other plainly is not. Who are the blond boy's parents?"

Secrets. I'll keep Secrets from you.

"The babe had emerged from his mother's body," she lied, "when I rescued him from the vigiles at

Ushushwana Bowl. I don't know who Jahnni's mother and father are."

"You lie," whispered the first Dark One angrily. "Seize her."

Two Inim's Beasts leapt onto the lamplit platform, fang daggers drawn. Salit flinched when a needle-sharp point pressed against the corner of her eye.

"His mother was an erotician from Atlan who toured with a traveling carnival," the Dark One said.

"His father has to be a magister. Look at his hair. His eyes. His stature even so young," said another.

Salit shrugged and refused to answer.

"Yet no one who traveled with the erotician ever pried her secret from her lips. Not even our courier who lived in the same wagon. It seems everyone else who had dealings with Tahliq has died or disappeared. Except the angel Lucyd, who denies knowing her. And you."

"How do the Dark Ones know so much about an erotician?"

"The Dark Ones know much about everything in the Imperium. You will answer."

"No."

"Take her eye."

"Go ahead. Maim me. Kill me. Kill my sons, if you wish, or keep them alive. It doesn't matter. Neither of them knows who Jahnni's parents are. I'll go to my grave before I'll ever say."

"Leave Salit alone," whispered the first Dark One. "She's much too valuable to lose."

My daughter, came Horan Zehar's whisper in her consciousness, *you have proven yourself a warrior this day.*

"Now, if you're finished with me, I have urgent matters to attend to in Our Sacred City," she said with a smirk. "I need passage across Sausal Bay. I'll require food, a waterskin, a wineskin. And half a dozen of these excellent cheroots."

"You never did say what brings you back to Atlan," said the elderly voice.

"Dark One," Salit said, "that's no one's business but my own."

Allpure Square, the Sacred Center of Marketplace. Our City of Atlan:

Not my city. Not anymore.

The familiar sights of the city filled her heart with a chill. In Allpure Square spacious bleachers had been constructed, and benches and witness stands of a makeshift courtroom. She marveled at the torturers' implements. Gallows and bloody racks had been left to marauding insects, birds, and the view of all who passed.

She found what she was looking for.

She would know the skull of her bonded one anywhere. One huge fanlike ear remained uneaten by insects.

She withdrew the flask of cooking oil from the food sack the Dark Ones had given her, doused Asif's head, the insects, the impaling pole. She took out the tin of matches.

With trembling fingers lit one, two, three, four, *five* matches.

Till the abomination ignited in a burst of fire.

"Beloved comrade and bonded one," she whispered, "even death will never part us. I swear I will follow you into the Eternal Flames of Inim."

She stood for a moment and watched, beyond tears. A squad of vigiles marched toward Allpure Square. She ducked into shadows and was gone.

She had decided. There was only one more duty of conscience she needed to fulfill. Then she would leave Atlan for the roaming life till her sons grew up. Only then, if Regim Deuceman still lived, would she fulfill her vow of vengeance.

You, Salit Zehar, with a conscience? she mocked herself.

Yes. Because Dubban Quartermain once told me he

had something to live for. And because I, too, know
what it's like to have loved and lost someone.

Deep shadows and clots of fog still hung over Misty
Alley at midmorning. Salit heard the click of half a
dozen locks before Plaia opened the door. She swallowed hard when she saw Plaia's face twist with horror
and grief the moment she saw Salit's face.

"It's Dubban, isn't it?" Plaia said and dropped onto
the rumpled cot as if she'd been shot. She choked out
words. "It's been nearly half a season since Asif came
for him. He should have been back by now." She
glanced up and registered Salit lugging two babes. Salit,
alone. "What about your Asif?"

"Gone, too. Oh, Plaia, I'm sorry."

The two women embraced each other against the on-
slaught of tears.

Plaia looked gaunt and wan with long days of worry,
nearly as pale as an angel. Her reddish gold hair tumbled below her waist in a disheveled mass. Salit couldn't
help but stare. Plaia was one of the most beautiful
women she'd ever seen, neither as ethereal as the angel
Danti nor as blatant as the erotician Tahliq. Her fingertips were stained blue, Salit realized in another moment,
with ink. Books and papers lay strewn on every surface
of the cottage. A knife and sheath had been slung on a
hook by the door.

Salit couldn't blame the academe for her caution. She
had seen detainment warrants with Plaia's face amid
the flutter nailed to many a lamppost. By the look of all
those warrants, half the folk of Atlan were sought by
Vigilance for questioning.

Then there was the megalopolis itself. The place had
gone mad. Many had fled the city, taking their chances
on the open grasslands where one could see a rift yawning open beneath one's feet and the perils of falling
walls and flying glass weren't quite so acute. Yet for as
many refugees who had fled, more from the countryside

had swarmed in, seeking the shelter and food Atlan Prefecture doled out with increasing reluctance.

What was left of Rancid Flats teemed with rootless people, strange subpures, outlanders, and plenty of criminals. Tension was thick in the lanes—hostile eyes, voices raised in incomprehensible dialects, ready fisticuffs. Salit stopped on every other street corner to listen to an Apocalyptist perched on a hay bale, exhorting the crowd about Ground Control's ultimate solution. When she asked a saloonkeep on Treadmill Lane what that meant, he told her that the Imperium meant to blow up the rifts and stop earthshocks forever.

Salit lit two cheroots and handed Plaia one, which the academe took without a word.

"Dubban helped me in my hour of need. He and his mother saved my life. The life of my son. And the life of my other son. He was courageous, if that means anything. He stood up to Regim and died with honor." Salit swallowed her words, tasting their bitterness.

"I just can't believe it," Plaia whispered. A fever lit her eyes. "Did you see how it was done? Did he suffer? Did you see his corpse? I *must* know."

"No," Salit said. "I saw my Asif. . . . But, no, not Dubban. I did not see his corpse. I saw the vigile take him away. That was all. Ah, but Plaia, it does no good to imagine otherwise. The damned vigiles killed everyone who had not fled when they could. My Asif. The camp mistress. Gravid women. Little babes. They were merciless. I saw no one alive when we left the cavern."

"Thank you for coming to tell me."

"It's the least I could do. I know Dubban stuck his neck out, stealing the threads for me. And you donated your own birthpods to the impure cause. The Alchemist was pleased."

"What did the Alchemist do with my birthpods?"

"I'd like to know that, myself. He's a difficult man to find, though. Very secretive. Moves his tentsite around."

"I want to know. Can we look for him?"

"Yes, we can try Blackblood Cavern, the causeway,

the pipeline. Other haunts of the impure. They're not pretty places. Are you sure you want to do this?"

"I've seen plenty of places that aren't pretty, Salit." The academe twisted her hair into a knot and pulled a cap over her head. She pulled on fingerless gloves, a cape of copper-colored cotton, and a thick leather belt with a knife and sheath. "I wouldn't want to think everything Dubban risked was all for nothing."

Salit with the two babes and Plaia with a sack of provisions meandered through Blackblood Cavern. Salit studied a covey of bloodbats hanging from the cavern's ceiling, but none of the beasts approached them or showed any sign of human intelligence.

They were hiking along the causeway, heading toward Big Derelict Duct when a couple of rough-looking qut smugglers sprang out from behind an outcrop. Plaia's shriek and Latif's wail echoed throughout the cavern, but the smugglers only handed Salit a wineskin and disappeared into the shadows. Salit struck a match. Plaia read by matchlight the kaligraphs that had been carved into the skin with a knife blade.

NEW CASCADE—A.

They found the huge magister leaning against a boulder at the bottom of the ledge, waiting for them. He led them up through a chimney in the wall of the duct. Ushering them into his new tentsite, he exclaimed in delight over the boys and expressed sorrow at the news of Asif and Dubban.

The tentsite perched on a narrow ledge above the New Cascade. A cloud of moisture hung over the roaring waterfall, drenching the tentsite and the Alchemist's possessions. Salit had no idea how he'd lugged everything to *this* aerie. They nearly had to shout to hold a normal conversation, but if the Alchemist was troubled by any of these discomforts, he gave no sign.

Jahnni gleefully poured colored sand from one

crockery jar to another, but Latif gazed pensively around at the Alchemist's tentsite and chewed his thumb. And Salit saw again the sarcophagus made of pot metal.

"So Asif and Dubban *did* bring the aetheric shell to you."

"They certainly did," the Alchemist said with a laugh. "Asif told me all about your experiment. And Horan Zehar's. Your father was a courageous Devil. More courageous than you know. You follow in his footsteps, Salit."

"Did you give it a whirl?" she said, jutting her chin at the shell.

"I confess I took my ease for a moment or two." The Alchemist showed her how he'd disassembled and rebuilt one instrument panel inside the aetheric shell. "I may be able to replicate this, Salit."

The Alchemist shined the magmalamp more brightly at the crystal sliver beneath the tube of the viewglass. "Yes, Salit, the magister threads Dubban first brought to you were probably precursors of disease. The threads of disease in Plaia's seeded birthpods had been marked by the natalists for removal. But there are many other markers that don't correspond to the known locations of hereditary diseases."

"Meaning what, Alchemist?" Salit said.

"Meaning the natalries have been removing certain characteristics from each purity. Meaning the Imperium hasn't merely shaped and bred the purities through the law of proximity and the institution of sharelock, but by the direct hand of the natalries."

"No!" Plaia cried, eyes wide with alarm. "The purities are the purities—"

"Always have been and always will be," the Alchemist finished dryly for her. "We know that the Ancient Ones established the natalries. That is one Secret all the High Council knows. I think we can conclude from this evidence that the Ancient Ones probably established which markers the physicians should watch for, for each particular purity. I say 'probably' because the natalries are to this day so riddled with Secrets that even those seated on the High Council aren't privy to them all."

"Even you, councillor?" Plaia asked gently.

"Even me," he said and bowed his head.

Salit stared from the academe to the renegade, astounded. "Do you know each other?"

"I recognize him from the illustration in my protocol texts back in fundamental school. You were younger, but you look much the same, Councillor Sausal."

"Coming from such a lovely young woman, I will take that as a compliment," the Alchemist said with a wry laugh.

"But why, Alchemist?" Salit said. "Why not allow the people of the purities to live their lives like we of the impure? We're far from perfect, of course, but we're free of all your rules and restrictions. We love freely and willingly, not like Plaia with her sharer posting warrants for her arrest."

"To create perfection." He reached out and touched Plaia's cheek. "To create utopia. 'Angels need drayers to haul buckwheat from Iapetus Plains, just as drayers need angels to dream. Purity sharemind facilitates protocol and enforces protocol. Prerogative ensures proximity is respected while enabling unequals to interact.' I wrote that." He sighed deeply and rubbed his eyes. "Once I believed it."

"Why do you no longer believe, Councillor Sausal?" Plaia asked softly.

"How can I believe in a lie?"

He'd had everything a man could want in the Imperium. Purity? High magister, councillor subpure, destined to rule and be obeyed. Family? The Sausals, one of the First Families of Atlan. Wealth and property rivaling the angels.' He'd been appointed Chief Advisor to the High Council on Impure Activities because he was incorruptible. Because he believed in proximity. Believed in Pan and everything Pan stood for.

"Yes, I became obsessed with the Orb of Eternity." He reached out and touched the orbs dangling from

Salit's neck. Jerked his fingertips away as if the orbs had scalded him. "I knew every rumor. That orbs were given to the impure by the Ancient Ones. That orbs cannot be manufactured. That orbs foretell. And may affect the future. If that were so, what a tool for the Imperium! But the orbs wouldn't respond to just any pure. I never could get one to foretell for me. The orbs Vigilance has captured don't do anything at all. They don't even gleam."

"Were you banished, then, because of your obsession with the Orb of Eternity?" Salit said.

"And then the High Council forbade the orb to us all," Plaia said.

"No, Plaia, the irony is, my interest in the orb was merely an excuse. The ban, the result of the High Council's jealousy that the orb shunned all magisters. It couldn't be used as a tool for the Imperium, except for my commentaries on the oracles. And I wasn't banished. I fled for my life."

"I remember that night well," Salit said. "You ran into Blackblood Cavern. Vigilance chased you. You were beaten. Vigilance harassed everyone in the cavern and arrested a dozen young men. Still my father hid you."

"Your father was a very wise man."

"But I don't understand," Plaia said.

He took Latif from Salit's arms and gently cradled the small blue babe. "I said the purities are a lie. A horrible distortion of human nature masquerading as perfection. The purities became my undoing when I found myself in love with one of another purity. A woman much higher than I and a woman properly pledged in sharelock. Her name was Milady Danti. We shared our forbidden bed for eighteen years."

Plaia gasped. Even Salit sensed the shock of the Alchemist's words.

"The most beloved woman in the Mind of the World was a hypocrite!"

"You have a blunt way of putting things, Salit Zehar." The Alchemist smiled sadly. "But you're right.

Oh, we suffered our fair share of guilt. We tried to stop, but we couldn't. Lucyd didn't know, or if he did, he didn't care. He shared Pannish love with Danti. That was enough for him. And I? I loved Danti in every way. I had no interest in entering sharelock with one of my own subpure.

"In the meantime, the earthshocks were worsening. Your proctor Tivern brought us disheartening discoveries about movements in the rifts. That she might ameliorate the shocks, but no one could stop them. Each wave of destruction provoked more discontent among the purities." He heaved a sigh, filled with infinite regret. "So the High Council commissioned an assassination. The assassination of Danti and the angels at the Hanging Gardens of Appalacia."

"*What?*" Salit and Plaia exclaimed together. "But why?"

"To deflect the people's attention from the earthshocks. From the Imperium's powerlessness. The High Council has long collaborated with the foes when an enemy is needed to unite the purities. To reinforce their sense of duty. Their faith." He laughed without mirth. "I understand your astonishment. It was an Imperial Secret few knew. *I* had never known it. My family had occupied their time and attention with parties and games. I had occupied myself with Danti.

"I found out by accident.

"We had just held a council. I'd forgotten a gift—an atlantium clip for Danti's hair—aboard Capitol Ship. I went back to retrieve it. And there stood Claren Twine, speaking with Horan Zehar, the most notorious Heaven's Devil in all Pangaea.

"I overheard their plans. When the Devil had left, I confronted Claren. He argued that only a spectacular foe atrocity would accomplish the Imperium's purpose. I loved Danti. I threatened to expose him, to expose this collaboration for the horrible wrong it was, not just against Danti, but against all the people of the purities. I wanted to call for a complete overhaul of protocol. I wanted to rewrite all of my commentaries.

"We parted with angry words, but still I could not believe my own fellow councillor would betray me. I went home to my villa. And met a brawny pack of vigiles who'd come to arrest me and haul me to the Chamber of Justice, dead or alive. I fled to your father to plead for Danti's life."

"But, Alchemist, you accompanied my father and me to the Hanging Gardens," Salit said. "You formulated the cherry laurel vapors. You detonated the vapors with your own hand."

He bowed his head. "Horan told me he could not prevent her death. But I could prevent her pain. She died of the vapors almost instantly. She barely felt the devil stars."

Salit fell silent, ashamed she had once fretted that Danti hadn't suffered more. That the blooding at the Hanging Gardens hadn't been brutal enough. At last she said, "The Dark Ones have twice warned me of Vigilance raids. What does that mean?"

He raised his eyebrows in genuine surprise. "Someone of the Imperium must want you to stay alive. But take care of yourself and your sons, Salit. The loyalty of the Imperium is not to be relied upon."

"Alchemist," she said, "are you a Dark One?"

"No. I only learned of the Secret of the Dark Ones from your father."

"Was Horan a Dark One?"

"We became friends, your father and I, and shared much conversation. But if he was a Dark One, he took his Secret to Eternity, Salit."

"Alchemist," Plaia said, and gingerly touched his arm. "What is this scar?"

"It's the bore left behind from my security number. I asked Horan to remove it. Everyone's security number contains the code that permits receiving and transmitting sharemind in all its forms. And with all its limitations. It's what enables you to dream in the Mind of the World."

"Purity sharemind isn't a natural characteristic?"

Plaia said. "Given by Pan? Passed on through one's Imperial materia?"

The Alchemist laughed sadly. "Sharemind is the great gift of the Imperium, Plaia, and coded into your security number. Which was manufactured and installed in your arm when you bobbed in the brine of your ges tank. Sharelock chips are much like security numbers, but specially coded for the sharers who wear them."

He shuffled some jars filled with vile-looking liquids and withdrew a crystal dish. Inside lay a tiny blue dot. He plucked the dot with tweezers and placed it beneath the viewglass. "See for yourself."

Plaia peered through the viewglass, then Salit took her turn. She saw the tiny blue dot magnified a hundred times, the tiny maze of canals etched into the hard blue substance.

Plaia said, "Dubban told me once he witnessed inductor-surgeons from the Security Number Administration drop a tray filled with security numbers."

"And an erotician I knew," Salit said, "a drud of the lowest subpure, possessed allpure sharemind. No one else of her family or subpure ever had. Manifesto of the Apocalypse, Edict Four: Eliminate security numbers and sharelock chips. Now I understand."

The Alchemist nodded. "My magister sharemind was so unique that my fellow subpures, the council itself, could have traced me to my sanctuaries. I didn't trust myself to refrain from sharemind. One lapse, and my life would be in danger."

Plaia tore off her cape and her tunic. "Remove my number, then." She drew her own knife from its sheath, thrust her bare arm and the weapon at him.

"Dear lady, why?"

She brandished her scarred hands. "Dubban cut the sharelock chips from my hands, but he didn't have the proper instruments. He couldn't remove every remnant. Pieces of them are still embedded in my flesh. My sharer was a terrible man, Alchemist. He abused me in every way, including in sharemind. Sometimes I can still feel him when I invoke purity sharemind or dream in the Mind of the World. If what you say is true about security numbers, Gunther won't leave me in peace till the number is gone. Cut mine out at once."

"Do not, Plaia," the Alchemist said.

"Please! Between the remnants of my sharelock chips and the slightest exercise of my sharemind, there's a chance he could find me. Isn't that so?"

"Yes. Nevertheless, don't do it."

"Why not?"

A tear slid from the Alchemist's eye. "I cannot tell you how much I miss sharemind. The rich joys of shared consciousness, the ease, the wealth, the pleasure of it to this . . . silence. This darkness. I'm *lonely* without sharemind. I thought I'd go mad, at first. Worst of all, I cannot dream the angels' dreams. I can never dream of Danti again. I implore you, Plaia. Do not. You'll regret it one day."

"Perhaps, Alchemist," Salit said with a nod at the dismantled aetheric shell, "you'll dream again in the Mind of the World *without* your security number."

Salit fed Latif while Plaia played a hand-slapping game with Jahnni and the Alchemist puttered about with his viewglass and crystal slivers.

"Plaia, are you satisfied," she said, "with what the Alchemist has discovered? Satisfied that the risks Dubban took were worthwhile?"

"The Alchemist's discovery would change the Imperium if the purities knew," the academe said. "That, and my proof of how Pangaea is changing. But, Salit, I don't know who has the means to disseminate such discoveries. That person will wind up as a heretic on the Imperium's torture rack."

"Someone will tell the people," Salit said confidently and shifted Latif to the other breast. "Someone must."

"I don't know," Plaia said quietly.

Salit could see the grief weighing heavily on the academe. Her golden green eyes filmed with sorrow.

Salit felt terrible about her part in Dubban's death. It gnawed at her still.

What else can I do for the academe to assuage that terrible debt?

"Plaia," she said, "the night Asif and I met you and Dub at his cottage on Misty Alley, you said if only you could see the whole world archipelago from a great height, you might be able to tell where a safe haven may be."

"I believe I could."

"But our windships don't fly high enough."

"Not high enough for me to see the whole world archipelago, that's true."

"Would the view from the moon be high enough for you?" Salit said.

Plaia laughed. "I suppose it would be. But the Imperium doesn't possess the technology to go to the moon. Not yet, anyway. Isn't that right, Councillor Sausal?"

"I'm afraid our poor windships aren't powerful enough to escape our planetary atmosphere," he said. "Let alone fly all the way to the moon."

"That's just a rumor in the taverns, Salit," Plaia said. "People cannot *really* go to the moon."

Salit grinned till she thought her face would split.

"Uh-huh, they can."

FACET 27

> Heart: Love or hatred.
> Passion inspires sharelock or murder.
> The action is desire.
> The forbearance is vengeance.
>
> **The Orb of Eternity**

Commentaries:

Councillor Sausal: We have observed that all energy originates in Pan, yet energy is neither good nor evil, but dynamic. We have also observed that good and evil emerge in the world when humanity exerts its will and unleashes the passions of the heart.

So, too, the Imperium is the source of all wealth and power yet Imperial functions are carried out by people of the purities. [*Deleted from The Contemporary Commentaries of Sausal (15th ed.) Thus the Imperium may be as capricious as the human heart.*]

Therefore the prudent person should cultivate serenity. Beware of passions that steal reason.

Guttersage (usu. considered vulgar): The torrents of the heart may blow hot or cold, but blow, blow they will.

South Appalacia Peninsula, three and a half leagues southwest of Central Atlan, the Iapetus Plains:

"But . . . it's a *barn,* Salit," Plaia whispered and blew out an exasperated breath. "Who could possibly go to the *moon—*"

"Sst!" The Devil girl crept to the edge of the buck-wheat field where cultivated rows of grain gave way to unruly clumps of laceweed and choke grass. Salit moved with the single-minded sinuosity of a feral hunting beast. Her cloak shivered around her scrawny shoulders as she parted the stalks and peered out.

Plaia peered out, too. The sky rose into a sooty vault, the golden brown fields stretched all around, and, plunked amid the buckwheat like a ruin someone had forgotten to demolish, stood the stable. The sway-backed terra-cotta roof and concrete walls stained deep turquoise blue looked as if they might collapse in the next tremor. The place was unimaginably old.

Muscular drayers, bronze skin sleek with oil, bright tattoos of gladiatorial conquests adorning their biceps and thighs, churned up billows of dust as they approached the structure. Some wore blinders and bridles as well as harnesses. Shouting and groaning, they pulled gigantic sledges heaped with the offal of civilization—crushed beer jars and cracked cookpots, ruined linens and wrecked machines, broken geegaws and smeary barrels buzzing with flies.

Drivers cursed and berated the drayers, flicking whips over the glistening shoulders. Streetsweepers, veiled head to toe in traditional qaftans of grey sacking, trudged beside the sledges.

That was the traffic streaming *in*—a tremendous crowd that couldn't possibly all fit inside the modest stable.

And streaming *out*?

Now and then a sledge and drayer trudged through the barn doors, northward bound on the Imperial road. Glittering bars of opalescent purple metal were neatly stacked beneath formidable security nets studded with virulently orange security monitors.

"Is that atlantium?" Plaia whispered.

Salit nodded and rubbed the bulb of her thumb across her fingertips. "Sure like to get my hands on some of *that*. But we didn't come here to steal atlantium, did we?"

Security officers stood watchfully at the barn doors, fiddling with sheathed daggers, tapping batons into the palms of their hands, smoking cheroots, gossiping. Their slack faces and dull eyes told of hours of boredom.

Everyone—the drayers, the drivers, the laborers, the officers—wore brilliant scarlet protocol chips firmly implanted between their brows.

"See those chips?" Salit whispered. "That's so they don't tell the Secret except to anyone who asks 'em first."

Plaia glanced at Salit and blinked. For a moment the trailing black hem of the cloak, the Devil girl's shoulders, her legs doubled over in a kneel, and booted feet metamorphosed into the pattern of buckwheat stalks stirring in the breeze.

She recalled the girl's proud demonstration of the cloak's power in Dubban's cottage. Salit's skill at camouflaging had become effortless.

But the memories of that night when the Devils had leapt out of the shadows released a tidal wave of memories of Dubban. Every whisper. Every kiss and caress. Everything they'd done in his bed after the Devils had left them.

She choked back her wail of disbelieving grief. *You cannot be dead, my love.* Not after all they had risked. All Dubban had done for her. How much she'd come to depend on her bold boy. How much more than a boy he'd become during their time together. She didn't just miss him in every way a woman missed a man—she dreaded each day he would never stand beside her against the Imperium.

And then the carpal bones of her hands throbbed painfully, and a sneering sharemind clawed at her consciousness as if the grief made her vulnerable. *I'll find you, you seditious bitch, and when I do, you'll regret the day you were born.*

She shuddered. Gunther, exercising his prerogative, invoking his slightly superior subpure sharemind.

She vowed never to invoke sharemind again, not

even to dream in the Mind of the World. Lest even the exercise of Imperial sharemind became sullied by traces of her sharer's sharemind emanating from the remnants of the chips.

And allowed Gunther to track her down.

"Imperial Mining sends drud miners to Sanguine. That's where they excavate atlantium ore. Imperial Sanitation and Maintenance sends streetsweepers to the moon," Salit was saying and flicked her forefinger against Plaia's shoulder. "Are you listening to me?"

"Oh, I see. The Imperium goes to the red planet *and* the moon?"

"That's what I'm telling you."

Plaia shook her head. She had heard the same rumors in every boardwalk saloon where she'd ever raised a beer jar.

"Now, listen, here's my plan," Salit whispered. "I'll camouflage myself. Nab one of the security officers. That skinny little bored one over there, see her? You'll need her uniform and especially her protocol chip." The Devil girl withdrew a wad of filthy chewing wax from her pocket. "Just kind of stick the chip on your face with this. Once we outfit you, I'll camouflage next to a streetsweepers' sledge, you march through like you know what you're doing, and we're there. Got it? Good. Let's go."

"Wait a minute." Plaia caught the girl's arm. Her mouth felt parched, her fingertips cold. She shifted the burlap sack on her shoulder and tightened the strap. "You don't mean to tell me we're going inside. The roof's ready to fall on our heads."

"Gah, academe," the Devil girl said and shook her head. "Still don't believe me now we're here?"

After the Devil girl had proposed an expedition to the moon, they had returned to the cottage on Misty Alley. Plaia had collected her maps and texts, her new data and extrapolations, Dubban's farglass, and the finger cymbals he'd given her. She'd dug up the safe box he'd buried beneath the floor and taken his secret stash of ten thousand ores. She'd also collected gloves, socks, a cap, warm leggings, and two thick sweaters.

The Devil girl had said the moon was cold.

"Yeah, we're going inside," Salit said. "Tahliq showed me the way to the Doors last summer. One of the Doorkeepers told her the Imperium built the Doors in times lost to antiquity. But Tahliq always believed it was the Ancient Ones who knew how to fold space."

"Fold space?"

"The space between Pangaea and Sanguine. The space between Pangaea and the moon. I didn't understand, at first, but you know?" She tapped her forehead. "I think I'm beginning to. I've had dreams. *My* dreams. I've seen the Ancient Ones with their little machines. The machines bend the sky up and up and up, and then *boom*, it folds. So there's no distance when we walk across the threshold. The power doesn't propel us, it just bends the sky inside the Folds."

"The Folds?"

"That's the crack in the threshold. If we get past consortium security in one piece, you'll see for yourself. The Door looks just like a big old barn door. When you step through, you'll walk right over the Fold. It *is* a bit scary, really dark and deep, and it smells strange. There's a few loose floorboards, but don't worry. The Doors are still sound."

"And who is it we'll meet there?"

"My cousin Whieta. She's the sharer of the jarmaker at Al-Muud who was maimed by Regim. Whieta's half-drud, half-impure. When Regim harmed her sharer and their family, she fled Al-Muud and sought labor as a streetsweeper in Mara Mamba. Now she labors at the waste-disposal factory on the moon."

Plaia had been nodding through the girl's story, but at that juncture she stopped. "How did you discover all this, Salit?"

"Oh, Whieta sent word through our people. She'll be pleased to help us. I saved her from Regim's wrath that terrible day. I only wish I'd been able to help her sharer and children."

Still Plaia frowned. "But if the moon laborers wear protocol chips that suppress the Secret, how could Whieta send word? Wouldn't the chip prevent her from speaking about it to someone who hadn't asked first?"

"I told you, she's half-impure. She wears no security number so protocol chips don't affect her. We impure can do all sorts of things you pures can't." Salit winked. "For instance, I can steal into thoughts. Without a security number. I peeked in at the Alchemist's thoughts. He's fascinated with my sons. I know he'll take good care of them while we're gone. And boy, the thoughts he's got about *you*, academe."

"What thoughts could the eminent Councillor Sausal possibly have about me?"

The Devil girl silently rose to her feet and slunk out of the buckwheat field, cocking her head toward the unfortunate security officer she meant to snare. She tossed the wad of chewing wax and a wicked grin over her shoulder. "The Alchemist really, really likes your . . . eyes."

The moment they stepped onto the Plain of Vapors, her teeth commenced clattering so violently Plaia wondered if she'd crack her jawbone.

"Ho, this way." The Devil girl seized her wrist and yanked her out of the queue. "Be quick, get down, and shut *up*."

Plaia dived off the road and dug in her bootheels. She slid on fine, slick powder into the pitch-black bowl of a crater the size of a large bathtub. She gasped at the needle-sharp cold air. Hot fluid flooded her sinuses, the back of her throat. She leaned over, struck with vertigo and a swell of nausea. The protocol chip sent sharp little punishing jolts into her forehead even though she'd only affixed it with Salit's chewing wax. Her chattering teeth didn't help, either, an ache already palpable in her gums. The sudden loss of body heat nearly made her swoon. In another moment she knew what the fluid choking her was: Blood gushed from her nostrils, spat-

tering onto the glassy grey dust in bright floral
splotches.

"Damn." Salit shoved a handcloth at her. "What's
the matter with you, academe? You want to get us arrested before you've even had your chance to look at
the world?"

"Air," Plaia choked out and pinched the handcloth
over the bridge of her nose. "So thin, I can hardly
breathe." Her lungs burned, and every motion seemed
slightly exaggerated, as if she'd suddenly become twice
as forceful and didn't know her own strength. "How
are you faring?"

The Devil girl shrugged. "Doesn't bother me." She
glanced around. "I remember this place."

"You've been here before?"

"No, I've seen it in a dream."

Plaia tore open her sack, wrenched out another pair
of socks and a heavy sweater. She tore off the security
officer's uniform, jammed thick clothes over the thick
clothes she already wore beneath the uniform. Her
chattering teeth eased. She ripped off the stolen protocol chip and stuffed it in a pocket.

The freezing cold had already stanched her bloody
nose.

Salit stood on tiptoe, peering over the rim of the
crater. "We'd better shake a leg, academe."

The Devil girl hopped up and out of the crater. Plaia
scrambled up after her, seizing the sharp, raw edge of
swept rock, boosting herself over, and tumbling onto
the slippery plain with an awkward bounce. She kept a
keen eye on the Devil girl, who was already gliding
across the desolate landscape. That cloak of hers
melded into the stirring grey dust, the harshly lit hill-
ocks, the starkly shadowed shallows. Treacherous craters, large and small, scarred the barren ground, which
looked as if it had been target practice for a vengeful
giant with a slingshot and a bucketful of asteroids. The
blue-black vault of the sky yielded to the awesome
reaches of outer space.

They were bound, Plaia saw, for a factory. One of

several that reared smoking profiles against the severe
lunar horizon. A thousand spewing smokestacks jutted
up from a tremendous squat of bunkers. Tiny black
figures swarmed in and out and all around the great,
dark blocks like insects tending a hive. Plaia saw in
another moment that the crawling forms, rendered tiny
by distance, were the waste-heaped sledges and veiled
streetsweepers.

Thousands of them. Hundreds of thousands.

A gigantic roar suddenly rumbled, booming louder
and louder, jamming her head with thunder. Plaia
stuffed fingers into her ears and wondered if her skull
would burst. The bleak moonscape lit up, and blinding
blue-white shafts of light thrust from beneath the thick
metal lids of immense incinerators. Furious blasts of
flame leapt from the towering smokestacks.

If she had never believed in the Eternal Flames of
Inim before, Plaia did now.

"Ho, Whieta, my cousin," Salit said and embraced a
wizened little woman with the purple-black hair and
grey complexion of the druds at Ál-Muud, the misshapen limbs and lopsided features of the impure. "This
is Plaia Triadana. I know, I know, she's a *pure*. We need
to stay a couple of days while she looks at the world.
That *is* what you're going to do, isn't it, academe?"

Plaia gazed out the tiny portals of the barracks. The
place smelled of wood rot and mold and was very cold,
scarcely warmer than the air outside despite the glowing cookstones in corner braziers. Salit's cousin's ill-lit
cubicle offered a comfortless cot, a chamber pot in one
corner, a washbasin in the other, and a tiny writing
table set before a portal. The uncertain privacy of sliding canvas curtains was all that shielded them from the
eyes of other laborers and the consortium's security.

Communal kitchens, dining rooms, bathing facilities,
and proper latrines were accommodated in facilities
down the hall.

A sheet of crystal paper covered the portal, and rawhide strips had been tacked around the edges. Still, gusts of bitter cold leaked through.

Plaia gazed and gazed through that little window, unable to tear her eyes from the gorgeous blue globe poised in deep blackness over the lunar horizon.

Pangaea. Rich, moist clouds formed a living scrim of swirling foam—snow-white, eggshell-white, pearl-grey, charcoal, delicate brown, and the most amazing pearlescent pink. The world archipelago was as recognizable as the face of a cherished friend.

A sensation surged through her, overwhelming her more intensely than any act of human desire. Love. Fierce and uncompromising. An unfathomable, depthless love for the planet. *Her* planet. The only home people had ever known.

This was why she'd sought her mastery in earth-shock prediction and prevention.

Steadfast purpose filled her.

"Yes," she said over her shoulder to Salit and her cousin. She spilled maps and texts from her sack, fished out the farglass, spread everything out on the tiny table. Her hands were already chilled to the bone. "That's exactly what I'm going to do. I'm going to look at the world."

Salit promised her four days on the moon, and then the Devil girl wanted to return to Atlan and to her young sons.

"Four days it shall be," Plaia vowed, unwilling to face the consortium's security alone.

She began at once, comparing the world spinning before her with Tivern's maps. This turned out to be a dizzying enterprise since the moon ceaselessly meandered through its orbit around Pangaea, and Pangaea itself rotated. The world, in reversal, appeared to undergo the waxing and waning of the moon, darkness blotting out a hemisphere at a time. Confounding her observation further, the clouds teased her with a visual hide-and-seek that, before too long, had her eyes watering and her head reeling.

Still, she could plainly see the discrepancies and errors riddling Tiv's maps. Plaia arduously penciled in renderings of the eastern Appalacian coastline right over the original map. By the time the Cordilleran coast had spun into view, she no longer wasted precious time exclaiming in amazement and dismay, but swiftly sketched the true shape and features of the landmass before her as accurately as she could.

Salit pulled up her hood, closed the chameleon cloak, and stole away, visible in the barracks hallway only as a mysterious shimmer. In a while she returned to Whieta's cubicle with steaming-hot caf and butter cakies. Whieta herself chatted with the security guards who patrolled the barracks and bribed them with one of Salit's Orbs of Eternity.

The Devil girl parted with her contraband, a noncommittal shrug arching her scrawny shoulders. "Don't worry. I'll steal it back before we go."

After twelve hours, the Panthalassa Ocean swung into view. Plaia gasped at the awesome sight: the vast variegated sea that drowned the other side of the world. The complexity of the currents cried out for its own topographical rendering. Streams of pale blue, deep indigo, moss-green, gentle brown, or ice-grey depending on their warmth, coolness, or mineral content, whirled and surged in formidable patterns that rivaled the magnificence of the clouds.

The appetizing scents of roast rock hen and hot flatbreads taunted her empty belly.

"Packing up for the night?" Salit said, suddenly standing beside her in the cubicle.

Plaia wearily gathered up the maps and her drafting materials and stowed everything beneath Whieta's cot. "Well, I'd better. I need to be fresh and clear-eyed when Tasman Province rolls around"—she checked the tiny water clock next to the cot—"in another ten hours." She knuckled her eyes and yawned. The Devil girl stood two paces before her, now a slight dark figure, now no more than another fold in the canvas curtains. "Could you please not do that? I really *will* go blind."

Salit chuckled and dropped to the floor in a double-jointed crouch. She extracted from beneath the cloak basket after basket of food and flask after flask of drink. "Hungry? Want some wine? Ho, this isn't what the sweepers get to eat. I paid a little visit to the security officers' mess."

Plaia gratefully seized a flatbread and a flask of kapfo. "No one will miss this?"

"Sure they will." At Plaia's groan, she said, "I'll dump the flasks behind the officers' mess after we've had our fill. By the time their supers finish interrogating their own, we'll be back on Pangaea."

"Thank you, Salit. For the most wanted foe terrorist in all Pangaea, you've been a chum."

"Well, our detainment warrants *do* share the same lamppost in Marketplace." Salit whipped her dagger from its sheath. "Just remember, I'm repaying a blood debt for your man. Salit Zehar, Heaven's Devil extraordinaire, always repays her blood debts." The Devil girl sliced off a chunk of rock hen, speared it, and seized the chunk off the knife tip with her teeth. "See anything interesting down there? Y'know, like the Highest Councillor bedding the Cardinal of the Mind of the World?"

Plaia grinned. "I'd need a *much* stronger farglass to see that. But, yes, what I've seen so far is *very* interesting. Appalacia and Cordillera exhibit patterns of folded and extruded mountains. No one has ever gotten such a clear view of them before. Between the reports I've been collecting on earthshock and volcanic activity and my adjustment of Tivern's magnetic wander curves, I believe I'll be able to plot just where the world shell is moving. And where catastrophe will strike."

Salit furrowed her brow. "What kind of mountains?"

Plaia took out her map and sighed at her scribbles. She wished she'd had another copy, but the task of transcribing Tiv's original the first time had taken her nearly all winter. She tapped her forefinger on Appalacia. "Look here. Some mountains are formed when one piece of the world shell pushes against another. See the collisional structure? They're called folded mountains."

Salit seized two sides of her cloak, folded the fabric, and placed the folds side by side. "Like the Folds in the Doors?"

Plaia eyed the Devil girl's demonstration. "Very much like that. Other mountains are formed by magma erupting through a crack in the shell—those are extruded, or volcanic, mountains." She traced the curving ridges with her fingernail. "The Appalacian range forms rows of peaks placed neatly side by side. The peaks are orderly, almost uniform, showing a similar degree of erosion. But here"—she tapped the Hercynian Sea— "the peaks are solitary. Randomly scattered. The configurations unique, the erosion indicating large differentials in the age of formation."

"Like the Isle of Pyrber where the Hercynian Vent used to be," Salit said. "Say, look at these other islands north of Pyrber. They volcanic, too?"

"Exactly right. They must have erupted long before Pyrber. The Appalacian landmass must have shoved up against Caledonia Province, here to the north. Shoved a couple of times, causing magma to erupt out of the molten core below the world shell. I'm still not sure where the intruding shell *goes*. But I'd say there must have been other vents at the bottom of the Hercynian Sea."

Salit nodded buoyantly, her colorful mop of hair flopping around her ears. "So if you could plot where the mountains of Pangaea have folded and where they've spurted up, you could guess where the world shell might tear open in the future and where it's going to bang into another piece of itself. Then maybe you could find a haven where the shell won't do any of those things."

"Salit, you deserve a seat on the board of Ground Control."

"Ho, academe, are you insulting me?"

Plaia shook her head and tipped the flask, drizzling sour kapfo down her parched throat. "Not hardly."

Plaia jolted awake.

Sunlight burned through the portal like a Vigilance spotlight. Whieta had curled up behind her and nestled in the small of her back. The dark huddle on the floor was Salit, wrapped in her cloak and coiled as if ready to spring. An unsheathed dagger lay on the floor flush with her face, her hand poised over the hilt.

No sooner had Plaia heaved a waking breath than the Devil girl *did* leap to her feet, dagger gripped in her fist.

"It's just me, Salit."

"*Sst!*"

Plaia heard the clomp of bootheels. The barracks suddenly came awake. Sleepy sweepers bolted upright in their cots, rattling the metal struts and murmuring in alarm. Magister voices shouted brusque interrogatories.

A trio of consortium security officers stood just outside Whieta's curtains, haranguing the sweeper in the next cubicle. Plaia heard something about a jar of beer the sweeper had allegedly swiped, and the protests of the accused thief in answer. She heard curtains being flung open, objects flung about. Marching bootheels again.

Then they were gone.

Plaia surveyed Whieta's cubicle in the morning light and saw nothing that would land their accommodating little hostess in trouble with the consortium. Her head throbbed. Her mouth tasted sour. Her eyelids felt as if their insides were coated with glassy moon dust—and perhaps they were. She yearned for a cup of hot caf, but rose, withdrew her maps and papers from beneath the cot, wiped a film of vapor from the crystal paper, and set to work.

Cloud cover over Pangaea was thankfully sparse, and a low procession of elongated landmasses swooped into view. They had to be the far eastern outlands Plaia had only heard about in school: Arctica, Tasman, Borno, Chinee, Buruma, Himal. The coastlines before her differed radically from Tivern's map. She hastily sketched what she saw, methodically resketching the whole on a blank sheet of parchment, before the planet's rotation swung the outlands over the horizon.

She stared in disbelief at Himal Rift, an abyss of fearsome dimensions even from this height. The suture zone stitched across the entire south perimeter of Himal Province and held fiery swirls of magma in its trough, intermingled with brown sludge. Blue rivers of seawater seeped through a massive trough between Borno and Tasman. Steam clouds several leagues in length billowed where cool ocean collided with molten disgorgement from the hot depths of Pangaea.

Suddenly Salit stood at her elbow again. The Devil girl plunked down a covered cup of hot caf and a hard-boiled egg wrapped in a handcloth.

"Bless you, my child," Plaia said. "Bless your children and their children and their children."

"I'll add it to your tab." The Devil girl studied her sketches. She plucked the sheet of parchment and held it next to the portal. She frowned with mock disapproval as if judging the artistry of the work, turning the sheet this way and that. "See anything good?"

Plaia blew on the caf, taking care not to scald her mouth, and contemplating the hard-boiled egg. *Consider the egg. When is the shell not the shell?* Tivern had posed. She answered Salit, "I saw Himal Rift. It's phenomenal." She cracked the shell and gently squeezed it. *Where does the landmass go?* A fragment of the shell popped off and fell in her lap.

"You're supposed to eat the thing, academe, not enter sharelock with it," Salit said. She produced another egg for herself and followed her own advice. "Say, look at this." She fitted the parchment sketch next to Plaia's new rendering of the Cordilleran coast on Tivern's map. "It's like a picture puzzle. I love picture puzzles, don't you? Once my father and I made our own puzzle. I painted a picture of our tentsite on a sheet of wood. Horan cut the whole sheet apart into pieces. Then he scattered the pieces every which way, and I had to put the picture together again. Did you ever make a picture puzzle? I'll have to make my sons—"

It was impossible. Unbelievable. It had to be a trick of the light.

But there it was, a picture puzzle scattered by the Hand of Pan for humanity to piece together again.

"Dear Pan and Inim." Plaia seized the sketch from the Devil girl's hand. *I knew it. I knew it before I knew it.* Her heart hammered in her breast so violently she feared her rib cage would burst open and set every yearning of her lifetime free.

The opposite coastlines of the world archipelago fit together.

Not *perfectly.* How could anything formed millennia ago, in times lost to antiquity, remain exactly the same? She took her time, studying how the extrusions of the far eastern coast fit into the involutions of the far west. There and there and there. In such minute and astonishing detail she couldn't have faked the correlations if she'd wanted to. There was an inward swerve in the Chinee coastline that wouldn't mesh by many leagues with the inland shore of the Bay of Dilran, leaving a large roundish gap between that portion of the coastlines.

Not perfectly. No. But close enough.

"Isn't that strange?" Salit was saying. "I mean, the whole damn ocean of the *world* lies between them."

"Yes, it does." Plaia laughed, and her cheeks were drenched with tears. "I *love* picture puzzles."

"And I say we go *tonight.*" Salit deposited a dinner basket and wine flask at Plaia's elbow. "This morning was a close call."

"You promised me four days."

Plaia massaged her lids in hopes her eyestrain would ease. Her right eye had blurred and refused to clear. She had sat before the portal for another fourteen hours, observing, scribbling, sketching. Gondwana, Siluria, Scanda, the Far Reaches. And back around again to Our City of Atlan, the Great Wall, the Bog, Appalacia. She'd taken to peering through Dubban's farglass, an undertaking that had reconfigured her headache from the back of her skull to right between the eyes.

"We've got two days left. You promised, Salit."

"I take it back. Whieta says security is getting restless."

"I've got money. How much more do they want?"

"They don't need your ores. They need cookstones, hide gloves, healing herbs, better skee."

"Take one of my sweaters."

"You'll freeze yourself solid in the snap of two fingers without your sweaters, academe."

"Two more days."

"Nope. There's talk about who's stealing food and drink from the officers' mess. No one among these druds has got that kind of nerve. And, come morning, they'll be wondering where *this* is." She brandished her fourth Orb of Eternity, strung the thong over her neck, and nestled the orb between her breasts.

"I thought you said you'd steal it back before we leave."

"That's right. We're leaving. I'm anxious to see my sons again. And I don't think *you* want to get arrested."

That silenced her.

"So pack up your gear, have some caf, and enjoy the view. Don't fall asleep and don't let anyone see you."

"All right, all right."

"We leave at midnight. I've got to go and make arrangements. See who's going through the Door tonight and who needs to be bribed. Or, y'know, taken *care* of." Smirking, Salit slashed her fingertip across Plaia's throat. Opened the curtain, closed her cloak—and was gone.

Plaia set about packing her gear. Foreboding filled her at the prospect of the harrowing trek to the Door. She gobbled the last of the cakies, drained the caf, and sat down to wait for her escort.

After the feverish hours and deep exhaustion of the past two days, her wakeful idleness slowed to an unbearable crawl. Her eyes strayed irresistibly to her beautiful blue world. Pangaea, half-shrouded in night, hung slightly to the right of the portal. She nestled up, peering out. The Panthalassa Ocean reclined before her like a great cosmic bath. Such lovely colors. Such patterns.

For the past two days she'd slept when the world ocean showed its face. Now she stared, fascinated anew by the soothing blue. *Look at that pale green current. It must be leagues wide. Why, it wends its way across the whole world. There it melds with paler, warmer waters. There flows with deep, grey waters. There flows side by side with waters so cold and indigo blue they look black.*

And with a jolt she saw something where the great green current flowed with the black: another green. Not a meandering aquatic green but the green of vegetation amid the watery hues. A solid patch that wasn't flowing somewhere else.

Dear Pan, that's . . . land.

An island. . . . A continent! On the other side of the world.

She nearly shouted with excitement, ripped off two layers of gloves, and fumbled in her sack, searching for stylus and parchment. *I've got to chart it. Trace the green current. It must eventually flow near some coast of the archipelago. Or lie in relation to other currents flowing near land. Then trace the current back to the black current—*

A clawlike hand closed over her wrist.

"Damn, academe," Salit whispered. "What are you *doing*?"

"I found something," Plaia said. "I've got to chart it—"

"Are you crazy? We've got to go!"

She grabbed Plaia's parchment. Plaia grabbed it back, and they struggled briefly for possession of the flimsy paper.

Suddenly the floorboards trembled beneath their feet, setting the curtains swaying and the cots rattling.

"What in hell was *that*?"

Salit said, "The factory's probably blasting another load of waste."

"No. No, I've never felt movement like this after a blast. It's . . . a foreshock. Salit, does the moon have its own shocks?"

"How would I know?" The Devil girl exchanged a rush of words with Whieta. The half drud's eyes darted fearfully. "Whieta says there are moonshocks sometimes. Nothing this strong. Let's take our leave, academe."

"You're right." Plaia reclaimed and hastily rolled the parchment, jammed the scroll into the sack, and yanked the drawstring shut. She stole one last yearning glance at the world poised above the lunar horizon, but the landmass—whatever it was—had disappeared beneath a whorl of clouds. She buttoned the stolen officer's tunic more tightly over her breast and warmed the chewing wax in her mouth, grimacing at the taste. She pressed wax and the scarlet protocol chip between her brows, wincing when the chip thrust needles of suppression into her mind. "I'm ready."

They slipped into a brigade of streetsweepers hobbling on the road toward the Door. Many had been injured. Some wore splints or mud casts over fractured limbs. Others reclined on litters carried by fellow sweepers. Plaia wrapped a kerchief over her nose and mouth and averted her eyes. She joined the escort of weary security officers, moving where she was told to move, answering queries with a noncommittal grunt.

Suddenly the ground rocked beneath Plaia's feet, lurching so violently she nearly fell to her knees.

"Plaia, what's going on?" Salit muttered.

Scaffolding of a silver metal framed the Door to Pangaea. Precise beams and gleaming crossbars formed lintel, jambs, and threshold. The Fold loomed wider here, a depthless abyss as wide as Plaia's arm was long that emitted energy distorting the air above it. No one had taken the time to conceal this Secret in a stable. No one needed to. Everyone wore the scarlet protocol chip ensuring their silence.

The lunar road jolted again. Whieta whimpered. The druds moaned. Plaia counted *one thousand, two thousand, three thousand, four* . . .

And again, a nerve-jangling oscillation.

"Peace and calm," a security officer growled. "We shall return to the barracks till the motion subsides."

"No," Plaia called out, "we must go through the Door."

The hulking magister subpure stepped in her path. He shoved the palm of a meaty hand against her breast and leaned so close they nearly touched noses. "I say we return."

"And I say we go on."

The ground shuddered again, jolting the Door. Plaia saw metal struts dangling loose, bolts that had worked free of their moorings, and joints that gaped where one beam no longer fit another. The scaffolding was, on closer inspection, frail and pockmarked with age.

Plaia sidestepped the security officer, shoved Salit and Whieta before her, and sprinted for the Door. "Go, go, go!"

Plaia leapt over the threshold. Swords of shimmering energy thrust out of the Fold, lancing her as palpably as a weapon. She tumbled to the ground and rolled, shaking badly. Sultry air struck her face like a towel soaked in hot water. The animal smell of a stable assailed her senses. She tore off her heavy clothes to see if she was bleeding or had lost limbs.

Shouting and a distant clanging sound filled her ears. In a moment she realized she heard the distant tolling of the Harbinger. She struggled to rise, but couldn't move her limbs. Perspiration drenched her. She glanced up at the startled faces of security guards and saw drawn weapons. She crawled on her hands and knees away from the Door.

The floor pitched beneath her, bucking so violently she tumbled across the stable. People were shouting, staggering crazily. Someone tackled her, and she hit the floor, kicking and flailing. She struggled to face her attacker but his hand gripped the nape of her neck and shoved her facedown.

And then she was free. She rolled over.

Salit Zehar was yanking a dagger from a burly guard's back and shoving him into the scattered straw. Plaia scrambled against the wall and crouched there, examining herself. She saw no blood, though she ached in two dozen places. She drank in the rich Pangaean air, nearly fainting from the surfeit of oxygen.

An earthshock. She cocked her head, listening to the toll of the Harbinger. *Seven mags.* The ceiling above her groaned, and a huge beam fell, smashing the drayers below it. Roof tiles cascaded and shattered on the floor. The concrete walls shivered.

Plaia glanced, horrified, at the Doors.

She could see clear through the Door to Sanguine. A range of harsh mountains poised against a blue-black sky, a reddish brown plain reclined below them, and the silver ribbon of a river. People looked back at her from the other side, peculiar little drud women with downy faces.

Through the Door to the moon she could see the dusty grey hills and severe shadowed craters, the great waste-disposal factories teeming with sweepers. The entourage of injured sweepers poised tentatively at the threshold.

The earthshock convulsed again. Vibrations shuddered through the other worlds, surging across the plains as if solid rock were water. The Folds rippled and widened. Rippled and widened again. A crackling blackness spilled out of the Folds.

Then a thunderous detonation exploded across Sanguine, and another explosion across the moon. A force swept away the atmosphere, leveled landscapes, scooped up mountains and human monuments, barracks and factories and laborers, and flung them into the void.

The blackness unfolded, a vast, sparkling ribbon uncoiling, flicking out with the snap of a whip. The enormous force pushed the other worlds before it, driving them farther and farther out. The moon's visage, once so huge and hearty, hung distant and forlorn, no more than an ornament in the night sky. The succulent plum of Sanguine had receded in the heavens, too, till it was no more than a dusky red twinkle in the vast firmament.

The ancient turquoise walls burst apart.

The Doors collapsed, lintels and jambs crushed in the explosion of rubble.

Plaia pulled herself to her feet and darted through the mob. She shoved aside terrified drayers and dodged security officers, sprinting around ceiling beams crashing down all around her. Till her heart hammered in her throat and her lungs heaved.

As the stable fell, she ran out and headed for the buckwheat fields. She dived into the wildly tossing stalks, sinking hands and knees into fertilized mud.

A dark shimmer coalesced beside her. Salit appeared, heaving for breath. Whieta joined them, crawling through the stalks like a feral creature. Salit embraced her, and they exchanged tearful words. Devil girl and half-pure cousin kissed and embraced, reassuring themselves they'd actually gotten *out*.

Plaia stood on unsteady legs and peered through the buckwheat.

Smeary curtains of force rippled and radiated away from the ruins, adding their stain to the polluted sky.

Salit stood next to her, watching sadly. "No one will ever believe us that the Imperium once went to the moon and Sanguine, will they?"

"No," Plaia said. "I can hardly believe it myself."

"Stand back, it's *him*," Plaia whispered.

"Who?" Salit said.

"Got walkabouts with him." She held up her scarred hands.

Dawn rose, and Rancid Flats was waking. Plaia and

the Devil girl pressed themselves against the side of canvas slung from a ridgepole and staked to the ground. A refugees' tentsite, the canvas mud-stained and quite the worse for wear, the grounds collecting broken jars and litter. Plaia had never seen the eyesore before, which had been erected on the corner of Misty Alley and Winding Lane during their two-and-a-half-day trek on the moon. Strange rough servs gathered at the front flap, still up from the night before, sipping skee from flasks and leering at passersby.

Her snug little cottage stood half a block away.

Dubban would have been outraged. He would have chased the roustabouts away with a brandished fist and a no-nonsense scowl.

But strange servs were the least of her troubles.

Gunther stood before the cottage with an escort of half a dozen heavily armed walkabouts. He wore the rich robes of a high-ranking bureaucrat and a fancy cap over his pate.

"You can open up, Plaia," he called through the door, "or we can break it down. Take your pick."

"We've got an Imperial search permission," a vigile shouted.

Two sacred surgeons and their assistants from the Temple of Sacred Sharelock stood behind Gunther, bearing scalpels and anodyne on a tray.

Plaia's hands ached at the thought of sharelock chips. She tapped Salit's stringy shoulder. "Let's go."

"Didn't you leave a lot of stuff in there? Proofs and such?"

"I retrieved everything I need, thanks to our moon trek. Come. I've got a friend, a fisherwoman, who lives down the lane. She'll shelter us till Gunther leaves the flats." Plaia recalled Rando, Nita's quick-fisted sharer, with a shiver of distaste. "But only if her damn sharer is out on the town with one of his bedmates."

Plaia pulled her cap down low, and they mingled with the crowd, giving a wide berth to Dubban's cottage and Gunther. Plaia strode up the alley for Nita's place and spied the thatch-roofed hovel. There was a tumbledown look of neglect and unhappiness clinging to the daub-and-wattle walls.

Nita's rugged, deeply tanned face peered out from behind three chain locks securing her front door. At the sight of Plaia peeking out from the low brim of her cap, she gave a little scream and clapped her hand over her mouth. "Oh, Plaia. That sharer of yours has been poking his mug around here, looking for you. Offering ores for information."

"I saw him. Is Rando home? Let us in, quickly."

The fisherwoman shut the door, unhooked the locks, cracked opened the door again, and ushered them inside. She gazed at Salit, eyes widening as she recognized the Devil girl from the Mind of the World. She glanced questioningly at Plaia.

Plaia patted her friend's arm. "It's all right, I know her. Salit," she admonished the Devil girl, "this is my friend, Nita. You behave yourself, all right?"

"Oh, sure." Without further introduction, Salit strode to Nita's ice box and pantry. She was soon snout-deep in the box and cupboards, plucking out flat-breads, salt cheese, jars of cold beer. She stuffed a fruit ice between her teeth with a satisfied sigh and bore her booty to Nita's dining table. She handed beer jars to Nita and Plaia and tucked into her repast.

Plaia kneaded her forehead. "My Dub is dead."

"We heard," Nita said and wiped a tear from her eye with her rugged knuckle. "Rumors have been buzzing. Such a good man. I know the two of you had something special. The Imperium wouldn't have made it easy. Thanks to you, Dub started acting way beyond his purity. Don't glare at me, please, Plaia. I cared about Dubban, too. I never was any good at talking about things I don't understand." She sipped her beer. "Perhaps *you* haven't heard. Your fathers are dead. Their villa collapsed in the last seven-mag. Pleasant Valley got hit hard. I'm sorry, Plaia."

It was a sudden grief, of course, but somehow, on the moon, Plaia had left her old life behind, once and

for all. Looking at Pangaea from on high, she knew
what she had to do.

Nita peered anxiously. "Are you all right, Plaia? You
spoke many times of your love for your fathers."

"Trenton and Cairn were good fathers, but in the
end they betrayed me. They made a mockery of the
family I thought I had. What does parental love mean in
Pangaea?"

Plaia gazed at the Devil girl as she devoured food.
Salit knew. This ravenous, cheeky, dangerous terrorist
girl knew the unconditional loyalty that parental love
required. Her love for her sons, even the beautiful
bronze boy who had not issued from her body, was
unquestionable.

"Salit, go back to your sons, once you've refreshed
yourself." Plaia pulled out her worn, much-scribbled-
upon copy of Tivern's map, rolled and sealed it, wrote
an address along its length, and handed the scroll to
Salit. "I need you to deliver this to an administrator at
Ground Control. Maiselle Trey is her name. She keeps
rooms off of Southwest Marketplace. You must make
certain to place this in her hands when no one else is in
her company. Will you do that for me, Salit? And then
your blood debt to me will be fully repaid."

Salit reached for the scroll. "I'll do it."

"Thank you. With any luck, Maiselle may be able to
stave off Gunther's ultimate solution. We can hope."
Plaia smiled fondly at her fisher friend. "We had some
good conversations, didn't we, Nita? But Atlan has
nothing left for me. I'm leaving. Can you smuggle me
aboard one of those transoceanic ships you told me
about? One that explores the other side of the world.
I've got some money for bribes, but I'm willing to
crew."

"But you're an academe," Nita said. She stared,
aghast, at Plaia's delicate hands. "Beg your pardon, but
what can you *do*?"

"I'll pass as a cartographer subpure. Don't exploratory ships map the currents?"

Nita eyed her. "They do. But crewing is hard labor,

Plaia. The sun will roast you alive. The food is terrible, the water worse. Forget sleeping soundly. And explorations last *forever*. It takes years to cross the Panthalassa. If your crew turns out to be a barrel of rotten apples, you're stuck with them. They're mostly druds and servs, who cannot abide middle pures and will take pleasure in making your life miserable. And *some* ships," she added, "never return at all. The torrents are treacherous. Even the Imperium has never conquered them."

"I shall manage, Nita. There's only one thing left for me to live for."

"What's that?"

"The lost continent." Plaia laughed, and her laughter felt like bubbles bursting open, letting loose the heady spice of a quest. "I know it's out there. On the other side of the world."

III

DRIFT

FACET 28

    Open Eyes: Objective intellect or selfish ego.
    A sapphire in the sunlight becomes like onyx
      in the moonlight.
    The action is logical investigation.
    The forbearance is dogmatic belief.

                    The Orb of Eternity

Commentaries:
Councillor Sausal: We have seen that Pan illuminates the day with the sun and the night with the
moon. Yet clouds may obscure the sun at noon,
and the night is dark when the moon is new.

    So, too, the Imperium preserves the truths of
the Ancient Ones for the benefit of all the purities.
[*Deleted from The Contemporary Commentaries of Sausal (15th Ed.)* Yet some truths have been
lost to antiquity, and some truths have yet to be
found.]

    Therefore the prudent person should observe
clearly and reason objectively.

    Beware of opinion that purports to be fact.
Guttersage (usu. considered vulgar): The academe
sets forth a theory and calls it philosophy.

    The priestess sets forth a theory and calls it
truth.

*Our Imperial Province of Andea, the Township of
Peruvia, Our City of Dalel. Zateca Alley, the Fiery
Phoenix Saloon:*

"Plaia. Plaia Triadana. Dear Afrodite, is it really you?"

Flushed with a hot-pepper sunburn and miserably aching in muscles she hadn't known she possessed, Plaia glanced up from her shot of skee. She'd been pressing her beer jar against one cheek, then the other, rolling it across her forehead and throat, taking what comfort she could from the chilly ceramic.

The autumn turning had blasted the southern provinces with fierce heat and becalmed the pale turquoise waters of South Panthalassa Ocean. For days she'd been marooned in Dalel, watching burly construction crews excavate ruins of the seaport by day, sipping rum at the Fiery Phoenix by night. With the help of Nita's friends in Andea, she had secured a position aboard a transoceanic vessel, Our Sacred Imperial Seaship the *Leaping Dragon,* but had been unable to depart. The magister-captain refused to set sail on an exploration without an inaugural boost of steady wind.

Andea. Cursed Andea.

It was small satisfaction that she could finally witness with her own eyes what the Imperium had long denied. That here magma had burst forth in a tremendous eruption where no magma chamber was supposed to have been. Here a living city had been buried in bleeding rock. Here Tivern had died, under suspicious circumstances.

And here Gunther had force-flooded a rift for the first time, setting off major earthshocks and cleaving new rifts that had decimated this part of the archipelago.

Andea was the last place in Pangaea she wanted to be marooned.

"Dear *Afrodite*?" Plaia turned, astonished. "Since when does a maiden-chasing roustabout like you invoke the name of She who rules women's fertility?"

"Since I've found good reason to thank She who succored me during my travail. So you recognized me, after all this time?"

"Well, of course!"

In truth, Plaia would *not* have recognized her colleague Paven had he not spoken first over the earsplitting din. That brash voice, that mocking guffaw, had been indelibly imprinted in her recollection. Evoking fond memories of simpler, gentler days—though her life as a mastery student had hardly seemed simple or gentle at the time. She still found herself bewildered that she could have ever thought otherwise.

"I thought you were dead," she added bluntly.

"And I thought you'd run off to commit heresies with a handsome black-haired serv," he shot back.

"I did. But you're not, my dear old chum."

Paven guffawed, dispelling any lingering doubt it was really him.

How naive we all were. She hoped the abashment didn't show too plainly in her eyes. Paven had once been a scientist-musician on his way to a mastery and a good position with Ground Control, just like her. Once a slender, elegant academe with the polished glow of privilege.

Standing before her now was a burly, blistered fellow, with the look of hard prison labor about him and long hours in an exercise yard with little else to do but lift weights. Paven wore his new ruggedness well.

She felt comforted. Her smile faded, though, when she looked at his face and hands. The top joints of each of his little fingers had been removed and two joints of the middle finger of his right hand. The handiwork of a Vigilance torturer. His eyebrows and luxuriant mop of brown hair had been shaved off so many times he'd acquired a premature baldness, a prison tattoo above his partially amputated left ear, and a painfully naked look to his eyes. Those sardonic eyes held sorrow in their depths, the haunted look of one who had faced ruin.

I suppose he could be thinking much the same of me.

Paven's academe sharemind teased her. *Child, you're as beautiful as ever.*

She yearned with a palpable ache to enter mutual consciousness with him. Subpure sharemind with Paven had always been effortless, delightful, and deeply satisfying. How she missed exchanging bawdy fantasies, contentious philosphies, sensations as immediate as her own perceived by another set of senses.

She did not enter.

The Alchemist had been right. Life *was* lonely and dark and isolated without the joys of common consciousness. Without the angels' dreams in the Mind of the World.

Her one consolation? She touched her arm, feeling the little mole of her security number. She had retained that which the Alchemist had sacrificed. She still *could* enter sharemind, in all its myriad forms.

Someday, she would.

But not yet. Even on the Andean Coast thousands of leagues from Central Atlan, even after the arduous, sunlashed journey sailing south, she did not believe she had gotten far enough away from Gunther. She'd awakened every night in her narrow bunk bed aboard the Imperial Fisheries skiff that had sped her away from Atlan. Awakened parch-mouthed and perspiring, apprehension jolting through her limbs. Certain she'd heard the stomp of Vigilance bootheels coming for her and Gunther's sardonic laugh.

But the sounds disturbing her slumber had only been the sea slapping against the skiff's sturdy hull.

"Damn, child," Paven exclaimed. She could tell from his distracted look that he'd been *trying* to enter sharemind and found her resistance puzzling. She worried he would ask why, but he only said, "Look at those scars on your pretty hands."

"Hardly pretty anymore. These hands are as callused and sunburned as yours, Pav." And as mutilated, but she didn't want to say that.

"That's just like you, Plaia, searching for more compliments. Don't tell me *you,* Plaia the Plaything, entered sacred sharelock?" His eyes widened with astonishment. "Don't tell me it was with that bastard Gunther. I never could abide that smug, proximicist excuse for a—"

"What's this I hear spilling from your mouth,

Paven?" shouted another familiar voice over Plaia's shoulder. "Discussing sharelock in the Fiery Phoenix with a beautiful lady?"

She turned. A dark-haired, dark-eyed, hardily built fellow stood smiling before her, as untouched by time and brutality as Paven had been maimed. "Rulian?"

"Sweet Plaia!"

She threw her arms around her former fellow prisoner and embraced him so tightly that he gasped and choked with disbelieving laughter. "My sweet cellmate."

"Say, Rul is *my* cellmate now," Paven declared and embraced them both so exuberantly he sent Plaia's beer jar flying across the bar, drenching the grizzled fisherwoman seated next to her.

"Hai, the three of ye take your grappling upstairs to a proper bed," the fisherwoman shouted, angrily swiping at her leggings with a handcloth.

"Let's snag a table," Paven said, ordering rounds of beer and skee, slapping a handful of ores on the bar.

A lively crowd of hard-bitten servs jammed the Fiery Phoenix, mostly weathered fishers and shippers with the occasional gang of pugnacious drivers, wrists bound with leather bands, bullwhips coiled at their belts. Plaia and company fit in well enough. She wore a sailor's tunic and leggings of rough copper-colored linen, Paven and Rulian the copper-colored uniforms of serv laborers.

Still, as they wended their way to the rear of the saloon, she averted her eyes and moved stealthily, acutely aware they were the only middle pures present. Their stature, demeanor, even the shapes of their faces, might give them away. She wondered how Paven could tolerate the risk. He had paid the price that night at the Serpent Sect rave.

"Nope, I'm not dead yet," Paven shouted in her ear as if he *had* discerned her memories in sharemind. "Atlan Vigilance tortured me a bit. Then they shipped me off to Andea. Tossed my butt in Tertius Jail. Been bummin' around the south coast ever since. It ain't

Atlan, child, but then again you won't get arrested just for drinking in a serv saloon."

He claimed a great squat of a darkwood table, its sticky surface cluttered with beer jars and shot glasses, ashtrays overflowing with cheroot ashes and rapture-root butts. Plaia began plucking the debris, but Paven stopped her.

"The Fiery Phoenix is *my* dive, sweetie. Here's how we locals clear the table."

He swept the back of his arm across and sent everything crashing to the floor.

They sat, and a server came with a tray. Plaia seized a shot of skee, clinked it against her fellow academes' glasses, and gulped half, wincing from the bite.

"Now what's this I hear about you and sharelock?" Rulian said, his dark eyes somber and questioning.

He'd been disappointed when she'd declined his sharelock offer. Disappointment clouded him still as he took her hands and examined them. "Did you cut the chips out all by yourself?"

"Scars look that bad, do they?"

"Never mind. Was it Gunther who came for you that afternoon they took you away?"

"Yes. With a petition for my release and a discipline chip. Which Gun planted on me with a trumped-up custody writ. All signed and sealed by Regim Deuceman himself. Gun's prostrated himself so many times at our Chief Commander's feet he's been appointed advisor to Vigilance on Ground Control matters. Can you believe it?"

"Easily. Gunther always did yearn for more than a proctor's position," Paven said.

Was that my flaw? Plaia wondered. *That I didn't yearn for enough?* "In any case, I was half-conscious for the sharelock ceremony. Our begetting was even worse."

Rulian took her hands again. "I worried when you didn't return to our cozy cell. I've seen too many colleagues disappear. Actually, I did more than worry. I raised holy hell."

"I looked for you after I ran away from Gunther," Plaia said. "Same story as Paven. No one at Tertius would admit to ever seeing you there. I can't tell you how many hours of sleep I've lost over both of you."

"Warden packed me off," Rulian said. "No notice. Incommunicado. The good news is Atlan Vigilance lost my papers in a seven-mag earthshock. Never did stand trial. After a while, no one here knew what to charge me with. The warden offered to dismiss me if I agreed to serve as a lockkeep. That's when I made sure that our Paven lost no more of his extremities."

"Good ol' Rul kept track of my good behavior and secured a dismissal of my proximity violation," Paven said. "So after all that book learnin', milady, that's what we do in life. The night shift at Tertius Detainment."

"You *and* Rulian, lockkeeps?"

Paven shrugged. "Academe positions are scarce around Andea. It's not so bad. We've got a cottage downtown where the rubble's been cleared away. We strike our own small blows against the Imperium every chance we get."

"I'll bet you do."

They all laughed again. But none could conceal the regret of so much lost opportunity. Of bright futures shattered by circumstances.

"Come and stay with us," Paven said. "Rulian and I will take care of you. Our hovel's not some fine villa, but it's comfortable. I guess we both love you, don't we, Rul?"

"Pannishly and every other way," Rulian declared.

"Say, why don't we all enter sharelock?" Paven said.

She grinned at the delightful prospect of living with these two devoted academes, who had both been good friends. She had no doubt they would take care of her, protect her, probably spoil her no end. How blissfully she could live in the obscurity of Andea, find work as a clerk or a priestess, and fulfill her Imperial duties at last.

She sighed and thrust the vision away. "I thank you, my dear colleagues, but I won't be staying long."

"Oh, no," Rulian said and exchanged a dark look with Paven.

"I've signed on to crew aboard the *Leaping Dragon*. We're only waiting for the magister-captain to set the departure date."

"The *Leaping Dragon*," Paven said. "That's an exploratory ship. Sails across the torrents of the whole damn world."

"I sure hope so," she said.

"You never told me you wanted to run off on a fisheries skiff like *I* did when I was a child," Paven said. "Plaia, you've never harkened to the call of the sea."

"No, I haven't," she said. "I admit, the prospect is a bit daunting."

"Then why?"

She thought of all she'd seen and done and searched for in the pursuit of the truth. "Pav, I've never given up trying to prove Tivern's theory. And there's something on the other side of the world I've got to find. Something that no one will be able to deny. Not Gunther. Not Ground Control. Not even the High Council. Something *big*."

"You know I loved Tivern, too," Paven said bitterly. "I believed in her theories. I believed in resonance. But, Plaia, Tivern and her theories have been the ruin of everyone who comes near them. Don't throw the rest of your life away on Tivern. It's not worth it. Give it up."

"I can't give it up, Pav." She took a deep breath. "Tivern was murdered. Here, in Andea Rift."

"No, no, Plaia," he cried. "That's just a rumor."

"She was ordered down into the observation chamber. Faber and Helden admitted as much at my expulsion hearing. I have proof, written proof, that she anticipated a magma eruption. Her wander curves show that Andea Province is, without a doubt, vigorously pushing south."

"Then she was foolish," Paven said. "Tiv liked fast bedmates and danger."

"No, Tiv loved life. Ribba once told me she would

never have gone into a rift that she knew was on the verge of exploding. Something happened down there."

"You know," Rulian said, "after force-flooding failed, Ground Control crews refilled the sea trench. Homely piece of work it was, too. The prefecture was hopping mad over the loss of revenues from admissions to the beach."

"No more trench?" Plaia said.

"Nope. Rumor says that after the crews restored the beach, the seawater left behind just up and disappeared. Whoosh, bathwater down a drain. Rumor says these days Andea Rift is as dry as an old abandoned well."

"Rumor says that, does it, Rul?"

"Would I lie to you, child?"

"Not in five thousand years. Say, Paven, old chum," she said and punched her colleague on his biceps, "feeling nostalgic for the good old days?"

"Maybe," he said warily. "What's hopping through that beady brain of yours?"

"How long has it been since you've gone calling on a rift?"

Plaia stepped off the platform at the bottom of the well shaft and held her breath, fear and longing competing for her heart.

"Damn, Plaia, maybe this isn't a good idea," Paven whispered. His voice bounced off the ceiling of the Imperial observation chamber. He dropped into a crouch and followed her, cautiously crawling beneath collapsed beams and chunks of rock.

"Probably not," she whispered back. "But now that we've gone this far, let's take a look."

They had lowered their voices out of long habit. *No decibel is inconsequential,* Tivern had taught her students of resonance theory and application. *Observe how the great soprano's vibrato shatters the crystal goblet.* And they had descended into the rifts—Paven with his drums, she with her cymbals, Ribba with her flute, Donson with his zitar, Julretta with her meters—

to play beautiful resonance into chasms filled with disharmony.

Were we fools?

No. They *had* restored harmony. If only for a little while.

She heard the unspoken question in Paven's voice.

Will we find Tiv's bones?

The Andean chamber had been carved, as all such chambers were, out of superhard basement granite and girded with metal struts. Some struts had collapsed, others melted into impossible twists. Knee-high sooty water pooled around pearlescent coils of cooled magmatic rock. The haze of ashes nearly suffocated her. An ominous booming noise sounded deep in the chasm at the chamber's melted edge.

No sign of a body. Bodies. The first rumors said Tiv's resonance team had died with her. The next rumors, after the cover-up, accounted for the disappearance of the team members one way or another: a runaway wagon, a suicide, a capsized pleasure boat. Perhaps Vigilance had removed any evidence after the magma had cooled. More likely Tiv and her team had been incinerated.

Plaia thought she detected a whiff of burnt flesh. *No, it's my imagination.*

She crawled to the chamber's edge, lifted her lamp, and studied the rift. Dim amber lamplight flickered up and down the basalt walls, casting rainbows across the cooled sprays of magma. The mouth of the caldera nearly half a league above her permitted a glimmer of sunlight into those depths. A massive portion of the opposite wall had collapsed into the spent magma chamber, yawning into a depthless blackness.

She didn't want to contemplate what this rift would look like when Ground Control detonated gigantic firebolts. As much as the "ultimate solution" struck her as madness, still she could see the logic of collapsing this chasm in upon itself. Empty spaces always invite chaos into their midst. But the logic made sense only if the world shell truly was a single formation, and the rifts mere cracks in the shell.

A tremor shook the rift. Shook the ground where Plaia stood.

"Damn, it's a shock," Paven shouted. "Let's go!"

Plaia dashed to the back of the observation chamber, crawled into the well shaft, and mounted the platform. She searched for the main cable that carried the platform up and out of the shaft. Dread clenched her throat. "Pav, I can't find the main cable!"

"Stay calm. There's always a backup."

Paven searched in the shaft. "Here it is." He yanked on the backup cable.

The platform did not budge.

"Pull," Plaia shouted. "Pull harder!"

Paven pulled till sweat popped out of his brow. Plaia seized the cable above his hands.

Suddenly the cable gave way beneath her hands and collapsed, showering a confusion of slack coils. Plaia sifted through the coils and seized the end that should have been secured to a pulley above.

The end had been neatly severed.

"I didn't know if I believed you," Paven said.

"Oh, Pav. Do you, now?"

She embraced him as a massive earthshock shivered through Andea Rift. She wondered if she would die as Tivern had died, by the same treachery. She and Paven dropped to a crouch, still clinging to each other. A monumental groan issued from the rift, as if the planet was in pain.

Plaia thought of the beautiful blue world she'd glimpsed from the moon, and love overwhelmed her. She began to sing the soothing lullabies of the Fires of Longnight, lifting a quavering soprano against the monstrous *boom*.

Paven joined her in his shaky tenor.

"Oh, daar-aar-kest night," they sang. "Holy night. All is calm. All is right."

Their small human voices echoed and echoed again,

and the shaking gentled. The roar quieted, and the ground was still.

"Oh, Pav," Plaia whispered and pressed her cheek to his. "Maybe we made a difference. We tried, we tried—"

"Listen," he whispered.

Another groan issued from the chasm.

Another movement shuddered beneath them.

Plaia rose and crept to the edge of the chamber.

She gazed down at a bewildering sight. The entire edge of the chasm had buckled and tilted. A slow-motion avalanche, it was sliding *beneath* the opposite edge. The gigantic plate of rock pushed down beneath the opposite plate, shoving deep into the magmatic core.

She stifled laughter, pressing the palm of her hand over her mouth. "When is the shell not the shell?"

"When it moves sideways," Paven answered.

"The shell isn't one formation, it's a collection of pieces, each piece with its own movement."

"The whole damn plate . . . pushes *under* another."

She rubbed her eyes. "So the planet really is *alive*. Like Tiv always said. Always moving and changing, one plate yielding to another, maybe new plates rising from the depths. Transforming. Revitalizing. That's why Pangaea is a living planet. Not dead."

"It's . . . hard to believe."

She gestured at the astonishing sight before them. "Belief, my friend, has nothing to do with it."

A tiny, distant voice echoed down the well shaft. She scrambled back to the platform, Paven close behind her. Together they shouted up the shaft. Several long moments later, a stout cable dangled into Plaia's hands. She seized it, tested its strength and resistance, and set about knotting the end round the pulley in the center of the platform.

"Aren't you glad Rulian was superstitious about accompanying us into the very realm of Inim?" she observed.

"Unlike you and me, Plaia," Paven said, leaping off the platform and hoisting her up to safety, "Rulian is an academe of nice judgment."

"Say, Dame Cartographer," called the first lieutenant of the O.S.I.S. *Leaping Dragon*, "you're the one stuck on currents. Hoist your skinny buttocks up to the mainmast-trees and take a gander at *this* strange beast."

For days the *Leaping Dragon* had forged through a train of young waves. Wind-whipped into steep peaks, the waves seemed to take delight in flinging the massive vessel about like a child's float toy.

After two seasons of languorous calm in South Panthalassa Drift, Plaia had cultivated reasonably sound sea legs and a stomach of iron. But as the ship sailed ever westward and north toward the Great Pan Stream—the vast green current she sought—the seas had grown increasingly turbulent. By the time the vessel had entered the agitation of Capra Current, she'd begun to wonder if she'd ever eat solid food or sleep a restful hour again.

"May I have permission to leave the navigating bridge, Captain Duowom?" Plaia asked.

Purity protocol aboard ship was riddled with necessity exceptions, and Plaia routinely spoke first to magister pures like the captain and the first lieutenant.

A great dragon of a woman, Captain Duowom glanced up from her charts and compasses with icy annoyance. With stern indigo eyes nested in a magister's complexion so sun-soaked it had turned deep bronze, the captain presented an intimidating mask of unbroachable authority.

In two seasons of sailing, though, Plaia had learned that the captain's demeanor concealed a profound private passion for the rigors and joys of sea life. The captain had found greater satisfaction in her Imperial duty of labor than in any of the other duties. Rumor said Duowom had generated twenty sons, twenty daughters, and twenty clovens and supported them all in a rambling villa in North Scanda. How many days, though, in her forty years of sailing, had the captain spent with her progeny? Not many, rumor said.

"Permission granted, Dame Cartographer," Captain Duowom replied.

"Thank you, Magister Captain Duowom." Plaia rose and walked backward out of the bridge, according to maritime protocol.

She'd been laboring over the captain's charts, as she had for the past two seasons. The chartwork required that her eyes remain clear and her hands clean and supple. She had been exempted from the hard physical labor required of the crew, even the other middle pures aboard.

She chewed another mintstick, rubbed kernel oil on her face and hands, and pulled her cap low over her forehead. She seized a fresh databoard, a stylus, and Dubban's farglass, stuffed everything into her jacket pocket, and sprinted from the navigating bridge.

She strode across the deck to the mainmast, boosted herself up the spurs, and joined the first lieutenant in the top mast-trees.

"This had better be good, First Lieutenant Montate," she said, clutching the guardrail. "I may lose Master Chef's fine lunch again."

Montate grinned. A burly magister subpure with bleached white hair, a huge sunbrowned face, and a dubious reputation, he slipped his hand around her waist. "Why, Dame Cartographer, this is your cup of tea. Have yourself a look to starboard."

"Dear Pan," she whispered.

A monstrous wave surged nearly half a league high, a blue-black pyramid topped by a crown of churning foam. In another moment she heard the ship's bells sounding urgent alarm. Crew scrambled up masts and riggings, letting out main- and topsails, shouting curses when several sails commenced to luff. Captain Duowom and her Chief Lieutenant wrestled with the steering wheel, and the great rudder shuddered beneath them.

Plaia turned to descend the spar. "We should assist them, First Lieutenant. And get out of here!"

The huge magister seized her wrist in his two fingers and pulled her back into the mast-trees. "Oh, no, stay and watch. Our captain has seen waves before, and our crew is top of the barrel. We'll travel the trough and slip round that big beauty, sure enough."

The wave loomed right before her, the *Leaping Dragon* lolled deep in the trough, and the wave's crest rose nearly at a level to where she stood. "First Lieutenant, what the devil is it?"

"Like I said, what you're looking for. I've seen many a giant wave thrust herself to the skies where two of the great currents collide."

The *Leaping Dragon* lurched to lee, defying the directions of up and down as it skipped sideways between heaven and ocean along the length of the trough. Then the wave curled over where the vessel had sailed just a moment ago and collapsed with a deafening *crash*.

" 'Tis a collision between flighty Capra and the Great Pan," Montate shouted in her ear. "The Great Pan is where we're bound, to be sure."

"The Great Pan," she said. "The green current?"

"The same."

"Will the Great Pan take us to the indigo-blue current?"

"To the Black Stream, you mean? Now, how does a land slug like you know about the Black Stream? And how do you know the Great Pan meets ol' Blackie?"

"I saw it on the captain's charts," she lied.

"I doubt that. I know the captain's charts better 'n' you. How could you see what don't exist? At least, nobody knows if it does."

"Perhaps," she said, climbing down the spar, "I possess the power of sight."

Possess the power of sight? Maybe she did.

For that night, she had a dream.

Captain Duowom called for a celebratory dinner.

Mounting the Pan, the crew called the practice of entering the vast green current at the violent interstices with lesser currents, and it was no mean feat. The belly of a monster wave had been the last earthly sight of plenty of other ships' crews.

The low-ceilinged mess had been garlanded with straw flowers. Master Chef had outdone herself, adorning the monotony of cod with salt hind and potted vegetables. Wine was uncorked and strong beer unkegged. Flirtation ran high among proximate subpures.

Yet Plaia sank into melancholy, despite the merriment or perhaps because of it. No one had stirred her since Dubban. She'd resigned herself to the reality that no one ever would. If she had stayed with Paven and Rulian and entered sharelock with them, their union would have been a Pannish one. Never again would she know the love she'd had with Dubban.

She should never have let Dubban go to the Far Reaches. She should have followed him and the Heaven's Devil. Should have overpowered Asif and sent him packing. Reason protested that she couldn't have done that. That Asif wore devil stars, and neither she nor Dubban had been a match for the terrorist.

But reason didn't soothe the ache in her heart.

She excused herself from the middle-pure table and returned to her tiny cabin. She flung the bolts home and collapsed in her bunk bed, tossing and turning, too exhausted to read or draw, too perturbed to sleep.

I need to dream the angels' dreams. Surely Gunther cannot reach me here.

She closed her eyes and invoked Imperial sharemind. Nothing happened. She might as well have tried to open a door whose hinges had rusted shut. After several scarifying moments of unrewarded effort, she finally glided into the glimmer of the Mind of the World.

Two dozen orderly dreampaths of the great aetherists lay before her as they always did: gigantic boulevards paved with luminescent dreamstones extending into tenebrous mist. She could choose any dreampath, glide down it, and enter the angel's dreams.

But riddling the boundaries between the great boulevards was something she had never seen before: tiny, ragged lanes and mysterious alleys. The famous visages of the angels stood before their dreampaths the way they always had. But now the monumental faces competed with two dozen tiny, cavorting figures of people Plaia had never seen before.

Her dream-eye glided amid this astonishing confusion. For a moment she blamed herself. *I haven't dreamed in so long I don't know what the Mind of the World looks like anymore.* But in another moment a more shocking astonishment struck her, unthinkable and baffling.

The Mind of the World has changed!

She roamed among the strangers, keeping her distance. She nearly leapt out of her skin when she glimpsed a giant magister standing beside a path. His blue-green eyes brimmed with glee. A sardonic smile lit his regal face.

The Alchemist?

How the devil can Councillor Sausal appear in the Mind of the World?

Plaia sped to the next dreampath, her dream-eye blurring with confusion. Next to the broad dreamstones of Milady Fandango lay another little path, raw and new.

At the entrance to the path stood a sarcophagus made of metal. A young man lay within. His black hair had been loosened from its customary thong and swirled across the pillow like smoke. His bold face was still in the repose of death, his eyes closed, a faint worry line furrowing his forehead. His dark lashes lay thick against his cheeks, his hands crossed over his chest.

Her heart lurched so painfully she couldn't breathe.

My beloved Dubban. What is this torment in the Mind of the World?

She noticed, then, the flash and strobe of an instrument panel across the inside wall of the sarcophagus.

Dubban opens his eyes.

He whispers, "My love."

She sprang from the bunk bed with a cry. She could hardly breathe. She paced, bare feet slapping on the floorboards, heartbeat battering in her breast.

Who put Dubban in the Mind of the World?

Someone rapped softly on her door. "Dame Cartographer?" said one of the stewards who waited on the higher purities. "Is anything the matter?"

"No," she whispered raggedly through the door.

"I heard you scream. . . ." The steward paused. "May I bring you something?"

"Could you rustle up a flask of d'ka?"

"I shall return at once, my dame."

Plaia sat on the edge of the bunk bed, shivering. She pulled on a heavy woolen sweater, but the chill came from deep within.

I must never, never dream again.

But after the steward brought the flask, she relocked the door, and took what ease she could, a tantalizing memory filtered through her beleaguered consciousness.

The Alchemist. The Alchemist's tentsite. He'd had a large oblong box, but it had been torn apart, an instrument panel torn apart, too, and spilled every which way on the ground. "I may be able to replicate this," the Alchemist had said to Salit.

What had Salit said? "Perhaps, Alchemist, you'll dream again in the Mind of the World *without* your security number."

And what, Plaia thought as she plunged into d'ka-soaked sleep, had they called the device? The same device her beloved Dubban had reclined within?

They'd called it an aetheric shell.

Six seasons came and went before Dubban's dreams began in earnest.

The *Leaping Dragon* sallied forth on the Great Pan Stream, ever westward, mainsails and topgallants swelling with good, steady wind. The ship swept down, poleward, as the vast green current branched and surged into its South Arc. There surf crashed upon the beaches of Outer Tasman and plunged into the Imperial sea trench and the coastal rift.

Two years at sea. Two and a half? When Plaia gazed in a looking glass she saw how grief had etched solemnity in her features.

In two and a half years of sailing, she never did glimpse the Black Stream. She'd despaired of ever locating the place where the stream met the Great Pan.

Captain Duowom chafed to find the place, as well, which no one had charted before. She plotted a return course eastward along the North Arc of the Pan Stream where the black waters were rumored to flow.

" 'Tis dangerous seas, Dame Cartographer. The gales blow rambunctious, the waves rise ferocious, and many an Imperial seaship has been lost in the great storms."

"But you'll sail there?" Plaia said.

"That I will. Will you accompany me?"

"Yes."

"Well, we shall see," the captain said shrewdly. "You're either a shipper or you're not."

Plaia knew she was not.

When the seaship sailed into the shabby little port of Geelong, and she set foot on the cheerless marshlands of Outer Tasman, she had knelt on the ground and kissed the sour soil.

She and the middle pures took rooms at an overpriced inn on the Geelong boardwalk. Idyllic days of shore leave ensued. Plaia's knees steadied and her stomach settled. The prospect of more years at sea filled her with revulsion and trepidation.

She was not alone.

She and the middle pures dined together on their first night ashore, too weary to brave the rowdy streets of Geelong. Earthshocks had reduced whole sections of the seaport to rubble, and desperate refugees roamed the ill-lit streets and alleys. Even local Vigilance had made itself scarce, the walkabouts reluctant to patrol.

"I shall return to Our Sacred City on the roads. I don't care about earthshocks, foes, rifts, or summer rains," the accountant declared. An apple-cheeked woman to start, she had not sustained sea life well. "Especially if Captain Duowom means to sail the northern seas."

"I'm going with you," the second physician said. "It's been four years since my daughters emerged in the North Appalacian natalries and I've never seen their faces."

The first physician asked, "What about you, Plaia?"

"Oh, I'm eager to chart the northern seas with our captain," she said, yet her heart felt anything but eager. The yearning for land overwhelmed her. She set down her fork and excused herself. She climbed the stairs to her chamber, marveling that her stomach didn't drop below her feet.

Then, as if to mock her, an earthshock of perhaps four mags rattled through the inn. She dropped to her knees on the landing, gripped the handrail, and cursed.

"Care for some company tonight?"

The first physician stood at the foot of the stairs. His sharelock chips winked in his hands. Longing shone in his eyes.

"No." Wasn't entirely sure she meant it.

"Are you sure?" the first physician said. "I've seen the scars on your hands when you remove your gloves. Surely these"—he brandished his own hands—"don't deter you."

"Why don't they deter *you*?" she asked.

"Because there were times during our voyage when I thought I was going to die. Because my sharer is leagues away in Gondwana Valley, and if I crew up with you and our captain for the eastward exploration, it will be years before I see her again. And because our captain may insist on protocol aboard ship, but she has no say about what you and I do here tonight."

"Those are all excellent reasons, Rogiere."

"Your answer is still no."

"Yes. Thanks for the offer just the same."

She watched him go with some regret. Then she strode down the hall, found her chamber, entered, and securely locked the door. She knew what she wanted to do this night of homecoming to solid ground.

I want to dream.

She lay back, trembling slightly, and closed her eyes. *The Mind of the World.*

The great dreampaths of the angels.

And the strange tiny paths: so many of them now.

She glides toward Milady Fandango's dreampath. Half a dozen tiny paths riddle the mists surrounding the grand boulevard.

And there he is: Dubban.

Reclining in the sarcophagus. His eyes open, he sits up.

"My love, I will cast this dream over and over and pray that you dream of me. I cannot contact you. Only a handful of us have acquired the shells, and I know you are not one of us. So you cannot cast your own dream to let me know where you are and whether you're safe and well.

"Know this, my love: I am not dead. I am *not* dead. Here is what happened."

Suddenly Plaia veered into another dream, violent and staccato.

A cavern. Tents of black sacking, impure women with distended bellies, babes, and young children. Blood, blood, and Salit Zehar. Women screaming, wild-eyed with terror, running into the shadows.

Tall, golden vigiles, heavily armed. The terrible face of Regim Deuceman. A burst from a firebolt. A little girl, perched on a caretaker's shoulder, watching. Regim calls her "My daughter."

Dubban, his face gaunt with horror.

"Superior Father Dubban," Regim calls him and marches him out of the cavern. They board a Vigilance windship.

Dubban pleading, "I'm the Superior Father who begot your child, lieutenant captain."

Plaia's throat clenched. She started up, unwilling to witness more. But Dubban swore he wasn't dead. She lay down again, trembling, and entered another dream, deep grey yet serene.

Brooding buildings. Over the lintel of the door to a cheerless granite bunker: DETAINMENT CENTER FOR THE TERTIUS, NORTH SCANDA.

Deep drifts of snow. Stiff winds scatter sprays of ice crystals.

Salit Zehar, shrouded in heavy hides, creeps along a high wall. She carries a tiny blue boy strapped to her back. A robust boy with a copper complexion and bright golden hair follows her closely.

Salit and her sons huddle next to the waste disposal behind the detainment center. They warm their hands before the incinerators leaping with flames. Dubban, in prison garb, tosses in refuse. He glances down and suddenly sees Salit there. She gazes back at him, openmouthed with wonder.

The dream abruptly shifted back to the alley next to Milady Fandago's dreampath.

Dubban gazes deeply into Plaia's dream-eye. "Salit told me of your meeting with the Alchemist. That you kept your security number. That you can still dream in the Mind of the World. That you've left Atlan on a quest across the torrents.

"Come to North Scanda, if you can. Find me. The warden has taken me out of solitary confinement, and I may receive visitors. Plaia, I have never loved another. Our time together at Misty Alley were the best days of my life. I will love you for Eternity, even if we never meet again."

He furrows his forehead in thought, his worry line deepening. "So that you may prove this dream is real before you risk the northern seas journeying to Scanda: I was told that half-human beasts are generated in a natalry in Outer Tasman. Find it, if you go there."

He strides to the sarcophagus, lies inside, and crosses his hands over his chest.

"Salit sent a message to the Alchemist through qut smugglers that I'm alive. He had this aetheric shell smuggled to me. A repayment for bringing him the

*stolen shell. This is one of the first shells he's built.
There's talk of a huge shadow market. Of producing
shells in great quantities. Impure smugglers have begun
selling them among all the purities. We have yet to
dream as skillfully and powerfully as the angels, but
give us time.*

"It's the highest Imperial crime to own an aetheric
shell. I've hidden my shell in a crawl space below the
basement of the library at the detainment center.

"I face danger every time I dream. But I will cast this
dream over and over and pray that you dream of me."

He closes his eyes.

Then he was gone.

"I've never liked the natalries, you know," said
Rogiere. He gingerly slapped the reins and clucked to
the burly drayer pulling the sulky. "My Imperial duty
of the healing arts succors those who require assistance
after they've been generated. I've always thought those
physician-natalists have got quite the big stick stuck
way up their bums, with their self-righteous airs and
their superior—"

The drayer set off at a breakneck canter.

"Never mind, Rogiere, can you get me *in*to the
place?" Plaia seized the handgrip next to her seat and
prayed the sulky didn't hit a dip in the road. She smiled
at Rogiere's indignation. She really did like the first
physician.

"I said I could, and I will." He jerked on the reins,
inspiring a lively stream of invective from the drayer.

"Splendid. Um. Do you want me to drive?"

"I said I have vast experience handling drayers, and I
do. Whoa. Whoa, there, I say!"

"Get up!" she shouted. The drayer glanced over her
massive shoulder in bewilderment, big brown eyes rolling. "I wouldn't want our captain to set sail this afternoon without us, would you?" Plaia said when Rogiere
glowered at her.

She had dreamed Dubban's dream three nights in a

row. Her heart soared with intense, improbable joy—and knotted in terrible frustration. *Dubban, my beloved Dubban.* Had the dream amounted only to the concoction of her febrile imagination? Her yearning for the impossible?

So that you may prove this is real:

A natalry in Outer Tasman where half-human beasts are generated.

A terrible sight met them as they sped up a broken road to the natalry complex. Earthshocks had decimated the gentle hill, which was only sandy soil flung over a kernel of deep bedrock. Fissures gaped in the high brick walls at the gates of the complex. The foundation tilted, half-submerged in the sandy soil. Fire had destroyed a dozen outbuildings. The blackened teeth of charred ruins thrust up among frail clumps of new milkweed.

"This facility is deserted," Rogiere said.

"They must have relocated on firmer bedrock," Plaia said. Apprehension shivered across her skin. For though the facility *seemed* deserted, she sensed something still there. "What was *that*?"

She heard an eerie, mournful keening.

She sprinted across the deserted courtyard, ignoring Rogiere's protests, searching for the source of the sound. She passed below a soaring archway, the sturdy architectural feature intact, the wall once surrounding it crumbled to ruins.

She strode down a deserted hallway, hushed and forbidding, the air thick with whirling motes of dust. She turned a corner.

It was a high-ceilinged chamber. Everything had been violently flung about. Viewglasses toppled over on high tables. Spilled vials of anodyne and runny yellow nopaine. Curettes and surgical forks. There were ges tanks, emergence trays, jars of rancid amniotic fluid that struck the air with a noisome stink.

Threaded through the chemical smells was the smell of beasts. Stale bodies and excrement and decay.

Wire cages had been stacked floor to ceiling, the

heavy padlocks imprinted with Imperial seals. Some cages had toppled and lay heaped on the littered floor. Water bottles and trays of food still provisioned some cages, even toppled ones, and the bone-thin prisoners within drank and fed. The provisions of others had been shaken loose in the earthshock. In those cages the prisoners lay limp, some curled up on cage bottoms, others splayed across the wires.

She had seen such creatures only once before when she'd trekked through Blackblood Cavern with Salit Zehar.

Ten dozen bulbous eyes stared. Now and then a prisoner hissed, baring curved yellow fangs and rheumy red gums. The reek of rotten meat joined the other smells. Plaia pressed her fingertips to her throat.

A bloodbat stretched her skinny arm between the wires of her cage and scrabbled claws against Plaia's shoulder. Plaia stepped back. The bat pressed her cheek and her slack little breasts against the wires.

"Sssss . . . ussssss . . . frrrrrr," the creature said, gazing into Plaia's eyes. "Sssss . . . ussssss . . . *frrrrrre.*"

"Plaia, I beg you, let's go," Rogiere whispered in her ear. "These are *bloodbats*. They feed on human blood."

"Perhaps not if they're half-human."

"What the devil do you mean?"

"Rogiere, look in her eyes."

The bat said, "Sssett . . . uusss . . . frrreee. Pleassse."

"Rogiere, she's *talking* to us."

"You're mad."

"Listen!"

Other bats took up the refrain. "Set . . . us . . . free . . . please!"

"This is lunatic," Rogiere cried. "I won't help you."

"Go, then." She tore through the laboratory, spilling drawers, flinging open cabinets, searching for keys to the padlocks.

Rogiere added, "You open those cages, and they'll kill us. They'll eat us alive."

"You have a point, first physician."

Plaia seized a chair and swung it against the glass of a long window set in the wall. The glass shattered, and the hot, stale air of Tasman rushed in.

She seized a lamp, lit it, seized another, and lit that. She thrust the lamps into Rogiere's hands. "I remember that bloodbats cannot abide bright light. That's why we never see them in daylight, true? Well, swing those around after I break open their cages. And let's duck under that examination table."

She found no keys, but she did seize a stout carpenter's hammer and chisel that had been abandoned on the floor. She fitted the chisel point into the hasp of each padlock, struck the hammer, and broke the locks, one by one.

At last she was done. She kicked the cages open.

Leathery wings slithered. Long claws scrabbled in her hair. Breath blew hot on the nape of her neck, and she dived beneath the examination table. She seized the lamp Rogiere thrust into her fist and brandished it.

Bloodbats leapt to the edge of the broken window and streamed through. A swarm of stubby dark bodies and elongated wings took off into the pale blue sky. The beating of their wings sounded like grind wheels chopping through sandstone.

Suddenly a bat leapt and stooped beneath the table. Plaia stared into a bestial face. A fanged mouth stretched open in a terrifying grimace.

"Thththththank you," the bloodbat said. The bat's paw reached out and seized a hank of Plaia's hair. "Prrrretty!"

Then the bat sprang to its feet, levitated, and was gone.

So that you may prove this is real.

The *Leaping Dragon* plunged into waves peaked as tall as trees, the water the deep translucent green of cold thick glass. The formidable North Arc of the Great Pan

Stream had blown with icy storms for over two seasons by the time they approached North Scanda.

No one commanded an iron-willed magister like Captain Duowom except the Prime Admiral of the Bureau of Imperial Maritime Exploration. Few managed to suggest what the captain had not thought of first herself.

Thus the trick had been to persuade the captain to command a radical change of course and believe that she herself had conceived of the notion. Plaia had thought long and hard and then chosen the one segment of life at sea where the captain could not best her.

She'd resorted to shameless sentiment.

One night at dinner she'd begun to weep. "It's my fathers," she'd said to her colleagues. "I cannot tell you how I miss them." Soon the middle pures' table was awash in homesickness and tales of cherished parents, siblings, and clovens.

The captain had risen, depositing herself heavily in an empty chair at their table, and Plaia had implored her for stories of her prodigious number of children.

"It's true," Captain Duowom had said mournfully. "Twenty sons, twenty daughters, twenty clovens. Two sharers, both good men. Half a dozen caretakers. Up in North Scanda, they are. Our City of Slo. It's been five long years since I've seen them, the poor dears."

Plaia had whipped out her sketch of their eastward route, the first lap of the exploration that would take the *Leaping Dragon* to the North Arc of the Great Pan. "If we detour through the straits west of Uralian Archipelago, a port of call at North Scanda wouldn't be much farther. Then we could take the same route south, down the east side of Uralian and continue the exploration to the North Arc."

The captain had studied the sketch. "This will add half a season to the eastward exploration. Perhaps more."

"We could secure extra provisions in North Scanda, couldn't we, my captain? How many more long years

will it be till you see your family again?" She'd added,
"The poor dears."

"First lieutenant," the captain had called out, "plot a
course for Uralia and North Scanda, if you please."

"Dubban Quartermain naitre Quartius, do ye mean?"
the warden said. A buzzard of a man, he perched on a
stool behind a broken-down secretary at the entrance to
Tertius Prison.

"He's also known as Superior Father Dubban," Plaia
said. She glanced around at the interior of the cheerless
granite bunker Dubban had dreamed of so well. If
North Scanda, despite its harshness, impressed her with
its savage beauty, the prison possessed no redeeming
qualities at all: dreary beyond belief, nearly as cold inside as out, and smeared with layers of grime. Plaia
didn't know how anyone could face each day in such a
place without going mad.

She eyed the warden.

A scrawny magister subpure, the warden wore frost-
bite on his face and simple-minded cruelty in his ice-
pale eyes. He wrapped a coat of matted fur more tightly
around his shoulders and chewed on his bloody
thumbnail. "Wasn't even middle pure, but a lousy serv.
A midwife, he was. Clever charlatan, too, but we found
him out in the end."

"Where is he? What's happened to him?"

"Plenty." Cold, appraising stare. "Maybe you'll tell
me what your interest is in him first, my fine dame,
before I go about divulgin' Imperial information."

She drew herself up. "Superior Father Dubban presided at my Rite of Begetting in Our Sacred City of
Atlan, sir. He generated my first five unborns."

The warden nodded grudgingly. "Well, your fine Superior Father Dubban has been recalled to Atlan."

"Recalled to Atlan. By whom? Why?"

"The Imperial Natalries. Chief Natalist herself secured his release. If you want your Superior Father

Dubban for another begetting, you'd best head back to Our Sacred City."

Plaia heaved a sigh of relief. Fierce hope and fiercer yearning burned in her heart. "Warden, that's exactly where we're going."

"Look lively, Dame Cartographer, there's a marvel in the water off the larboard bow," shouted First Lieutenant Montate. "Hoist your skinny buttocks up to the mainmast trees and take a gander. And hurry up. Our marvel won't stay with us for long."

Plaia glanced up from her charts, standing at her drafting table on the navigation bridge. "Dame Captain, may I be dismissed from the navigation bridge?"

"Yes, yes," Captain Duowom said. "Go see what Montate has dredged up for you now." The captain yawned. "I shall be in my quarters, Dame Cartographer, but don't disturb me unless you need to. I solemnly promised my sharers I would try to get more rest."

"Thank you, Dame Captain." Plaia flung down her compass and stylus, eagerly sprinted from the navigation bridge, and mounted the mainmast, agilely shinnying up to the mast-trees. In eight years on the high seas, she had often climbed the spars.

Montate pointed and handed her a farglass. "There. Maybe fifteen degrees. A pod of leviathans. Good Pan, do ye see them? Why, I do believe," he said, clutching his forehead, "I'm getting a glimmer of leviathan sharemind."

There, skimming beneath the surf as if molding it, swam sleek, grey-skinned people. Each was nearly as long as the *Leaping Dragon*. Their brawny arms thrust and spread, thrust and spread in an effortless breaststroke. Their huge spatulate hands paddled the waves. Their powerful legs kicked deep below the surface. Wide-finned feet kicked up now and then amid the creamy foam.

Plaia glimpsed the gleam of a huge golden blue eye.

"Go ahead and try, Dame Cartographer," Montate said with a grin. "You wouldn't be the first."

"Try what?"

"Entering sharemind with our sea godlings yonder. Some claim they can."

She gripped the handrail till her knuckles turned white, braced herself, and closed her eyes, invoking purity sharemind. Invoking the Imperial sharemind that took her to the Mind of the World and Dubban's dreams. She even reached into the remnants of her sharelock chips and wrested a glimmer of sharer's sharemind.

SO . . . TINY BIRD. . . .

For a horrifying moment she thought the wily Montate had tricked her with his magister sharemind. Was about to dominate her consciousness and force her to do something she didn't want to do. Then she realized she didn't apprehend Montate at all. She hovered in sharemind, undisturbed. She extended the ambit of her consciousness and called out—

Leviathans. I . . . I have a question for you.

YES, TINY BIRD?

She gasped, heart hammering.

Leviathans, I seek the place where the Black Stream meets the Great Pan.

A pause. The sound of huge bubbles in deep water. A vast submarine gurgling.

WHY DO YOU SEEK THE CONFLUENCE OF LIGHT AND DARKNESS, TINY BIRD?

She squinted open an eye.

Montate was gazing at her, openmouthed with wonder. "Never mind me. Go back to them, damn you!"

Leviathans, I seek the lost continent of the world. I know that it lies amid the Confluence of Light and Darkness.

Silence.

She peeked through her lashes, saw the great grey bodies plunging away.

Leviathans. I implore you. I've risked my life.

Silence.

A train of stiff young waves surged behind the leviathans, the wake of their passing.

HOW DO YOU KNOW OF THE LOST LAND, TINY BIRD?

I saw it, once. From a very great height.

WHAT HEIGHT?

No point in keeping Secrets from them.

From the moon, leviathans.

Silence. Gurgling, hoots, and whistles, the signals of the sea.

WHY DO YOU SEEK THE LOST LAND, TINY BIRD?

Because it will prove Pangaea has changed before. Changed before and changes now. If I can convince enough people, perhaps we may stop the Imperium from blowing up the world. For, leviathans, that is just what the Imperium intends to do. The bureaucrats call it the ultimate solution. Even you will not be immune.

Silence.

Silence.

Silence.

The leviathans swam away, bent on their course. Their powerful bodies arched and fell, arms reaching and spreading, finned legs beating up and down in a rhythm of determined purpose.

Leviathans? Leviathans!

Plaia punched the guardrail with frustration.

POINT THE PROW OF YOUR SHIP TO THE LEE OF THE MOON WHEN SHE RISES TO-NIGHT. DO NOT DEVIATE AND YOU SHALL FIND THE CONFLUENCE OF THE BLACK AND THE GREEN. DO NOT DEVIATE AND YOU SHALL FIND THAT WHICH YOU SEEK.

Thank you, thank—

DO NOT MISUSE THAT WHICH YOU FIND, TINY BIRD. WE HAVE GUIDED MANY OF YOUR SEASHIPS AWAY FROM THIS PLACE. IT POS-SESSES . . . MANY SECRETS. . . .

I do not mean to misuse it. I hope only to convince—

A huge wave off the starboard bow hurtled at the

Leaping Dragon. All hands hit the deck. When the sea ran off and Plaia glanced again to larboard, the leviathans had plunged into the deep.

"I will punish you to the full extent of the bureau's regulations," Captain Duowom said, face quivering and eyes ablaze.

Plaia, Montate, and a brace of shipboard vigiles stood at attention on the navigation bridge. They swayed precariously on their sea legs as a train of waves stirred and slammed against the *Dragon's* hull and set the seaship pitching.

The captain paced heavily before them, hands clasped behind her back as if she did not trust herself not to strike someone.

To Montate, "You will return this ship to our original course, First Lieutenant. At once. And then you will join Dame Cartographer belowdecks." To Plaia, "I will have you thrown in irons for the remainder of this exploration. You are under arrest. You will be put to trial when we reach Andea under the bureau's regulations."

"With all due respect, Captain Duowom, I am a civilian hired at a wage, not an officer of the Maritime Bureau."

"Do *not* speak seditiously to me, Dame Cartographer. *No* one changes my course. Do you hear me? Changes it without my permission while I was sleeping. I cannot *fathom*," she said, spittle collecting in the corner of her thin lip, "how you could be capable of this treason."

"It's not treason, my captain."

"What do you call it, then?"

"A small detour in the course of our exploration. The leviathans told me—"

The captain sputtered with fury. "*Leviathans* cannot think or reason or invoke sharemind with human beings. That is lunatic rumor, nothing more. I have never, in forty years of sailing, entered common consciousness with a leviathan. Let alone *communicated* with a sea beast."

"Yet they told me that this course will take us to the confluence."

"Five-point-five degrees north by northwest of our present course, Dame Cartographer, will sail us directly into the High Black Pool, not the Black Stream. Where we will drift and meander helplessly unless we are lucky, and a catastrophic storm pries us loose, which will capsize and drown us all. Security?" she said to the shipboard vigiles. "You will take this woman below-decks and—"

"Halloo!" cried the second navigator, a wiry little woman who presently clung to the mainmast-trees, peering through a farglass. "The Black Stream, Dame Captain. I spy the Black Stream!"

"Impossible," Captain Duowom shouted back.

"There she runs, dark as ink, beside our fair green Pan."

"Nonsense. The Pan cannot possibly join the Black Stream for another fifty leagues east of our present location. Perhaps farther, after our Dame Cartographer's treason."

"Halloo!" the second navigator cried again, her voice hoarse with excitement. "I see the line of a cliff on the horizon, Dame Captain. I see land!"

Plaia gazed up at a cobalt-and-vermilion sky, oddly depthless and studded with stars. The sun shone as small as a child's flung tossball, but the heat of it burned her cheeks. She breathed deeply, savoring the dustless air. Thin dry soil frosted with ice crystals crunched beneath her bootheels. Dwarf willows and birches huddled in the lee of gentle hills. A cluster of brilliant blue wildflowers brought tears to her eyes. Birdcalls unlike any she'd ever heard before formed a scrim of sound in the chill afternoon.

She heard a distant roar.

"No, we cannot lay over long enough for ye to map

the whole damn island," Captain Duowom grumbled but Plaia could tell the stolid magister fairly bubbled with excitement.

"But I need to verify that the coastline conforms to the gap between the Chinee and Cordillera coastlines. That would prove, you see, that this land and those provinces were once joined."

"I haven't the slightest idea what you're ranting about, Dame Cartographer. And my answer is still no."

"Plaia! Halloo, Plaia. Come have a look."

She sprinted over the ridge and caught her breath.

A magnificent waterfall roared like thunder, plunging a league into a crystalline lake. Montate stood amid a rainbow of spray at the base of the cataract, gesturing *Come here*.

She galloped down and joined him.

"Look at this," he said.

She examined a precise rectangle cut into the cliff, nearly hidden beneath a sweep of vegetation and the cloud of vapor. She pushed at the corner of it. The rock yielded to her touch. She pushed again and a door silently swung open, revealing a dark passageway covered, simply covered, with kaligraphs.

She strode inside. Stale air struck her in the face. She saw gold and atlantium. She saw the flickering lights of a databoard. She stood before a work of art painted across the entire chamber wall, the colors as vivid as if they'd been dipped by a brush just yesterday.

Tall, regal people gazed down at Plaia, slanting sapphire eyes in beautiful angelic faces. Their complexions shone a deep rich blue. Other people stood beside the giants. Smaller in stature, they possessed misshapen eyes and lopsided limbs. Yet their complexions were the same rich blue. A tiny blue woman held a databoard punctuated with kaligraphs in one hand and a faceted atlantium orb in the other. All around her shimmered waves of dark energy like the draperies of a chameleon cloak.

Two huge blue disks had been painted across the opposite wall of the chamber. Plaia saw landmasses resembling Appalacia Province, Cordillera, Gondwana, the Reaches, Scanda, Tasman. All of the provinces of the world. But they did not cluster together in the archipelago she knew so well.

"What is it?" Montate whispered.

"It's a map," she whispered back, "of once upon a time."

FACET 29

>Closed Eyes: Resting or death.
>The councillor must execute the sentence
>   required by the law.
>The action is regeneration.
>The forbearance is stillness.

The Orb of Eternity

Commentaries:
Councillor Sausal: As Pan is Eternal, so one's Essence lives in Eternity.

So, too, the Imperium permits that which is proper and forbids that which is improper. [*Deleted from The Contemporary Commentaries of Sausal (15th Ed.). Yet when Pan manifests the myriad things, dualities appear: light and darkness, life and death. And that which is considered proper and that improper are defined by the Imperium.]

Therefore the prudent person must accept that life is limited.
Guttersage (usu. considered vulgar): Sleep is the little sister of death. The good news is you're refreshed for another day.

Death is the big sister of sleep. The good news is you never struggle through another day.

Our City of Atlan, the crest of Prime Hill. Milord Lucyd's cloudscraper, the Villa de Reve:

"Close your eyes, milord," Danatia said with a smile.

"They're closed, milady," Lucyd said.

"Splendid! This will cheer you. I want you to be happy today."

"You have made me very happy every day in twelve years of sharelock, Danatia. You've been the best codreamer I've ever had. But, as for today, well—"

She pressed her cool fingertip over his lips. "Hush, now. And you're peeking."

He closed his eyes again, fraught with foreboding despite her sweet smile and teasing tone. They had dreamed of this: Closed Eyes.

From the dreamchamber at the apex of his cloud-scraper, Lucyd could hear revelry rising in the half-repaired streets of Atlan. Another celebration of the Festival of Spring Moontide in the megalopolis, the quadrants of Marketplace strewn with garlands and ruins. The air blew thick with the reek of the Bog, volcanic ash, and the stinging powder of festival flares. The people of the purities, boisterously giddy, capered in costumes, sang in ragged voices, and banged drums and cymbals and small gongs.

So many small gongs. Like ten thousand warnings of Apocalypse.

Since times lost to antiquity the festival had celebrated the fecundity of the world and the promise of the vernal turning. Celebrants had praised the great gift of the natalries and all the ways in which the Imperium served the citizenry, asking only the purities' fulfillment of the Imperial duties in return. Priests and priestesses offered prayers of thanksgiving for the beauty and joy of life in Pangaea.

They had dreamed that morning, he and Danatia, of great explosions. Of walls of rock bursting open, of gravel raining from the skies. He had invoked the Orb of Eternity and a smiling young man, someone Lucyd had never seen in his life, had stridden into his dream. The young man had flung an orb, and the orb had fallen and tumbled the way it always did, coming to rest with a facet in view. And then two enormous eyes, closed in repose or death, had filled his dream-eye, and Lucyd had awakened, shaking.

Danatia had embraced him tenderly, stroked his cheek, and murmured soothing words but, hours later, he felt unsteady still. He could not dispel the terrible foreboding in his heart, despite her smiles and soft whispers.

"Am I going to die?" he said.

"Not today, milord," she said.

"It's impossible, Danatia. I can no longer dream as the Temple of the Mind of the World wishes. Nothing is the same in the Mind of the World, and it is not my fault."

"I know, milord. My love."

Today, on this high sacred day, the Imperial Bureau of Ground Control had announced that the first gigantic firebolt buried deep in Appalacia Rift would be detonated and thus secure Our Sacred City, now and for times lost to the future. Gunther Triadius would announce the exact moment of detonation at an inaugural ceremony in Allpure Square.

Ground Control had tested the giant firebolts in the deserts of Central Gondwana and out at sea. The criers had shown in public sharemind awesome images of the blinding blast, the stunning fireball, and resultant cloud like a colossal mushroom wrought of swirling smoke and fiery ash.

The sheer force of the Imperium now rivaled the mysterious powers of Pangaea, Ground Control proclaimed. The powers that had decimated the world archipelago would be themselves decimated by Imperial might. The ceaseless earthshocks and magma eruptions that had plagued the megalopolis ever since the Big Shock nearly fourteen years ago would cease forever.

I can no longer dream of tranquility without end.

Lucyd sighed heavily. Today, the Festival of Spring Moontide, was also the celebration of his eightieth year of life. His mothers had carefully planned his emergence. Family anecdotes related that when Lucyd had been unready to emerge on this day, the physician-natalists, Superior Mother, and Superior Father had removed him from his ges tank and birthsack anyway.

And he, an angel infant, had presided as the guest of honor at a tremendous feast and revel held by his mothers. Whereupon he'd been reinstalled by Primus physicians in a tank of warm air for the next three weeks, nearer to death than he'd been to life. "We were infuriated with you for being so stubborn," his mothers had laughed. "For almost departing for Eternity just because you didn't want to emerge into this world."

He wondered, now, eighty years later, whether that trauma might have caused his lifelong sensitivity to the mundanity. His inability to tolerate sunlight or lamplight or the breaths of other pures.

"Now, now, milord, I said no peeking."

"Danatia, you know how I loathe surprises."

"Even from me?"

"We've had too many surprises in twelve years of sharelock, milady. Many of them unpleasant."

When he and Danatia had announced their sharelock and secured the proper approvals, Lucyd's eldest cloven had renounced them and bitterly refused to attend their sharelock ceremony with his brothers. He'd hired a crier and conveyed a long, furious sharemind berating Lucyd for abuses, both real and imagined.

Then Tonel had jabbed a needle of allpaine into his arm and taken his life.

Lucyd had wanted to weep. He'd *tried* to weep. But could not. After the other clovens had sent him an atlantium heart engraved with their thanks for his generosity, and five of his sons had announced their sharelocks with lovely angels, Lucyd gradually forgot about the embittered man with a face like his own.

As for life in Our Sacred City, earthshocks struck and struck again, and crime among the purities soared. Chief Commander Regim Deuceman staged raids and purges. A fearsome figure, he would appear with bodyguards and an elite squad, exact summary punishments and tortures, then disappear into seclusion.

No one had been immune from Regim's wrath, not even the angels. Milord Sting himself had been called to the Chamber of Justice for impure thoughts. Lucyd had never liked Sting, but when he called upon the aetherist's villa to inquire after his health, the majordomo had stiffly informed him that the angel had been banished.

"I promise this won't be unpleasant," Danatia insisted with a giggle.

"All right."

In another moment he heard a soft mewling, felt soft, soft fur, and a supple body rubbing against the palm of his hand. *Two* bodies.

He gasped and opened his eyes, tears starting.

Two gorgeous little sphinxes smiled up at him. One female—an exotic Tugora subpure—boasted fluffy white fur, a shapely little figure, and face, ears, fingertips of a pale coral pink. Her eyes—large ovals of golden green—sparkled with a mischievous intelligence. The second female—an equally exotic Tonkese—was as sleekly furred in silver bristles as the first was fluffy white, her tiny sculpted face demure, her almond-shaped eyes a fiery magister blue.

Danatia laughed and clapped her hands. "You are in dire need, milord, of a new pair of mood muses."

Sitla and Arvel had died two seasons ago. As Lucyd had grown older, death had become no easier, and he had grieved deeply for his beloved sphinxes. Their eighteen drud years amounted to well over a hundred and twenty angel years, and their lives had been filled with comfort and happiness.

He knew this. Yet the loss of their companionship still struck him keenly.

"They're beautiful," he whispered. "Where did you get them?"

"Never mind," she said. "Perhaps they'll ease your dreams, milord."

"It isn't your fault as my codreamer that I can no longer meet the terms of the temple's commission."

"Then your commission is summarily withdrawn, milord," rasped a harsh magister voice.

A voice that sent dread through Lucyd's blood.

"I'm sorry, milord," his majordomo whispered.

"They demanded entrance. They brought an armed escort."

"Yes, we did. As is befitting to apprehend a dangerous traitor and a vicious heretic. It's time you angels were taught a lesson."

Chief Commander Regim Deuceman stood at the door to the dreamchamber, hand in hand with his daughter, Regima Clere. Lucyd glimpsed the glint of weapons, the gleam of pitiless eyes. The promised squad stood behind father and daughter.

Ever the recluse, still Lucyd had heard the sordid rumors whispered about Regim and Regima Clere. How the father had entered sharelock with his daughter and spoke to her as if she were her dead mother. Who knew what else their sharelock entailed? Lucyd's eyes strayed down to their clasped hands. Up to their chiseled golden faces, golden hair, eyes blazing like blue fire. So tall, both of them. What a pair. He glimpsed the sharelock chips winking among their carpal bones.

Lucyd drew himself up. "You have no authority to withdraw my commission, Chief Commander. That commission is issued by the Cardinal on behalf of the Temple of the Mind of the World. Pan preserve you. You may go."

"Oh, I don't think I'm to be dismissed this time, milord."

"Magisters and vigiles rule the Imperium with firebolts and daggers," Regima Clere declared in a high, ringing voice. "Not the angels with their dreams in the Mind of the World and their indolent riches."

Lucyd laughed at the girl's brash words, obviously aped from her parent. "Well, I certainly must agree the angels no longer rule the Mind of the World, Mistress Regima Clere. And neither does the Imperium, despite your edicts and acolyte-auditors and proclamations. Thousands, tens of thousands, perhaps hundreds of thousands of people among all the purities possess illegal aetheric shells and cast their own dreams in the Mind of the World. I'm not certain how it's happened, but it's quite a splendid chaos."

"Through the sedition of angels like you. You dream of the Orb of Eternity over and over," Regima Clere said. "I dreamed your dream just this morning."

"Excellent," Danatia said. "We do hope you enjoyed it."

The magister girl huffed indignantly, but her father held up his hand. "Never mind her, my daughter." To Lucyd, "Your ceaseless dreams of the Orb of Eternity amount to sufficient evidence of your treason, angel." To Danatia, "And so, my spy, where does he keep his orb?"

Spy? Lucyd's heart clenched. An icy chill swept over him, and he stared at Danatia. *Beloved Danatia.* "My . . . love?"

Regim snorted with laughter. "That's right, your beloved Danatia is an Imperial spy. She was hired by my father-in-lock years ago, but she takes my money now." To Danatia, "Mistress spy, Lucyd's dreams are not acceptable now that we stand on the verge of the ultimate solution."

"We have come to arrest the traitor," Regima Clere said.

"We wish to make him a part of our grand ceremony today announcing the detonation of the first firebolt," Regim said. "He will recant his dreams of destruction, and then he will be executed for all the purities to witness. Tender me sufficient cause, and you may be dismissed."

"I can tender you no sufficient cause," Danatia said. She took Lucyd's icy hand in her warm ones, gazed into his eyes.

"Is it true, milady?" Lucyd asked.

"Yes, it's true Councillor Twine hired me when I first came to live with you at Villa de Reve. To . . . spy upon you. He convinced me that you may have collaborated with the Heaven's Devils who murdered Milady Danti and . . . well, she was my sister." She gazed at Regim, regal and serene. "He does not now nor has he ever collaborated with the Heaven's Devils or any other foe. He loved Milady Danti, though she returned his love little. He would never have harmed her or participated in her harm."

"We have evidence," Regim said.

"What Horan Zehar said to taunt you? I don't believe it. I don't believe *you*."

"But his dreams of Salit Zehar, of the orb—"

"Milord Lucyd dreams of Salit and the Orb of Eternity because Horan Zehar put the orb and his daughter into the Mind of the World thirteen years ago. Milord Lucyd does not possess an orb. You have no cause to arrest him."

"Give me cause, spy," the vigile bellowed. "Denounce him, as you've been paid to do."

"I cannot. I *will* not!" she shouted. "He is my sacred sharer, and my dreamer, and my love. Begone, and trouble Lucyd and me no more."

"Look, my father," Regima Clere spoke up, whispering in her father's ear, brushing a kiss against his cheek, and pointing—to Lucyd's horror—at the beautiful little sphinxes. "The angels possess illegal sphinxes. Sphinx breeding is a shadow-market enterprise. Owning sphinxes, a violation of the repeal of the mandate of indenture. We have our cause."

The Chief Commander brushed a kiss on his daughter's cheek. "That's splendid, my darling. You've learned your lessons well. But you forget he's still an *angel*, our only superior pure, not to mention he's an *aetherist*."

"My father, he's in violation of proximity," the magister girl said with stunning coldness. "Even an angel cannot escape the law of proximity."

The Chief Commander claimed her mouth in a kiss. "My Regima Clere, how you have fulfilled your promise as my daughter." Regim's blue-fire eyes blazed with overweening zeal.

"Thank you, my father," Regima Clere said.

"Milord Lucyd Sol naitre Primus," Regim said and gestured to his squad, "you're under arrest."

• • •

"As the highest subpure of the highest pure, you are accused of the highest heresy, Milord Lucyd," intoned the Supreme Sayer. She swung her stitched-blind face back and forth, avidly entering and departing from sharemind with her official seers. The huge, dark, saucer-shaped eyes of the seers stared, unblinking. "Your blessed dreams of love and duty have transformed into abominations. You have brought destruction and impure things to the Mind of the World. How do you plead?"

Lucyd stood on the gallows, head held high. Danatia stood beside him, her arm around his shoulders, her sapphire eyes blazing defiantly.

Hooded hangmen and Vigilance torturers stood next to them, shifting their ropes and knives from hand to hand, in anticipation of a spectacular execution.

"Oh, I'm sure I am quite guilty," Lucyd said.

The crowd howled.

Lucyd had never ventured out to see the barricades and bleachers at Allpure Square. He looked now with great sadness at the screaming people, the high bench of the Supreme Sayers, the torturers' rack and gallows, Regim and his daughter, with their bodyguards and private vigiles.

A podium dedicated to the Imperial Bureau of Ground Control stood beside the gallows, and he saw Gunther Triadius seated there. Heavily armed bodyguards surrounded a second magnificent podium. A contingent of high councillors was seated there, waving and smiling at the crowd. Lucyd spied the tall, angular physique and long, stern face of the eminent Councillor Claren Twine.

Kaligraphs announcing the detonation of the first gigantic firebolt and the salvation of Pangaea skittered across expensive Imperial banners.

"What happened to your dreams, Milord Lucyd?" came a strong clear woman's voice.

"My fellow Pangaeans," Lucyd said. His voice sounded rusty and thin. Danatia took his hand. "I do believe I've just heard the first good question I've heard all day. Not from Vigilance. Not from the High Council. Not from the Supreme Sayers. From one of *you* standing there, in the crowd." His voice grew stronger. "What is happening to my dreams?"

"Yes, milord, can you tell us?" came the woman's voice again.

A hush fell over the crowd.

"Simply this: I can lie to you no longer," Lucyd said. "I dream of the Orb of Eternity because the orb has become part of the Mind of the World. I dream of Apocalypse because the Apocalypse is here."

"The false dreams of the angels, or any other dreams in the Mind of the World, no longer matter," Gunther shouted from the Ground Control podium and brandished a water clock. "Every Pangaean will witness the ultimate solution . . . *now*."

A gigantic *boom!* vibrated through the feverish festival air, both deeply distant and immediately below Lucyd's feet.

And then silence. Complete, devastating silence.

The trembling ground stilled.

Lucyd embraced Danatia. He whispered, "I'm sorry, my love. Closed Eyes. The oracle has come true."

Regim climbed onto the gibbet, leaning on Regima and two bodyguards. He brandished a scroll. "I think we need hear no more testimony. In the name of Our Sacred Imperium of Pangaea, I pronounce this angel guilty of the highest treason. My father-in-lock," he called to the councillors' podium, "will you sign this death warrant on behalf of Vigilance Authority and the High Council?"

Now Claren Twine mounted the gibbet. He took the stylus and hastily wrote upon the scroll that Regim held for him.

Time seemed to move very slowly. *That's because I'm about to die,* Lucyd thought. Yet he became aware the tension on the gibbet had changed.

The Chief Commander gazed at the scroll, then at his father-in-lock, and a stunned expression flooded his face. He slowly withdrew a crumbling scroll from the pocket of his uniform. He brandished the document and the writing Claren had just made.

"Behold the fancy hand of treason," Regim said to the crowd.

"What is he doing?" Lucyd whispered to Danatia.

"I'm not sure," she whispered back.

Lucyd caught a glimpse of the death warrant, the fanciful loops and swirls of Claren Twine's kaligraphs. The second scroll had been inscribed in the same type of kaligraphs, rendered in high Imperial style with distinctive serifs. On the second scroll was a cryptic message—

VIGILANCE COMES FOR YOU

"I want to know the meaning of this, my father-in-lock," Regim said. When the high councillor only smiled and stepped down from the gibbet, Regim shouted to his squad, "In the name of Vigilance, seize Claren Twine for questioning." To the Supreme Sayer, "Is this edict in order?"

The Supreme Sayer nodded and intoned, "Execute the angel."

A hangman slung a noose over Lucyd's head.

Bong. Bong. Bong. Bong. Bong. Bong. Bong. Bong. The Harbinger began to toll.

A massive earthshock struck the megalopolis.

A gang of middle pures tore down the barricade sequestering southeast quadrant. People surged into Allpure Square, surrounding the gallows. The hangmen and torturers brandished their knives and weapons, fending off the frenzied mob.

A slender woman leapt onto the gibbet. She wore the tunic and leggings of a sailor and carried a rucksack over her shoulder, but possessed the carriage and assurance of a high-middle pure. Her golden green eyes blazed. She swept waves of reddish gold hair away from her face and brandished her hands for silence.

Diamond shapes scarred the backs of her hands.

The crowd fell silent.

"I say to you," she said in a strong, clear voice, "the

angel speaks the truth. I have sailed across the torrents and discovered this: The world as we know it has not always been the same. The world has changed before, and it is changing now. The shocks are a sign of that change."

"Plaia Triadana," Gunther shouted. "Seditious bitch."

"Oh, yes," she said, "Gunther Triadius knows me well. But he can no longer coerce me into saying what he will, abusing sharers' sharemind." She brandished her hands. "I cut out your damn sharelock chips, Gunther. I will say what *I* will."

"You still say the same lunatic things you said years ago when you were an ignorant student. There is only one shell, just as there is only one Pangaea. Only Pan and only one Imperium. Only one world on which humanity lives—"

"There are many worlds," she said, "above and below us."

Plaia strode to Lucyd, loosened the noose, and flung the hangman's rope away. "Go now, and go quickly," she whispered to Danatia, who nodded wide-eyed.

She dug into her rucksack and withdrew a map. She exhibited the map to the crowd, turning to face each quadrant so each purity could see what she had to show.

"You see, Milord Lucyd?" she said and graciously held the map toward him. "The eastern coastline of Chinee fits the western coastline of Cordillera. Once Chinee and Cordillera were one province on the other side of the world."

Gunther shouted, "She makes no sense."

"I don't understand, Dame Academe," Lucyd murmured.

"Pangaea is drifting apart," she said, "just as Pangaea drifted in the past. As Pangaea will drift again one day. The Imperium will come to an end, and another Imperium will rise. As an Imperium rose in the past when the world was a different place." She dug into the rucksack again. "Behold! I have proof."

"Show us your proof, academe," a man shouted.

Gunther turned to Regim and Regima Clere. "*Do* something, my Chief Commander. Arrest her. She's a runaway sharer."

"Seize her," Regim commanded of his squad.

The academe blanched when vigiles mounted the gibbet and surrounded her. "Go," she said again to Lucyd. "You are vindicated, milord."

Lucyd climbed down from the gibbet, leaning on Danatia's arm. "Thank you," he said, and his heart swelled with joy and sorrow. "Pan preserve you, Plaia."

"You see, my love?" Danatia whispered. "You don't have to dream anymore. Closed Eyes. The oracle has come true, and you may sleep peacefully. Let's take the windship and leave this place."

It was *her*.

"Let the academe speak." Dubban cupped his hands around his mouth and shouted above the roar of the crowd and tolling of the Harbinger. "Let's see her proof."

"Gah, let the academe speak," Salit Zehar shouted and punched Dubban on his biceps. "Is that really her, midwife?"

"Yes," he said, his heart tightening with equal measures of elation and alarm.

Had Plaia dreamed the dreams he'd cast? He didn't know.

Among the thousands of people among all the purities who bought and sold illegal shells, many had become shellmasters and cast their own dreams. The Mind of the World had become a vast confusion of dreams. Even the dreampaths of the angels, established for millennia, no longer lent structure to the aether.

The Alchemist had cast dreams in the Mind of the World. Dubban had dreamed several, sensational dreams accusing the Imperium of misusing the natalries. Shocking revelations that beneficial threads among the tangled strands of drud and serv birthpods had been marked by physician-natalists and removed by midwives. A startling dream that the Imperium controlled sharemind through the design of security numbers.

Dubban had heard the talk in the taverns. Not everyone among the purities believed the Alchemist's dreams. Others refused to dream his dreams at all. Still others had kept their sons and daughters at home when they reached the age of ripeness instead of sending them to be harvested.

Dubban had cast his own dream over and over.

Dream of me. Please dream of me.

And there she stood.

"You'd best be careful, Salit," Dubban said. "The place is swarming with vigiles."

"Nah, they're too stupid to recognize me." She flung the hem of her shawl over her shoulder. "You see, midwife? Or should I call you priest in that natalist gear? The rumors among my people were right, eh? Your woman returned from her quest. And this ludicrous ceremony has flushed Regim Deuceman the Butcher out of hiding. Ho! The intelligence of the impure is the best."

"Not so loud, my mother," Latif said. The boy wore a qaftan that covered him from head to toe. He peered out through eyeslits, looking all the world like a tiny impure woman.

"I agree, my mother," Jahnni said. Salit's other son was not so easy to conceal. He stood as tall as a magister.

"Listen to your sons, Salit," Dubban said and cupped his hands around his mouth again. "Let's see her proof."

Plaia raised her head, and their eyes met as they had met during the Festival of Spring Moontide long ago. The overwhelming love that had resonated in him then resonated now a thousandfold. She was older, wearier; well, so was he. Her travels had honed her. She stood as slim as a reed. Her eyes were exactly the same, though, and her hair, rendered more gold by the sun, held no grey.

Her lips curved in a smile. He had never seen such a beautiful sight.

"My proof!" She brandished a shard of pottery inscribed with strange kaligraphs. "There is land, another continent, on the other side of the world. My captain and crew and I discovered this continent. We discovered a chamber millions of years old. The chamber is filled with treasures of another Imperium. Another civilization that existed when the provinces of Chinee and Cordillera were neighbors, and the lost continent an island between them. This shard is from that chamber."

Gunther seized the shard, flung it to the flagstones. The shard shattered into dust.

Plaia laughed. "There's more, Gunther. More than even you and the Imperium can destroy. There are paintings of the Ancient Ones. The ancestors of the angels. And the ancestors of the impure. They're from the same people, before the natalries created the purities. And there's a map of the world. It shows the vast ocean that once lay between Appalacia and Gondwana and another ocean between Tasman and Cordillera. It shows how the provinces were scattered all over the world."

"She's insane," Gunther shouted. "What she claims is impossible. She's a heretic."

The Harbinger commenced tolling, and another earthshock struck, flinging people to the pavement.

The Ground Control podium collapsed in a haystack of plywood, crumpled banners, and bloodied bureaucrats.

"Vigilance, pacify these people," Regim shouted. "My squad, seize the heretic and my father-in-lock, and follow me."

Regim and his daughter strode away, pushing through the mob.

"I'm going after her," Dubban said to Salit and her sons.

"We're coming with you, priest," Salit said. "I wouldn't miss a meeting with Regim the Butcher for all the atlantium in Pangaea. I've got a vow I've been meaning to fulfill."

Dubban peered through the ancient trapdoor in the corner of the Chief Commander's chambers. His mouth felt parched, his hands clammy. He couldn't stop the trembling in his innards.

From this vantage point, he could see Gunther's loathsome grin, the squad of vigiles. Regim paced, assisted by his bodyguards as he circled the torturers' racks, shouting questions. Claren Twine had been bound wrist and ankle to one rack, Plaia to the other. Regima Clere brandished a dissecting knife over the councillor. The magister girl's bodyguards, protocol chips winking in their foreheads, watched their mistress impassively.

"Sure you don't want a dagger for yourself, priest?" Salit whispered in his ear.

"I'm not a warrior," he replied. "What would I do with it?"

"You stab it in the damn magister's face."

"I'll leave that to you and your sons. You *will* defend me?" he asked anxiously for the tenth time.

The robust copper boy, Jahnni, smiled and squeezed Dubban's arm. "Priest, my little brother and I owe our lives to you. Take the academe woman and get out of here as fast as you can."

"We'll take care of the magister beasts, Father Dubban," Latif added.

Dubban noted that the impure boy's high melodic voice quavered. *I know exactly how you feel, Latif.*

"Remember what I told you, Dubban," Salit said.

"Yes, yes. Take the passage hidden next to the door out of here. Go all the way down to the basement, through the waste-disposal chamber to the rear of the building. Up one floor, and we exit in the back lot of the windship hangar. I know which kind of ship to take," he said wryly. "Asif and I had practice."

Salit's eyes flashed in fury. "This is for my bonded one." She punched open the trapdoor, singing shrilly—

> *Farewell, sighs and sorrow,*
> *Farewell, tears and grief,*
> *Welcome, blood and death.*
> *Welcome, Heaven's Devils*
> *Who wreak wrack and ruin*
> *On the Imperium!*

The Heaven's Devils burst in, Dubban following.

"Death to the Imperium," Jahnni shouted.

"Death to magisters," Latif shouted.

"Seize them!" Regim roared, and his elite squad surrounded the Devils.

Dubban sprinted to Plaia's side, but Regima Clere stood in his way, her knife brandished.

"Step aside, Regima Clere," he said.

"Why should I?" she said in a haughty voice. "Who are you?"

So cold for one so young. Dubban met the girl's eyes. "Because I am your Superior Father. I held you and dried your tears." He said to Regim, "Chief Commander, as the priest who assisted you and begot your daughter, I demand that you release Plaia and allow us to take our leave."

Regim hobbled before him. "I've honored my debts to you twice, Superior Father Dubban. You've exhausted my patience."

"Is what he says true, my father?" Regima Clere said.

"Yes," Regim said.

The girl's thin lips trembled. "Let them go, my father."

"Very well," Regim said wearily.

"No!" Gunther shouted. "Plaia belongs to me. I paid for her. She wore my sharelock chips."

Dubban dipped into his pocket and scooped out the chips he'd removed from Plaia's hands. He flung them at the academe's feet.

"Here are your sharelock chips. Take them."

He unbuckled Plaia's restraints, seized her, and lifted her off the rack.

They ran.

"We're going to steal a *windship*?" Plaia asked as they crouched beneath the exit portal of a small cruiser festooned with light blue warning kaligraphs.

Dubban thumbed the urgency switch concealed beneath the lintel of the exit portal. The portal silently slid open. He boosted her inside. "Yes."

Vigiles sprinted across the airfield, shouting, brandishing crossbows.

"Sit there," he said, pointing at the seat. "You'll want to fasten those restraints over your lap."

He plunked himself into the pilot's seat, closed the portal, fastened his own restraints.

"You actually know how to fly this thing?" she said.

He surveyed the instrument panel before him. A sturdy rod topped with a huge pliable black bulb protruded from the center of the panel. "Yes."

A walkabout leapt onto a side deck.

Dubban stared at the walkabout and gestured with his thumb, *Going up*. The walkabout leapt down.

"Are you sure?" she said.

Dubban punched the red button overlaid with the kaligraph for GO, and then the one that promised UP. In less than a minute, they had levitated straight up two leagues high or more. The ship soared through the dust of the collapsing megalopolis into the western horizon.

"Yes," he said with a grin.

"Dubban," Plaia said, eyes wide with wonder, "have I ever told you I love you?"

He said, "We have a lot of catching up to do."

FACET 30

Skull: Certainty or chaos.
No one rules the stars.
You may choose to roll the orb once again
   but the oracle signifies whatever you
   choose.
The action is free will.
The forbearance is anarchy.

The Orb of Eternity

Commentaries:
Councillor Sausal: Thus we conclude that Pan
manifested All that ever was, All that is, and All
that will ever be. May Pan preserve you for Eternity. [*Deleted from The Contemporary Commentaries of Sausal (15th Ed.)*—

Yet what created Pan? What preceded Pan?
What will succeed Pan?

What created that which preceded Pan? What
will create that which will succeed Pan?

So, too, we must conclude there was a time
before the Imperium ruled. And there will come a
time after the Imperium rules no more. For like
Pan, the Imperium has a beginning and the Imperium will come to an end.]

Therefore the prudent person should treasure
life.

For you will never pass this way again.
Guttersage (usu. considered vulgar): One thing is
for certain: Nothing is for certain.

Our City of Atlan, Southeast Marketplace, the Vigilance Authority cloudscraper, the Chief Commander's chambers:

The Harbinger tolled ceaselessly now, the great gong echoing throughout the megalopolis. In Jahnni's ears, in his *head*, like the sound of doom made manifest.

"Get behind me, my sons," Salit commanded after Dubban and Plaia had fled. She brandished a folded devil star. The chameleon cloak swirled around her, appearing and disappearing in agitation, and Jahnni could *feel* his mother's rage like a crackle of lightning.

She said, "Ho, Regim Deuceman, I have come to fulfill my blood vow to you."

He spit back, "Not before I fulfill my vow to *you*, impure wench."

"We shall see," she said in a mocking singsong and flung the star at the vigiles restraining her.

With a *hiss!* the star hurtled through the air and sliced clear through a vigile's waist. He crumpled, head, shoulders, and torso separating from the rest of him.

Regim's squad shouted and scattered for cover.

Latif stepped behind Salit's crouching figure, but Jahnni stood his ground, defiant and protective in equal measure.

"I shall stand beside you, my mother," he said.

Another gigantic earthshock shuddered through Atlan, and the entire Vigilence cloudscraper shivered like a house made of paper. Fissures shot through the west wall of the chamber.

Jahnni had witnessed Salit Zehar's combatcraft many times, knew her speed and ferocity and strength. But the scowling vigiles towered above his mother. They were magister brutes with bulging muscles and Imperial weapons. Especially Regim the Butcher who, despite his prosthetic leg and middle age, a notoriously dissolute life behind him, still amounted to a formidable foe.

And Salit, for all her skill as a warrior, stood no taller than a child. Next to Regim, she was a tiny creature. The roaming life had taken its toll on her: She'd grown scrawny and weathered and arthritic. Grey had added its touch to her variegated hair. Deep lines grooved her face. She was nearly thirty years of age. Among the impure, she was geriatric.

"My Jahnni," she had told him just yesterday as he'd massaged the ache out of her gnarled little hands, "I do not know how much time I've got left."

When *he* stared back at Regim and Regima Clere, though, the gamefield was a little more level. Jahnni met their eyes. *Ha! I stand taller than the Butcher and his daughter by a handbreadth.* The roaming life had trained his muscles more rigorously than any Imperial gamefield. Had sharpened his senses and strung his nerves tight.

Another earthshock rocked the chamber. The west wall collapsed, stone and glass shattering.

One vigile leapt out from behind the desk where she'd taken cover and bolted from the chamber. Another vigile followed, another, and another.

"Halt, deserters," Regim shouted. "I'll have you flayed alive on Allpure Square."

The vigiles fled, leaving Regim himself and his fierce-eyed bodyguards, his loathsome daughter and her bodyguards, and Gunther Triadius.

Claren Twine lay trussed to the torturer's rack.

A sea breeze cleared the dust. Jahnni could see the whole panorama of Atlan and Sausal Bay. The fallen wall revealed a very fine view.

"Halt, or I'll kill you myself," Regim shouted, but the vigiles were gone.

Excellent. Our odds improve by the minute. Jahnni drew his dagger. He glanced at Latif and saw that his little blue brother brandished a devil star.

Only recently had Jahnni's disappointment that he could not master stars ceased stinging his pride. His mother had explained that Heaven's Devils alone could master devil stars.

When he'd protested, "But I'm a Devil, too!", Salit

had smiled and touched his cheek. "You certainly are, my fine copper son. But not of the impure."

Very well. Let Latif have his star. Jahnni had mastered daggers and caltrops and crossbows and battle hammers. Salit had taught him well how to hunt and how to kill. Latif, with his dreamy black eyes and delicate stature, had often wept when Jahnni pulled out a slingshot and brought down a bird or a beast. But Jahnni relished spilling blood with his own hand.

"My mother, let us dispose of these magisters and take our leave before Atlan falls into the fires of Inim, eh?" He nodded at Regima Clere. "I'll slit that one's throat."

Regim's daughter gazed haughtily as if no one and nothing could ever harm her. A peculiar attitude even for a magister, Jahnni thought, since, at the moment, she bore no weapons of her own and her bodyguards stood trembling in terror.

She looked to be about his age, a tall, golden girl on the cusp of womanhood. She might have been beautiful, with her father's chiseled features, bright hair, and golden complexion. But her beauty was marred by her arrogance and by her eyes. They were pale blue, slanted, and slightly crossed, as if, overcome by vanity, she wished to gaze only at herself.

"Watch your manners, boy," Regim said.

Jahnni stared down the barrel of a Vigilance firebolt.

"Gunther," Regim called to his advisor, who cowered in a corner, "take Regima Clere to the windship field. My daughter," he said to her, "you know how to fly a ship. Go to the Twine fortress in Majestic Heights and wait for me there."

"But my father—" she began to protest.

He held up his hand. "I have urgent matters here. I won't be long. But you must go before the cloudscraper collapses. It would seem," he said to Gunther, "that Ground Control's ultimate solution has failed. Take her safely."

"Yes, Chief Commander," Gunther said.

"My granddaughter," called Claren Twine from the

torturer's rack. The rasping whisper of his voice filled the whole chamber. "Unbind me, child, and take me with you. As high councillor and your superior, I command you."

"I think not, my father-in-lock," Regim said. "You are a traitor, and traitors must be punished to the full extent of the law. Even high councillors. Especially high councillors. Regima Clere, go now."

Gunther seized Regima Clere's hand and yanked her along. Jahnni saw how she grimaced with disgust at the academe's touch. He didn't blame her. The two strode to the door, her bodyguards trailing.

"Just a minute," Jahnni said and blocked their path. "My mother, do you release them?"

Regima Clere stared, face-to-face, with that haughty look Jahnni wanted to wipe right off her. Yet he felt strangely as if he was gazing into a looking glass. A warped looking glass. For though her eyes and coloring were most foreign, her hair and features seemed so familiar.

She in turn raked her gaze over him. "Your impure strumpet of a mother does not command here. My father does."

"You will not insult my mother."

He reached out and slapped her shapely cheek. Her mouth flew open in astonishment. As swift as a serpent striking, she slapped him back. He caught her wrist, brandished his dagger in her sneering face.

"My mother?" he repeated. "What is your command?"

"Let them go," Salit said, smirking as she gripped another devil star and idly twirled the weapon through her fingers. "I have no quarrel with the Butcher's spawn or his advisor. We shall find them again easily enough, my son, when we decide to assassinate them."

"As you wish, my mother," he said and shared his mother's smirk. *How fine to witness these vigiles tremble before Salit Zehar.* He flung Regima Clere's wrist away as if her touch disgusted him.

With a final glance of pure malice, the magister girl, her bodyguards, and Gunther strode out.

"If my own family will not help me, perhaps you will, Salit Zehar," Claren Twine called out again. "Unbind me, help me, as I have so often helped you. 'Vigilance comes for you,' eh? On the wings of a bloodbat."

Jahnni glanced in bewilderment at Salit, then at Regim, as his Heaven's Devil mother and her sworn enemy *both* stared at the high councillor.

"Then you confess, my father-in-lock?" Regim said. "To the highest treason in the Imperium? You, the Chief Advisor on Impure Activities to the High Council? You collaborated with the Heaven's Devils?"

"My son-in-lock, I personally ordered the execution of Milady Danti." Claren sounded weary. "Just as I ordered the execution of Clere Twine."

Regim choked. "You *ordered* the execution of your own daughter? At our sharelock ceremony?"

"Seemed like a good place. The Temple of Sacred Sharelock is riddled with secret passages and exits into the water ducts. The foes have used them for a thousand years."

"How *could* you?"

"No one is sorrier than I, my son-in-lock."

"But *why*?"

Salit barked with laughter and strode to the rack. With two strokes of her dagger, she slashed the councillor's bonds. "Yes, tell me, Dark One. Why?"

Claren sat up, rubbing his wrists. He climbed down off the rack. "Many thanks, Salit. I've often admired you from afar."

Jahnni could feel his mother's shock and, beneath her smile, the surge of her rage.

"What's it all about, Dark One?" she said.

"Ah, Salit, in the end, it's all about preservation. Horan possessed blood of the Ancient Ones. He remembered things, and he *saw*. So do you. There's no telling how Latif will turn out. You have discovered your powers, haven't you?"

"Yes, Dark One."

Claren chuckled. "I thought so. I apprehended as much with my magister sharemind at Labrad."

Powers. The magister calls my mother's gifts powers.

Jahnni had witnessed his mother do many strange things. She could steal into the thoughts of pures, for instance, frightening them witless when she wanted to or merely discovering where they'd hidden the key to their larder. He knew just how they felt, for she could enter *his* thoughts whenever she wanted, and did so to command him in a pinch or chastise him when he wouldn't listen. Though she'd assured him many times, "My son, I will not invade your privacy."

Then there was her chameleon cloak and the mnemon pocket. In all the years he had traveled among the impure with Salit and his blue brother, Jahnni had met only a handful of others who wore cloaks. Most had appeared just like the other impure—palsied, frail, and diseased.

Salit had told him those people might or might not truly *be* that way. "The most skillful among us," she'd said with a laugh, "can persuade their cloaks to camouflage *them*."

By which she meant they could change their shape and appearance and not merely disappear into the world the way Salit did. She'd said, "This cloak loved my father, the great Horan Zehar, far more than it loves me."

The Orbs of Eternity she possessed were more of a puzzlement. Though she wore four orbs around her neck, she possessed no special mastery over them. "Neither did Horan Zehar," she'd told him. "He resorted to orbcasters among the purities when he wished a foretelling. I've never had the patience to study the facets and discern their meaning. The most I can say is, they sting me."

Which wasn't the case with Jahnni and his brother.

When as boys Jahnni and Latif had played with their mother's pretty purple jewels, an orb had stung Latif so viciously he had never wanted to touch one again. Jahnni had cradled his distraught brother and sung him to sleep while Salit went hunting. Neither boy had told her of their play.

Whereas when Jahnni had cupped an orb in his hands, he would suddenly see fiery comets plunging through space or leviathans diving into oceans. And *that* had frightened him so much *he'd* never touched the orbs again, either.

Though he gazed and gazed at them whenever he got the chance.

Claren Twine lit a cheroot. The scent of expensive bacco stirred ancient memories.

"There are those who understand that the impure must survive," Claren said. "Of all Pangaeans, only the impure have not been tampered with by the natalries." Claren chuckled. "After all our Imperial obsession with purity, *you,* the impure, are the pure ones. Purely untouched by the Ancient Ones' technology."

"You speak blasphemy," Regim whispered.

"I've no doubt my daughter Clere would have said the same. Regim, we of the High Council know that the Ancient Ones possessed knowledge and powers which have become lost to us. Even with our Imperial power. They possessed an understanding of things beyond our comprehension. How to fold space. How to travel to the other worlds. How to manufacture suspensions and firebolts and cloaks and orbs."

Claren sighed as if his lungs could not grasp enough air. It was a horrible sound.

"Even the angels were committed to the natalries," Claren said, "to preserve their beauty and their power of dreaming. Such riches! As part of the scheme, the Ancient Ones gave certain technologies to certain purities and not to others. But only they could master all the technologies."

"So the Ancient Ones loved us as sons and daughters, too, Dark One, because we *are* their sons and daughters?" Salit said.

"Yes. I'm sorry, Salit. Perhaps one day the impure may become masters of us all again."

The councillor strode to the chamber door.

"Halt, traitor," Regim said, aiming his firebolt.

Salit and Latif brandished their devil stars at Regim. Jahnni strode to the vigile and held his dagger before the vigile's throat.

"One more thing, Dark One," Salit asked quietly. "Why did you order the execution of your own daughter?"

The councillor sighed heavily. "Clere was only an adjunct prefect. She wasn't yet privy to many Imperial Secrets. She didn't understand that only the impure may still carry the ancient blood and the ancient memories. Even though she was my daughter, I was sworn to secrecy. Poor Clere. She had learned her lessons as a magister only too well. She was arrogant and proximicist and despised the impure with a deep, abiding hatred. I knew of her plans to exterminate the impure in Atlan, perhaps in all Pangaea. I tried to dissuade her without arousing her suspicions. But then Milady Danti was murdered, and she became infuriated beyond all reason. Milady Danti," he said sardonically, "was Clere's favorite angel in the Mind of the World. Clere adored her. In Danti's memory, Clere was about to launch a campaign against the impure. She had drawn up plans to kill every impure in Blackblood Cavern. Another Morn of Savagery. I *am* sorry, Regim, but she had to be stopped. The very future of Pangaea was at stake."

He poised on the threshold. "Just as *you* had to be monitored. And finally stopped. But you outmaneuvered us all, Regim, with your bodyguards and secrecy and paranoia. Even I couldn't get near to our Chief Commander of Vigilance, eh? I would have killed you myself, years ago. Salit Zehar, I command you to carry out your blood vow. Good-bye, my son-in-lock. May you live in Eternity."

Claren Twine strode out the door.

Regim started after him, but Jahnni thrust the dagger nearer to the golden throat.

"Let me give you some advice, stupid boy," Regim said, aiming the firebolt at *him*. "Never threaten someone with a dagger when he aims a weapon at you that could blast your guts away. I once killed an impure man not much older or bigger than you that way."

Salit gave an infuriated scream, and Regim started in surprise. Jahnni felt the rage boiling out of his mother. As Regim started at her, Jahnni lunged and seized the barrel of the vigile's firebolt, thrusting it toward the ceiling.

Regim gripped the weapon more tightly and they grappled, stumbling across the chamber in a terrible dance, dragging the bodyguards with them.

Regim peered intently at his face. "Who are you, boy?"

"I am Jahnni of the Far Reaches."

A colossal groan rose up from the waterfront. Everyone in the chamber gawked through the collapsed wall, and Jahnni saw an impossible sight: The entire boardwalk was rising and rising as if it were a child's gameboard tipped by a titan's hand.

Chattering in terror, Regim's bodyguards seized the firebolt from the grip of man and boy and fled from the chamber.

Regim paid them no attention, but only stared. "Who generated you, Jahnni of the Far Reaches?"

"My mother gave birth to me like a beast," Jahnni spit back.

The golden vigile shook his head and shoved Jahnni away, breaking his grasp. "That impure wench is not your mother."

Jahnni stumbled back, astonished at the vigile's unexpected strength. "Of course she's not. Any fool can see that. I was born of the body of an angel who fled from the world because she could not bear the cruelty of the Imperium. My father was the great Pan." Inexplicable tears rose in his throat but he swallowed them.

Salit had told him that story many times as they'd warmed themselves around a campfire. He'd taken comfort in it over the years. Though he wasn't sure he believed the part about his father, he'd understood with a child's knack for hidden messages that his father had been both an important man and a grief to his mother.

"You lie to the boy, Salit Zehar," Regim said. "How did he come to live with the likes of you? How is it he calls you his mother? That freak of a boy"—he pointed at Latif—"is plainly of your body, but not this one." He gazed at Jahnni as if he might devour him.

"You will never know, Butcher," Salit said.

"He's my son, isn't he? Tahliq, his mother. He's got her skin, her beauty. You were there, you and her, at the confinement camp in the Far Reaches. She knew as well as I her child was mine. She told you, didn't she?"

"She told me nothing."

"Is she dead, then? Tell me, Salit."

"I will go to my grave before I tell you that which is most dear to you, Regim Deuceman."

"Then go to your grave you shall."

The vigile leapt at Salit, seizing her tiny waist and flinging her to the floor. She kicked up, aiming for his crotch, catching only his kneecap, but it was a good move. Regim winced and hobbled, more reliant on his leg than his prosthesis.

"Kill him, Latif," Jahnni shouted. "Throw the star."

"No!" Salit shouted. "He's mine to take. He murdered my father *and* my bonded one."

She leapt to her feet, flung her star.

The star plunged into Regim's chest with an audible *thunk!* and commenced its bloody spiral.

But to Jahnni's astonishment, the vigile seized the weapon through the aperture at its center and ripped it from his flesh, smashing it flat against the rigid thigh of his prosthesis. The star cracked in half and plunged to the floor, its sentience stilled.

Jahnni circled around their mother and the vigile, signaling to Latif to do the same.

Enraged, Regim roared and lunged at Salit, who lunged back, and they clasped each other in a deadly embrace, staggering across the floor. Regim seized her wrist, oblivious of the metal claws she raked across his chest, and broke it.

Jahnni heard the *crack* of her frail bones. "Latif, my brother, we must kill him. Never mind what our mother says."

Salit grasped her limp wrist, her face twisted in anguish. Regim drew a small, curved knife from his boot top, shoved her arms away, and plunged the blade into her belly.

She shrieked, fell on her back, and he leapt atop her, straddling her, tracing the bowl of her hipbones with deep ragged jerks of the knife.

"This is for you, my beloved Clere," he shouted. He leaned over, shouted, "Who is that boy, Salit? Tell me!"

"Burn in torment, Regim," she gasped back. "I shall love both my sons for Eternity."

She shuddered, then, and fell still, her eyes staring wide.

Regim rose shakily to his feet, blood staining his uniform. He staggered once, then lunged at Latif. He seized Jahnni's little brother with one hand, his devil star with the other, and smashed both against the chamber wall. Latif kicked and shouted, but he was smaller and frailer than Salit and struggled helplessly in the vigile's grasp.

Regim dragged him to the collapsed wall and swept Latif into his arms, swinging him out over the edge.

Jahnni leapt on the vigile's back and dragged him and Latif into the chamber. But Regim wouldn't release Latif. He shrugged away from Jahnni's grasp, circled his massive fingers around Latif's slender throat and squeezed.

"Jahnni, help," Latif said, gagging, beating his fists on the vigile's broad chest.

Jahnni leapt on the vigile's back again, bearing down with all his weight, sank his teeth into Regim's ear, bit, and ripped. Circled his own massive hands around the vigile's thick neck, fingers searching for the vulnerable place between his collarbones the way Salit had taught him.

Regim roared again, flung Latif against the wall, whirled, and grappled Jahnni.

And Jahnni stared into a familiar face, fiery blue eyes into fiery blue eyes.

"Do not force me to kill my own flesh and blood," Regim whispered.

"I am not your flesh and blood. I will avenge my mother."

Jahnni shoved, and they fell to the floor, rolling over and over, Jahnni's knife poised at the vigile's throat, the vigile keeping the blade at bay with a hand wrapped around Jahnni's wrist.

"You cannot break me like you broke my tiny mother," Jahnni cried and he could feel the vigile tremble, the poison in the startips beginning to work.

"She was not your mother," Regim ground out. "Your mother was the most famous erotician in Atlan. Tahliq Jahn Pentaput naitre Quintus. She gave you her name, Jahnni."

"No." Jahnni violently shook his head. "No!"

Suddenly a caltrop plunged into the vigile's forehead. Face drenched in tears, Latif crouched beside them.

The vigile's hand faltered, and Jahnni plunged the dagger, gouging the blade deeply into the golden throat. Latif's small blue hands joined his copper ones, and together the boys dragged the dagger through the vigile's windpipe.

"I . . . would have loved you." Regim Deuceman collapsed, the Butcher butchered.

Jahnni rolled off the corpse and embraced his brother, who sobbed in great choking gasps, trembling violently in his arms.

"Ssh, ssh, now," Jahnni murmured. "Salit is avenged. Our mother can go to the Eternal in peace now."

"Do you really think she will?" Latif said in a small voice.

"Yes, I do." Jahnni smiled tenderly at his brother. Despite their quarrels and competitions, he'd consoled his little blue brother many times before when troublesome dreams had awakened him. He would console

him again. "Come, let's collect our mother's cloak. The
orbs, too."

The terrible shudder of another earthshock shook
the cloudscraper. Jahnni gazed out at mighty temples
and pyramids collapsing all around them. The Imperial
purple and gold Pagoda of Pan wobbled over the ruins
of Marketplace. Fissures gaped open in the proud boulevards. Whole sections of the megalopolis sank, others
rose, and magma sprayed showers of burning rock like
festival streamers.

Jahnni blinked as the horizon disappeared.

A gigantic wall of seawater rose up in Sausal Bay.
The crest touched the sky.

"Come, my brother," Jahnni said. "Let's see if we
can steal one of those windships down below, eh?"

"Jahnni," Latif said, "I'm afraid."

Wild exhilaration swelled in him. "Ah, Latif, we're
young. We're strong. Old Pangaea will fall. But one day
a new Pangaea will rise."

"No one will ever know our glory. Nothing will ever
be the same. The Imperium will vanish forever."

"Yeah," Jahnni said as the north wall of Vigilance
Authority sheared away. "It's a great time to be alive!"

ORB OF ETERNITY

Drawings by Tom Robinson

FACET 1

    Darkness: Nothing or all.
    Night endures till dawn breaks.
    The action is being.
    The forbearance is doing.

FACET 2

    Light: All or nothing.
    The day shines till twilight covers it.
    The action is doing.
    The forbearance is being.

FACET 3

    Point: Central or static.
    The rock endures in the restless river.
    The action is concentration.
    The forbearance is scattering.

FACET 4

Line: Guidance or division.
A stone wall surrounds the magister's house.
The action is inclusion.
The forbearance is separation.

FACET 5

Circle: Distinction or confinement.
The magister selects a sacred sharer.
The action is choice.
The forbearance is constriction.

FACET 6

Spiral: Infinity or repetition.
The magister reviews the law and repeals the
   mandate that oppresses the people.
The action is evolution.
The forbearance is extinction.

FACET 7

Square: Order or rigidity.

The aetherist enters into sacred sharelock with a barren mathematician who proposes a great theorem.

The action is perfection.

The forbearance is sterility.

FACET 8

Triangle: Ascent or descent.

The ax splits a log.

The action is construction.

The forbearance is destruction.

FACET 9

Sun: An angel or a devil.

The sun nourishes or scorches vegetation.

The action is enthusiasm.

The forbearance is wrath.

FACET 10

Moon: A devil or an angel.
The moon illuminates or obscures the night.
The action is nurturing.
The forbearance is smothering.

FACET 11

Comet: A genius or a lunatic.
The comet comes once in a lifetime.
The action is inspiration.
The forbearance is insanity.

FACET 12

Clouds: Gathering or dispersal.
Clouds signify uncertainty.
Roll the orb twice to complete the oracle.
The action is fulfilling potential.
The forbearance is idle speculation.

FACET 13

Rain: Watering or deluge.
The pauper receives an inheritance.
The action is investment.
The forbearance is gambling.

FACET 14

Lightning: Sudden illumination or catastrophe.
The vigile's sword may hew the foe's chains or cut
off her head.
The action is insight.
The forbearance is confusion.

FACET 15

Mountain: Lookout or barrier.
At the foot of the mountain, the plower looks up
at the peak.
At the mountain's peak, the angel looks down at
the whole valley.
The action is perspective.
The forbearance is dogma.

FACET 16

Volcano: Release or cataclysm.
The sharer punishes the corrupted child, who
thrashes a younger sibling.
The action is forcefulness.
The forbearance is paroxysm.

FACET 17

Lake: Ownership or greed.
The angel drives the pauper off her property, but
gives him a loaf of bread.
The action is amassing wealth.
The forbearance is selfishness.

FACET 18

Island: Sanctuary or prison.
The hermit ponders the nature of existence and
tells no one.
The action is contemplation.
The forbearance is delusion.

FACET 19

Tree: Providing nourishment or supplying poison.
The red fruit sustains one, sickens another.
The action is survival.
The forbearance is corruption.

FACET 20

Fire: A hearth or a conflagration.
A blaze staves off the cold or burns a child's hand.
The action is watchfulness.
The forbearance is ruin.

FACET 21

Wheel: Hauling or trampling.
Mobility fosters contact, near and far.
The action is forming friendships.
The forbearance is inciting hostilities.

FACET 22

Lodestone: Attraction or binding.
The vigile meets a brilliant erotician.
The action is union.
The forbearance is entrapment.

FACET 23

Bird: Liberty or heedlessness.
The philosopher encounters a nihilist.
The action is exhilaration.
The forbearance is delinquency.

FACET 24

Spider: Craft or terrorism.
The magister cultivates the wilds, capturing beasts
    and foes.
The action is trapping.
The forbearance is brutality.

FACET 25

Serpent: Wisdom or treachery.
The stealthy angel hides in the tall weeds where no
    one would think of looking for him.
The action is diplomacy.
The forbearance is espionage.

FACET 26

Fish: Family or feud.
Cod swim the sea in their numbers and are netted
    by fishers.
The action is maintaining alliances.
The forbearance is genocide.

FACET 27

Heart: Love or hatred.
Passion inspires sharelock or murder.
The action is desire.
The forbearance is vengeance.

FACET 28

Open Eyes: Objective intellect or selfish ego.
A sapphire in the sunlight becomes like onyx in the
    moonlight.
The action is logical investigation.
The forbearance is dogmatic belief.

FACET 29

Closed Eyes: Resting or death.
The councillor must execute the sentence required
    by the law.
The action is regeneration.
The forbearance is stillness.

FACET 30

Skull: Certainty or chaos.
No one rules the stars.
You may choose to roll the orb once again but the
    oracle signifies whatever you choose.
The action is free will.
The forbearance is anarchy.

ABOUT THE AUTHOR

A Phi Beta Kappa scholar and a graduate of the University of Michigan Law School, Lisa Mason is the author of five previous novels: **Arachne** and **Cyberweb**, published by AvoNova, which are cyberpunk tales taking place in a future California; also, published by Bantam Spectra, **Summer of Love** (a Philip K. Dick Award finalist) and **The Golden Nineties** (a *New York Times* notable book of the year), which are time travel tales, and **Pangaea Book I: Imperium Without End.**

Mason published her first short story, "Arachne," in *Omni* and has since published acclaimed short fiction in numerous publications and anthologies, including *Omni, Year's Best Fantasy and Horror, Full Spectrum, Asimov's Science Fiction Magazine, Magazine of Fantasy and Science Fiction, Universe, Unique, Transcendental Tales, Unter Die Haut, Immortal Unicorn, David Copperfield's Tales of the Impossible, Desire Burn, Fantastic Alice,* and *The Shimmering Door.* Her novels and short stories have been translated into French, German, Italian, Japanese, Portuguese, Spanish, and Swedish. She optioned her 1989 *Omni* story "Tomorrow's Child" to Universal Pictures. Mason lives in the San Francisco Bay area with her husband, the artist and jeweler Tom Robinson.

Readers who want to correspond with Lisa directly can reach her via e-mail at LisaSMason@aol.com.